The School of Hard Knocks

(Schooled in Magic V)

Christopher G. Nuttall

Twilight Times Books
Kingsport Tennessee

The School of Hard Knocks

Copyright © 2015 Christopher G. Nuttall

Paladin Timeless Books, an imprint of
Twilight Times Books
P O Box 3340
Kingsport TN 37664
http://twilighttimesbooks.com/

First Edition, May 2015

ISBN: 978-1-60619-306-8

Library of Congress Control Number: 2015937653

Cover art by Brad Fraunfelter

Printed in the United States of America.

Prologue

The Council Chamber was two miles below the desolate wastelands surrounding Mountaintop, hidden from prying eyes and accessible only through the most powerful magics. Generations of Councillors, even in the glory days of the Empire, had layered spells over the chamber, ensuring that no one could enter save with the permission of one of their fellows. It was the most secure location in the world. And the only way to access it was to walk through a series of caves that were hellishly dangerous to the unwary.

Aurelius, Administrator of Mountaintop, stepped into the chamber and looked around, his gaze passing over the fourteen men and women who made up the Star Council. Collectively, they were the most powerful group of magicians in the world, certainly in political terms. A Necromancer or a Lone Power might have access to more raw magic, but the former would lack the skill and the latter the inclination to turn it into political power. And even the greatest Lone Power could not stand against the united Council.

He took his seat at the stone table, etched with runes to discourage hostility and looked up at the map drawn on the back wall. A good third of the continent was shaded black, representing territories dominated by Necromancers and lost to the Allied Lands. The remainder were divided into political and magical sections, the kingdoms ruled by monarchs and the cities ruled by local councils and the Great Houses. It was a chilling reminder, he knew, that the Necromancers were slowly winning the war. The average peasant in the fields, even the monarchs on their thrones, could forget, but magicians never could. If the Necromancers had banded together, the war would have been lost long ago.

Or they *had* been losing, he reminded himself. Two years ago, something had changed. A new factor had entered the war. And two Necromancers had died at the hands of a single magician. Despite himself, despite the clawing fear that had gnawed at his heart since he'd been brought into the Council, Aurelius had taken heart. The opportunity in front of them could not be ignored any longer.

"The MageMaster is dying," he said, without preamble. "He has turned most of his official duties over to me."

"But not the oaths," Cloak observed. His tone was lightly mocking. "You're practically a free agent."

Aurelius kept his face impassive with the ease of long practice. The Councillors were supposed to keep their identities secret, but few secrets lasted long when powerful sorcerers were probing, searching for answers. He knew the identities of thirteen of the fourteen other Councillors—Masters of Great Houses, Guild Leaders—yet it galled him that he had never been able to uncover Cloak's true identity. Someone so powerful—and power was a given for anyone capable of reaching the chamber—should not be able to remain unidentified.

And yet Cloak was anonymous.

Even his appearance was bland, an illusion of mundane normality that hid his true features under a glamor. It was rude, Aurelius knew, to attempt to see through the disguise, yet he had tried, more than once. And he had always failed. Cloak was very practiced at keeping his identity to himself. He'd been on the Council for over seventy years, longer than all but three of his fellows, yet none of them knew his name.

If I had been on the Council when you joined, Aurelius thought darkly, *I would have demanded to know your name. Or at least what you want to be called.*

He looked at the others, putting Cloak out of his mind. "We have an opportunity to bring the Child of Destiny to Mountaintop," he said. "She would be under our tutelage."

"It would be risky," Master Ashworth commented. "Particularly after the events of last year."

"But necessary," Master Ashfall snapped. "The Lady Emily is the greatest force for change—for *hope*—that we have seen since the Fall of the Empire. We *need* to shape her, to steer her towards our thinking, particularly now that she is a Baroness of Zangaria. Mundane power must not be allowed to go to her head."

"Power has gone to yours," Master Ashworth said. "Do you not understand the dangers of provoking a confrontation with Whitehall—or Void?"

Aurelius smiled as the two magicians bickered. No one quite knew why House Ashworth had fragmented, allowing some of their number to form House Ashfall, but the two Great Houses had been at daggers drawn ever since. Cooler heads had not been able to dampen the hatred that flared whenever the two families met. Indeed, House Ashworth sent its children to Whitehall while House Ashfall sent its children to Mountaintop, just to prevent them from continuing the feud in supposedly neutral territory. And what one Master supported, the other opposed on principle.

He cleared his throat, catching their attention. "We would not threaten her life," he said. "To threaten her in that manner would trifle with destiny itself."

Cloak snorted. "And do you believe in destiny?"

"I do not *disbelieve*," Aurelius said, coolly. "The Lady Emily has killed two Necromancers in single combat. She has turned the Kingdom of Zangaria on its head. The changes caused by her mere presence have rippled out, producing unintended consequences and side effects. But what else does a Child of Destiny *do*?"

"They upset the balance of power," Master Zane said. The ancient magician leaned forward, one hand resting on the table. Unlike the others, he wore no glamor, only his lined and wizened face. "We should kill her now."

Master Ashworth slammed one hand against the table. "Are you mad?"

"There are risks in keeping her alive," Master Ashfall noted, smoothly.

"She's an inexperienced child," Cloak said. "She can be manipulated."

"A child who has killed two necromancers," Master Ashfall said. "Trying to keep her prisoner might prove disastrous. Is it really worth the risk?"

Aurelius pointed to the map. "Two years ago, we knew we were losing the war," he said, flatly. "And then the Necromancer Shadye died at Whitehall."

He knew they understood. They might have their differences with the Grandmaster of Whitehall–and his faction in the White City–but they knew that Whitehall should have been able to remain secure indefinitely. And then Shadye had burst into the school, smashing that old certainty beyond repair. If he hadn't been killed shortly afterwards, Aurelius knew, the gateway to the Allied Lands would have lain open and Shadye's army of monsters would have laid the land waste.

"A Child of Destiny *must* tip the balance against the Necromancers," he said, quietly. It would not help to show his desperation so openly. "She would not need to exist if Destiny intended them to win."

"True," Master Toadstool agreed.

"But what does it profit us," Master Zane asked, "if she destroys *our* stability too?"

"Then we teach her how we think," Aurelius snapped. "And why we *have* to be the way we are."

"A seduction," Cloak observed. His voice sparkled with amusement. "Or are you planning a *conquest?*"

"*No,*" Master Ashworth snapped. Magic crackled around his eyes, shimmers of power that tingled through the room before slowly fading into the wards. "My grand-daughter is the same age. I will not have that tradition resurrected, not now."

Aurelius nodded. "I do not believe that would end well," he said, lightly. "We merely wish to show her how we live, not push her into a stand against us. We will not hold her for long against her will. If worst comes to worst, we will graciously allow her to leave, armed with knowledge she can use against the Necromancers."

"You assume she will remain focused on them," Master Zane observed. "But as a Baroness of Zangaria she would have more... *mundane* interests."

"My spy reported that she has little interest in her new responsibilities," Aurelius said. "We may well be able to convince her to abandon them."

"Which would cause problems in Zangaria," Master Ashworth said.

"Which would be none of our concern," Master Ashfall countered. "I believe the Compact is still in force, is it not?"

"For the nonce," Aurelius said.

"But we are talking about breaking it," Master Zane pointed out. "If we succeed she will join us, thus forsaking Zangaria."

"That is why we have to act now," Aurelius said. "Before she becomes too involved with mundane interests."

He looked around the chamber. "It is time to vote," he said. They had debated the plan endlessly, ever since Shadye's death. But it hadn't been until the MageMaster weakened badly enough to pass most of his duties to Aurelius–and access to the wards running through Mountaintop–that it had become practical. "Do we vote aye or nay?"

Cloak's illusion never wavered, but there was a definite hint of amusement in his tone. "I believe we are forgetting one tiny detail," he said. "A Lone Power. How... *careless* a thing to forget."

"Void... will have other issues to keep his attention," Aurelius said, stiffly. "But I do not believe he would object, provided she was not harmed. And she will *not* be harmed. Merely... re-educated."

One by one, they voted.

Aurelius smiled as the votes were tallied. All of them, even Masters Ashworth and Ashfall, had voted in favor, some more enthusiastically than others. Some probably had plans to draw advantages from the whole scheme, others because they intended to use it as leverage in later negotiations, but in the end it didn't matter why they'd agreed. He knew, even if they didn't, that it didn't really matter *why* they'd voted in favor.

All that mattered was that they *had*.

Chapter One

EMILY GLANCED BOTH WAYS UP AND DOWN THE CORRIDOR, THEN KNELT IN FRONT OF THE heavy stone door and reached out with her mind. There was no physical lock holding it shut, merely an incredibly complex spell woven together from literally hundreds of spell components. It would pose no barrier to the person who had set the spell, but anyone else would find themselves either unable to enter or be forced to unpick the spell piece by piece, just to gain entry. The spell was so well-crafted that it was already reacting to her intrusion.

She felt a moment of admiration for the professor who had created the spell–she had hardly any time to study it to determine how best to proceed–then plunged her mind into the spell, trying to sniff out its weak spot and destroy it. A spell so complex would have no shortage of components that could be removed, weakening the spell; she pushed her mind forward, feeling magic crackle around her as the spell continued to react. To stop now would leave her exposed to the spell–and whatever it was designed to do to unwanted intruders.

It felt like hours before she saw the knots of spell components holding the whole network together, but she knew it was no more than a few seconds. Time always seemed to slow down when she thrust her mind into a web of magic. Summoning a dispersal spell, she pushed it at the spell component and watched it evaporate into nothingness. The magic chasing her seemed to fade at the exact same moment. Emily felt a flicker of triumph, which faded as she realized the remainder of the network of spells wasn't collapsing. Instead, it was reconfiguring itself...

Horror flashed through her mind as she recalled the Mimic, then she realized–too late–what she was seeing. The professor had been clever, very clever. His spell had been designed to collapse into another pattern when someone removed the vital component. The magic powering the spell hadn't evaporated; it had merely fallen into another spell and charged the new pattern instead. And there was no time left to deal with the new configuration. Magic flared around her...

...And she found herself back in her body, utterly unable to move.

Damn, she thought.

It had been Lady Barb's idea to have Emily test her skills against the defenses various professors mounted on their doors. Trying to break into professorial offices was an old tradition at Whitehall, after all. Emily had cracked three doors in the last two days, but they'd belonged to professors known to be weak in magic or magical skill. Professor Lombardi was neither.

She gathered her magic and tried to break the spell holding her firmly in place, but it refused to budge. It was difficult to tell if the spell was simply resistant to the magic she was using or if there was something about it that broke up and absorbed the spellwork before she could even trigger it. The professor's defenses were clearly far more complex than the simple freeze spells students practiced on one another in First Year.

"Well," a voice said. "What do we have here?"

Emily had to wait until Professor Lombardi stepped into her field of vision before she saw him. He was a short man with lightly-tanned skin, wearing–instead of the robes of professors and students–a leather jacket and trousers that seemed to catch and reflect the light in odd ways. The scars on his hands, a reminder of failed experiments, seemed to look worse every year. And he looked far from happy.

"Emily," Professor Lombardi said. "You do realize that trying to break into the office of a Charms Master could be very dangerous?"

Yes, Emily thought. It was a point of law in the Allied Lands that magicians could do anything they wanted to anyone who tried to break into their homes. A magician's home was his kingdom and he could defend it however he saw fit. The Grandmaster wouldn't allow his professors to use anything lethal to defend their offices, but anyone caught in the act of trying to break in could expect harsh punishment at the very least.

"Let us see now," Professor Lombardi said. He inspected the door, then turned to meet her frozen eyes. "You got past the first level, but the second caught you. I'd expect better from a student with more advanced tutoring in charms."

He paused. "Of course, the third or fourth levels were primed with nastier defensive spells," he added. "The third level would have turned you into a slug, while the fourth level would have knocked you out and kept you out. And you really don't want to know what the fifth level would have done. Now... *punishment*."

Emily cringed, mentally, as Professor Lombardi assumed a contemplative pose. He wasn't an easy-going professor, not by any definition of the term. Emily had seen enough accidents, even in a carefully-supervised classroom, to find it hard to blame him. A moment's carelessness could inflict permanent damage on an idiotic student. At the very least, she could look forward to a short uncomfortable session with the Warden.

"I'm afraid that won't be necessary," Lady Barb's voice said. She sounded to be coming down the corridor, but Emily couldn't turn her head to see. "Emily was acting on my instructions."

Professor Lombardi's face darkened. "And do the two of you have an excuse for setting a student loose on my wards?"

Emily felt a flicker of surprise. *Two* of them?

"Yes," Lady Barb said. "It's called practice."

Emily heard her fingers snapping. A second later, the spell holding Emily in place shattered, releasing her from its grip. She staggered and would have fallen to the ground if Professor Lombardi hadn't held out a hand and caught her. Her heartbeat was suddenly very loud in her ears, as if all involuntary functions had come to a halt while she'd been held by the spell. Or perhaps there was some function included in the spellwork that had kept her calm, despite being helplessly trapped. She knew she couldn't ask the professor until he was in a better mood.

She turned, forcing herself to stand upright. Tall and blonde, Lady Barb's patrician composure broke slightly to wink at her. Her silver armor glittered in the light emanating from the walls. Beside her, Sergeant Miles looked like an amiable gnome.

His short brown hair seemed damp, clinging to his skull. Emily's eyes narrowed as she realized he was standing too close to Lady Barb, his sleeve brushing against hers...

It was selfish, she knew. But she couldn't help a pang of bitter jealously and fear at this fresh evidence that Lady Barb and Sergeant Miles were lovers.

"This is outrageous," Professor Lombardi said. "You do *not* turn a student loose on my wards for *practice*."

"You were the first professor who managed to stop her," Lady Barb pointed out, mildly. "I think you should be proud of your success."

Professor Lombardi glowered at her, but Lady Barb cut him off before he could say anything.

"Emily, the Grandmaster wishes to speak with you," she said. "Go to his office. I'll speak to you afterwards."

"And you can tell him that I object in the strongest possible terms to allowing *anyone* to practice on my wards," Professor Lombardi said. "And if you hadn't been encouraged by your *tutors...*"

"Testing wards is hardly an unimportant part of her training," Sergeant Miles said. As always, he seemed utterly inoffensive. If Emily had met him without his armor or uniform, she would never have taken him for a soldier, let alone a combat sorcerer. "And besides, testing the defenses here is an old rite of passage for students."

"And so is hideous punishment for those who get caught," Professor Lombardi snapped. "Emily; *go*."

Emily nodded apologetically and fled down the corridor. Behind her, she heard the argument getting louder, then fade out as Whitehall's wards absorbed the noise. She slowed as soon as she turned the corner and walked up the stairs to the Grandmaster's office. Whitehall felt eerily quiet to her, although she wasn't sure if she was imagining it. She knew it would be another month before the majority of the staff and students returned from holiday and resumed their studies.

She paused outside the Grandmaster's office and checked her appearance in the mirror hanging from the wall. Her dark brown hair had grown longer, reaching down to the small of her back. She was tempted to keep it that way, although she knew she would need to cut it before classes resumed in the fall. But her face no longer looked pale, even compared to the dark shirt and trousers she wore, while her body looked stronger and healthier than ever. And she felt more confident too, despite the certain knowledge that she would have been in real trouble if Lady Barb hadn't intervened. She could have endured whatever Professor Lombardi chose to dish out as punishment.

The Grandmaster's door was solid wood. Emily hesitated, then tapped once. It creaked open a second later, allowing her to enter the office. Surprisingly, there was a large bookshelf mounted against the far wall, something that hadn't been there the last time she'd visited the Grandmaster's office. The Grandmaster normally kept his office completely barren, which no longer surprised her. He was blind.

"Emily," the Grandmaster said, rising to his feet. "Take a seat."

Emily sat and studied the Grandmaster as he returned a book to the shelf. He was a short man, barely taller than Sergeant Miles, yet he radiated power that blurred into the wards surrounding Whitehall. As always, a white cloth was wrapped around his eyes, a reminder of his blindness. Emily knew he had to see in some form, perhaps through magic, but she had no idea how it worked. She'd asked, once, and had been told she would have to wait to learn when her own magic was strong enough to use the technique.

Perhaps I should introduce Braille, she thought, morbidly. There were spells to cure blindness, but they were only available to the rich or well-connected. Poorer victims couldn't hope to have their blindness cured. It made them completely useless to their families, nothing but an additional mouth to feed. Braille might make the difference between them having a chance to live or being thrown out into the gutter to die.

But she didn't know how to recreate Braille from what little she knew of it...

The concept might work if I passed it on to someone, she thought. *They'd have a clue how to proceed...*

The Grandmaster cleared his throat. Emily started in embarrassment.

"I trust you have been enjoying your time at school without actually having to attend classes," the Grandmaster said. "You've certainly been keeping the librarian busy."

Emily flushed. She'd spent over half of each day in the library, just reading her way through the colossal collection of books on magic and the Allied Lands. The remainder of the days had been spent with Lady Barb or Sergeant Miles, exercising and practicing newer forms of magic. Some of them had been so tricky she doubted she would be able to master them for years to come.

"Yes, sir," she said.

The Grandmaster hesitated, then got to the point. "You will recall the events of last year, of course," he said. "Lin stole some of your notes and almost killed you."

Emily nodded, even though the Grandmaster couldn't see it. She still had night-mares about how close she'd come to death, time and time again. The Mimic would have killed her outright, then stolen her form, but the Gorgon's magic would have leeched away her thoughts piece by piece, eventually leaving her as nothing more than a stone statue. It was a thoroughly horrifying way to die.

And the Gorgon would have been blamed for my death, she thought. *Lin would have covered her tracks very neatly.*

"We have been investigating since then," the Grandmaster continued. His voice sounded oddly awkward. "We have uncovered a plot to kidnap you."

Emily blinked. "Kidnap *me?*"

"You *are* quite important," the Grandmaster pointed out, sardonically. "If you didn't have such a powerful guardian, it is quite likely there would be *more* plots to kidnap or assassinate you. Your mere presence has turned the world upside down."

Emily took a long breath. "And what should I do? Hide?"

"No," the Grandmaster said. "We want you to let yourself be kidnapped."

He went on before Emily could say a word. "The kidnap plot seems to come from Mountaintop," he said, referring to one of the rival schools of magic. *Lin* had come from Mountaintop, along with a number of other exchange students. "They actually asked for you to be considered for the student exchange program in Second Year. Now... we believe they are moving to find a way to bring you to Mountaintop without our permission."

Emily frowned. "By *kidnapping* me?"

"They would probably make it look like an accident," the Grandmaster said. "Or perhaps have someone else do the kidnapping, then claim they rescued you. The point, Emily, is that they would have you at Mountaintop. At that point..."

He hesitated, noticeably. "At that point they will try to seduce you."

Emily felt herself blushing. Male attention had always bothered her, although she had a feeling that it was more of a legacy from her stepfather than anything more fundamental. But the thought was absurd. Did they plan to send a handsome young wizard to woo her?

"They'll offer you knowledge and power," the Grandmaster said. "Lin... will have told them that you have a habit of pushing the limits. They'll give you access to forbidden books, show you magics you are not yet ready to handle and encourage you to progress forward as fast as you think you can go. Mountaintop does not have a reputation for turning out excellent sorcerers without cause, Emily. There is a great deal they will be able to offer you."

"Oh," Emily said. She swallowed, nervously, as it dawned on her that it *would* be tempting. She'd resented the librarian's flat refusal to show her some of the forbidden books without permission from the Grandmaster more than she cared to admit. "But what will they want in exchange?"

"They'll want *you*, on *their* side," the Grandmaster said.

Emily frowned before she looked up at him, staring at the cloth covering his eyes. "And why do you want me to... to *let* them kidnap me?"

The thought was nightmarish. She *hated* being helpless. Being trapped by a professor's wards was one thing, but deliberately letting herself be taken... it was horrifying. She felt her heart start to pound as it dawned on her she could be walking into a trap.

"There's something going on at Mountaintop," the Grandmaster said. He picked a file up from his desk and passed it to her. "Spying on us is one thing, but there are other—worrying—rumors. The MageMaster hasn't been seen in public for over a year and we have picked up hints that there's a power struggle underway within the school. This plot to kidnap you may be part of it, Emily, or it may be something more sinister.

"We have tried to discover what is happening, but none of our sources have been able to provide answers. And yet Mountaintop produces a fourth of the combat sorcerers and trained magicians available to the Allied Lands. We *must* know what is wrong, *if* something is wrong. And we have been unable to slip someone through their defenses."

"But they *want* me there," Emily said, remembering the story of the Trojan Horse. "They'll take me in because they *want* me."

"Precisely," the Grandmaster said.

"And you want me to do *what?*"

"Look around," the Grandmaster said. "Find out what's happening, if you can. We don't expect you to do anything else."

"That sounds vague," Emily told him.

The Grandmaster smiled. "There's no point in issuing precise instructions you might not be able to follow," he said. "We don't know *what* you'll find when you enter the school."

Emily stared down at her pale hands. "And what... what if they just *kill* me?"

"They'd be out of their minds," the Grandmaster said.

Emily just *looked* at him. She'd been in the Allied Lands for just over two years. In that time, she'd met far too many people who could be described as being out of their minds. Shadye the Necromancer, the Iron Duchess, Hodge...

"They believe you to be a Child of Destiny," the Grandmaster said. "Right now, the Necromancers are slowly winning the war. Your presence must swing matters in our favor because there's no other way it can go. Your loss would mean all of us losing everything to the Necromancers.

"And besides, for you to suffer an accident would start another war," he added. "You are a student of Whitehall, after all, and entitled to our protection. And your guardian would hardly take your death lightly. No, they won't kill you. But they *will* try to seduce you."

He paused. "And you already know there are far too many ways to tamper with a person's mind."

Emily nodded. Lin had been a mistress of Subtle Magic. So had Mother Holly. And, done properly, it was incredibly difficult to prove that someone had been under the influence at any time. She might go to Mountaintop and find herself slowly bewitched, never knowing she wasn't acting entirely of her own volition. It wasn't a pleasant thought.

But Lin had her notes. Who knew what she could do with them?

Gunpowder, Emily thought. *Steam engines. Everything else I thought might be worth considering...*

And she could copy them, easily, her own thoughts reminded her. *By now, there could be hundreds of copies. You can't put the genie back in the bottle.*

"You don't have to decide immediately," the Grandmaster said. "And we won't hold it against you if you decide to turn down the task. But we need an answer within two or three days."

"I understand," Emily said.

"You can consult Lady Barb or Sergeant Miles, if you like," the Grandmaster told her. "And don't worry about Professor Lombardi. I'll have a few words with him."

Emily nodded, ruefully. All of a sudden, spending the next few weeks in detention didn't seem like a bad thing. It might be dirty and unpleasant, but it didn't carry the risk of death.

"How long will you want me to stay there?" she asked. "A month?"

"They will try to tempt you into spending your entire Third Year at Mountaintop," the Grandmaster said. "It won't affect your grades, I think."

"I see," Emily said.

"You may go," the Grandmaster said. He tapped his desk, then looked at her with his sightless eyes. "You're excused from everything else for the rest of the day. But think carefully before you give us an answer."

Emily nodded, then stood and left the room.

Chapter Two

EMILY PAUSED TO WIPE THE SWEAT FROM HER EYES AS SHE REACHED THE LEDGE, THEN SAT down on the grassy knoll. Jade had shown it to her, two years ago, back when they'd first started exploring the mountains surrounding Whitehall. He'd claimed that it made an excellent place to sit and think, well away from the school yet close enough to get back quickly if necessary, but in hindsight Emily sometimes wondered if he'd had other motives in bringing her to the secluded spot. It assured privacy... at least to magicians. But it hardly mattered now.

She shook her head, then gazed down at the school. From high overhead, Whitehall shimmered in the sun. Brilliant flickers of light seemed to dance around the castle, giving it an atmosphere of fragility, almost like a fantasy palace from a Disney movie. And yet the wards protecting the building were far stronger than any merely physical defense. It was impossible to break them without inside help.

And Shadye had inside help, she reflected, bitterly. *Me.*

The memories of Shadye's attack on Whitehall still felt nightmarish, even now. It was odd how her memories of Earth had faded as she'd grown accustomed to the Nameless World, but she'd never quite been able to rid herself of her darker memories. Shadye had used her, manipulating her sleeping body like a puppet, forcing her to lower the wards and allow him access to Whitehall. And he'd come far too close to success to suit her.

She sighed before forcing her churning thoughts to slow down. Shadye was dead, forced into a pocket dimension that had then been deleted, wiping him from existence. Few people knew how he'd broken into Whitehall and fewer still knew how he'd been defeated. Emily's success had made her a hero, yet it had also started ripples of change running across the Allied Lands. The innovations she'd introduced, ideas from Earth, had spread far out of her control. It was no wonder, she admitted privately, that she'd been targeted by spies, kidnappers and assassins. The knowledge in her head could change the Allied Lands for the better—or the worse.

"You shouldn't come up here alone," a familiar voice said, from behind her. "This isn't a safe place for *anyone*, let alone you."

Emily flushed as she turned to see Lady Barb pulling herself onto the ledge. The older woman looked tired, yet surprisingly understanding as she strode over and sat down next to Emily, staring out over the castle below. Emily sighed inwardly—she'd hoped to be alone for a good while, long enough to have a proper think—then started to rise to her feet. She wanted to pace.

"Sit down," Lady Barb said, without turning her head. "You really *shouldn't* have come up here."

"I wanted to be alone," Emily confessed. "I..."

"There's an entire castle full of empty classrooms and abandoned dormitories," Lady Barb pointed out, snidely. "You could have sneaked into a Year Six study and claimed it as your own."

"It wouldn't have been the same," Emily said. She knew just how closely the interior of Whitehall was monitored. Anyone who had wanted to find her quickly could have just asked the wards. "And besides..."

She waved a hand, indicating the natural beauty surrounding them. On Earth, she had never left the city, never seen anywhere closer to nature than a park. But here... Sergeant Miles and Jade had introduced her to the joys of walking for pleasure, even though the mountains surrounding Whitehall were home to all manner of creatures, some of them more dangerous than anything walking on two legs. But she'd been careful not to go anywhere near the truly dangerous areas.

"You should have asked one of us to accompany you," Lady Barb said, firmly. "Particularly now. The Grandmaster told you what he had in mind, I assume?"

"Yes," Emily said. She felt her cheeks heat with embarrassment. It had never really occurred to her that *anyone* would need to give up their work to accompany her up the mountain, even now. Some of the teachers had more time for her now it was outside term time, but others had left the building for a well-deserved holiday. She hadn't wanted to intrude on their business, whatever it was. "I'm sorry."

"So you should be," Lady Barb said, firmly. She turned, allowing her bright blue eyes to meet Emily's. "Have you come to a decision?"

Emily frowned and looked away. "I don't know," she said. "Part of me wants to do it, to recover the notes Lin stole; part of me thinks it's too dangerous..."

"This from the girl who challenged Mother Holly," Lady Barb said, dryly. "And has the most fearsome reputation in the Allied Lands."

"Apart from Void and the others like him," Emily said. She looked around, half-expecting the ancient sorcerer to appear. "Do you think he would approve of this?"

Lady Barb snorted. "Do you need his permission to go to the bathroom?"

Emily looked back at her, refusing to be distracted. "This is a little more complex and dangerous than going to the bathroom," she said. "And I don't know *what* he would make of it."

"Sink or swim," Lady Barb said. "*That* will be his attitude."

She shrugged. "Emily," she added, "there's one thing you need to know right now. If you refuse this mission, no one will complain and it will certainly not be counted against you in the future. You have no obligation to help us deal with the puzzle surrounding Mountaintop, or anything other than being a good student and graduating with a respectable number of awards and plaudits."

"But it's partly my fault," Emily said. "Lin... Lin wouldn't have come to Whitehall if I hadn't been there."

"True," Lady Barb agreed. "But that doesn't make it your responsibility to deal with the aftermath."

Emily shook her head, slowly. The great advantage of everything she'd introduced to the Allied Lands was in how easily everything could be duplicated. Kings and princes had barely realized there was a new system of reading and writing–to say nothing of numerals and printing presses–before it had already swept the Allied

Lands. People who had been forced to memorize hundreds of thousands of symbols to read and write—and even those interested in basic learning had needed to master thousands of symbols—had no trouble at all with the English alphabet. Their spelling might be chaotic, but it was far superior to the previous system. And there were other innovations on the way.

But she had no idea how many of her notes Lin had copied or stolen over the months they'd shared a room. Had she copied the plans for steam engines, rifles and machine guns... or something far more dangerous? The nuke-spell? Mother Holly's death had been largely explained, according to the Grandmaster, by her losing control of the magic she'd stolen, but Emily doubted the cover story would be universally believed. Mountaintop might put her notes together with the observed end results and draw the correct conclusion.

"We don't know much about Mountaintop," Lady Barb said, breaking into her thoughts. Her voice was oddly pensive. "The exact location of the school is unknown. We don't even know the names of most of the teachers who teach at Mountaintop. The only thing we know for certain is that almost all of the magical families send at least one or two of their children there to study. *And* that they graduate a sizable percentage of the combat sorcerers available to the Allied Lands."

Emily frowned. "You don't even know where to *look* for the school?"

"We have a rough idea," Lady Barb explained. "But we don't have a precise location."

"Oh," Emily said.

She rolled her eyes. Magicians seemed to have a somewhat childish obsession with secrecy, even though she had good reason to be grateful for the law that insisted that no magician could be forced to share his inventions and innovations with his peers. Apparently, spying on one's fellow magicians could take up a great deal of an up-and-coming magician's time, something Emily found a little depressing. *Earth* had only progressed as far as it had because ideas were shared, then improved upon and shared again. There was no such thing as crowd-sourcing for magicians.

It was something she wanted to change. But, given how hard it was to encourage magicians to work together, she knew it wouldn't be easy.

"I thought everyone knew where Whitehall is," she said. "How can they be unaware of Mountaintop's location?"

"Different priorities," Lady Barb said. "Back in the days of the Empire, Whitehall was meant to introduce the magical and non-magical families as much as it was meant to teach, while Mountaintop was dedicated to turning out combat sorcerers. They were allowed to hide themselves from detection."

She shrugged. "And now... we don't know where to look for them," she added. "They don't seem to have a nexus point for us to track. But neither do any passing necromancers."

Emily shuddered. Shadye had torn Whitehall apart in his bid to capture her, despite the presence of hundreds of magicians of varying levels of power and training. The battle had been savage and would have been lost if Emily hadn't thought very fast on her feet. It was quite understandable that Mountaintop would wish to hide. But it was also very worrying.

"They could kill me or keep me prisoner indefinitely," she said, numbly.

"They would be fools," Lady Barb said, bluntly. "Holding you indefinitely, let alone killing you, would certainly provoke a reaction from your... from your supposed father. The more blatant methods of controlling your mind would also be considered far beyond the pale. If they weren't desperate, I suspect, they would never be considering any form of blatant attempt to grab you."

Emily *looked* at the older woman. "Desperate?"

"They're taking a risk," Lady Barb said. "A *serious* risk. This could spark off a civil war among magicians, draw the wrath of a Lone Power or even hand the Allied Lands to the necromancers on a plate. They wouldn't be committing themselves this openly if they didn't have good reason to believe it was necessary."

"I see," Emily said.

She sighed, knowing she'd already made up her mind. "How are we going to do this?"

"If you're willing to take the risk," Lady Barb said, "you and I will travel to the White City. I have an open invitation to meet up with several prominent figures in the White Council and I intend to introduce you to them."

Her lips quirked. "It will be completely hush-hush, of course," she added. "The entire city will be aware of your presence within hours."

Emily had to smile. "And they'll try to kidnap me?"

"They'll certainly have no better chance," Lady Barb said, smiling back. Her expression vanished a moment later. "However, they'll probably want to make it look like an accident that you ended up in Mountaintop. They wouldn't kidnap you violently and then expect you to play the role of a normal student."

"I suppose not," Emily said. The Grandmaster had said the same thing. She had a sudden mental vision of being chained to a desk and being expected to pay attention to a faceless teacher. It didn't seem like an environment that would be conducive to learning. "They'd want me to think I'd been rescued from a worse fate."

"It's quite likely," Lady Barb agreed. She reached out and gripped Emily's shoulder. "You have to understand the risks, Emily. We will give you all the protections we can, all the little precautions that most magical children learn from the day they start practicing magic, but it would be easy for them to play games with your mind. You, of all people, know how easy it is to influence a person's thoughts."

Emily nodded, eyes downcast. Blatant mind control spells were noticeable, but subtle magic, pushing a person's thoughts in a particular direction, was incredibly hard to spot, let alone counteract. A victim might never realize that he or she wasn't acting of his own volition. If Lin hadn't used such magic on her, Emily reflected bitterly, the spy might have been discovered before the Mimic had been destroyed and the wards lifted, allowing her to make her escape.

She looked down at the two bracelets on her arm. One was her familiar, trapped in an inanimate form; the other was a protective bracelet she'd sewn herself, back

during the days they'd stayed in the Cairngorm Mountains. The second bracelet protected her from subtle magic, she knew, but the first thing any kidnappers would do
if they wanted to make her vulnerable would be to remove the bracelet and everything else. Her lips thinned at the thought, then relaxed.

They'd have a very nasty surprise if they removed the wrong bracelet, she thought,
morbidly.

"There are other forms of temptation," Lady Barb told her. "You could be offered
power beyond your wildest dreams."

"I have power," Emily pointed out. "But I never wanted it."

Lady Barb lifted an eyebrow. "You never wanted to reshape the world to suit
yourself?"

Emily flushed red. On Earth, she would have given her eyeteeth for enough power
to protect herself from the outside world, but she'd never wanted power over other
people. But being a baroness was all about having power over her subordinates... her
serfs. In a very real sense, she *owned* hundreds of thousands of people. It wasn't something she was comfortable with, nor did she really want it. Yet, as far as she could tell,
there was no way to put it down.

"Not like that," she said. If she'd been able to choose, she would have gone into a
library and just stayed there. "Can they offer me something beyond being a Baroness
of Zangaria?"

"Yes," Lady Barb said, flatly.

Emily waited for her to elaborate, but the older woman said nothing, withdraw-
ing into her thoughts. There was a peal of thunder in the distance, loud enough to
surprise her. When she looked up, she saw dark clouds gathering over the mountain
peaks in the distance. The weather surrounding Whitehall, thanks to the nexus
point under the castle, was variable and subject to change without notice.

Lady Barb climbed to her feet. "We'd better get down off the mountain," she said,
as she held out a hand to help Emily. "We don't want to get caught in a rainstorm."

She kept talking as they found the path and made their way downwards, passing
endless bushes of prickly thorns and trees that seemed to reach upwards to infinity.
"You won't be able to change your mind afterwards," Lady Barb warned, as Emily
followed her. "I don't think we will be able to get someone in to help you. Picking you
for this mission is clever, but it has a great many risks."

Emily frowned. "Clever?"

"Anyone else—any normal exchange student—would be kept under tight supervision," Lady Barb said. "He would never be shown any of the innermost secrets of
Mountaintop. You, on the other hand... they'd want to seduce you to their side. They
will have good reason to show you everything they can."

A low rumble of thunder interrupted her words. Moments later, raindrops started
crashing down around them. Emily cast a basic ward to protect herself, then kept following Lady Barb as water started to pool around their feet. Lady Barb didn't bother
with a ward. She didn't seem to care about the water, Emily realized. All that mattered to Lady Barb was getting back to Whitehall as quickly as possible.

"You need to watch your back carefully," Lady Barb warned, as they reached the edge of the wards protecting the castle. Lightning flashed as they stepped through the wards and ran towards the heavy doors. "You cannot trust anyone there."

Emily canceled her protective spell as they tumbled into the castle. "Is there no one who could advise me?"

Lady Barb hesitated. "There is someone," she said, finally. There was something in her voice that made Emily reluctant to press the issue. "I will speak with him and see if he will assist us."

She took a breath before casting a spell to dry herself. "You can join me and Sergeant Miles for dinner tonight," she said. "Then you can go to bed. There will be quite a bit of preparation to do before we turn you loose on Mountaintop."

Emily nodded, feeling a sudden surge of affection for the prickly older woman. "Thank you," she said, sincerely. She paused. "Did you know about this before we left for the mountains?"

"Yes," Lady Barb said. She held up a hand before Emily could say a word. "And I didn't tell you, to answer your next question, because you didn't need to worry about it during our holiday."

"Holiday," Emily repeated. It had been muddy and unpleasant and she'd seen more than she'd wanted to see of how the poorer parts of the Allied Lands lived. But it had also been educational, and she'd enjoyed having Lady Barb to herself. It was almost like having a proper mother. "Thank you, I suppose."

"Thank me when you come back," Lady Barb said.

She turned and headed towards the stairs, then stopped and looked back. "Join us in my apartment at three bells," she told Emily. "I'll have a book sent to you, one from the forbidden section. I want you to read it thoroughly, as I will quiz you over dinner. And then you will have some hard choices to make."

"I understand," Emily said, even though she didn't. But she also knew she'd get nowhere by badgering the older woman. Students at Whitehall were expected to do more than just memorize something long enough to pass an exam and then forget it. "I'll see you at dinnertime."

Chapter Three

IUNDERSTAND THAT YOU READ THE BOOK," PROFESSOR ELEAS SAID, THE FOLLOWING MORN-ing. "Do you understand what we're asking you to do?"

Emily swallowed, and nodded. The book had made uncomfortable reading. There was one permanent defense against subtle magic, but it involved carving runes into her bare flesh, personally. The defense, for reasons the book's author had felt unable to specify, didn't work so well if someone else carved the runes.

She looked around the office, unwilling to meet the petite professor's compassionate gaze. It was a fascinating room, lined with overflowing bookshelves, enough books to keep Emily going for weeks. One wall was decorated with tiny knives and surgical tools that were part of the professor's craft, while a small chair sat in the far corner. Emily wanted to look away from it, knowing—thanks to her reading—what purpose it served. Reluctantly, she looked back at the professor. His gaze had never left her face.

He was a short potbellied man, wearing nothing more than a loincloth. His skin, even his bald head, was covered in runes, mostly carved by himself. Emily shuddered at the thought of pricking her own skin with a knife, let alone following a careful outline to complete the rune on her bare skin. The professor had carved so many runes into his body that a single mistake could have destroyed his life's work. Few magicians used so many runes, even to protect themselves. Emily understood why.

"Emily," the professor repeated. "Do you understand what we're asking you to do?"

"Yes," Emily whispered. "You want me to carve my own skin."

"Yes," Professor Eleas said, bluntly. "It will not be easy. One mistake, just one, and we will have to heal the skin quickly and start again. We cannot risk allowing you to walk away with an imperfect rune on your body. The results would be... bad."

Emily nodded, unable to speak. Her reading had told her precisely how bad it could be, if she made a single mistake. She might accidentally curse herself, leave her mind open and vulnerable or even blight herself with bad luck. There were too many dangers for anyone to accept it blithely.

"They'll know what I did," she said, quietly.

"They will," Professor Eleas agreed. "But how could they complain?"

They couldn't, Emily thought, gazing at the professor's bare chest. *Everyone who can uses protection against subtle magic.*

"Lady Barb will draw out the rune on your body," the professor said. He touched his chest, between his nipples. A large rune had been carved out there, glowing with a faint blue light. "But I will have to check it before you start carving."

Emily flushed. "There's no alternative?"

"I *am* the expert," Professor Eleas said. He didn't sound annoyed. "There's no time to call anyone else, Emily." He tried a reassuring smile. "Lady Barb will be in the room."

Emily cringed, mentally. She'd never liked undressing in front of anyone, even other girls. Growing up in a house where her stepfather had watched her had left her mentally scarred, unable to wear tight-fitting or revealing clothing for fear of exposing far too much. And yet, somehow, it was no longer as horrifying a thought as it had once been.

But there was no time to dwell on her feelings.

"I understand," she whispered, gritting her teeth. "Let's get on with it."

Professor Eleas nodded, making a motion in the air with his left hand. Moments later, Lady Barb entered, her face utterly expressionless. Emily knew the older woman well enough to understand that she was worried, perhaps more worried than she was prepared to admit. She'd known just how hard it would be for Emily to expose herself to anyone.

"Draw out the rune," Professor Eleas ordered, passing her the chalk. "I will turn my back."

He suited action to words as Lady Barb stepped over to Emily and motioned for her to take the chair. Magic—barely powerful enough to be sensed over the constant background hum from the school's wards—shimmered around Emily as she sat down, doing what it could to prepare her for her ordeal. Lady Barb sighed, then pointed a finger at Emily's shirt. Flushing, Emily pulled it off, then removed her makeshift bra. Lady Barb rested one hand on Emily's shoulder and then started to draw on her bare flesh between her breasts. Looking down, Emily could see a simple rune taking shape. It looked like a slightly lopsided six-point star.

"Done," Lady Barb said. Compared to the complex, snake-like runes on the professor's bare back, it was simplicity itself. "Professor?"

Emily closed her eyes, feeling her face grow red and hot. There was a long pause, then she heard the professor turn away again. Lady Barb pushed something into her hand; Emily opened her eyes and saw a simple silver knife. She knew, from experience, that it would be spelled to remain sharp and clean indefinitely. And that it would cut through her flesh as easily as it would cut through butter.

"Be careful," Lady Barb said, as she rolled a large mirror over to allow Emily to see what she was doing. "And if you make a mistake, put the knife down *at once.*"

"I know," Emily said, miserably. She had to do it. If anyone else did the carving, the rune could simply be healed, canceling the magic. The only way to embed it into her skin properly was to carve it herself. "I understand."

She couldn't help staring at her breasts as she lifted the knife, feeling just how solid it was in her hand. They were nowhere near as large or shapely as Alassa's—but then, she'd never wanted to have giant breasts in the first place. Her damned stepfather had left her with enough body issues to worry about what would happen, if they'd been any larger. And besides, she simply hadn't eaten enough as she was growing to make them grow properly, along with the rest of her body. She'd been more than a little malnourished when she'd arrived at Whitehall.

At least I'm not a D-Cup, she thought. *That would attract far too much attention.*

Carefully, she placed the blade against her chest, but hesitated. There was no way any form of pain relief spells could be used, not here. Magic always came with a price, she knew, and pain was part of the price for carving magical runes into one's own body. She gritted her teeth, then pressed the blade against her skin. It was hard, so hard, to overcome her body's reluctance to harm itself. But if it wasn't, she suspected, she might have killed herself long before she'd discovered the multiverse was far bigger than anyone knew.

This is my world now, she thought. *And I will defend it.*

She felt a prick as the blade pierced her skin. A drop of blood appeared around the blade, followed by a pain that seemed somehow greater than reasonable for a simple prick. But it was true that a simple paper cut could hurt worse than broken bones, she thought in an attempt to distract herself, although she'd never been sure why. It was almost more than she could do to move the knife, but as she drew it along her skin it was somehow easier and easier to make the cut. She twisted the knife to follow the drawn rune, sucking in her breath at the pain.

And then there was a flare of magic. It was done.

"Good," Lady Barb said. She produced a cloth and wiped Emily's chest, removing the blood. The wound itself was already healing with astonishing speed, the process accelerated by the magic surrounding the chair. "Good enough, I believe. Professor?"

Professor Eleas turned and inspected Emily's work. "Good," he said, coldly. "It will provide protection against light subtle magics—and warn you of the presence of more complex magics."

Emily nodded, suddenly feeling very lightheaded.

"Drink this," Lady Barb said, passing Emily a potions gourd. "It won't taste nice, but it will help."

It tasted horrible, Emily discovered, as she drank the potion. Potions *never* tasted very nice. But the dizziness slowly faded away, allowing Emily to stand and look down at the mess she'd made. Blood had stained her trousers, leaving her feeling uncomfortably messy and unclean.

Maybe I should have stripped, she thought. But she'd been unable to bear the thought of removing everything.

"There's a shower and clean clothes in the next room," Lady Barb said. She pointed towards a door in the wall Emily was certain hadn't been there a moment ago. "Wash yourself thoroughly, then get dressed and come meet me in the drawing room. Put the rest of your clothes in the basket and the household staff will dispose of them."

Emily nodded, feeling oddly disconnected from her body, then trudged through the door. Inside was a simple shower, almost like one from Earth. Whitehall was staggeringly luxurious compared to the rest of the Allied Lands, even the monarchs who dominated most of the kingdoms; indeed, she had a feeling that she was the only student whose living conditions had degraded since coming to the school. But she wouldn't have given it up for anything, she told herself savagely. Whitehall was the only place she'd ever felt truly at home.

She washed thoroughly before looking at her chest in the mirror. The rune was harder to see than she'd expected, nothing more than a set of lines on her bare skin, but she could sense its presence in the magic field surrounding her body. She checked herself carefully, making sure that she wasn't bleeding magic in all directions, then dried her body and reached for the robe Lady Barb had left for her. Once, she'd never worn anything like it. Now, wearing the long robes felt almost like second nature. She pulled it over her head, checked her appearance in the mirror again, then walked out the door and headed through the long series of corridors. As always, they changed when she wasn't looking.

"Emily," the Grandmaster said, as she entered the drawing room. It was a relatively simple room, set aside for the older students and their advisors. Emily suspected she wouldn't have been allowed to use it during term time. "I understand you did well."

"More than well," Lady Barb said. She smiled at Emily, then nodded towards a steaming jug on a side table. "Pour yourself a drink and sit down."

Emily obeyed. The teachers seemed somewhat more relaxed around her—and the handful of other students in the castle—over the holidays. She'd been warned, by Lady Barb, not to expect it to continue when term resumed. The teachers had their hands full keeping order and making sure their charges didn't accidentally kill themselves. They couldn't afford to show any kind of favoritism when magic could be extremely dangerous, except on rare occasions.

"You will be leaving tomorrow," the Grandmaster said. "There is a World Game Tournament about to commence in the White City. It will serve as a suitable excuse to have you attend, without arousing suspicions."

"A World Game?" Emily asked. "What's that?"

Lady Barb smirked. "You'll find out," she said. "But you won't be attending for more than a day or two. I imagine that allowing you to go back to Whitehall without an escort will give them an opportunity to strike."

Emily nodded, trying to remember if she'd read anything about World Games. She'd always had a good memory for facts and figures, something that had served her in good stead at Whitehall, but she couldn't recall anything about World Games. But then, she *had* spent much of her time studying magic and history rather than what passed for current affairs. It was just something else that everyone born in the Allied Lands would probably take for granted, and expect her to take for granted too.

The Grandmaster leaned forward. "There is a great deal we have to go over," he said, "but time is not exactly on our side. Or theirs, for that matter. You may well have to rely completely on yourself."

"I know," Emily said. Sergeant Miles had said the same thing, repeating the point time and time again. She had a feeling that Sergeant Miles privately suspected the whole affair was a fool's errand. "I am ready."

Lady Barb eyed her. "That's misplaced confidence and you know it," she said. "I expect you to keep your eyes and ears open, but not to do anything stupid. There's no point in wreaking a terrible revenge if you're dead."

"True," the Grandmaster agreed. He clapped his hands together, loudly. "We will eat lunch now, Emily, and you can spend the rest of the day being briefed."

Dinner was a surprisingly enjoyable affair, Emily discovered. Outside his office, the Grandmaster seemed almost a different person, someone happy to talk about magic, history and the mischief some of his students got up to when they thought he wasn't watching. Emily had never known that he'd once been the Charms Tutor, or that he'd accidentally turned one of his fellow teachers into a yak when he'd been demonstrating something altogether different to his students. She couldn't help wondering—and then damning herself for stupidity—if her teachers on Earth had had lives outside of school too.

Of course they had, she told herself. *Or did you just believe they slept in coffins under the school when there were no children around?*

"Take an hour to rest," the Grandmaster urged when dinner finally came to an end. Emily glanced at her watch and was astonished to discover just how much time had passed. "And then we will see you in my office."

Lady Barb followed Emily out of the room, pulled the door closed and caught Emily's arm. "I would advise you to write letters to your friends," she said. "I would also advise you to write a will. You might not come home from this little... adventure."

Emily agreed and walked back to her room. It felt odd to sleep alone, but she knew she would miss it when her roommates returned to Whitehall. Or so she'd thought before she'd been told she needed to go to Mountaintop. Finding a pad of paper, she sat down at her desk and started to compose a letter to Alassa. She honestly wasn't sure what to say. It looked like she would be away from Whitehall for at least *part* of Third Year, perhaps all of it. And if she didn't come back...

It would feel *wrong* to be without her friends, she thought, feeling a flush of shame. She hadn't been the best of friends to *them*, not when she hadn't really known what it was like to *have* friends. And what would they feel about her if she never came home? Would Alassa mourn her death or be privately relieved that Emily, who had turned her kingdom upside down, was no longer in a position to change things? But the pace of change probably wouldn't slow down much, even if she died.

Pushing that aside, Emily wrote a series of letters to everyone she knew, then another set to be delivered in the event of her death. Once that was done, she turned her attention to writing a will. On the face of it, she had little to leave to anyone, apart from the Barony of Cockatrice. King Randor might choose to override her wishes—Emily had no natural-born heir to take her place—but she left it to Imaiqah anyway. It would be good for Alassa to have at least one friend who wouldn't be afraid—now—to tell her when she was being a stubborn idiot. Besides, Imaiqah would probably have a better idea of what to do with the Barony than Emily herself.

Shaking her head, she sealed the letters before sorting them into two piles. One set would be sent from the castle tomorrow, the remainder would be held in storage until she either destroyed them herself or she died. She looked down at the reminder of her mortality, then rose to her feet and carried the letters out of the room, closing the door behind her. A pair of students were cleaning the floor as she passed, both looking thoroughly sick of being worked to death. Emily felt little sympathy for the two miscreants. She knew what they'd done to deserve being held over the holidays and forced to clean the school without magic.

"Emily," Lady Barb said, as she entered the mailroom. The older woman had written several letters of her own. "Are you ready to be briefed?"

"I think so," Emily said. She placed her letters in the box, knowing they'd be sent as soon as humanly possible. They'd get there, eventually, but the Allied Lands postal service left something to be desired. "Are you ready to brief me?"

Lady Barb nodded, then led her out of the room and through a maze of corridors to the Grandmaster's office. The Grandmaster himself was absent, Emily saw, but Sergeant Miles and a man she didn't recognize were seated at a desk, drinking Kava and talking in hushed voices. They stopped talking as soon as they saw Emily, suggesting they'd been talking about her. Emily couldn't help the flush that rose to her cheeks. She had never been comfortable with her unwanted fame, let alone the stories that had spread from one end of the Allied Lands to the other. Some of them were thoroughly embarrassing—or disgusting.

"There is a great deal to remember," Lady Barb said, as she motioned for Emily to take a seat. "Listen carefully."

She was right, Emily discovered. Hours seemed to fly past as they drilled her, time and time again, in everything from tradecraft to escape techniques. Some of them were linked to what she'd already learned at Whitehall, others were completely new. The only thing they refused to teach her was how to teleport. She just wasn't ready to master teleporting, Sergeant Miles said, and Lady Barb agreed. Emily accepted it, resentfully. Teleporting seemed vastly preferable to hours spent riding from one place to another, but channeling so much power while remaining focused was difficult.

"Make sure you get plenty of sleep," Lady Barb said, finally. There was no give in her voice at all. "We'll be leaving early tomorrow morning."

"I'll do my best," Emily said. She knew there was no point in arguing. Her sleep had been oddly peaceful since returning to Whitehall, but she knew that wouldn't last. She had a feeling she had been suffering from a form of PTSD. And, from what she recalled, PTSD could reoccur without warning. "I'm not sure I will remember all of this."

The stranger laughed, not unkindly. "Not many people do, unless they are forced to absorb it over long periods," he said. "Use memory spells later, when you're ready to remember. And then concentrate on what else you need to know."

Emily nodded, then allowed Lady Barb to lead her back to her room.

Chapter Four

E AT QUICKLY," LADY BARB ADVISED, AS EMILY ENTERED THE SMALL DINING ROOM. "WE don't have time to waste."

Emily nodded. She'd found a packed bag outside her room in the morning, although Lady Barb had already warned her that it was unlikely her bag would be taken to Mountaintop if–when–they took her. There was little inside, apart from a change of clothes and a handful of tiny potions bottles, the kind that every sorcer-ess would carry with her at all times. They hadn't even included a book! But they wouldn't have risked adding one, she knew. It might not be returned.

She took some porridge and fruit from the side table, then sat down to eat. As always, it tasted good, better than she'd expected. But then, she didn't have much to compare it to, not from Earth. She felt too nervous to eat, but forced herself to swal-low the food, bite by bite. Who knew when she would have a chance to eat again?

"We're moving awfully quickly," she said, carefully. Lady Barb wasn't one of the teachers who exploded with rage at being asked questions, but she did get sarcastic if she believed the question to be stupid. "Is there a reason for this?"

"There are two," Lady Barb said. She watched as Emily ate, her eyes silently order-ing the younger girl to eat more breakfast. "First, we would have problems creating a convincing kidnapping opportunity for them to take you as we get closer and closer to the start of term. Second, we have been able to make contact with someone who might be able to offer advice–but he is only available for two or so days. I would prefer you had a chance to speak with him before you left."

She stood before Emily could ask any more questions and strode over to the door. "Join me in the portal chamber once you have finished eating," she ordered, as she opened the door. "And remember to bring your bag."

Emily sighed–she hated stepping through portals, even though she now knew how to protect herself–but did as she was told. As soon as she had finished eating as much as she could, she rose to her feet, picked up her bag and walked through the door. It was a pity, she told herself, that she hadn't been able to bring her staff, but after what had happened in the Cairngorm Mountains she suspected that wasn't actually a bad thing. The advantages of having the staff were outweighed by the risks of using it too much.

There was no sign of the Grandmaster–or anyone else, apart from Lady Barb–as she entered the portal chamber. The portal itself was a square of light, shimmering in the center of the room, magic flowing into a tight knot that held it firmly in place. Emily closed her eyes for a long moment, making sure her defenses were ready, then opened them again and looked at Lady Barb. The older woman gave her appearance a quick once-over, then nodded wordlessly and held out her hand. Emily took it and allowed Lady Barb to lead her up to the portal, closing her eyes again. And then there was a sudden brilliant surge of magic...

"We're here," Lady Barb said. "You can open your eyes now."

Emily opened her eyes, fighting down a surge of embarrassment. It was a *good* thing, Alassa had assured her, that she'd had such a bad reaction to her first step through a portal. It meant she had plenty of potential for magic. But the sensation still felt awful when she wasn't ready for it. She clung to Lady Barb's arm and looked around. The chamber was very different from Whitehall.

They were standing in a massive chamber filled with glowing portals, spinning in and out of existence and maintained by powerful magical fields. The portals were surrounded by heavy stone walls, interpenetrated by countless large windows, with sunlight streaming through from the outside world. Emily hesitated, then walked towards the closest window, noticing in passing that the windows were made of actual glass. It was a sure sign of colossal wealth, she knew; there were rooms in King Randor's castle that were wide open to the elements. Outside, she saw a city that fairly *shimmered* with white light.

"The White City," Lady Barb said, softly. "Home of the Emperors—and now of the White Council."

Emily barely heard her. The city seemed almost like something from a dream—or a fairy tale, just like Whitehall itself. Most of the buildings were covered in white stone, casting brilliant reflections; several looked as if nothing held them up, apart from magic. Each of the mountaintops in view had a large castle built in the heights, as if someone had hollowed out the mountains and built their homes on the tops. And they all *glowed* with white light.

She looked towards the streets below and sucked in her breath with wonder. There were marketplaces, statues of the gods and giant apartment blocks and everything else she had come to associate with the city-states, but there was also a sense of grandeur that the city-states lacked, a sense of towering proportion that dwarfed her and everyone else. Here, there were no limits.

"I should have come here sooner," she breathed. "It's beautiful."

"It's also a place where few can come without permission," Lady Barb said, giving her a fond look. She seemed content to stand beside Emily and wait while her charge drank in the view. "The city fathers don't want any riff-raff around, Emily. Someone without a place here would be evicted very quickly."

Emily looked up at her. "What happens to them?"

"Depends," Lady Barb said. "There are plenty of other places they can go."

She pointed out a handful of places for Emily to see. The White Palace, where the Emperors had once resided; the Garrison, which had served as the heart of their military machine; the Temple of Light, dedicated to the God of the Sun; Langseeker College, heart of the educational infrastructure... Emily found herself becoming dizzy with all the places and sights below her. It was almost a relief when Lady Barb finally took her arm and led her towards the doors—and the stairwell leading towards the city below.

"I don't understand," she said, as they walked down the stairs. There was something *odd* about it, but she couldn't place her finger on just what was bothering her. "Why keep the portals so far from the rest of the city?"

"They weren't, at one point," Lady Barb said, quietly. She leaned close, so close that Emily could feel Lady Barb's breath against her ears. "Ask me about it when we are back at Whitehall."

The sense of overwhelming strangeness—and magic—grew stronger as they reached the bottom of the stairwell and walked out into the open air. Unlike every other city Emily had visited, there was no foul smell, nothing caused by countless people living together without anything resembling proper sanitation. And yet there was something strange about the city that bothered her. Currents of magic, uncomfortable to her senses despite living in Whitehall, flowed through the air, sometimes brushing unpleasantly against her mind. The population paid no attention to her. Emily couldn't help feeling more than a little relieved.

She studied them as they walked, noting just how finely most of them were dressed. Once, it would have impressed her, but she had a feeling that she was looking at people quite like the lords and noblemen of Zangaria. They dressed importantly, and *acted* importantly, in an attempt to convince others that they *were* important. The more she looked at them, the more she was reminded of some of the rich girls she'd known from Earth, the ones who had always had the latest fashions or cell phones. They'd acted important too.

"You have to be quite rich to establish a home here," Lady Barb explained, as they walked through a long market street. The prices, Emily noted, were several times what they would have been in Dragon's Den. "It's the ultimate sign of wealth and power to have a home in the White City. Even those who work as tradesmen have to have a sizable fortune before they can work here."

"Nice work if you can get it," Emily muttered. It reminded her of stores on Earth where the prices were always higher than other stores, but because they were seen as fashionable they attracted customers with money to burn. "Who lives here?"

"The Grandmaster is perhaps the only person you know who maintains a permanent residence here," Lady Barb said, as they reached a large building. "My family has their own establishment, but it belongs to the family rather than one person alone."

She led the way into the building, up a long flight of stairs and then smiled as they found themselves on a balcony, looking down at a large table dominating a room the size of a dance hall.

"This is a World Game, Emily," she said. "You may want to play yourself one day."

Emily stared in frank disbelief. She'd played Chess and Risk and several other board games on Earth, but what she was looking at rivaled computer games for complexity. The board below her showed the Allied Lands, with hundreds of playing pieces in position and notations showing everything from cornfields to populations and mining towns. She'd never really had the time or equipment for such computer games—and she would have sworn the game below her was impossible for any pre-tech society.

But they have to train their memories, she thought. *They don't have anything to jog their minds if they forget.*

She looked up at Lady Barb. "What is the *point* of this?"

"Plotting out the future, they think," Lady Barb said, with a shrug. "And also having fun."

She grinned, then led Emily along the balcony and into a side room. Emily sensed a flare of magic surrounding her for a long moment, but it faded away harmlessly. Lady Barb stepped to one side, allowing her to see the man sitting in front of them, his hands clasped in his lap and eyes cold and bright. And she realized, as she bobbed a curtsey, that she recognized him.

"Master Grey," she said. As before, Jade's master looked rather like a monk: bald, muscular and grimly determined to trample over whatever opposition barred his path to his destination. And there was a sense of abiding dislike in his eyes that bothered her more than she cared to admit. "I thank you for meeting us."

Master Grey rose to his feet and bowed, slowly, in return. "I have little to say," he said. "But what I have to say is important."

"Of course," Lady Barb said. She motioned for Emily to sit down. "We appreciate this meeting."

Emily wondered, as Lady Barb passed them both mugs of Kava, just where Jade was. But she had a feeling that Master Grey was just waiting for her to ask that question, purely so he could refuse to answer her. Instead, she clasped her hands in her lap and waited, patiently, for him to start talking.

"There is little I can tell you about Mountaintop," Master Grey said. "All students are expected to take Oaths of Secrecy upon entering the school, oaths that remain binding for the remainder of their lives. I cannot give you many details without breaking my oaths."

Then what good are you? Emily thought, nastily. Master Grey was a powerful magician, and Jade spoke highly of his master, but Emily simply didn't *like* him. He'd seemed to take a dislike to her the moment they'd first met and it hadn't improved since. *What is the point of this meeting if you can't help us?*

"We understand," Lady Barb said.

Emily frowned. No one had asked *her* for an oath. "Are Oaths of Secrecy expected from students at Whitehall?"

"Not until you reach Fifth Year," Lady Barb said, shortly. "Master Grey?"

Master Grey leaned forward. "There have been reports of shifts in the balance of power," he said. "The MageMaster is growing old and feeble. His ability to keep his subordinates in line may no longer be assured. Some of them may be acting independently of any authority."

Emily was still mulling over the oaths. There were some fields of magic, she knew, where oaths were expected from any would-be students, but she'd never heard of an oath so binding that it was expected of *every* student at a school. It rather suggested that Mountaintop had something to hide, something it wanted to keep from the rest of the Allied Lands. And *that* was more than a little worrying. There were horrors aplenty throughout the Allied Lands, horrors all the worse for few thinking they *were* horrors, yet Mountaintop had something to hide? What could it be?

She dragged her mind back to the present as Master Grey continued to speak. "I would caution you against becoming involved in any quarrels," he added. "They tend to end badly for all concerned."

"Obviously," Emily said, unable to keep the irritation out of her voice. "They always do."

"*Emily*," Lady Barb said, warningly.

Emily felt her face heat and looked down at the ground.

"I will be in position, as you requested," Master Grey continued. "But you do realize that any form of intervention will be tricky."

"But not impossible," Lady Barb said.

"Not impossible," Master Grey confirmed.

He stood up in one smooth motion, towering over Emily. "My apprentice will be seconded to Whitehall for the duration of your time at Mountaintop," he said, warningly. "I would advise against sending any letters out of Mountaintop. They will almost certainly be read."

And alert Mountaintop to my friendship with Jade, Emily thought. "I understand," she said, out loud. "I won't write any letters to him."

Master Grey eyed her for a long chilling moment, then stalked out of the room, closing the door quietly behind him. Emily watched him go, then turned to Lady Barb. Her tutor looked annoyed.

"Better not to insult someone like him," Lady Barb said, darkly. "He *was* pushing against his oaths."

"It was useless," Emily said, tartly. She had come to think of Lady Barb as a mother, a confidante who was also a strict disciplinarian, but she wasn't about to hide her opinion. "He told us nothing."

"He may have told you more than you thought," Lady Barb said. She pressed her lips together, then motioned for Emily to follow her. "And you should know just how dangerous it can be to press against a sworn oath. He could have sacrificed a great deal just trying to help us."

She paused. "And he will be in position to help, if possible," she added. "We should be grateful that he is willing to risk himself so extensively."

Emily was far from convinced, but left the matter alone. Instead, she accompanied Lady Barb to a hostel–Lady Barb had flatly refused to use her family's establishment in the city–and dumped her bag on the bed, then allowed Lady Barb to show her some of the sights. The sense of abiding *strangeness* surrounding the White City only grew stronger as they walked the streets, leaving her utterly unsure of what she was sensing. She tried to explain the sensation to Lady Barb, but the older woman said nothing. Emily honestly wasn't sure if she was keeping her mouth shut deliberately or simply didn't understand Emily's halting explanations. Perhaps it was yet another thing that only made sense to someone born in the Allied Lands.

The next three days passed slowly, too slowly. Emily rapidly found herself bored, but tried to simulate alertness as they walked from room to room, inspecting the different World Games and admiring the players, though most looked half-dead as they played, as if their minds were elsewhere. She honestly couldn't understand how the players kept so much complexity in their minds, and wondered why they played at all - although they definitely seemed to get something from it. In fact, two players became so wrapped up in the game, they ended up throwing curses at each other and had to be separated by the Mediators. By the time Lady Barb said she could walk back to the portals and go home, Emily was thoroughly sick of the whole affair and the strange city.

"Remember to look unhappy at being sent home," Lady Barb advised, as Emily picked up her bag. "There isn't a magician in the Allied Lands who wouldn't be happy at having a chance to network here. Or a mundane. You fit into both worlds, and you should love it."

Emily sighed. She would have preferred being completely unnoticed, but that would have defeated the point of visiting the city. Instead, she'd had to endure a constant stream of attention from various magicians, some old enough to be her great-grandfather, all of whom were interested in talking about Shadye, Mother Holly or Void himself. If Lady Barb hadn't been providing chaperonage, Emily suspected she would have fled the city days ago. The written marriage proposals had largely dried up since she'd become Baroness Cockatrice, but a handful of the younger magicians hadn't been shy about asking her to consider taking their hands in marriage.

She walked up the long flight of stairs to the portal chamber, wondering—again—why they didn't charm the staircases to move automatically. *She* might have no difficulty walking, but other visitors had real problems. One old man had been trapped in a magical wheelchair and *he* would have been unable to get down the stairs under his own power. Perhaps it was just tradition... tradition, it seemed at times, was a force more powerful than the strongest magics she knew.

She pushed the thought out of her head as she reached the portal, readied her mind and then stepped through it...

...And something went wrong. Very wrong.

There was a sudden surge of magic, a thunderous crash that slammed into her thoughts... and then she plunged into darkness.

Chapter Five

FOR A LONG MOMENT, AS SHE SLOWLY RETURNED TO AWARENESS, EMILY WAS SO BADLY DISoriented that she honestly wasn't sure of where she was or what had happened. Her head hurt, so terribly she thought she was dying, while her entire body was twitching uncomfortably. What had happened?

And then she remembered stepping through the portal. Had she forgotten to prepare herself for the jump? Or...

Her eyes opened, but her vision was so blurry that she could barely see anything. Panic flickered at the corner of her mind, but she closed her eyes again and forced herself to try to think straight. Her stomach heaved as new stabs of pain flared through her head, then settled down. Something was very badly wrong.

Mountaintop, she thought, numbly. *They jiggered the portal.*

"Emily," a voice said. "Can you hear me?"

It took Emily several tries to respond. "Yes," she said. "What... what happened?"

"You stepped through the wrong portal," the voice said. It was female, soft enough to avoid setting her head off again. "Can you open your eyes and sit up?"

Emily obeyed, slowly. Her vision was still blurred, but as she forced herself to sit up it started to clear, revealing a tall girl sitting beside her. Emily's hands twitched uncomfortably as a glass was pressed into her hands, then she lifted it to her mouth and took a sip. The water felt wonderful against her cracked lips, then tasted heavenly as she swallowed it. It occurred to her, a moment too late, that it might have been drugged, but she couldn't stop herself finishing the glass. She needed the water too badly.

"You'll be fine," the girl said. "I have a potion for you to drink too, when you're ready."

"Thank you," Emily said. They didn't want to kill her, she told herself, and they could have drugged when she was unconscious if they'd wanted to. "I..."

Her head swam as she finished the water and looked around. She was lying on a bed in the middle of a large room, which looked to have been hewn from dark stone. The only source of illumination was a light globe floating over their heads, casting a dull radiance over the room. She glanced down at herself and discovered that she was still wearing her robes, although they felt unclean against her skin. At least she didn't seem to have thrown up, she reassured herself. Maybe she'd just sweated so badly she needed a wash.

"Drink this," the girl said. She pressed a small glass into Emily's hand. "It's something to help you recover."

Emily took it, gratefully. It tasted as foul as she'd expected, but her head cleared once she'd taken the first few sips. The girl watched her intently until she'd finished the glass, then took it and placed it on a side table. Emily shook her head, running her hand through her long hair, then forced herself to swing her legs over the side of the bed and stand. Her legs threatened to buckle for a long moment - the girl caught her arm and held her for a long moment - then steadied.

"You're recovering quickly," she said, "but you should really stay on the bed until you are ready to move."

"I'm ready to move now," Emily assured her. A quick check revealed she was still wearing her snake-bracelet. The charm she'd placed on it to make the bracelet impossible to remove seemed to have worked. "And... where am I?"

"You're at Mountaintop," the girl said. She let go of Emily's arm, then held out a hand. "I am Nanette, Head Girl."

Emily took Nanette's hand and studied her. She was tall, with tanned skin, long dark hair and a face that reminded Emily somehow of herself, perhaps a few years older. And yet... Nanette carried herself with a confidence and an easy grace that Emily couldn't help admiring. Nanette was surrounded with a haze of magic that marked her out as a powerful and well-trained magician. Emily couldn't help being reminded of Lady Barb, without the weariness and cynicism that marked the older woman. She wanted to be like Nanette when she grew up.

"I'm Emily," she said, shaking Nanette's hand. "How did I get here?"

"Accident, as far as we can tell," Nanette said. She let go of Emily's hand and stepped backwards. "But the Administrator will explain all that, once you speak with him. I'd advise having a wash and a change of clothes first."

Emily felt herself flushing. Magicians were encouraged to wash regularly, in stark contrast to just about everyone else on the Nameless World. Even the nobility didn't bathe more than once or twice a week, something that had disgusted her when she'd first heard about it. They had a tendency to smell quite badly, particularly the men. She allowed Nanette to show her into a small washroom, where she discovered a spare pair of dark blue robes. It was no surprise to discover they were the right size for her. She checked the robes for unpleasant surprises, then went to the toilet, washed herself and then pulled on the new set of robes.

You're a prisoner here, she reminded herself, as she stepped back out of the washroom. Her companion was waiting patiently. *You cannot afford to relax.*

"Follow me," Nanette ordered. She paused. "I assume you can cast a light globe?"

Emily nodded, a little insulted. Light globes were among the simplest spells in the book; she'd mastered them within the first few months of her time at Whitehall. She also knew how to cast a spell to allow her to see in the dark, like a cat, but she kept that to herself. It wasn't so commonly taught to students below Fourth Year, despite its obvious advantages.

"Good," Nanette said. She led the way towards the door and out into the passageway, her light globe bobbing ahead of her. "Cast one if you feel the urge."

Emily wasn't sure what she'd expected from Mountaintop, but she certainly hadn't expected dark, claustrophobic passageways. The darkness pressed around them like a living thing, so shadowy that she had to force herself to refrain from creating a light globe of her own. She couldn't help the impression that they were walking through an abandoned mine—there were marks on the stone walls that suggested as much—or that there could be anything lurking out there, within the darkness. Even the light globe didn't seem to illuminate more than a few meters around them. The shadows seemed absolute.

She closed her eyes, feeling out with her mind. There was an omnipresent background hum, a sense of magic, just like in Whitehall, but there was something very different about it, something that nagged at her mind. The magic currents seemed less intense, yet also considerably more focused. She opened her eyes again as she sensed magic flaring in front of her, then started as she caught sight of a hooded figure emerging out of the darkness and sweeping past them. It was all she could do to remain calm as magic warped and twisted around the figure.

"A proctor," Nanette said, bluntly. "You get used to them."

Emily swallowed. "What do they do?"

"Keep order," Nanette said. "Don't get on their bad side."

They reached a heavy stone door. Nanette paused, then pressed her hand against it, muttering a spell. There was a glow of light from where her hand touched the stone and the door slid open, allowing more light to spill into the passageway. Inside, it was warm and cosy, almost like Whitehall. Emily felt a surge of relief as Nanette led her inside and closed the stone door behind her. They walked through another stone door without incident, then stopped in front of a third. Nanette knocked, and waited. A moment later, the door opened and she motioned Emily inside.

"Lady Emily," a masculine voice said. "Welcome to Mountaintop."

Emily saw a man rising from a stone desk. He was tall, taller than her, seemingly in his early forties. He had a thin line of gray hair, but his scalp was bare, reminding her of a monk. His body was strong and powerful, the fine robes he wore doing nothing to hide the muscles under his skin. A wand hung at his belt, suggesting that he felt powerful and experienced enough to risk using one on a regular basis. Beside it, there was a sharp silver knife and a tool she didn't recognize. His entire body was surrounded by a haze of magic, as if he couldn't be bothered trying to hide his presence—or if he wanted to impress her with his power.

She couldn't help feeling a little intimidated, but she took the proffered hand and shook it, firmly. His hand felt warm, yet hard and calloused. Emily was mildly surprised, then mentally cursed herself for not realizing what it meant. Most magicians disdained mundane work, but combat sorcerers had to be skilled in physical arts as well as magical ones. Both Lady Barb and Sergeant Miles had the same sense of combining magic with raw physical strength and skill.

"I am Aurelius, Administrator of Mountaintop," the man said, motioning her to a chair. "It is a great pleasure to make your acquaintance, Lady Emily."

"Thank you," Emily said. "I wish I'd expected to come here."

Aurelius smiled openly, then returned to his desk. Emily took a moment to survey his office and fell in love at once. Every wall was lined with bookshelves, each one crammed to bursting with tomes of magic. Some were familiar from what she'd seen in Whitehall's library, but others had only been mentioned in reading lists or were completely unfamiliar to her. She had to fight to resist the urge to rise to her feet and survey the bookshelves more closely, picking out titles and volumes she hadn't read.

She'd never been happy with anyone telling her there were books she shouldn't read, no matter how dangerous they were. Ideas alone were rarely dangerous on Earth.

But that's a temptation too, she reminded herself.

"Several of our more... experienced magicians were due to return from the White City," Aurelius explained. "One of the portals was actually modified to allow them to return directly to Mountaintop and, unfortunately, you stepped through it and triggered the wards intended to keep out uninvited guests. The surge of magic knocked you out, but you arrived safely. I have to confess we weren't expecting you."

It sounded convincing, Emily knew. She might have even believed it if she hadn't known to prepare herself for a possible kidnap attempt. Stepping through the wrong portal was more imaginative than simply knocking her on the head and transporting her to Mountaintop, with the added advantage of giving the Administrator plausible deniability if Void came knocking, demanding to know what had happened to Emily. They could simply swear blind that it had been a terrible accident.

"I wasn't expecting to arrive here," she admitted. "How do I get home?"

Aurelius smiled. "I have something of a proposal for you," he said. "Are you aware that you have frightened a great many people?"

Emily nodded. There were too many question marks over how she had defeated Shadye for anyone's peace of mind. They'd hailed Emily as a hero, but they'd also wondered if she was a budding necromancer herself. If she hadn't been used to social isolation on Earth—and had Alassa and Imaiqah as friends—she might have found it more worrying. And then she'd defeated Mother Holly too. They thought she'd cracked Mother Holly's wards, releasing her power in one burst. The truth was far worse.

"You're the daughter of one of our most powerful—and eccentric—Lone Powers," Aurelius continued. "As a young girl, barely schooled in magic, you defeated a necromancer, then made yourself a Baroness of Zangaria. You have introduced ideas that are threatening to reshape the world. They have responded by trying to slow your magical development and limit your training. You shouldn't be held back by convention, Lady Emily, but encouraged to spread your wings and fly."

He leaned forward. "We need you," he added. "And so I am inclined to view your arrival here as a gift from the gods."

Emily fought to keep her face expressionless. She'd never had a sense she was being held back, quite the opposite. Whitehall had pushed her into Martial Magic well ahead of her peers, as well as offering her private training from Lady Barb and other teachers. But she had to admit it was a good sales pitch for someone like her. If there was one thing she wanted, it was to know everything there was to know about magic. And to test the limits as much as possible. What could magic do if she combined ideas from Earth with the power of the Nameless World?

"We have actually tried to contact you before," Aurelius said, seemingly unaware of her thoughts.

"You sent Lin to spy on me," Emily said.

"Lin... is no longer here," Aurelius said. "Her actions were dictated by... another faction."

Emily didn't believe him, but she held her tongue.

Aurelius went on, calmly. "It was strongly suggested we offer you a term at Mountaintop, where you could experience more of the world and explore your birthright," he said. "You are a child of magical society, as much as I am or your Grandmaster. You should be learning with fellow magical children, not mundane aristocracy or common-born magicians. We could offer you that term, here and now."

Emily frowned, trying to look hesitant—and yet tempted. If she'd actually *been* Void's daughter, she knew she *would* have been very tempted. It might even have been the best thing for her. Magicians needed a wider base of learning than could be provided by one tutor, no matter how powerful. But she knew she couldn't accept too quickly.

"I have obligations at Whitehall," she mumbled. "And what of my studies?"

"We follow a similar curriculum," Aurelius assured her. "You wouldn't need much revision to re-enter Whitehall in Fourth Year, if that was what you wanted. Or you could stay here and complete your Fourth Year exams with us, then return to Whitehall later—or never, if you saw fit. We would be more than happy to have you stay with us."

I bet you would, Emily thought, sourly. They looked very different, but there was something about Aurelius that reminded her of King Randor. Alassa's father meant well—she was sure of that—but he also placed the good of his kingdom ahead of the good of his daughter, let alone Emily herself. To him, people would always be pawns first and people afterwards. Aurelius was probably much the same.

She allowed her frown to deepen. "But wouldn't Whitehall object?"

"They'd have no choice but to comply if your father honored your wishes," Aurelius said, dryly. "You could write to him and request permission to stay here. Or you could simply write to them directly and explain you want to stay here for at least part of a term."

He smiled at her. "There is a great deal we could teach you," he offered. "And there are a great many contacts you could make within magical society. Whitehall, for all of its best efforts, simply lacks the students who could help further your future career. There are even tutors who might be interested in advancing your studies privately. *No one* is held back here."

She *was* tempted, Emily had to admit. Under other circumstances, without the awareness they wanted to seduce her, it might have succeeded. There would be nothing for Aurelius to gain by holding her back, not if he wished her to join magical society. If nothing else, she would have the chance to further her studies and read about fields of magic denied to her at Whitehall. And she would learn much more about the magical side of the Allied Lands, as well as trying to figure out just what was going on at Mountaintop. She couldn't do that without accepting their offer.

But she couldn't accept *too* quickly.

"I would be happy to stay, at least for a term," Emily said, slowly. "But I don't know how well I'd fit in here."

"Everyone has that problem," Aurelius assured her. He gave her a smile as he rose to his feet. "And, in light of your acceptance, I have a present for you."

He led her through a side door into a small library. Just like his office, the walls were lined with books, most completely unfamiliar to her. A small table sat in the middle of the room, surrounded by comfortable chairs. Another door was set within the far side of the compartment.

"This is my private library," Aurelius said, simply. "I personally own seven hundred volumes of books on magic. There are books here that aren't even in the main library."

Emily stared at him, her mouth opening in shock. Seven hundred volumes, all produced before she'd introduced the printing press to the Allied Lands, were a staggering display of wealth. Even if they'd probably been passed down through the ages, with each custodian adding a handful of new volumes, it was still astonishing when each book had had to be produced individually.

He smiled at her reaction. "You may come here whenever you please," he said, motioning towards the other door. A quick spell granted her access to the compartment. "There are books here, I believe, that even your father would be unable to find. You may read them at your leisure."

"I..." Emily stumbled. Aurelius had given her a gift beyond price. Magicians hoarded their knowledge jealously, keeping what they knew to themselves. For one magician to allow another free access to his private library was almost unprecedented. If she hadn't been warned about seduction, she suspected she would have fallen at that moment. "Thank you."

"You are more than welcome," Aurelius assured her. He led the way back into his office, then opened the other door. "Nanette will show you to your dorm and help you with settling in, Lady Emily. I shall expect great things from you, I think."

"Thank you," Emily said. He hadn't asked her to take the oaths. *Why* hadn't he asked her to take the oaths?

"And try to make friends," Aurelius added, as Emily stepped through the door. "You'll find true allies at Mountaintop if you know where to look."

And other surprises, Emily thought. But she kept that thought to herself.

Chapter Six

Y OU SEEM TO HAVE PLEASED THE ADMINISTRATOR," NANETTE SAID, AS THEY MADE THEIR way through another series of darkened corridors. "Will you be staying with us for a term or two?"

"I think so," Emily said, reluctantly. She didn't want to talk, but Nanette seemed determined to make conversation. "Where *are* we? Precisely?"

"Somewhere in the old Dwarf Caverns, deep below the ground," Nanette said. "No one knows *precisely* where we are."

Emily blinked in surprise. "Dwarves?"

"Most of them were driven out or exterminated during the Faerie Wars," Nanette explained, as they reached another pair of stone doors. "The remainder burrowed deep underground and were never seen again, at least not by us. And that is all that mattered."

That wasn't a surprise. The Nameless World had no conventional racism, in sense of black against white or vice versa, but it *hated* magical creatures with a passion. Gorgons, werewolves and dwarves... none of them could expect anything more than reluctant tolerance at best, outright hatred and extermination at worst. They'd been created, she'd been told, as weapons of terror during the wars. The terror lived on even though the Faerie were long gone.

Nanette opened the door and led Emily into the chamber. There were a handful of light globes hovering high overhead, casting their usual radiance over a barren room with nothing more than a handful of doors set within the walls. They were all marked in the complicated script the Allied Lands had used before Emily had introduced English letters, the script she could barely read more than a few hundred letters from. One door had the image of a raven overflying the markings, the others were blank.

"Welcome to Raven Hall," Nanette said, as she opened the raven door. "This will be your home for the next six months."

Emily nodded.

Nanette held up a hand. "There are rules," the older girl said, "some of which are taught to students as soon as they enter Mountaintop. You may not invite anyone into the dorms without permission from the other occupants—and you may not invite anyone *male* into Raven Hall itself, *ever.* You *will* be caught and you *will* be punished."

"I understand," Emily said, slowly.

"There are study rooms and spellchambers to either side of the hall," Nanette continued, pointing towards the other doors. "They are assigned on a rota basis, although you may swap with other students if you need to use them outside your designated study period. Right now, you will have near-complete access to them, as you are the only student here, but that will change in a week. The others will arrive in the hall then."

She paused to gather herself, then led the way into Raven Hall. Emily hadn't been sure what to expect, apart from the ever-present light globes, but the hall surprised her. It was far larger than her room at Whitehall, with ten large beds arranged along the walls. Each of the beds looked large enough to sleep three or four people comfortably, but only two looked to be made and ready for someone. The Administrator, she thought, must have been very certain that Emily would accept his offer.

Up close, the beds looked odd. There was one large bed and another, smaller one at the foot of the larger bed, as if someone else would be literally sleeping at her feet. The smaller bed was barely large enough for Emily herself, let alone someone bigger. She frowned and turned to Nanette to ask, but the older girl was already striding down towards the end of the room. Emily sighed, mentally filed the question away for later study, and followed Nanette through another set of doors. Inside, she saw showers, toilets, mirrors and washbasins. They all looked far cruder than what she was used to at Whitehall.

"The showers operate on a first come, first served basis," Nanette said. She pointed towards a pair of doors set within the rear of the compartment. "The bathtubs inside are operated on a rota basis too, just like the study rooms. You get to fight over them on weekends."

She smiled, rather humorlessly. "You can find soap, towels and everything else you might need in the cupboards," she added. "I assume you know how to deal with blood?"

Emily flushed, but nodded. The last thing she wanted was to leave samples of blood lying around at Mountaintop. After Shadye had used her own blood against her, she'd mastered several spells for breaking the connection between herself and any blood she happened to spill, and used them religiously. She made a mental note to check herself for any unexplained pinpricks that might have suggested they'd taken blood, then she followed Nanette back into the dormitory. It didn't look any better than it had when they'd first stepped inside.

She cringed as she realized what the beds meant. At Whitehall, she'd shared a room with two other students—one other, after Lin had made her escape. Here, she would be sharing with nine other students, perhaps more. There would be almost no privacy at all, even if they were all girls. The thought was upsetting, even now. But there was nothing she could do about it, unless she wanted to risk asking for a private room. She had a feeling, somehow, that it wouldn't be granted.

Desperately, she sought something else to fix on. "How are students selected for the dorms?"

"It's random," Nanette said. "Every year, the students are resorted into different dorms, forcing them to get used to new roommates. Not too different from Whitehall, Emily, but just on a larger scale. Most of your new roommates will *know* one another, I think, yet they won't have shared quarters before. You only get to choose roommates when you reach Fifth Year, while Sixth Years either supervise dorms or get private rooms."

Emily looked at her. "And which do you have?"

Nanette pointed towards one of the beds. "That's my bed there," she said, "right at the edge of the room. If you want to sneak out at night, you'll have to sneak past me—and I'm a very light sleeper." She smirked. "By tradition, I'm not allowed to say anything if you *do* manage to get past me and into the corridor, but you're still not safe from the proctors or wandering staff. Try not to get caught."

Emily had to smile. Sneaking around at night was an old Whitehall tradition—and, it seemed, one that Mountaintop shared. Trying to roam the corridors undetected, avoiding teachers on the prowl, perhaps even breaking into classrooms or having a midnight feast... Alassa had been particularly fond of it. Emily had gone along with her a few times too.

But there hadn't been any older students supervising them in their rooms.

"This is very different from Whitehall," she mused. "What else should I know?"

Nanette shrugged. "You're not allowed to fight in the dorms," she said. "If you do, I have to stop you and that won't be pleasant for anyone. You can play pranks, but if you manage to keep someone from getting to class you will both be punished. And that will make me look *very* bad. I will not be happy."

Emily understood. The prefects at Whitehall had the same problem. They were meant to help the teachers maintain order, but anything that got so far out of control that the teachers noticed would almost certainly cost the prefect his or her position. Someone failing to turn up for class because her roommate had turned her into a frog would make the hall's supervisor look either lazy or incompetent.

Nanette jabbed a finger at the far corner of the room. "That's the Silent Corner," she said. "If I tell you to get in there, you will get in there without any backchat. And you stay there, without speaking to anyone, until I tell you that you may leave. No one is allowed to speak to you either."

Sent to Coventry, Emily thought.

"So try to get along with your fellows," Nanette added. "Or, if you must fight, keep your disagreements verbal."

"I'll do my best," Emily assured her. She cast around for another subject to discuss. The Head Girl would be a goldmine of information if Emily could only figure out what questions to ask her. "What are the teachers like?"

Nanette smiled. "You've already met the Administrator," she said. "He's strict—very strict—but fair. He doesn't take many classes though, only a handful of students who require advanced tutoring of one kind or another. You may be one of them. If you are, remember not to ask stupid questions. He *hates* that."

Emily nodded, wordlessly. Lady Barb was just the same.

"I don't know what classes you'll be taking, so it's hard to say which teachers you'll have," Nanette added. "Mistress Mauve takes Charms; she's also incredibly strict and doesn't take any backtalk at all. *Do not* dispute your grades with her unless you're absolutely *certain* she's marked you poorly, or you'll regret it. Professor Clifton takes Wards and Warding; I think you'll probably have him, perhaps at a more basic level than some of your roommates."

She smiled, again. "He's a decent teacher, but we think he spends too much of his time hitting the bottle," she warned. "Students like me probably drive him mad regularly. Try not to deal with him outside class. It isn't a very pleasant experience."

"I know," Emily said, remembering her mother. She'd been a drunkard too. "And the others?"

"Mistress Granite takes Healing," Nanette said. "You took Healing last year so I imagine you'll be expected to continue with it. She's *nasty*; you really *don't* want to get on her bad side. Strict, unpleasant and some of us think she actually searches out excuses to punish us for misbehavior. Try to keep your head down in her class and learn as much as you can, without making mistakes. She used to make us heal each other in the name of practice."

Emily swallowed. She'd studied Healing under Lady Barb and she had to admit that Lady Barb had been short-tempered and permanently cross with her students in class too. But then, there was far too much scope for Healing to be abused—or simple carelessness to leave a patient far worse off than before he'd met the healer. Lady Barb hadn't tolerated any mistakes either.

"And then there's Professor Zed," Nanette added. "He's..."

"*Zed?*" Emily interrupted.

"Professor Zed, who takes Alchemy," Nanette confirmed. "Do you know him?"

Emily hesitated. It could be a coincidence, she knew. Zed might easily be a common name in the Nameless World. *Emily* was largely unique, as far as she knew, but then she'd come from a whole different world. It was possible that it *was* a coincidence, that there were two different people with the same name who happened to be Master Alchemists, yet somehow she was sure it was no coincidence. The first Zed she'd met had been Zangaria's Court Wizard...

...And it had been Emily who had cost him his position.

Oh, it hadn't been *completely* her fault, she knew. Zed had been a poor Court Wizard by any reasonable standards. He'd certainly been completely incompetent at teaching Alassa magic, if nothing else, almost leaving her completely dependent on a wand rather than using her own inner magic. But he'd been a skilled Alchemist who had preferred to research rather than teach. If he was here, at Mountaintop, with a good reason to hold a grudge against Emily...

Nanette touched her arm. "Are you all right?" She asked. "You've gone quite pale."

You can tell? Emily thought, waspishly. Her skin had always been pale, even after spending two years in the Nameless World. She shook her head, cursing her display of weakness. It was all too easy to see how Nanette might use it against her at a later date.

"Tell me," she said. "When did he come to the school?"

"I believe he replaced Professor Nutt a year ago," Nanette said. "But I didn't have his classes at the time."

Emily felt her blood run cold. If he'd taken up his post at Mountaintop a year ago, it would be directly after *her* Zed had been fired from Zangaria. It was quite likely that he was the same person. And that meant that Alchemy, hardly her best subject, was likely to become hellish. But she would just have to tolerate it. She'd endured poor treatment before, from both her stepfathers and teachers at school on Earth. She could be patient.

"Thank you," she said, slowly. "Are there others?"

Nanette smirked. "There are dozens," she said. "But it really depends on what classes you take. I imagine you'll keep up with your classes from Whitehall, but also try some new ones."

"That makes sense," Emily agreed.

She allowed Nanette to lead her over to her bed, but frowned when she saw the drawer underneath. One of them was stuffed with clothing, ranging from simple underwear—no bra, she noted sardonically—to long dresses rather than robes. Nanette pulled one of them out and held it up for Emily to inspect. It was a long black dress that would fall to her ankles, she realized, surprisingly elegant compared to the shapeless robes of Whitehall. One arm had three white bands just below her shoulder, where Nanette's dress had six. Emily guessed they represented years of schooling.

"This is your regulation uniform," Nanette explained, dryly. She shook it out, revealing a stylized V-shaped badge hanging from the collar. "You are entitled to four dresses and assorted underwear drawn from the school's stockpiles; if you want something more fashionable, you are obliged to purchase it for yourself. I suggest you choose something a little more elegant, if you wish to make a splash among your fellows. A good fashion sense is a sign of both wealth and power."

Or of a desperate attempt to fit in, Emily thought, remembering how she had never been able to wear anything fashionable on Earth. Her mother had never been able to afford to buy anything new. They'd been completely dependent on charity shops, even for the basics. It had been one of the many—many—reasons why she'd been a social outcast back home. *I don't think I will be replacing the dresses anytime soon.*

"That's your father's emblem," Nanette said, pointing to the badge. "You'll discover that around half of the students will have badges of their own, signifying their family names and suchlike. Those that don't are scholarship students like your friend Imaiqah. They won't be able to help you with contacts and suchlike, but they will be able to help you study magic—if, of course, you wish to be seen with them."

"Oh," Emily said. "Do I *want* to be seen with them?"

"It depends," Nanette said. "What do you want from your time at this school?"

Emily shrugged, resolving to think about the issue later. Instead, she shucked off the set of replacement robes, and pulled the dress over her head. It was shorter than she'd realized, coming to an end just below her knees. The badge fell off the collar, then Nanette caught it and pinned it just above her right breast. There were no spells on the dress, as far as she could tell, but there was a spell on the badge. It wouldn't glow, Nanette explained, for anyone else.

"Don't forget your underwear and stockings when you dress properly," Nanette said, once Emily had inspected herself in the mirror. The dress was tighter around her chest than she would have preferred. "Flipping someone upside down is a common trick here, I'm afraid, so watch yourself. Most senior students learn to protect their dresses very quickly."

Emily nodded. She knew some of the spells from Whitehall. Others... she would have to learn, very quickly. She had a nasty feeling that Mountaintop was more clique-ridden than Whitehall... and Whitehall had far too many cliques for Emily's liking.

"Now," Nanette said, when Emily had tested everything else in the drawer, "I think it's time we had something to eat."

She kept up a steady stream of information as they made their way to the refectory, where they were served a stew and bread meal that was surprisingly tasty. Emily found that she was hungrier than she'd realized after stepping through the portal, something that puzzled her more than she cared to admit. Just how long had she been completely unaware of her surroundings? They could have done anything to her while she'd been asleep... she gritted her teeth, pushing the thought aside. There was no point in worrying about it now.

"Markus," Nanette called. "Come and join us."

Emily looked up. Markus was a young man around the same age as Nanette, if her guess was accurate, his face on the far side of handsome. And yet she had to admit he had character, the same character as many other magicians. Standards of beauty were different on the Nameless World, she reminded herself, as Markus sat down next to Nanette. Somehow, she had to admit that she found his presence disarming—and immediately likable. This was an honorable man.

"This is Emily, the Necromancer's Bane," Nanette introduced her. "Emily, this is Markus of House Ashfall, Head Boy of Mountaintop."

She lowered her voice and winked. "There was a shortage of other suitable candidates," she added, *sotto voce*.

Markus didn't look offended. "Pleased to meet you, Emily," he said. "I understand you'll be taking exams over the next week?"

"Don't scare her," Nanette said, quickly. "They're just placement exams."

Emily groaned, but she understood. Whitehall and Mountaintop probably *didn't* match up completely, not when it came to how their students passed through their studies. They'd need to know where she was before they started teaching her newer and more interesting magics.

"I'm looking forward to them," she said, instead. "And to learning more from both of you."

Markus smiled. "That's the best attitude you could have," he assured her. "But I hope you keep it for longer than a week or two after term begins."

Chapter Seven

MARKUS HADN'T BEEN JOKING, EMILY HAD TO ADMIT, AFTER SHE'D SPENT HER FIRST WEEK at Mountaintop Academy. The exams had been harder than she'd expected, pushing her to the limit as she struggled to pass without showing off everything she could do. They were very practiced at judging a student's true level, unlike the exams she'd taken on Earth. But then, it was very difficult to fake competence in magic. Stupid magicians normally managed to kill themselves very quickly before they could cause harm to anyone else.

Nanette was a surprisingly good companion, Emily had discovered, but she only rarely allowed Emily any true privacy. There was no way to be sure if she was watching Emily for the Administrator—who Emily hadn't seen since the first interview in his office—or if she was merely wary of letting Emily out of her sight, yet, in the end, her motivations didn't matter. All that mattered was that it was irritating. Emily was relieved when Nanette—and Markus—warned her they couldn't spend so much time tutoring her once the term began. The other Third Year students wouldn't like it.

"You'll be expected to join the other Third Year students in the Main Hall after lunch," Nanette warned, as she stepped into Raven Hall. "Most of them will arrive beforehand, but they'll probably be quite tired and a little disoriented. Don't worry about helping them, just stay out of the way. There's enough chaos when students return to the dorms without you adding to it."

Emily eyed her, warily. Nanette was rarely so snappy with anyone... but she looked harassed, her eyes dark and shadowed. It dawned on Emily, suddenly, that Nanette had had to catch up with her own work quickly, after spending so much time supervising Emily. Markus could do some tutoring too, yet he wasn't allowed in Raven Hall. He'd told her, after she'd asked, that any boy who tried to cross the line into the sleeping dorm was automatically turned into a slug. Emily hadn't asked what happened to girls who tried to enter the male dorms, but she had a feeling it wasn't anything nicer.

"I'll stay out of the way," she said. "Do you want me to go to the library or somewhere else?"

"You'd be better off staying here," Nanette said, briskly. She nodded at the book in Emily's hand, an introduction to pocket dimensions. Nanette had suggested it, somewhat to Emily's surprise. It was rather more detailed than the book she'd borrowed from Yodel, although not as instructive as the books Lady Barb had let her read. "Keep reading and planning for the coming semester. You'll find it very hard work."

She was right, Emily suspected, as the older girl turned and swept out of the room. Whitehall had been hard too, but this Mountaintop was going to be different. She would have to study—to learn—while plotting how best to discover just what was going on. And, perhaps, to explore the rest of the cave systems. Supposedly, Mountaintop occupied only a very small portion of the caverns. There was much more for any enterprising student to explore. Part of her couldn't wait.

The next few hours were as chaotic as Nanette had warned. Students entered the room, stuffed their boxes and trunks under the beds, and took quick naps. None of them looked very awake or aware, something that worried Emily. How carefully was Mountaintop protected from detection? She'd read about a spell that could be used, if there was enough power, to hide something as large as a castle from prying eyes... had someone used something similar to hide Mountaintop? Or were they merely the local counterpart of jet-lagged, as they had stepped through portals from a dozen different time zones?

By the time they were called for lunch, then into the Great Hall, Emily also felt tired. But her new fellow students looked much better after eating a large meal and drinking various odd-smelling potions.

She stood at the back of the Great Hall and hunted for Lin, as well as silently trying to count heads. There were no less than a hundred Third Year students, she estimated finally, which suggested there were five or ten Third Year Halls. The numbers seemed to be evenly divided between boys and girls, although she suspected there were slightly more boys. Several cast curious glances at her, although they kept their questions to themselves. Emily, who hated being the center of attention, was relieved. She wouldn't have to answer questions until much later.

And there was no sign of Lin at all.

But they would be fools to allow us to meet, she reminded herself. *They'd expect me to want a little revenge.*

A ripple of magic ran through the hall, calling her attention to the stage. Aurelius stood there, looking impressive in red and gold robes. Compared to his students, he seemed to glow with light and power. Emily glanced from side to side, tearing her gaze away from Aurelius with an effort and gave everyone around her a careful look. It was easy to realize that almost all of her fellow students wore dresses that were specifically tailored for them. A couple of girls even had slits in their dresses that exposed their legs when they moved. It was so unlike Whitehall, where everyone wore the same robes, that Emily had to force herself not to stare.

Status symbols, she reasoned, remembering what Nanette had told her. *The ones who wear better clothes are richer.*

"Welcome back for Third Year," Aurelius said. There was a subtle compulsion in his voice that drew their attention to him. Emily had to work to break it. "Many of you, I'm sure, will be relieved to hear that you have passed your first set of exams and are now free of the duties of being young students"—several of the students muttered excitedly—"and that you will take your rightful places as mentors to students younger than yourselves."

Emily frowned. What did he mean?

"You will notice, of course, that not all of your fellows passed their exams and had to be held back a year," Aurelius continued. "Those of you who *have* passed would be wise to concentrate on your future studies, rather than the past. Third Year is harder still, then Fourth Year will come before you know it. And it is *those* exams that will determine your future."

He paused, his bright eyes sweeping the room in an almost paternal manner. "The staff has determined your timetables, your hall supervisors and suchlike," he added. "They will be distributed after you return to your halls. You will have one day to grow accustomed to your return to Mountaintop—we advise you to write letters to reassure your parents that you actually arrived—and then you will resume classes. As always, nothing but the best will be expected from you."

His voice softened, slightly. "You will also have noticed that several other students have joined you from other schools. Do your best to make them welcome."

Emily flushed as several more glances were aimed at her. She couldn't pick out anyone else new... or perhaps she could. They were the ones wearing the school-issued dresses, without any frills at all. She found herself studying the black uniforms worn by the boys and shuddered despite herself. They were far too akin to the uniforms worn by the SS. But it couldn't have been deliberate. Black was considered a suitable color for sorcerers, after all.

"Your Shadows will meet you in your halls," Aurelius concluded. "Remember your side of the agreements, if you don't do anything else. Dismissed."

Emily frowned. What was a Shadow?

There was no time to ask. The throng of students poured out of the Great Hall, pulling her along with them. They made their way through corridors that were still dark and shadowy, despite the sudden profusion of light globes. There was little lighting outside the halls and classrooms, providing an incentive for students to learn to produce their own light as quickly as possible. It didn't seem a very wise thing to do, Emily thought, but maybe the school board felt differently.

But then, Whitehall tolerated an alarming amount of practical jokes and pranks in the name of teaching students how to defend themselves. Mountaintop probably did the same thing.

Nanette was waiting for them as they filed into Raven Hall, her gaze silently pausing on Emily before she looked at the next girl in line. Emily felt an odd stab of bitterness, despite her relief; Nanette was clearly going to pretend she had no prior relationship with Emily or anyone else. And she wouldn't know any of the other students personally, Emily suspected; *she* didn't know many students outside her own year at Whitehall.

She blinked in surprise as she saw the girl sitting on her bed... no, on the smaller bed attached to *her* bed. The girl was young—Emily would have placed her at thirteen or fourteen on Earth, although she knew that meant nothing on the Nameless World—with a pale, but vaguely Indian face. Her eyes were dark brown and fearful; she wore a black dress that seemed a size too large for her, with her hair in two pigtails hanging down the side of her face. One hand played with a wooden wand.

She met Emily's eyes and shivered. The nervousness in them made Emily fearful, too.

"Gather round," Nanette ordered, before Emily could ask the girl any questions. "Shadows to the front, Third Years to the rear."

Emily wasn't the only girl who had picked up a Shadow, she realized; there were ten Third Year students and ten Shadows, all of whom knelt in front of Nanette. Emily wondered if she was expected to kneel too, but she took her cue from the other older students and remained standing upright, clasping her hands behind her back. There would be time to ask Nanette for explanations later.

"Welcome back to Mountaintop," Nanette said, without preamble. Her gaze swept the room. "I believe you have all spent time in other halls, so I won't bother to explain anything you should have picked up last year. Your class schedules are on your beds, the rotas for everything from bathtubs to spellchambers are posted in front of them. Please bear in mind that while you *can* swap periods with other students, you cannot do this without their permission. I will be *most* displeased if you try to steal rota time from its proper owner."

She paused, then looked dispassionately at the kneeling Shadows. "As Third Years," she added, looking back at the older students, "you are assigned a Shadow, a younger student who will serve you in exchange for tuition and education in how to become a part of magical society. Their duties have already been explained to them. I strongly advise you to be careful they don't miss classes or anything else that might provoke the ire of their tutors. It will reflect badly on you."

Emily looked down at the kneeling girl. Was she *Emily's* Shadow? Whitehall had nothing like it; hell, there was a strict ban on importing servants from outside the school. She had heard of a few older students offering money to the younger students in exchange for servitude, but no one had ever asked *Emily* to serve them. But then, she *had* defeated Shadye...

She pushed the thought aside as Nanette kept speaking. "But we have a famous newcomer amongst us today," she said. One hand indicated Emily, who suddenly found herself the center of attention. "Lady Emily, Void's Daughter, Necromancer's Bane."

Emily shifted from foot to foot uncomfortably as they stared at her. Magical lineage was important, she knew, and Void was among the most powerful magicians in the Nameless World. Their belief that she was his daughter would give her some prestige, she was sure, although it was very far from true. But it was better they believed she was a literal bastard than having them try to figure out the truth.

"Emily is responsible for the deaths of two necromancers," Nanette continued. "Her presence here is... reassuring."

She paused, then pointed her finger at a tall girl who didn't seem too pleased to see Emily, for no apparent reason. "Claudia," she said. She moved on to the next girl. "Olive. Janus."

She rattled through twenty names in just under a minute, leaving Emily hopelessly confused. She'd never been good at memorizing names—she barely knew the students in her classes at Whitehall—and these were completely new. The only name she managed to memorize was the name of her Shadow. Frieda, Daughter of Huckeba. That, Emily suspected, indicated she was a scholarship girl. Imaiqah had been introduced the same way too, back when they'd first met.

"You know the basic rules, so follow them," Nanette concluded. "Lights out is at twenty-two bells. You may keep private lights for yourself within privacy wards, if you wish, but you will be awoken at eight bells precisely if you are not already awake by then. I suggest you try hard not to be late for class"–her voice hardened–"as oversleeping is not accepted as an excuse. Do not mess around with someone else's property, particularly their Shadow. If you have familiars, you are required to tend to their care and feeding yourself. Do not bring outsiders into the dorms without permission."

She paused. "And *do not* mess around with someone's coursework," she warned. "*No* excuses will be considered acceptable. Are there any questions?"

One of the girls–Helen, if Emily had matched her name to face correctly–held up a hand. "Are we responsible for the care and feeding of Shadows, too?"

There were some snickers from the older girls. Nanette glared them into silence.

"You are responsible for making sure they eat, drink and appear presentable at all times," she said, tartly. "I suggest you remember how you felt as a Shadow and adjust your behavior as you see fit."

She took a long breath. "Go back to your beds," she ordered, "and unpack. You will be expected to attend High Tea in the Dining Hall, tonight, then sort yourselves out tomorrow before starting your classes. If your homework has eaten the dog again and had to be destroyed, I would strongly advise you not to go to classes without at least *trying* to recreate it."

Emily had to smile. Clearly, the *my homework ate the dog* excuse wasn't confined to Whitehall.

She sighed to herself as Nanette shoed them all back to their beds. Emily sat down on the coverlet and reached for the book, then looked up as Frieda cleared her throat. Standing upright, her hands twisting in front of her, the girl looked tiny, almost like a child. And yet Frieda had to have matured before she could use magic and go to a magic school. Her clothes were so drab and worn that Emily was sure they were at least third-hand. Emily sighed, inwardly. She'd never been a Shadow, and had no idea what to do with one. And she had never been comfortable with the small army of servants she'd inherited in Zangaria.

"Go unpack," Emily said, tiredly. It would probably be better for Frieda if she spent as little time with Emily as possible. Besides, it was quite possible that Frieda had been sent to spy on her. "Or go do whatever you have to do."

"I have to wash your clothes every week," Frieda said. Her voice was quiet, too quiet. "And I have to change the bed, sort out your possessions and look after your books. And anything else you might want me to do."

Emily looked around the room. Several beds had vanished behind shimmering hazes, indicating the use of privacy wards, but she could still see several of the other girls ordering their Shadows around–or, in one case, berating one of them for some imagined offense. It didn't seem that the life of a Shadow was a very pleasant one, even at the best of times. She thought about some of the girls she'd known on

Earth—or Whitehall, for that matter—and shuddered, inwardly. There was too much temptation to abuse the system for anyone to be trusted with a Shadow.

And besides, she was used to doing everything for herself.

But was that true any longer? She had washed clothes during the trip to the Cairngorms, she recalled, but at Whitehall she'd had everything washed *for* her. But she'd washed her own clothes on Earth, too... in hindsight, that probably explained why some of her clothes had shrunk after she'd washed them in the sink.

"Do whatever you want, at the moment," she said, and paused. There were a pair of envelopes on her bed. One was addressed to her, the other to Frieda. "You might want to start by reading these."

She opened her letter and skimmed it quickly. It was nothing more than a time-table, organized along the same basic lines as Whitehall, although she noted that class periods were definitely longer. Some spaces had been marked for private study, others had been left completely blank. A note at the bottom stated that further classes would be assigned within a week or two, depending.

Charms, Alchemy, Healing, Warding, Dueling, Life Magics, Death Magics and Rituals, she thought, reading the list twice. There was no mention of Subtle Magic, unless it was covered under Rituals. Thankfully, there was also no mention of Artwork. *But what are Life and Death Magics?*

She shuddered. *Necromancy?*

But it seemed unlikely, she was sure. Necromancy was hellishly dangerous, but it was also very simple, horrifically so. Any fool could be a Necromancer, as long as they mastered the basic rite. It was only then that trouble started.

"You have to sign this," Frieda said, interrupting her thoughts. "You have to say I read the list."

Emily took Frieda's piece of paper and read it. She had the same basic classes as Emily had taken at Whitehall in her First Year, but with a couple of additions. Wandwork and Chanting. Emily was surprised that Mountaintop taught Wandwork to such young students, while she had no idea at all what Chanting was. Perhaps it was using music to work magic, she speculated, or perhaps it was something completely different. She'd have to ask Nanette when she had a moment away from the other girls.

She signed it, then passed the paper back to Frieda and checked her watch. It was almost time for dinner. Afterwards...

Sighing, she shook her head. This was going to be harder than she'd thought.

Chapter Eight

EMILY COULDN'T HELP FEELING NERVOUS AND ALONE AS SHE WALKED INTO THE CHARMS classroom, only to discover that three quarters of Raven Hall had already chosen seats. The nervousness she understood, but the loneliness was something new—or very old. It had been strange to have friends at Whitehall, yet it was stranger still to miss them. If she had Alassa or Imaiqah at her side right now, she wouldn't feel so isolated at Mountaintop.

But they couldn't have accompanied her, she knew all too well. It would have made it impossible for her to do her job.

Her stomach churned as she sat down, picking a seat midway from the teacher's desk. She had never encountered a Charms Tutor who wasn't a stern disciplinarian, all too aware of just how much could easily go wrong. And when it did, it could be very difficult to fix.

She watched as the remaining students filed into the room, inspected the books and equipment on her desk. The books were largely unfamiliar, apart from one she'd read at Whitehall, but the wand lying on the edge of the desk was an unpleasant surprise. She'd worked with staffs, in the past, and knew how dangerous they—and wands—could be.

"Rise," a sharp voice ordered. The students rose to their feet. Emily followed them, reluctantly, as a tall woman swept past her and took her place at the front of the classroom, her eyes scanning the room dispassionately. "Those of you who are new here, move to the front of the room. I like having my eye on new students."

Emily didn't want to move, but she obeyed, joining two other girls and a boy. Up close, Mistress Mauve looked cold and hard, her face utterly stern and unforgiving. Emily felt her stomach clench as cold eyes met hers for a long moment, then looked past her as if she wasn't really there. A moment later, the remaining students sat down, their eyes boring into Emily's back. Mistress Mauve had reminded them, if they'd needed the reminder, that she was new at Mountaintop.

"We will be spending the first four days reviewing material we covered last year, as most of you will have forgotten it," Mistress Mauve said, once they were seated. Emily privately doubted that anyone would *dare* forget anything she'd taught them. "Once I am sure you have remembered the *basics*"—she stressed the word darkly—"we will commence with Third Year studies. In particular, we will be looking at ways to string successive levels of spells together to produce decision trees."

She paused, daring them to comment. When no one said anything, she went on.

"These spells are an order of magnitude more complex than any you have worked with before," she continued. "Many of you will be tempted to skip these lessons, as you will feel you do not need to know how to spend time comprehending the spells you use—or you do not intend to use them in your later lives. Such a decision would be immensely stupid. These spells are the backbone of higher magic... and refusing to learn how to use them will leave you at the mercy of other, more studious magicians."

Her gaze met Emily's for a long moment. "You will need to learn, among other things, how to ward your own homes against all intruders," she warned. "It will be impossible to produce your own wards without mastering these techniques."

There was a long pause. "Take the first sheet of parchment on your desks and start working your way through it," she concluded. "I will be inspecting each and every one of your answers after they are handed in. Once done, you may read your assigned textbooks—and plan your raids on the library. Many of the textbooks on your reading lists are in very high demand."

Emily sighed, then reached for the first roll of parchment and unfurled it gently. As she had feared from Mistress Mauve's lecture, it was nothing less than a complex exam, with questions ranging from difficult to extremely complex. If she hadn't had additional tutoring from Mistress Sun over the last two years, she suspected she would have real problems trying to solve the questions. If Mistress Mauve was anything like Professor Lombardi, it would be safer to admit ignorance than attempt to solve a question she didn't understand.

She heard a muttered series of groans and curses as she bent her head to the parchment. Nanette had told her that Raven Hall's occupants had been selected at random, but Emily was starting to have her doubts. It was clear they all shared the same basic origin—Emily was the only outsider, and would've been even if she'd truly been Void's daughter—and perhaps the same level of academic achievement. Such a system, she decided, as she worked her way through the first question, would certainly make a great deal more sense than Earth's system of assigning students to classes by age alone.

The first question took nearly fifteen minutes to solve; the second seemed almost impossible. Emily had to fight down despair as she broke it into its component sections before putting it back together in a more workable form. *This* was no simple test where most of the spell components were useless, she realized dully. Each of the incants played a specific role in just how the spell worked, depending on circumstances. It was nothing less than a computer-style language in its own right.

Shadye should have kidnapped a computer nerd, Emily thought as she finished writing down her answer and moved on to the next question. *One of them would have been able to master the spellwork coding by now and turned himself into a master magician.*

She gritted her teeth as a headache built behind her temples, but forced herself to proceed. The next three questions were all deceptively simple, but they had nasty stings in the tail. One had the magical counterpart of 'times zero' midway through the spell structure, invalidating everything that had gone before. Another made no sense at all; finally, she gave up and admitted defeat. By the time the bell rang, signifying the end of the period, she had sweat trickling down her back. Had they sneaked her into a class for magical geniuses by mistake?

"You will return here after refreshing yourself," Mistress Mauve ordered. Her gaze showed no hint of mercy. "By then, I will have studied your answers and determined how much you have remembered."

Emily rose to her feet, noting to her relief that only a couple of students had started to read their textbooks. Several of the other girls looked as shell-shocked as Emily, muttering to themselves quietly enough to keep Mistress Mauve from hearing their words.

The curriculum at Mountaintop couldn't be *that* different from Whitehall's, could it?

"Um... hey," a voice said. Emily looked up to see a girl she couldn't place. "Do you want to join me for Kava?"

Emily hesitated. The girl seemed *too* bright and cheerful, as if she were trying desperately to cover her nervousness behind a show of confidence. She'd seen girls like her before, when a famous singer had visited her school on Earth, but why would anyone show such an attitude towards *her*? The suspicious part of her mind, the one that had been hurt too many times, insisted that it was a trick. But the rest of her was curious.

"Why not?" Emily asked. "What would you like to be called?"

The girl blushed, brightly. "Lerida," she said. Her voice stuttered as she tried to speak the next few words. "You're my hero."

Emily felt herself blushing too as Lerida led her out of the classroom and down into a small study room. A large jug of Kava, spelled to remain warm and drinkable, sat on the table, which was surrounded by chairs and several bookcases. Emily hesitated, then sat down and poured them both mugs of the hot, foul-tasting drink. She'd never quite acquired a taste for it, but she had to admit it was good for keeping students awake. There was probably more caffeine in it than anyone on Earth would consider safe.

"I'm not a hero," she said, as she took a sip. "I just..."

"You killed a Necromancer–*two* Necromancers," Lerida insisted, sitting down far too close to Emily for Emily's liking. "And you saved a Princess and won a throne. If that doesn't make you a hero, I don't know what does."

"I didn't win a throne," Emily pointed out. She wasn't entirely clear on how the Barony of Cockatrice related to the larger Kingdom of Zangaria, but she was fairly sure that she wasn't an independent monarch. "And..."

She sighed, inwardly, as Lerida continued to bubble on. She'd known there were people at Whitehall who admired her, but they'd also feared her. It hadn't made her feel very comfortable, yet... part of her was almost pleased by Lerida's straightforward hero-worship. It was almost like being a cheerleader, with the added bonus of actually having done something to make the worship deserved. But the rest of her disliked the thought of *anyone* fawning over her. Lerida had an ideal in her head that Emily knew she could never match in person. She was just... *Emily*.

"There are so many people who admire what you've done," Lerida was saying. Emily realized, to her embarrassment, that she'd tuned out the girl's words. "You really should come and meet us."

Emily felt herself flush, again. If she didn't already have a fan club here at Mountaintop, she was sure that Lerida would start one, given half a chance. The thought of an Emily Fan Club was horrific. There was no such organization at Whitehall, but everyone there knew she was as human as the rest of them. They'd seen her stub her toe and make mistakes just like everyone else. And she was grateful for that.

"Maybe I will," she said, knowing that her words would be taken as a firm commitment. She knew she should shoot the whole idea down, yet she couldn't bring herself to be cruel–and it *would* be cruel. "But I have to do a great deal of catching up first."

"Oh, don't worry about the exam," Lerida said. "You're the Necromancer's Bane. You'll pass it easily."

"I don't feel like I passed," Emily confessed. "I feel as though I failed."

"Everyone does that after taking one of her exams," Lerida told her. "I always feel as though I messed up completely. I think it is how she welcomes us back to school."

There was a cough at the door. "How *who* welcomes you back to school, Lady Lerida?"

Emily jumped, almost spilling her Kava. Mistress Mauve was standing there, looking annoyed. It was a truly fearsome expression.

"I... I was talking about the Head Girl," Lerida said, desperately. "She..."

"Was not in her post last year, as she was absent," Mistress Mauve said. There was something in her voice that suggested she thought that being absent was a crime deserving nothing less than a good old-fashioned hanging. "Report to me at the end of the day, Lady Lerida. And do not corrupt the newcomers with your dreams."

She turned on her heel and swept out of the room.

"She's strict," Lerida said, softly. "But she does know what she's talking about."

Emily didn't doubt it. Whitehall–and, she suspected, Mountaintop as well–placed a great deal of focus on practical work. It was impossible for anyone to fake competence when they had to demonstrate the spellwork on a regular basis, although she knew from bitter experience that knowledge alone didn't make someone a good teacher. She had started off poorly with Master Tor, and their relationship had never really improved.

"We'd better get back to class," Lerida said, finishing her drink and placing the mug in a sink. She didn't bother to wash it. "We don't want to be late, not now."

"No," Emily agreed. She hesitated, then swallowed the questions she wanted to ask. Lerida might be a good source of knowledge, but she would also be talkative. Too talkative. And it would be dangerous to underestimate her anyway. "Let's go."

They walked back into the classroom and took their seats, just in time to avoid being caught trying to sneak in late. Mistress Mauve handed out detentions with a vicious glee that surprised and terrified Emily, then closed and locked the door before striding up to the front of the room. If the rules of Mountaintop were anything like Whitehall, anyone who turned up after the door was locked would be denied entry–and given good cause to regret it. None of the teachers tolerated interruptions after classes resumed.

"Most of you are at an acceptable level," Mistress Mauve said, once silence had fallen over the classroom. "A number of you require more of a review"–she waved a hand in the air and several rolls of parchment flew off her desk, dropping down in front of a handful of students–"and a couple of you have shown rare promise. However, it will only get harder from here."

She paused, menacingly, then waved her hand again. This time, the rolls of parchment went to everyone, including Emily.

"Read them now, and prepare yourself for a private discussion with me tomorrow," Mistress Mauve ordered. "We will discuss your mistakes in considerable detail."

Emily nodded, and reached for the roll of parchment and unfurled it slowly. There were actually five sheets of parchment, the top one ordering her to report to Mistress Mauve at eleven bells the following day. She didn't *think* she had anything on her timetable that would clash with the appointment, but she reminded herself to check before anything else happened and she found herself expected to be in two places at once. It had happened, more than once, at Whitehall.

She opened the remaining sheets and read through them carefully. She'd managed to get more of the questions right than she'd thought, but two of her mistakes were terrifyingly bad and–as Mistress Mauve noted in neat precise script–would have caused disasters if the spells had actually been triggered. Emily swallowed the reaction that came to mind, and checked some of her work against the textbooks. Mistress Mauve was correct. She'd missed several variables in one question and it could have been disastrous.

"You will find your homework assignment in the baskets by the door," Mistress Mauve said, coldly. "I expect it handed in by the beginning of next week–Monday at the latest. I suggest you work on it carefully, as it will merely be the start of a series of assignments that will each build on the previous assignment. Thirty percent of your final grade for the year will depend on your work outside class. I would *suggest*"–she smirked, rather coldly–"that you think ahead before committing yourself."

She paused. "My office will be open from four till six for anyone who wishes to ask questions," she added. "Stupid or useless questions, however, will not be tolerated."

Emily winced, inwardly. Somehow, she doubted that anyone would visit Mistress Mauve unless they were truly desperate. It might cut down on the number of people who bothered them outside class–she had the feeling that quite a few of the teachers she'd known had disliked children and teenagers intensely–but it also meant that someone in trouble would be unwilling to seek help until it was too late. She sighed, then got to her feet with the rest of the students. There was nothing she could do about it. If she needed help, she'd just have to brace herself and visit the teacher's office.

Outside, Lerida caught her arm before she could make her escape and half-dragged her to the refectory. Unlike Whitehall, the room seemed to be far less ordered; Emily caught sight of students from all years and halls jumbled together, their faces blurring slightly as they used privacy wards to hide their words. Lerida pulled her to a chair, waved to a younger girl to bring them plates of food, and started to bombard Emily with questions. Emily sighed and started to ask questions of her own.

"Most students have older or younger siblings in the school," Lerida explained. "Outside classes and halls, they tend to sit together. And if you happen to have a boyfriend, the only place you can sit with him openly is here."

Emily frowned, surveying the crowd. Now that Lerida had pointed it out, she could see that the students were gathered in groups, some of them clearly cutting others dead. It reminded her of the aristocrats of Zangaria, who were seated according to who was feuding with whom at the moment, but somehow different.

Or perhaps it wasn't different at all. Magic crackled through the air, as if the students were about to start hexing each other. Emily fought down the urge to dive under the table and forced herself to eat, instead. She could dump Lerida later.

"We have Alchemy next," Lerida said, checking her timetable. "It's always more fun than Charms."

"Maybe," Emily said, doubtfully. Her success rate at Alchemy was poor... and that was with a crazy, but likeable teacher. Zed, she suspected, would be grateful to find any excuse to have her punished. "I used to *like* Charms."

"You still can," Lerida said. "Most of us study privately as well as attending classes. You would be welcome to attend."

"I'll see," Emily said. She had liked studying with Alassa and Imaiqah, but neither of them treated her as anything special. Lerida would be very different. "But give me some time to get used to the school, please."

"Whitehall must be very different," Lerida said. "Why didn't your father send you here, instead?"

"I think *he* went to Whitehall," Emily said. It was odd; she'd looked Void up in the school's rolls, but she'd found nothing. Of course, she knew, he probably hadn't called himself Void at the time. "And so he chose it for me."

Chapter Nine

Emily wasn't sure what she'd expected when she stepped into Zed's Alchemy classroom, but she hadn't expected a handful of desks—ten in all—surrounding a central table. Each of them had a wok, rather than a cauldron, and a wand placed neatly on the table. A roll of parchment sat within the wok, while a small pile of ingredients rested within the drawer under the table. It was enough like Whitehall's arrangement to make her feel homesick, while being different enough to be disconcerting.

She sat down at a desk and forced herself to remain calm. Zed might have good reason to dislike her, even to *hate* her, but he couldn't actually kill her, not when his bosses wanted Emily to join them. She might have to endure a tongue lashing, or having her work marked down unfairly, yet she'd endured worse. Her stepfather had been a master at getting under her skin and making her feel weak and helpless. Somehow, she doubted Zed could be any worse.

The remaining students from Raven Hall filled the classroom, chatting quietly amongst themselves as they waited for the teacher. Emily had to admit that the idea of having fewer students to a class, particularly when the class included various substances that exploded when someone looked at them the wrong way, made a great deal of sense. But it also meant there were fewer students for her to hide behind if Zed tried to be genuinely nasty. She pushed the thought to one side as the door opened one final time, then closed and locked itself. A man strode past her and up to the front of the classroom. The students rose to their feet in respect.

For a moment, Emily was sure she'd been wrong and that it wasn't the same Zed after all. He was tall and thin, rather than the jovially plump man she remembered from Zangaria, wearing stained robes rather than fine outfits suited to a Court Wizard. And then she saw his eyes and realized that she'd been right all along. The eyes were very familiar indeed. And, as his gaze passed over her and froze for a long second, she knew he knew who she was.

He looks thinner, the compassionate part of her mind noted. *Is that my fault?*

She was fairly sure he wouldn't have *starved*, even if he had been unceremoniously fired by King Randor. He was a trained Alchemist, after all, and the Allied Lands had a permanent shortage of trained Alchemists. If he'd been desperate for money, he could have produced potions for city-states or towns... or even moved to another Kingdom and traded his knowledge for a place to live and work. Coming to Mountaintop to teach might even be a step upwards, at least in magical society. They didn't always take Court Wizards very seriously.

But he still had good reason to dislike her.

"Be seated," Zed grunted. His voice was the same, although there was a harder edge to it than she remembered. "We have much to cover and very little time."

Emily sat, smoothing out her skirt, and waited. Whatever was coming, she told herself firmly, she could endure it.

"Safety is, always, the highest priority," Zed informed them, bluntly. "We will be working with both increasingly dangerous ingredients and several charms over the following months, so I expect each and every one of you to be very careful and not take risks. Those who do and are caught at it will not sleep comfortably for a week. Those who are not caught will probably end up wishing they had been."

Emily shivered. Professor Thande had said much the same, back when she'd taken her first lesson in Alchemy. A single mistake could cause an explosion—or worse; she knew, all too well, just how easy it was to screw up. And that had been when she'd *liked* the teacher. She forced her thoughts not to wander as Zed ran through the same lecture, almost word for word, as Professor Thande. The only real difference was his flat warning that they were *not* to teach anything they learned from his classes to any younger students without his permission.

But no one would have been interested in learning from me when I was a First Year, she thought. It still shocked her to recall just how ignorant she'd been, back when she'd first come to the Nameless World. *I barely knew how to do anything.*

Zed paused to allow his warning to sink in, then leaned forward. "Over the last year, you learned a number of potions from me, potions considered both easy and very useful. Indeed, some of them are so simple they can be produced by mundanes, with the right amount of care and modification. This year, we will spend most of it concentrating on something altogether different. We will be producing *Manaskol.*"

He spoke the word as though it should mean something to them, but Emily had never heard it before in her life. Or had she? It wouldn't be the first time that she'd discovered a concept, spell or potion that had two different names. She would just have to wait and see what *Manaskol* actually *did.*

"The disrespectful amongst us call it Magic Ink or Magic Glue, depending on precisely what additions are made to the baseline recipe," Zed informed them. "That is, as always, a way to trivialize both the importance of *Manaskol* and the skill involved in actually producing it from scratch. To be blunt"—his gaze rested on Emily for a long moment—"*Manaskol* is so important that producing several pints of it, in certain places, is considered a suitable way to pay tax. A few weeks of work would allow you to save all of your hard-earned money."

He smirked for a moment, then sobered. "The importance of *Manaskol* lies in its ability to absorb certain types of magic," he continued. "For example, in its ink form, it serves as the underlying structure for magical contracts—or secret messages, readable only by the intended recipient. Alternatively, in its glue form, it binds together stone walls, allowing the magician to create and secure wards that remain firmly in place. In many ways, it is the base of our entire society."

Emily thought fast. There had been references to... *something...* that might serve the same role in the books she'd read, but they hadn't provided any details. Maybe the writers had expected their readers to know all about *Manaskol* anyway, she thought, or maybe the details had been deliberately obscured. After she'd managed to get into terrible trouble after borrowing a book from Yodel, she was fairly sure that *some* details were definitely hidden, just to make sure that anyone trying to use the books had a proper background education. But something as important as *Manaskol* couldn't be hidden indefinitely.

"I would be very surprised," Zed concluded, "if any of you managed to produce it correctly the first time. It is immensely complicated. The instructions are on the parchment; read them carefully, then commence. And don't hesitate to ask if you need help."

Emily nodded to herself, then reached for the parchment and removed it from the wok. The instructions were written in Old Script, unsurprisingly; thankfully, she'd memorized enough letters to read it without any real problems. If there was one definite advantage the Allied Lands had over Earth, it was that there was a common language, both spoken and written. Even the alchemical notations were identical everywhere. She could be fairly certain she could read and understand anything she found in the Allied Lands.

Unless some dotty old sorcerer wrote the book, she thought, recalling Lady Aylia and her stories of adventures as a junior librarian. Some sorcerers used their own notation, often altering the figures to the point where their recipes and spells were useless or actively dangerous, while others often scribbled down nonsense as well as useful information, forcing researchers to check everything before actually trying any of the spells. *That won't happen here, will it?*

She looked up and shivered as she realized Zed was watching her. For a moment, she wanted to leave the class and never return. But she knew it was impossible.

Gritting her teeth, she bent her head back to the wok. The instructions for *Manaskol* were, as he'd said, extremely complex. She'd never quite seen anything like it, let alone instructions to use a wand during several stages of the brewing process. The wok itself, she discovered when she examined it, was actually designed to hold spells too. It was very different from the cauldrons Professor Thande had insisted they use for brewing potions.

Carefully, she started to sort out the ingredients she needed, refusing to allow her nerves to push her into making mistakes. Lady Barb had taught her, more than once, that an unflinching refusal to be bullied and manipulated could save her from making all sorts of stupid choices. People would always want to see her stumble, Lady Barb had warned... and she'd talked about people who had no personal grudge against Emily. Zed would probably be delighted if she managed to kill or injure herself while brewing a complex mixture.

She finished sorting out the ingredients and swore under her breath as she realized she didn't know how to use the wok. It wasn't something she'd been taught at Whitehall. She hesitated, wising there was someone else she dared asked, then raised her hand to call the teacher. Zed stepped over to stand beside her, his gaze cold with disdain, and quirked an eyebrow. Emily gritted her teeth and forced herself to meet his eyes.

"I don't know how to input spells into the wok," she said. Now she was looking, she realized there was no candle under the basin. Normally, heating charms or candles were used to heat cauldrons. "I haven't used one before."

"Something that would normally be covered at the end of Second Year," Zed said. His voice was dry, but there was a hint of cold amusement at Emily's expense. "Why didn't you learn how to use them?"

Emily felt her cheeks heat as she flushed with anger. "I wasn't told that it would be necessary," she said, keeping her outrage in check. There would be worse to come, she was sure. "It was not mentioned on any of the preparation materials for Third Year."

"It is generally assumed to be obvious," Zed muttered. He held a hand over the wok, and cast the first spell. Emily watched as it sank into the wok. "I have prepared the wok for you, *this time*, but I suggest you learn how to do it yourself in future."

Emily nodded, a little surprised. She'd expected a scathing lecture on her own incompetence.

"Thank you," she said, softly. Another thought struck her. "It's been a long time since I used a staff, sir, and I have never used a wand."

"So I was led to believe," Zed grunted. He picked the wand up and held it in front of her face. "Use the same basic procedure as you would use for a staff, but be gentle when you allow power to flow through the wood. If it starts to splinter, drop it at once and then..."

He broke off as one of the woks exploded into a sheet of fire. Emily stared as the classroom's wards fought to contain the blast, directing it up and away from the students, several of who took their eyes off their own woks to watch the flames. Moments later, two other woks went the same way. One of the students jumped backwards, cursing out loud; the other seemed rather less surprised.

"You overpowered the blending spell," Zed said. He waved his hand, clearing up the mess and disposing of the remains of the wasted ingredients. "Remain behind after class so we can discuss the matter more thoroughly."

Emily forced herself to look away, then started to put the first ingredients in her wok. Magic flared to life almost at once as the ingredients mixed, much to her alarm. She'd seen quick-reacting potions before, but this was different. Hastily, she charged the wand with the first piece of spellwork–thankfully, she'd had enough practice with her staff not to overdo the spell–and started to use it to stir the mixture, allowing power to flow through the wand. She braced herself for another explosion, but all the mixture did was start to bubble.

She glanced at the sheet of instructions, then picked up a vial of Basilisk Blood and started to drip it into the mixture. The reaction was immediate; one moment the mixture was bubbling like cream, the next it started to glow with magic. Emily jumped backwards, just in time to avoid having her face singed when the wok exploded. As before, the blast was contained by the wards, but the smell wasn't. Emily wrinkled her nose, and cringed mentally as Zed made his way back to her seat. He didn't look happy.

"Too much Basilisk Blood," he said, angrily. "The precise level of blood required changes depending on just when your mixture starts to boil. You need to tighten your senses to detect the changes within the brew."

"Yes, sir," Emily said. She cursed under her breath. Cooking had been bad enough, yet it had been easy compared to Alchemy. But then, she'd always been more interested in feeding herself than trying to make her food taste nice. And she hadn't always had the ingredients to follow the recipe precisely. "I didn't catch it in time."

"No, you didn't," Zed agreed. He gazed down at her for a long moment, but simply waved his hand, banishing the mess. "Start again. This time, pay closer attention to the magic as it swirls around the wok. You don't want to lose more ingredients by missing the signs that indicate it is about to blow."

Emily nodded in relief. She had few illusions about the cost of Basilisk Blood–or many of the other ingredients in the recipe. There *were* breeders who reared such creatures as casually as farmers reared sheep or cattle, but it was an immensely dangerous occupation. And some of the other creatures they raised made Basilisks look as dangerous as kittens. She knew that Whitehall and Mountaintop were immensely rich, by the standards of the Allied Lands, yet she'd just wasted a sizable amount of money. It would be hard to blame Zed for being angry with her.

"Thank you," she said, instead.

Zed gave her a sharp look, then marched away to deliver a sharp lecture to Claudia. The girl looked annoyed; she'd managed to make it through the first three steps, only to lose control of her mixture as she started to add several other ingredients. Emily turned her attention back to her wok, primed the wand with the spells she would require later on in the mixture, and started again. This time, the third step turned into something corrosive; she dropped the wand as it started to melt in her hand.

"You used too much power," Zed said, stamping back over to glare down at her wok. "Did you prime the wand ahead of time?"

Emily winced at his accusing tone, but nodded.

"This is rather more complex than anything *simple*," Zed said, making the word a curse. "A staff is poor preparation for using a wand in alchemy. I would suggest that you have a word with one of the Wandmistresses. They will be able to teach you the finer points of handling a wand."

Several of the girls tittered. Emily felt her cheeks heat, realizing that he'd finally managed to take a shot at her. She had a feeling, given just how many wands she'd seen in Mountaintop, that students were taught to use them earlier than at Whitehall. He'd just managed to send her back to the local counterpart of kindergarten. But, given the dangers of using wands too frequently, surely it wasn't worth the risk.

But he was right. She *did* need the lesson.

"Yes, sir," she said, subdued. "And..."

"Wait," Zed said, as three more woks exploded into flame. "We will discuss the matter later, sometime later in the week."

He walked back to the center of the room, then turned to face his students. "As you can see," he said, with a sudden smile, "this is *quite* a complex brew. None of you got past the fourth step."

There was a long pause. Emily heard one of the girls muttering unpleasantly, just loud enough to be heard. Zed waved a hand at her and she froze, unable to move or speak. Emily shivered–she *hated* that spell; even being turned into an animal was preferable–and forced herself to listen. It was clear that Zed didn't tolerate interruptions.

"We will be doing this again and again until you all manage to brew it successfully on a regular basis," Zed informed them. "I will be talking to some of you individually over the next few days, discussing how to improve your brewing skills. This is complex enough, after all, to defeat even experienced magicians. Only a skilled Alchemist can *guarantee* not to waste ingredients in a futile attempt to prepare *Manaskol.*"

He paused. "I would suggest you go back to your dorms and wash *thoroughly* before dinner," he added. "Those of you I told to stay behind, stay behind. Everyone else can leave."

Emily rose with the other students and–feeling as though she'd passed a test of some kind–stepped through the door and made her escape. It hadn't been *quite* as bad as she'd feared, but she knew it might get worse... that it *would* get worse. Zed had clearly spotted her weakness and intended to exploit it.

She sighed, but followed the other girls back to Raven Hall. Zed was right. They definitely needed to wash... and then she could do some research. She'd never studied the use of wands in Alchemy, after all, and it was clear that she needed to learn.

And besides, she told herself, the more she knew, the harder it would be for him to embarrass her in front of the class.

Chapter Ten

EMILY HAD FELT EXHAUSTED AND STRESSED AT THE START OF HER SECOND YEAR AT Whitehall, but Third Year at Mountaintop was worse. Five days of classes, some where she excelled and some where she was behind the other students, had taken their toll. Zed's constant gaze, when she was in his class, was unnerving, as was his habit of correcting her more blatantly than he corrected anyone else. And then there was the constant need to watch what she said...

She staggered into Raven Hall, feeling like a shower and an early bed without bothering to go for dinner, but stopped in annoyance as she saw an envelope on her bed. Frieda would have been given it, she knew, and told to place it there for Emily... she shook her head, fighting down the sudden surge of irritation, and reached for the envelope. Inside, there was a short note inviting her to the Administrator's office after dinner. It didn't look, despite the flowery language, as if she were being offered much of a choice.

Annoyed, Emily grunted to Frieda when the younger girl entered the dorm and walked out, heading for the refectory. Dinner, unlike lunch, was served between six and eight evening bells, with students invited to attend whenever they felt like it. Emily had a private suspicion that several of the students had held midnight feasts, perhaps in some of the passageways that weren't officially part of the school, but no one had invited her to join their gatherings. Besides, she'd also heard Nanette catch several girls trying to sneak out of the dorm on Wednesday and give them a sharp lecture. She wasn't sure that sneaking out was worth the risk *just* yet, not when she was probably still being watched closely.

Dinner was relatively simple compared to Whitehall's fare, but there was a lot of it. Emily ate quickly—she'd been eating much more since coming to the Nameless World—then walked out of the refectory and through the maze of passageways towards the Administrator's office. The wards pervading the school, as always, perplexed her more than she cared to admit. They didn't seem to monitor the students as closely as the wards pervading Whitehall, but they *did* prevent certain kinds of magic from being used in the corridor. Any night-vision spell seemed to fail completely.

It puzzled her. She could understand limiting the number of spells the students could use on each other outside class—bullying was alarmingly easy with magic—but why prevent students from using a spell to see in the dark? Unless they were afraid that students would walk into one another in the darkness... no, that made little sense. No matter how many other spells she tested, she hadn't found anything else the wards barred. She was tempted to ask Aurelius, but she didn't quite dare. There were several other questions she didn't dare ask him, either.

She stepped into the lighted administrative complex and winced, inwardly, as she saw a line of unhappy-looking students in front of a stone door. As she passed, a boy emerged, trying to look as though his punishment hadn't *really* hurt. Emily wanted to roll her eyes—young men seemed to be the same in both schools—but instead she averted her eyes as she walked up to the Administrator's office and pressed her hand against the stone door. It opened smoothly a moment later, allowing her to step inside. The office appeared to be empty.

"Come through here," Aurelius's voice called. It echoed from a third door, one that had been firmly closed the first time she'd visited his office. "It's quite all right."

Emily stepped inside and stopped dead. The room seemed to be a comfortable sitting room, complete with stuffed sofas and a small table, but it wasn't that that caught her attention. Ahead of her, covering the far wall, was a painting that seemed to glow, suggesting that the artist had worked magic into his work. Emily stepped forward involuntarily and stared. She had never cared much for art—her first art teacher had been unbearably pretentious—but this was something different.

"It catches everyone that way," Aurelius said. Emily flushed. She'd been so captivated by the painting she hadn't seen him lounging on one of the sofas. "Please. Feel free to study it."

"Thank you," Emily said. "What *is* it?"

Up close, more and more detail was revealed as she stared at it. The painting showed two men, one wearing monkish garb, the other wearing wizard robes and a pointy hat. Both of them stood inside circles drawn on the ground, which were surrounded by hundreds of demonic monsters, their claws trying to rend and tear at the two magicians. Both of them looked a little apprehensive, as if they'd bitten off more than they could chew. Emily leaned forward, trying to drink in every last detail. She couldn't help noticing that both magicians held books under their arms.

"They were the last of the DemonMasters," Aurelius said. "Back then, magicians summoned demons regularly, sacrificing a little of their lifeblood to keep a horde of monsters at their beck and call. The ones who had the most demons under their control were known as the DemonMasters. They were greatly feared by all who knew them."

He nodded to the book under one of the magician's arms. "That's a Book of Pacts," he said, flatly. "The details of each bargain were recorded in the magician's own blood, then stored for later reference."

Emily turned to look at him. "What happened to them?"

"Seven hundred years ago, according to legend, that one"—he pointed to the man in wizard robes—"challenged the other to a duel. They drew their circles of protection, then started summoning monsters and hurling them at each other. But the monsters grew more and more powerful until they finally broke through the circles. Both magicians were devoured. It was the end of an era."

He smiled at her, and pointed to one of the bystanders. "Do you recognize that man? The one standing next to the white-haired girl?"

Emily frowned. The bystander looked young, physically, but his hair was shockingly white and his face was lined and grave. His female companion had the same appearance of youth mixed with great age. He leaned on his staff and watched as the two DemonMasters met their ends. But his face was completely unfamiliar to Emily.

"No," she said.

"If legend is to be believed," Aurelius said, "he is Lord Whitehall. The founder of your former school."

"Seriously?"

"I am not in the habit of joking," Aurelius said, sternly. He shrugged. "But legend is often unreliable. There are too many records from that era that were deliberately destroyed–or lost in the chaos of the Faerie Wars. Even Mountaintop's origins are lost in a haze of lost documents, disinformation and outright lies."

Emily could well believe it. "And the girl?"

"No one knows," Aurelius said. "She's only mentioned in a handful of manuscripts dating from that era, all of which contradict themselves blatantly. There are some people who believe she never existed at all."

He turned and sat down on the sofa, beckoning for her to sit facing him. "I don't know if you've tasted this before," he said, pouring hot brown liquid into a glass, "but you might like it."

Emily sat, smoothing down her dress, and took the proffered glass. It felt warm against her bare hand, but there was clearly a charm worked into the glass to prevent it from burning her skin. A simple spell revealed it was safe to drink. When she tasted it, she thought of tea, strong sweet tea. And a faint hint of sugar.

"Nice," she said, slowly. She'd rarely tasted tea on Earth. "What is it and why don't we have this in Whitehall?"

"You probably have to ask for *Teh Tarik*," Aurelius said. "Not everything is provided; sometimes, you have to ask."

He poured himself a glass and sat back on the sofa. "You've completed your first week at Mountaintop," he added. "Are you enjoying yourself?"

"It's proving... very challenging," Emily said, after a moment. Mountaintop felt familiar enough for the differences to be truly disconcerting. She really didn't *like* having a Shadow hovering around her bed, as if she expected Emily to find her something useful to do. "But it's also proving very interesting."

"Good, good," Aurelius mused. He looked down at the glass in his hands. "The remaining students have all returned to school–those we haven't frightened off, that is. From now on, the wards protecting the school will be tightened. It will be difficult to leave until the end of the first semester. Do you want to remain here for the next three months, at the very least?"

Emily hesitated. She didn't want to seem *too* enthusiastic. And besides, part of her *wanted* to forget the mission and go straight back to Whitehall, where there were no Shadows, watching eyes and teachers who openly disliked her. She'd be safe there.

But you'd pass up the chance to learn just what is happening here, her thoughts rebuked her, gently. *And you do want to know what happened to Lin, don't you?*

"I have a question," she hedged. "Why didn't anyone tell me about the Shadows?"

Aurelius looked surprised. "Oversight," he said, finally. "The details are included in the prospectus we provide to all new students and their families. Some students serve as Shadows as a way to pay their tuition fees. Your father should have discussed the issue with you."

"I don't think he expected me to come here," Emily pointed out, snidely. Nanette had implied that *all* students spent time serving as Shadows. She would have to ask more questions and sort out the discrepancy later. "He sent me to Whitehall."

"True," Aurelius agreed. He looked up, meeting her eyes. "If there are other details you wish explained, Nanette will explain them to you. It is part of her duties."

She hasn't had time for me since the others returned, Emily thought, a little resentfully. *Jade* had always found time for her... but then, they'd shared a class. Nanette was in charge of the entire Hall, as well as serving as the school's Head Girl. She had no time for anyone, let alone Emily.

"I'll ask her," she said, instead.

"Please," Aurelius said. "Do you have other questions?"

Emily hesitated, then shook her head.

"Then we do need an answer," Aurelius said. "Do you wish to stay? You will be unable to leave until the end of the first semester at the very earliest."

"What happens," Emily asked, "if I get expelled?"

"You get turned into something inanimate for the rest of the semester," Aurelius said. She rather doubted he was joking. "There are other ways to deal with rowdy or disobedient students than simple expulsion."

"Yes, sir," Emily said. She took a breath. "I would like to stay."

"I'm glad to hear it," Aurelius said. He looked down at his glass and took a sip of his drink. "You will, of course, have to take the oaths."

He reached into his pockets and withdrew a sheet of paper. Emily took it and scanned the words automatically, feeling magic tingling around her fingertips. It *wanted* her to swear the words out loud, to bind them to her with her magic...

I swear, upon my magic and my life, that I will keep the secrets of Mountaintop, that I will uphold the traditions of Mountaintop, that I will honor the teachers of Mountaintop and that I will put my magic at the school's disposal, should I be called upon to serve.

She'd expected something worse, she knew, but the oath struck her as curiously imprecise. What were the secrets of Mountaintop - and what were its traditions?

Even so, it didn't matter. She couldn't swear the oath without fatally compromising her mission. But she did have a way out.

"No," Emily said. She winced at his suddenly dark expression, but forced herself to remain calm. "My father ordered me not to take any oaths without consulting him."

"That will not be necessary," Aurelius said, too quickly. For a second, so quickly she was half-convinced she was imagining it, he looked worried. "We would not ask you to go against your father. You will be spared the oaths for your first semester, at least. Should you wish to stay longer, we may have to open discussions with your father."

Emily kept her expression blank, but she was frowning inside. Aurelius had given in *way* too easily. She'd expected to be asked to take oaths, sooner or later; indeed, she'd been surprised when she realized she'd been accepted without being asked to swear even a basic oath of secrecy. Maybe he'd just been planning to dangle the joys of Mountaintop in front of her before insisting she took the oaths.

"That would be wise," she said. He *couldn't* talk to Void, not unless he intended to admit that he'd effectively kidnapped Emily from the White City. "I'm sorry..."

"Don't be," Aurelius said. "Your father's will comes first."

He leaned forward. "We've been monitoring your progress in your first classes," he said, softly. "In some, you did very well, better than I would have expected. In others... you lack the basic grounding you require to make progress."

"Yes, sir," Emily said. She'd done better in Charms than she'd expected—it turned out that Mistress Mauve had a habit of throwing advanced questions at her students, forcing them to put their brains to work—but she knew she was doing poorly in other classes. Only in Healing, it seemed, did she have any real advantage. "Whitehall and Mountaintop are very different."

"But you only require more training," Aurelius assured her. "You certainly don't have an inherent *inability* to learn or use more advanced forms of magic."

He paused, significantly. "I will be assigning you additional - private - lessons with various teachers," he added. "They will help you to overcome the... weaknesses Whitehall has programmed into your learning."

"Thank you," Emily said. She *enjoyed* private lessons, normally. "But why... ?"

Aurelius blinked at her, owlishly. "You are the daughter of a Lone Power," he said. Do you know how *rare* it is for a Lone Power to have a child? A child who *survives?*"

Emily shook her head, fascinated despite herself.

"Very rare," Aurelius told her. "They tend to develop magic early, *far* too early, and then fail to make it through puberty. But you... you made it. You belong with us, with magical society, not with a school that caters to all and sundry. We can help you grow to reach your full potential, while mundane society tries to hold you back."

He paused. "You do realize that King Randor is already trying to use you?"

"I know," Emily admitted.

It wasn't something she liked, but there seemed to be no way to avoid it. Her status as the Necromancer's Bane brought her power and influence—and Randor, who had maneuvred her into becoming a Baroness, had become her liege lord. If she'd known at the time that it would give him the ability to exploit her reputation, she might have turned down the offer, even though it would have embarrassed her friend in front of the people she would have to rule, one day. The only good thing that had come out of the whole affair had been Alassa escaping the threat of an arranged marriage, at least for a while.

"He has used your name as a threat, more than once," Aurelius said, softly. "And others have noticed. You might well find yourself targeted by... other sides in the White City. I dare say he hasn't really prepared you for your duties as Baroness either, am I correct?"

"Yes," Emily said, slowly.

"He would not want you acting independently," Aurelius said. "But only through acting independently could you attain your full potential."

He looked up and met her eyes. "Do you know the difference between a book of magic and a book *about* magic?"

Emily blinked, surprised by the apparent change in subject. "One of them is magic—it's a magical artifact in its own right," she said. "The other is just a textbook."

"Crude, but basically accurate," Aurelius said. "And do you understand that ownership of a book of magic would move from one magician to another, if the first happened to be defeated or succeeded by the second? If you happened to beat me in a duel, my books of magic would consider their ownership passed to you. The same would be true of any magical artifacts that happened to be in my possession."

"Yes," Emily agreed.

She carefully did *not* think about the book she'd stolen from Mother Holly. The Grandmaster had been reluctant to let her keep it. He'd practically insisted that it should be locked away while she was at Whitehall, yet he'd also been reluctant to let her store it at Cockatrice. But he hadn't been able or willing to take it from her.

"You defeated Shadye," Aurelius said. "What do you think that means?"

Emily stared at him. She'd known that no Necromancer had moved into Shadye's territory, but she'd never bothered to wonder *why*. The Blighted Lands surrounding Shadye's fortress were desolate wastelands. She'd never really considered that *she* might have a claim to the lands, or the fortress itself. The Grandmaster had certainly never mentioned it to her.

"You own his books now," Aurelius said. His eyes searched her face for a long moment, looking for something. "And you might wish to ask yourself why no one told you that before now."

Emily stared down at her hands. He was obviously trying to manipulate her. She *knew* he was trying to manipulate her. But it still felt as though she'd been betrayed by the Grandmaster and Lady Barb. Lady Barb was her *advisor*. She should have mentioned to Emily that there was at least a possibility that she had a fair claim to Shadye's fortress and whatever artifacts he'd left behind...

Perhaps he had none, she thought. *A Necromancer has raw power and madness, not skill.*

She shivered. Shadye had been mad, of that she was sure, but he'd also had a workable plan that had come alarmingly close to success. Who knew *what* he might have stored in his fortress?

"Here," Aurelius said.

Emily took the proffered handkerchief and wiped away tears. "I'm sorry," she said, feeling bitterly upset. They could have *told* her if she'd had a claim to Shadye's land. *Void* could have told her. He'd never shown any inclination to worry about whatever the Grandmaster might have thought about anything. "I..."

"Don't worry about it," Aurelius said. "We're here for you."

Oddly, she had the feeling he meant every word.

She blinked away tears, then placed the glass on the table and stood. "I need to be alone for a while," she said. She didn't want to break down in front of him. "Please..."

"My library is always open to you," Aurelius said. "And I will be here to talk, if you want."

Emily nodded, then stepped through the door and walked into the private library.

Chapter Eleven

Emily honestly wasn't sure just how long she spent sitting at the small table in the private library, trying to organize her thoughts. She'd known that ownership of certain magical artifacts passed from the defeated to the victor—it was how she'd come to own Mother Holly's spellbook—but it had honestly never occurred to her that she might have inherited anything from Shadye. Certainly, no one had mentioned the possibility to her...

And now she wondered why.

No other Necromancer had moved into Shadye's territory, no other magician had made it his home... they could have slipped into the Blighted Lands at any point and searched the remains of his fortress for books, artifacts or anything else he might have hoarded over the years. Instead, they'd been content to leave the remains of Shadye's fortress alone... no one had moved into Shadye's territory.

Could it have been left abandoned because *Emily* owned it?

It was hard, so hard, to think clearly. She wanted to go back to Whitehall and demand answers, to know why they'd kept the possibility from her. But there was no way she could leave just now, no matter how angry she felt. She knew she couldn't leave Mountaintop now and hope to return, at least not without arousing suspicion. Who knew what Aurelius would think if she returned from a brief visit to Whitehall?

She wiped away her tears and stood, resolving to ask the Grandmaster and Lady Barb when she next saw them. Aurelius had given her access to his library, after all, and she had no intention of wasting it. She paced over to the bookshelves and skimmed the titles, mentally cataloging the ones that were new to her. Quite a few books had no visible titles at all and crackled with magic when she touched the spines, so she left them for last. Aurelius might have to remove charms and hexes from the books before Emily could read them safely.

And there's probably a spell watching me, she thought, as she extended her senses as far as she could. Magic crawled along the rocky walls, shimmering in and out of her awareness; some spells preserving the books, others keeping them safe. *He will know what books I look at.*

Finally, she found a book on magical ownership rights and pulled it off the shelf. The book had little magic worked into the parchment, although she had the uneasy feeling that the cover was made from human skin. It wasn't uncommon in books of magic, but it never failed to make her feel queasy. Opening the book, she sat down and started to skim through it, using a translation spell to make out the more complex words. It rapidly became clear that magical ownership was a complex business. There was no hard and fast rule for when something became an artifact with ownership rights, nor was there any standard way ownership could be transferred. The only certain way to transfer ownership was to have one person defeat—and kill—the other.

If Shadye owned anything like that, she thought, *it's mine now.*

But the book didn't say anything useful. What happened if the new owner didn't *know* she owned it? The book didn't say. What happened if someone stole the artifact from an owner who didn't know she *was* the owner? The book didn't even speculate.

Emily ground her teeth in frustration, realizing that a more experienced magician would have known to ask what had happened to Shadye's properties. It had never occurred to her that she might have won anything from Shadye. But then, it was quite possible that Shadye didn't have anything she could *win*.

"Necromancers are not skilled magicians," Sergeant Miles had said, years ago. "They have raw power, but little else—apart from madness."

Emily closed her eyes bitterly. The only way to know would be to go to Shadye's territories and find out if there was anything there. But she couldn't do that alone... perhaps she could ask Void to accompany her, or maybe Lady Barb. Emily was sure Lady Barb would give her a straight answer, if asked a direct question. Emily briefly considered trying to write a letter, then dismissed the idea. The code phrases they'd worked out hadn't been intended for this situation.

She opened her eyes and returned the book to the shelf and, in the spirit of defiance, pulled a book on blood magic down from the higher shelves. Whitehall's librarians rarely allowed anyone below Fifth Year to read such books, no matter how curious they were. Emily opened it, recoiled at the stench of human blood that wafted up from the pages, then started to read. Some of the magic was alarmingly familiar, others were completely new. She hadn't known it was possible to perform an adoption using blood, one that would—literally—make someone the child of their adopted parents.

Pity it wouldn't satisfy King Randor, she thought, morbidly. She knew she would have to give Cockatrice an heir one day, a child of her body. The thought bothered her more than she cared to admit, even though she'd started to face up to the problems left behind by her stepfather. She'd never met a boy she thought she could fall in love with, let alone spend the rest of her life with. But then, she hadn't really been looking.

A soft cough made her jump and look up. Aurelius was standing on the other side of the table, regarding her with a faintly amused, almost paternal expression.

Emily flushed, started to try to hide the book, but recalled she had permission to read everything in the room. But he'd probably learn a great deal about her from what books she chose to read.

"It's quite late," he said, softly. "And even though it is the weekend, you really should be in bed."

Emily felt her cheeks grow warmer as she checked her clockwork watch. It was much later than she'd realized, well after curfew. Nanette was going to be annoyed... she sighed, returned the book to the shelf, then turned to face him and curtseyed. Aurelius half-bowed to her in return, then indicated the door. Emily stepped out into absolute darkness. The door closed behind her a moment later, leaving her alone.

She listened carefully for a long moment, hearing nothing, then created a light globe to illuminate her path back to Raven Hall. Her footsteps echoed loudly in her ears as she passed through the outer door and into the passageways beyond, the light globe giving the complex an eerie appearance that sent chills down her spine. She was completely alone, in absolute silence. There were parts of Whitehall that felt sinister, particularly at night, but this was different. Part of her just wanted to stay where she was until morning, when there would be other students around. But she knew that wasn't an option.

The darkness ebbed and flowed around her as she walked, barely pushed back by the glowing light. Emily wasn't scared of the dark, but she'd learned enough after two years in the Nameless World that she should be *very* scared of some of the creatures that could hide within the shadows. Mountaintop, like Whitehall, would have wards to keep out the worst kind of supernatural vermin, but she knew from listening to the other girls that the wards were far from perfect. The school was only part of a much greater network of caves and tunnels dug deep beneath the ground. Who knew what might be lurking there in the darkness?

She started as she heard the sound of running footsteps ahead of her, coming towards her. Quickly, she pressed herself against the wall, realizing–too late–that her light globe would reveal her presence to anyone who saw it. Moments later, a young boy–a First Year, she thought–ran past her, his face pale and wan. Two other boys ran after him, casting spells as they moved. Their aim wasn't very good, Emily noted; one of the spells came alarmingly close to her. They were gone before she could find the words to protest...

And then another shape loomed out of the darkness. Emily gasped in pain as a hand caught her by the upper arm. The hand felt as cold as ice; when she looked up, she found herself looking into the hooded face of a proctor. She couldn't see anything inside the hood, not even the suggestion of a chin. The proctor studied her for a long moment, then started to pull her down the corridor. It was futile to resist, Emily realized, although she had no idea where he was taking her. What happened to students caught out of bed in Mountaintop?

But I was with the Administrator, she thought, frantically. Aurelius could have given her a night-time pass or something, if she'd thought to ask. *I wasn't sneaking out of my dorm!*

The proctor reached Raven Hall and pushed her through the door. Nanette was standing beside the other door, her arms crossed under her breasts and a grim expression on her face. Emily realized, with a twinge of guilt, that she'd made the older girl wait up for her, even though she hadn't been *deliberately* remaining out of bounds. Nanette was unlikely to be happy at being denied sleep herself.

"Well?" Nanette demanded. "What do you have to say for yourself?"

She went on before Emily could say a word. "You are two hours late for bed," she added, darkly. "Where were you?"

"I was with the Administrator," Emily said. It felt odd to have anyone close to her age care about what she was doing after dark. Madame Razz had been much older than any of her charges. "We were talking, and then I was reading. I didn't realize it was so late until he told me to go to bed."

Nanette studied her for a long moment, clearly trying to sniff out a lie. "You do realize," she said sweetly, "that I *will* check with him? And that if you are lying, your punishment will be doubled? And public?"

"Ask him," Emily said. "He will vouch for me."

Nanette glowered at her, but finally nodded. "I will, tomorrow," she said flatly. "Until then, go to bed and stay there until morning."

The dorm felt strange in the semi-darkness, Emily discovered, as she stepped through the door. Most of the beds were surrounded by privacy wards, including several designed to block out the sounds of people snoring. Her lips twitched–Aloha had snored, although she'd always denied it–and her roommates had been forced to learn the spells to protect themselves just to get a good night's sleep. She heard a faint moan as she reached her bed, and frowned. Frieda was asleep in her bed, twitching uncomfortably. She must be having a nightmare, Emily realized. She knew she'd woken her roommates once or twice with her own nightmares.

Poor girl, she thought.

Emily changed rapidly into her nightgown, then went to the washroom and finally climbed into bed, closing her eyes. She must have been more exhausted than she'd realized, because the next thing she was aware of was the sounds of the other girls as they took down their privacy wards before starting the new day. Cursing her mistake–she'd been too tired to erect wards of her own–Emily buried her head under her pillow and tried to block out the sound completely. It didn't work.

"Hey, you're back," one of the girls called, shaking Emily's bed. "And you seem to be alive."

Emily groaned and sat upright, wincing at the bright light spilling through the room. She should have set up wards against that, too. Nanette always made the light globes too bright, either to encourage them to get out of bed or merely to force them to master the wards necessary to block out the light.

Claudia was balancing on the edge of Emily's bed, grinning down at her. A moment later, she cast a privacy ward so that no one else could hear them. Emily silently willed her to go away, but she didn't take the hint.

"I thought Nanette was going to kill you, she was so pissed," Claudia said, cheerfully. "And you're even sitting upright. What did she *say* to you?"

"Nothing important," Emily groaned. She reached for her watch and cursed again. It was barely eight bells in the morning... and it was the weekend! She'd planned to spend it in the library, reading and researching. And she could have slept in. "What did she say to *you*?"

"Go to bed," Claudia grinned. Her smile grew predatory, in a manner that reminded Emily far too much of the bullies from Earth. "I was wondering what you were going to be doing this weekend."

"Studying," Emily said. She sighed as she saw the envelopes placed on her bedside table. "I need to wash and eat."

"If you have time, come join us for our weekly gathering," Claudia said. "I'm sure you would fit in perfectly."

Emily frowned. "Fit in where?"

"With our quarrel, of course," Claudia said. She grinned brightly. "We consider ourselves honored to have the most talented witches of Mountaintop in our ranks and no one can deny you're talented. We would normally wait, but..."

She shrugged. "Can I tell the others you will be attending?"

Emily shrugged, then reached for the envelopes and opened them one by one. The first envelope was a note from the Administrator, telling her that she would be taking dueling classes with the First Years, as she had no prior experience of dueling. The second was a note from Markus, inviting her to lunch with him. Claudia let out a loud gasp when she saw it, obviously overacting. Emily rubbed her head in irritation and considered less polite ways to tell her to go away.

"The Head Boy is inviting you to lunch," she said. "You should go."

"Better than going to your quarrel?" Emily asked. "Or..."

"Oh, gods no," Claudia said. "But you really don't want to annoy the Head Boy."

She grinned, and did her impression of a male voice. "Your badge is one single micron out of alignment, do five hundred lines," she said. "Your dress is one inch too short; bend over and take six whacks. Your hair is too long; go serve in charms as an unwilling test subject."

She sighed and stalked off.

Emily glowered after her, then pulled herself out of bed, washed and dressed in her uniform. She had no idea what she should wear to lunch with the Head Boy, but she had a feeling she should at least look reasonably presentable. Claudia's suggestions ran through her head as she went to the library and did some research before heading down towards the Head Boy's private office. It was surprisingly far from the hall he was meant to be supervising, as well as his other duties.

"Come on in," Markus called, when she looked inside. "Food's on the table."

The office was bare, Emily noted, as she closed the door and sat down at the table. There were two large portraits: one showing a family of people who looked alarmingly like Markus, the other a family that had been drawn to appear as demonic as possible. One of the girls nagged at her mind; she looked oddly familiar, but how?

"Please, eat," Markus said. He grinned. "One of the advantages of being Head Boy is that you can bring in your own food, if you wish."

Emily nodded and tucked in. The food was definitely better than anything she'd eaten at Mountaintop—and much more suited to her taste than the endless banquets at Zangaria, where the aristocrats preferred quantity to quality. Markus chatted as they ate, talking about spells he was learning and asking how Emily was coping after a week in Mountaintop. He seemed more caring than Nanette, Emily noted. But then, he hadn't had to wait up for her the previous evening.

"I have questions for you, if you don't mind," Markus said. "I believe you know Melissa of Ashworth?"

Emily looked up at the portrait again. The girl was Melissa, all right, but drawn to make her look as unpleasant as possible. Emily disliked Melissa cordially, but she had to admit the girl was prettier than her portrait. Normally, in the Allied Lands, it was the other way round.

"I do," she said. "And she looks much nicer than that."

Markus snorted. "Tell me about her," he said. "Please."

Emily hesitated—she disliked talking about someone behind their back—but did as she was bid. Markus listened with some amusement, his eyes glittering with light as Emily described the minor prank war she and her friends had played with Melissa and *her* friends, and sighed when Emily had finished.

"She's the Heir of her family," he said, by way of explanation. "We're sworn enemies."

"How upsetting," Emily said, dryly. "Is that why Melissa went to Whitehall?"

"Yep," Markus said. "Or so I assume."

Emily blatantly rolled her eyes. Markus merely snorted in response.

"But I assume you have questions for me," he said, after a moment. "What can I offer you?"

"Claudia invited me to a quarrel today," Emily said. She rather assumed Claudia hadn't invited her to an argument. "What *is* a quarrel?"

"A social club," Markus said. He smiled. "You will, if you stay here, switch halls and roommates every year. In the end, you will be expected to know everyone from your generation in magical society. But your quarrel, which will be composed of people from several separate years and halls, will be with you for the rest of your life. You will help them, and they will help you."

His eyes darkened. "Melissa and I would never be allowed to share a quarrel," he added. "Too much chance of binding oaths getting in the way."

Emily frowned. "Should I go?"

"Of course," Markus said. "But..."

He held up a hand. "I'll give you a word of advice," he added. "There are over a dozen currently active quarrels at this school. Taste them all before you commit yourself. You may discover that one of them isn't suited to you."

Emily nodded, thoughtfully.

Chapter Twelve

T HE REST OF THE WEEKEND PASSED QUIETLY, MUCH TO EMILY'S RELIEF. SHE SPENT MOST OF
her time in the library, reading about Mountaintop's history and social structure.
Like Whitehall, she hadn't been able to escape the sense that a great deal of the
school's "official" history was little more than rumors and hearsay, while the truth
had been lost or deliberately suppressed by the people in power. But there was no
way to know for sure.

She gave up on history studies and read, instead, about the quarrels. As Markus had
said, they were social groups, although they tended to be more like the Freemasons
than any social club she'd known on Earth. A quarrel stayed with its members forever; they helped and supported each other, no matter the cost. There were even
hints that shared membership in particular quarrels had helped members patch up
arguments between their families that had threatened to lead to outright war.

But there were also some chilling drawbacks.

They were also restrictive. A member could never leave or transfer to another
quarrel. Their members were forced to swear binding oaths before being considered
full members. And many of the quarrels kept their business secret, adding secrecy to
the oaths their members swore. By now, magical society was thoroughly infiltrated
by quarrels, but it would be immensely difficult to identify all of the members. And
if someone chose to stand alone...

Someone like Void could remain apart, she thought. *But someone weaker would be
either forced to join for self-protection, or remain isolated forever.*

She was still mulling the issue over as Monday rolled around and she found herself, after a hasty breakfast, walking down towards the Dueling Chambers. Several
First Year students followed her, casting odd glances at the older girl. They clearly
didn't expect her to be joining them, not entirely to Emily's surprise. But Whitehall
didn't teach any form of professional dueling. Emily had looked it up, after seeing a
Dueling Championship before she'd gone to the Cairngorms, and discovered it was
an elective. Only a handful of students elected to take the course.

"Lady Emily?" Frieda asked in disbelief. "What are *you* doing here?"

Emily looked down at her Shadow. She hadn't realized—even though she should
have—that Frieda would be taking the same class. No wonder the younger girl was
surprised to see Emily entering the chamber. Perhaps she'd been pushed by her
classmates into asking, if it was rare for younger students to address older students
directly. It certainly was at Whitehall.

"I never took Dueling," she said, simply. "So I have to attend *this* class."

She followed the younger students through the main doors and into a large spellchamber. As always, she could sense the presence of powerful wards in the air, providing protection from magical accidents. They didn't feel as strong as the wards
she recalled from the championship, but the tutors probably felt that their students
would be nowhere near powerful enough to require such heavy wards. Emily had
to admit they were probably right. As a First Year, it had taken her quite some time

to learn how to use the more dangerous military spells—and, normally, she wouldn't have learned them for years.

"Class," a female voice said. "Be seated."

Emily looked up—and blinked in surprise. There were two tutors for dueling, she realized, and they looked strange. Both were female, but one was white with pitch-black hair and the other was black with brilliant *white* hair. Their faces were completely identical, right down to the patrician cheekbones and bright blue eyes. They might not have been conventionally pretty, Emily noted, but their faces definitely had character. And if they were twins...

Her eyes narrowed. There was no such thing as magical twins. She'd asked, once, and had been told that while twins were born in the Allied Lands, none ever had magic. It was one of those laws that everyone knew—everyone in the Allied Lands, at least—but had never been satisfactorily explained. Everyone just seemed to believe it was the way things were.

An experiment with bilocation that went wrong, Emily asked herself, *or something more sinister?*

She sat down at the back of the class, noting how short many of the younger students actually were. Emily had never been particularly tall on Earth, but she was quite tall—for a girl—by the Nameless World's standards. And quite a few of them looked as thin as she'd been when she'd gone to Whitehall for her First Year. She had no difficulty in placing them as newcomers to magic as well as Mountaintop itself.

"I am Mistress Hitam," the black woman said. She ran a hand through her long white hair, then nodded to her companion. "This is Mistress Putih. We are both Dueling Mistresses with over twenty years of experience, so we suggest you listen to us. Dueling is one of the greatest sports in the Allied Lands, with great honors and rewards going to the champions, but it is also one of the most dangerous. Failing to listen to us will result in severe harm."

There was a pause.

"There are three levels to dueling," she continued, once it became clear that no one would dare to interrupt. "The first level is for educational purposes; it is fought out until one of the contestants is unable to proceed any further. The second level is fought to satisfy minor points of honor and, as such, is fought to first blood. Finally, the third level, fought to satisfy *major* points of honor, is fought to the death. Two contestants will enter the arena, but only one will emerge. You will *not* issue any challenges above the first level while you are at this school. If you do, we'll kill you. Personally."

Emily swallowed. It didn't look as though Mistress Hitam was joking.

"Dueling acts as a check on society," Mistress Hitam said. "It teaches people that they are ultimately responsible for their own words—and that you have to be prepared to back them up with force, if necessary. There are levels of insult and accusation, indeed, where *failing* to issue or accept a challenge is taken as a sign of guilt. But once issued, a challenge cannot be retracted save by the discovery of certain proof it should never have been issued."

She paused again. "And such proof can be very hard to find."

Mistress Putih stepped forward. "You will be expected to research dueling in the library after classes," she said. Her voice was very like her twin's. "Next week, we want an essay from each of you on when a dueling challenge can be issued, when one *should* be issued and the potential consequences of refusing to issue or accept a challenge."

Emily winced, inwardly. The whole concept struck her as fundamentally wrong. It would be easy to contrive a situation where a challenge could be issued, then fought, with the intention of killing one of the parties. She understood and accepted that a person should be held accountable for their words or actions, but death seemed too steep a punishment. Or was that her Earth upbringing speaking? There were no laws covering libel or slander in the Allied Lands.

Mistress Hitam started to speak again, talking the students through what spells they were allowed to use in the spellchamber. Most of them, Emily noted, were relatively simple and completely non-lethal, at least by local standards. Someone from Earth would be horrified at the thought of being turned into an inanimate object, even if the transformation could be reversed easily. But it was apparently a valid way to win. Somehow, she doubted First Year students could cast many spells without moving their arms.

She jumped as Mistress Putih caught her arm and pulled her to one side. "You know many more spells than we teach the little ones," she muttered. Up close, Emily couldn't help noticing that her breath smelt faintly of roses. "Stick with the same ones we show them."

"I understand," Emily said. She noticed that several of the children—the ones from magical families, judging by their robes—didn't seem to carry wands. They also seemed to know more spells than their poorer counterparts. "Why do some of the students have wands and others don't?"

"Because some of them *need* the wands," Mistress Putih said.

Emily frowned - as far as she knew, that wasn't even remotely true - but said nothing.

Mistress Hitam called two of the students into the spellchamber, then ordered the remainder of the students to gather around the edge of the wards. Emily stood at the back, unable to avoid noticing her Shadow casting worried glances at her from time to time. Maybe Frieda might feel ashamed at having her superior watching, she realized dully, just as some of the students on Earth had felt embarrassed by their parents when they visited the school.

It wasn't something she understood. *She* would have been happy if her mother had bothered to put down the bottle long enough to attend.

"You smell," one of the female students said. It was, Emily supposed, a challenge of sorts. "And you stink of goats."

"And you have no imagination," the other student countered. He lifted a hand threateningly. "I challenge you..."

His counterpart shot a flare of green light at him—and missed. Her aim really wasn't very good, Emily noted, as the magic crashed into the wards and vanished. The second student threw a spell of his own, which missed as the first one jumped to one side, then came up with a wand in her hand. Emily snorted inwardly as she zapped her target with a spell that caused a minor electric shock. It would have been a good tactic if the victim had been dependent on a wand, as it forced them to drop the weapon, but useless against someone who didn't need one. His target threw a second spell... and scored a direct hit. The student shrank rapidly and became a frog.

"The duel is complete," Mistress Hitam said, after a moment. "One of the contestants cannot continue."

She let the victor out, then snapped her fingers, releasing the second student from the spell and returning her to human form. She looked embarrassed as the other students jeered at her and stumbled out of the wards. Emily couldn't help feeling sorry for her, even if the duel had been very tame by Martial Magic's standards.

Mistress Hitam didn't hesitate; she sent two more students into the wards and set them to dueling. They didn't seem much more capable than the previous two, Emily noted, although they'd clearly learned from watching their predecessors and kept moving, never standing still for very long. This time, they snapped spells at one another for ten minutes before one finally froze the other in her tracks.

Emily couldn't help feeling a little bored as the class wore on. The students became more practiced, but none of them seemed very capable compared to any of the First Year students she knew from Whitehall. But the more she watched, the more she thought she detected a disturbing pattern. The students from magical families were far more knowledgeable than the students from non-magical families... and they were often deliberately humiliating their victims.

She felt her eyes narrow as Frieda stepped into the spellchamber. Her opponent didn't even give her a chance to raise her wand before she fired the first spell, sending her staggering all over the spellchamber. It wasn't quite a victory—Frieda wasn't immobilized—but she didn't stand a chance. Moments later, her opponent finished the duel by turning her into a tiny statue of herself, then picking her up and carrying her out of the wards. When Frieda was released from the spell she couldn't meet Emily's eyes.

Emily cringed mentally. *She* would have hated to lose in front of her superior too.

"You will duel with me," Mistress Putih said, turning to face Emily. "It wouldn't be fair to the other students to let you duel with them. And stick to the spells we showed them earlier."

Emily nodded, feeling a sudden flush of anticipation as she stepped through the wards. She had enjoyed matching herself against the other students in Martial Magic, once she'd mastered enough magic to prevent them using her as punching bag, although there were no formal rules beyond a ban on inflicting any form of permanent damage. Sergeant Miles had warned her to keep her distance from the boys, though. Pound for pound, she was no match for them. Without magic, they'd beat her every time.

Mistress Putih bowed, then fired the first spell without bothering with a formal challenge or exchange of insults. Emily blocked it effortlessly–it was a very low-power spell–and threw back one of her own, trying to freeze the tutor in her tracks. The Dueling Mistress let it hit her, countered it before Mistress Hitam could count to ten and then fired a second spell of her own. Emily was unwillingly impressed. No matter how many times she practiced, she couldn't break that spell without moving her hands.

She jumped to one side as Mistress Putih fired something stronger at her, then threw back a set of spells of her own. If she had to stick with the basics, she could at least cast them faster than the other students. Mistress Putih looked pleased as she ducked, dodged or blocked her way through the spells, then fired two spells back at Emily. One was blocked, the other missed...

...And then Emily found herself frozen, utterly unable to move.

She almost panicked as she tried desperately to break the spell, hearing Mistress Hitam's voice slowly counting up to ten, but it refused to let her go. How the hell had Mistress Putih *done* it? She'd blocked the spell completely. She was *sure* she'd blocked the spell.

"Lady Emily is unable to continue," Mistress Hitam said. "The contest is over."

Emily staggered as she was released from the spell, then looked at Mistress Putih, lifting her eyebrows questioningly. Mistress Putih smiled, then pointed one long finger behind Emily, indicating the wards. Emily shook her head in disbelief. Mistress Putih had reflected the spell off the wards and straight into Emily's back.

"Congratulations," she ground out, annoyed at herself. She had seen some spells reflected off the wards. If students could do it accidentally, a tutor should be able to do it deliberately. "Well played."

"I've had twenty years of experience," Mistress Putih pointed out. "I think you will need additional practice, though. You have a great deal to unlearn."

"I don't want to fight duels," Emily said. Sergeant Miles hadn't said much about formal dueling, but he *had* warned them, enough that his students could repeat the speech in their sleep, that there were no rules in actual fighting. A Necromancer certainly wouldn't follow any rules. "I need to fight Necromancers."

"You are a sorceress of growing power and influence," Mistress Putih countered. "You will be challenged, sooner or later. And then you will need to know how to fight."

Mistress Hitam cleared her throat as the students gathered around her. "You will all have to practice the spells in the spellchambers," she said. "Make sure you have an older student supervising you when you do. The prefects are expected to make time for it if you require their assistance. We will continue formal dueling training over the next few months in this room. Outside this room, you are *not* to engage in any duels. Do you understand me?"

The students agreed, in chorus. "Emily, remain behind," Mistress Hitam ordered. "The rest of you can go get washed and changed before your next class."

Emily watched the students go, then looked at the two teachers. Up close, she was *sure* it was a bilocation accident that had separated one person into two, although she was sure they had different personalities. Lady Barb had cautioned Emily not to even *think* about using the spell herself until she was much older, citing all the horrific things that could go wrong. Discovering that she suddenly had an identical twin was the least of it. Her magic could be ripped apart by the strain.

"You should be testing yourself against students from Third Year," Mistress Hitam said. "You shouldn't be facing the younger students at all."

Emily frowned. "Why?"

"Because they are no match for you," Mistress Hitam said, with a hint of irritation. "It would be bad for their development to have you wipe the floor with them. And because we don't want them to wipe the floor with you."

"Oh," Emily said. The years were meant to be separate, after all. If she, a prospective Third Year, was soundly beaten by a First Year, it would reflect badly on her entire year. Given the degree of respect and deference given from lower years to the higher years, it would likely reflect badly on Mountaintop's social system. "I'll find someone to duel with, if I can."

"You will," Mistress Hitam predicted. "There are no shortage of members in Dueling Clubs who practice intensely outside class."

Emily sighed. She would have to ask one of the other girls for advice.

"Go get washed and changed," Mistress Putih ordered. "Your next class is... when?"

"Alchemy, after lunch," Emily said. The next period had yet to be designated. "And then Charms to round up the day."

"Study the books on dueling challenges," Mistress Hitam advised. "We expect the essay from you too, young lady. And you will need to know the basics as comprehensively as the other students, perhaps more so. Your father fought many challenges in his day."

Emily nodded. She knew that the link between her and Void—the *supposed* link between her and Void—was a form of protection. It also covered up her origins quite neatly. But it was also a major headache at times, either through people assuming she could influence him or through people taking her for her father's daughter and being too afraid of her to speak. Killing two Necromancers hadn't really helped with *that*, either.

"I will," she said, reluctantly. One thing she would happily introduce computers or even typewriters, if she could. Writing out a thousand words left her hands aching painfully, but her attempt at producing a magical typewriter had floundered on the high magic requirements. "And I'll try to get it back to you before the end of the week."

Chapter Thirteen

AFTER TWO MORE EXPLODED WOKS AND AN ACCIDENT THAT HAD COME ALARMINGLY CLOSE to burning her hair off, Emily was more than a little surprised that Zed hadn't handed out a horrific detention or simply sent her to the Administrator's office for more immediate punishment. But then, she *had* been trying, unlike one of the other girls. Helen had been talking to her neighbor when her mixture started to steam, and, before she'd even turned around to look at it, it had exploded with terrifying force. Zed had written Helen a slip and dispatched her to the office, and told her not to bother coming back. Emily found it hard to blame him.

She sighed in relief as the class finally came to an end. It was no consolation that—so far—no one had managed to get further than the sixth step in making the alchemical concoction, even students who had plenty of experience with wands. Zed had warned them, after all, that making anything this complex took months to master. She cleaned up her table, placed her empty bottles in the disposal bin, and then stood with the rest of the class. But then, Zed caught her eye.

"Remain behind," he ordered. "Everyone else, dismissed."

Emily flinched inwardly as the room emptied with astonishing speed, no one caring to stick around when the teacher was obviously in a foul mood. Zed waved his hand in the air, dispelling the stink of burning chemicals, then nodded to Emily to follow him. Emily obeyed, clasping her hands together in the hope that it would keep them from shaking. Right now, Zed was the last teacher she wanted to be alone with in Mountaintop.

She followed him into a smaller room that reminded her, all too clearly, of the office he'd used in Zangaria. It was a little larger than the one she recalled, with three cauldrons of potion bubbling merrily above a set of small fires and a large, leather-bound book sitting on the table. Emily glanced at the book, then frowned as she read the title. *Potions of Light and Darkness.* She'd heard something about that book once, years ago. It hadn't sounded pretty.

Zed's eyes gleamed with an unholy light as he indicated the first cauldron. "Love potion," he said, simply. "Or, rather, *fixation* potion. Brewed properly, fed to the right person, it will make him completely fixated on one other person, who will become the center of his universe. He will live and die for that person—and, once the target of his admiration is dead, he, too, will die. It has no cure."

Emily swallowed. His words sounded very much like a threat.

Zed smiled cruelly, then indicated the second cauldron. "This potion is very definitely on the banned list," he added. "We call it *pain*, liquid pain. A single drop of this potion would hurt the drinker far worse than the most unpleasant and fearsome of torture curses. And there is no cure for this, either. The victim would have to endure, suffering all the while, until the potion finally worked its way out of his body. They say the pain is worse than being burned alive by a dragon."

And how, Emily asked herself in a desperate attempt to remain calm, *would they know?*

"Very interesting," she said, through a suddenly dry mouth. "And what is the third?"

"Boiled water," Zed told her. "I prefer to have my cauldrons washed with water, rather than magic. It can cleanse them without leaving unfortunate traces of magic behind."

Emily wasn't sure she believed him, although Professor Thande had taught them the importance of keeping stray magic away from their cauldrons as much as possible. It was why they used flames rather than charms to heat their potions, at least in the first two years of schooling. But she supposed it was reasonably possible.

"Please, take a seat," Zed said. He sounded as though he was trying to be civil, even though it was clear he wasn't pleased to have Emily in his office. "There are some matters we have to discuss."

He walked around his desk and sat down, facing her. His expression was hard to read, but Emily was sure he was more than a little annoyed with someone, although—for once—she didn't think it was actually *her*. She took the seat and waited for him to speak. Patience wasn't her strong point, but she didn't want to say the wrong thing and accidentally upset him.

"You have problems combining magical spellwork and alchemical brewing," Zed said, without preamble. "You also have problems judging the precise moment a potion is ready for the next stage—or is about to destabilize and explode."

Emily nodded, not daring to speak. She wasn't the only one, if the constant stream of explosions from the other woks meant anything, but she knew Zed had a good reason to pick on her. The more advanced the brew, the greater the chance she would lose control and have it explode in her face. At least the wards had kept them all safe from serious harm, so far. That would change soon, she knew. There were stages in later brewing where the wards themselves would actively interfere with the alchemical process.

"I have been... *urged* to give you private lessons," Zed said. Emily suspected, by his tone, that he meant *ordered*. "Like many students with great magical potential, you have difficulty with the more subtle aspects of magic. Alchemy requires a light hand and a steady grasp on your magic, which is partly why we use wands at this stage of education. But you have almost no experience with wands at all."

"Yes, sir," Emily said.

Zed eyed her darkly, as if he suspected she was trying to annoy him, but continued. "I believe Whitehall reaches this level of development later," he added. "Mountaintop is more inclined to add Wandwork to the curriculum than Whitehall—and students your age would be expected to master a wand, rather than have a wand master them. If it had been entirely up to me, you would have entered Alchemy as a Second Year, not a Third. You need more experience than you actually have to pass this year."

Emily rather suspected that, if it had been up to him, the only place she would go would be somewhere on the other side of the world—or one of the myriad hells the different religions held in store for infidels, heretics, dissenters and those who didn't show their rulers the proper respect. But she held her peace. Zed was at least *trying* to help her, even if he'd been forced into it by his superiors. It was more than could be said for some of the other teachers she'd met in her life.

"If you still have free periods after my classes on Monday and Thursday, you will study with me immediately afterwards," Zed said. "There may well be a requirement for more private study later, but it will depend on how your timetable shapes out over the next few weeks. And how well your studies go with me. I will not waste my time if you are unwilling to learn."

"Yes, sir," Emily said. Briefly, she wondered if he intended to spend two or three classes with her, then tell his superiors that she was hopeless. "That would be satisfactory, but..."

Zed eyed her, unpleasantly. "But?"

"But I need to refresh myself after taking a two-hour class," Emily said, carefully. She was sure he would need to refresh himself too. "And I..."

"You would be able to have a cup of Kava and go to the washroom before returning, if you wish," Zed said. Perhaps he considered it a reasonable request. "However, we would need to spend at least a full hour if we are to get anything worthwhile out of this class."

"I understand," Emily said. She met his eyes. "I will do the best I can."

"Glad to hear it," Zed grunted. He jabbed a hand into the corner. "There's Kava in that kettle over there. Do you require the washroom now?"

"Um... no, sir," Emily said. "I..."

"Then pour yourself a mug and sit down at the table," Zed ordered. He nodded to a smaller, completely empty table. "We will go through one particular brew stage by stage."

Emily nodded, then did as she was told. Zed, whatever his other flaws, was efficient. By the time she'd poured herself a mug and tested it for unpleasant surprises, Zed had found a cauldron, a wand, several bags of ingredients and a parchment with written instructions, all of which he dumped on the desk. Emily sat down–Zed sat next to her, slightly too close for comfort–and motioned for her to begin.

Reading the instructions, it became clear that the potion was a general anaesthetic used in Healing, one that all healers learned how to brew. Unlike some of the simpler pain-relief potions, it actually required an antidote before the drinker awoke from his enforced slumber, an antidote that had to be brewed from the same batch of potion as the anaesthetic itself. Otherwise, they would sleep until they died. It was only used, Lady Barb had said, when there was no alternative. She'd also said that being able to brew it safely was a formal requirement for a Healing Apprentice.

Under Zed's watchful eye, she carefully sorted out the ingredients she needed, then worked her way mentally through the instructions. An ordered mind and attention to detail, Professor Thande had taught her years ago, was the key to successfully following the recipe and duplicating someone else's potion work. It took a different kind of mind, one willing to gamble and experiment, to come up with something completely new.

She picked up the wand and primed it with the spells she would need. Zed took it from her as soon as she was finished, inspected it carefully, nodded in approval and put it back on the table. Emily let herself have a private moment of relief, then poured a pint of water into the cauldron and lit the fire underneath. It wouldn't be long before it started to bubble.

"Tell me," Zed ordered, suddenly. "Why do we use water as a base for potions?"

Emily had to think to recall the answer. "Because water is magically neutral," she said, finally. "It allows the ingredients to combine without warping them."

"Very good," Zed said. His face flickered with approval. "And why *don't* we use water when we make alchemical brews?"

"Because the water dampens the magic... ah, it *would* dampen the magic if we used it," Emily stumbled, slightly. "And because some of the ingredients would be dampened to the point of complete uselessness."

"Very good," Zed said. "And why have we switched to woks in the classroom?"

Emily froze. She didn't know; hell, she'd never cooked with a wok on Earth. But she knew she would have to guess.

"Because the mixture is spread out more evenly over the heat?" She hazarded. "Or..."

"You should never guess," Zed reproved her. "But you're right. And what other problem does this cause for us?"

Emily looked down at the bubbling cauldron. "You can only make anything that requires a wok in limited quantities," she said, slowly. "There are always limits to how much you can make at a time."

"Correct," Zed said. He nodded towards the cauldron. "You can start adding the ingredients now. Try not to use the wand until you definitely need it."

Emily nodded, found a spoon to stir the brew and went to work. Piece by piece, the potion built itself up in front of her, slowly turning an eerie yellowish color. Emily couldn't help thinking of urine and shuddered, hoping she would never have to drink the potion in real life, no matter what happened. It smelt funny too, she decided, as she added the final ingredients and reached for the wand. She needed to be very precise as she released her magic...

The potion started to bubble alarmingly, but she held her nerve. There was a long pause, just long enough for her to start to worry, before the mixture thickened as she stirred it with the wand. Emily took a sniff, recoiled at the smell, then removed the flame from under the cauldron. The potion would remain useable for several weeks, she knew, without any form of preserving charm.

"Go back to the desk," Zed ordered. He stood and bent over the cauldron, sniffing it carefully. "And think about what you did right—and wrong."

Emily felt her eyes narrow as she rose and walked back to the desk. The potion was perfect, certainly better than anything she'd brewed in classes at Mountaintop. But if he wasn't satisfied...

She shook her head, rested her hands in her lap, and forced herself to be patient. He'd tell her what he thought was wrong soon enough.

"Your technique is serviceable, if uninspired," Zed said, as he walked back to the desk and sat down facing her. "You will probably never make an Alchemist if you are unwilling to modify the techniques to suit yourself, although as a Third Year student it is impossible to be *sure*."

Emily scowled, rebelliously. She'd been taught, right from the start, to follow the instructions religiously. Changing something–anything–to suit herself might have been disastrous. But was she expected–at Mountaintop–to change her techniques if she found something that suited her better?

Zed seemed to read her thoughts. "The way you were taught to approach Alchemy is the standard way," he said. "They put safety ahead of daring recklessness. But if you want to become an inspired brewer, you will have to study the reasons behind each of the techniques and understand where you can cut corners or improve upon them. It is daring recklessness that produces the most advanced alchemical brews."

Or kills Alchemists without a healthy sense of self-preservation, Emily thought, rudely. She'd also been taught that Alchemists who kept pressing the limits were exiled to somewhere isolated to get over it–or at least carry out their experiences well away from everyone else. But she'd never really considered just how much of a margin of safety had been worked into the standard techniques. Not *everyone* wanted to become an Alchemist when they grew up.

"I see," she said, out loud.

"You also need to work on your Wandwork," Zed added. "Have you been taking lessons?"

"Yes," Emily said, "but..."

"Keep working on them," Zed said. "You need to produce *precisely* the right amount of magic or the results will become dangerously unpredictable. I chose this potion because it is quite forgiving, as Alchemical brews go. Others... would have exploded in your face when you inserted the wand."

Emily flushed. She didn't *like* using a wand. It was far too easy to become dependent on it... and then to lose her magic if–when–she was denied access to a wand. The staff had been quite bad enough, but the wand was worse. She'd honestly prefer to use her own magic without a wand.

Zed seemed to read her mind, again. "Very few magicians can use magic in alchemy without a wand," he said, dryly. "You could try, but the resulting explosions could seriously harm you–if you were lucky."

He snorted. "I can try to teach you techniques, if you like," he added. "But I would advise against it."

But you won't take back the offer, Emily thought. There would be no protective wards if she tried to use her magic without a wand. The resulting explosion might kill her... and Zed could swear, quite honestly, that it had been a terrible accident and that he'd tried to warn her it was a bad idea. And it would be her own determination to avoid using a wand that had killed her.

She took a breath. "Can't I practice with water first?"

"Not unless you want to scald yourself," Zed said. He rose to his feet. "You would blast the water to instant steam."

He turned and walked back to the caldron, then turned to look at her with wary respect. "Go back to your hall and have a shower—wash thoroughly," he added. "There are chemicals in the air that shouldn't be allowed to rest on your dress longer than strictly necessary. In Fifth Year, you will be expected to shower before and after class, using showers right next to the classroom."

Emily frowned. Professor Thande had never made a big deal about showering after class, although he had lectured his students on other safety precautions. Perhaps it was something to do with the more dangerous concoctions they were making, she decided, or perhaps there was something else involved. The lesson plans were quite different to Whitehall's.

"Thank you," she said, standing. "It was an interesting lesson."

Zed smirked, rather sardonically. "I will see you on Thursday," he said. "Until then, make sure you concentrate on your essay writing. I expect a decent follow-up to the last essay you wrote."

Emily sighed. She had yet to meet a teacher who hadn't handed out an essay as a way of welcome his or her students back to Mountaintop. In that, at least, Mountaintop was entirely like Whitehall. But the essays did force them to think, instead of regurgitating facts and figures as she'd done on Earth. She would still have traded half her fortune for access to Wikipedia, though. Earth's basic knowledge was more precious than gold on the Nameless World.

She curtseyed to him, trying to push as much respect into her motion as she could. Maybe he didn't like her and probably never would. He could still teach her something new.

"Dismissed," Zed said, quietly.

Emily nodded and walked out of the room, back towards Raven Hall. A handful of students, their passage illuminated with light globes, ran past her, shouting and screaming. She sighed—she couldn't help thinking of them as children, even though the youngest was no younger than fifteen—and shook her head. There was no time to think about it, she told herself, as she entered the hall. She had too much work to do.

And start sniffing around, she reminded herself, firmly. *That's why you're here, isn't it?*

Chapter Fourteen

EMILY FELT THOROUGHLY UNCLEAN AS SHE STUMBLED AWAY FROM HER FIRST CLASS IN DEATH Magics, following several other students with equally stunned expressions. *None* of them had really comprehended what Death Magics might be until they'd watched Professor Yagami take a corpse, cut it open and start explaining the many weird and thoroughly unpleasant uses for dead human body parts. Emily had seen Shadye use reanimated skeletons as servants, but Professor Yagami's work was far worse. She hadn't wanted to know how the skin of a recently dead magician could be used to produce a book of magic.

When she returned to Raven Hall, Frieda was sitting on her bed, reading a book. Emily nodded to her, then saw an envelope resting on top of *her* bed. When she opened it, she discovered that it was another invitation from Aurelius. It ended with a suggestion that she showed the note to Nanette ahead of time.

She must have asked him about Friday night, Emily thought. The Head Girl hadn't said anything to her since then, which Emily had taken for a tacit announcement that Emily had been telling the truth. *And he doesn't want her to wait up for me.*

She sighed, then undressed and stumbled into the shower. The hot water washed the grime from her skin, but she still felt vaguely dirty. Working with Alchemy had included dissecting frogs and other small creatures, yet it had never involved dead human flesh. But that would change, the professor had pointed out, with an unpleasant gleam in his eye. Human flesh, particularly flesh from a magician, had all kinds of interesting and unpleasant uses.

After showering, Emily donned a spare uniform and then took the note over to Nanette, who was lecturing two of the other girls. The Head Girl didn't seem pleased by something, but she took the note without comment, skimmed it quickly and then returned it to Emily with a nod. Emily gave her a nervous smile in return, then walked to the refectory, where she ate dinner before making her way to Aurelius's office. The note had specifically told her to eat before she met him. Emily couldn't help finding that a little strange.

A pity we're not supposed to store food under our beds, she thought, as she knocked at the door. Whitehall allowed students to buy food at Dragon's Den and bring it back to the school, but Mountaintop had no such tradition. But then, Mountaintop was far more isolated than Whitehall. Whatever had caused the desolation above the school, if the reports were to be believed, had destroyed every human settlement for miles around. The dwarfs had only survived by digging deep below the ground.

The door opened, revealing Aurelius standing in front of a table and reading a heavy tome. He slammed it shut as Emily entered the room and curtseyed, then placed the book on the table and bowed to her, before motioning to the chair. Emily nodded and sat, resting her hands in her lap. Aurelius looked normal, but there was a faint hint of... *excitement* surrounding him that bothered her. The last person she'd seen who'd had the same air had been Hodge.

"Another week gone," Aurelius said. It sounded as though he were trying to make conversation before the big event. "And how are you finding your studies?"

Emily looked down at her hands. "Death Magics is a disgusting class," she said. No matter how hard she'd scrubbed her hands, she still thought she could smell the stench of dead flesh embedded in her fingernails and warped into her skin. "But otherwise they're proceeding well."

Aurelius smiled. "And your private tutoring?"

"It is actually helping," Emily said. Zed might still regard her with bitterness, but she had to admit he was a good tutor, one-on-one. She'd learned more from him, as treacherous as it seemed to admit it, than from Professor Thande. But then, she'd never had private Alchemy lessons at Whitehall. "But it may be a long time before I complete the class project."

"It's worth doing," Aurelius said. "A skilled brewer can support himself indefinitely if he can master the more complex concoctions."

He sat down facing her. "There is a specific reason I asked you here so late at night," he said, bluntly. "Do you know what it is?"

Emily tried to think of a possible explanation, then shook her head. There would have been more time right after classes if he'd wanted to summon her immediately–or he could simply have called for her during her free periods. Unless, of course, he had something unpleasant or outright illegal in mind... it struck her, suddenly, that she had no idea what Mountaintop thought of student-teacher relationships. They *were* frowned upon at Whitehall.

"No," she said, out loud. Surely Aurelius wasn't trying to seduce her physically as well as mentally. He had to know from Lin that Emily had.... *issues* with men. "Unless you *want* me to read more books in your library?"

"Not tonight," Aurelius said. He paused. "It is my intention to introduce you to one of the oldest and most dangerous branches of magic in existence. Only the most powerful of magicians, including your father, dare to dabble in such matters–and even *they* can get into real trouble if they make a mistake. You would *not* be introduced to such magics at Whitehall. If your apprenticeship contract deemed them necessary, you would be taught them by your master."

Emily frowned. "*Should* I be learning them now?"

"You are very far from a normal student," Aurelius pointed out. "And you never know which piece of information, which forbidden skill, will come in handy until you actually need it."

"I know," Emily said. Lady Barb had said much the same, normally before assigning reading materials and essays on a whole series of different subjects. "I'll do my best."

Aurelius gave her a toothy smile. "You cannot afford mistakes," he said. He picked up the tome with one hand and passed it to her. "Demons are prone to taking advantage of the slightest mistake."

Emily looked up sharply. "*Demons?*"

"Oh, yes," Aurelius said. "Demons."

"I was taught that summoning demons is a Black Art," Emily objected.

"Lord Whitehall *would* say that," Aurelius countered. He gave her a twisted smile. "They prefer to ban the magic completely rather than give people the training they need to do it safely. It might give people ideas."

Emily frowned. She couldn't dispute that some governments in the Allied Lands tried hard to censor knowledge they considered dangerous, but everything she'd heard about demons suggested that they were always chaotically evil. They just couldn't be trusted. And yet... the prospect of learning something unknown to most of her fellow students was terrifyingly seductive.

She took the book, feeling torn in two. Part of her recalled Shadye's bargains with a demon—or something he'd called the Harrowing—and recoiled in fear. The other part of her was fascinated. Demon-summoning had rarely even been *mentioned* in the books she'd read at Whitehall and, when it had been, it had included strict warnings never to even *try* to summon a demon anywhere near the school. After her near-disaster with the pocket dimension she'd tried to build, she hadn't been inclined to try to design a summoning ritual.

"The more ordered magicians rarely call on demons," Aurelius said, as Emily opened the book and began to parse out the text. "But those who are forced to rely on their own resources often use demons to assist their spells. They can be quite practical, but they have a nasty habit of getting out of control... the DemonMasters often wound up dying at the hands of their own creatures."

The book was difficult to read, even with a pair of translation spells. Emily couldn't help thinking that the author had had orders to write a specific number of words, for he never used one word when he could use three and a single sentence when he could write an entire paragraph. His words were a mixture of practical advice and demented raving, reminding her of some of the other ancient books she'd read. By the time she had finished, she couldn't help having second thoughts about the whole affair.

"Put this on," Aurelius said. "And come with me."

Emily looked down at the piece of cloth he'd given her. It felt like a scarf, but one that seemed designed to fit over her head than wrap around her neck. She'd seen something like it before, she recalled, but it took her some thought before she placed it. A Muslim girl she'd known, vaguely, had worn something like it to keep her hair concealed. It saved her having to pin a scarf in place.

Aurelius smiled at her expression. "Demons are prone to grabbing someone by the hair, if they feel they have a chance," he said. "It's better to wear protection than risk losing your hair—if you're lucky."

Emily looked at his close-cropped skull. "Is that why you wear your hair so short?"

"More or less," Aurelius said, as he opened a hidden doorway at the rear of his office. "It also got in the way when I was naught but a young apprentice."

He led her down a long flight of shadowy steps into a single darkened chamber, then cast a light spell. Emily frowned, feeling more than a little apprehensive as she saw the circles carved in the ground, reminding her of the ritual chamber Lady Barb had shown her months ago. One large circle would keep the demon sealed in, she reasoned from what she'd read; the two inner circles would provide protection for the DemonMasters. Once the circles were active, the writer had warned, they could not be crossed. To do so was to court death.

"Take this," Aurelius said, holding out a tiny vial of reddish liquid. "Blood. Payment for the manifestation."

Emily took the vial automatically. "Whose blood is it?"

"Mine," Aurelius said.

Emily felt her mouth drop open in shock. Magicians *never* shared their blood, with good reason. Aurelius had given her a gift beyond price, even though she suspected she wouldn't be allowed to take it out of the chamber. Whatever he intended her to do, with a demon, he definitely wanted it to happen.

Aurelius smiled at her stunned expression. "You will be summoning a demon I have in thrall, which is safer than trying to call something new out of the Darkness. But as you are the principal speaker, you will have to do the talking. I won't even be able to *hear* the demon unless you allow it."

He paused. "You know the words of summoning?"

"The ones written in the book?" Emily hedged. "Which one of those is the demon's name?"

"None of them," Aurelius said. He stepped across the outer circle, then knelt down and drew out a glyph on the stone floor. "This will ensure that only the demon we want has access to the circle."

He's done this before, Emily thought, disquieted. Aurelius moved with an easy precision that spoke of long practice. Whatever the dangers of summoning demons, he'd chosen to take the risk many, many times.

She was having second thoughts—if not third, fourth and fifth thoughts—as she took her place inside the secondary protective circle. All of the stories about idiot apprentices who accidentally summoned demons, but were then unable to dismiss them suddenly seemed very real, even though she'd also memorized the words of banishment. Aurelius reminded her—again—not to step out of the circle without his permission, then motioned for her to begin. Emily took a long breath, then started chanting the words over and over again, feeling more than a little silly as the minutes ticked away and she lost track of time. But the sudden surge of tainted magic around her was no joke.

She felt dizzy for a long moment as *something* materialized in front of her. It was hard to look at it, harder still not to stumble back until she accidentally broke the circle, but somehow she remained still. She wondered, an instant too late, if she shouldn't have used magic to stick her feet to the floor... yet it might have damaged the ritual. Demon rites seemingly had to be quite precise.

"WELL," a voice boomed. "WHAT HAVE WE HERE?"

The demon slowly took on shape and form as Emily stared at it, silently willing the creature to assume a shape she could tolerate. Massive bulging eyes, a grinning mouth of unkempt teeth, a dark outfit glittering with chains and metal skulls, a shock of uncombed hair... it looked oddly familiar, in a way that shouldn't have been possible. And yet... she knew what she was seeing.

"You took that image out of my mind," she accused. There was no way it could be a coincidence. The books had said it was possible—and that the demons couldn't share what they saw without permission. "Didn't you?"

The demon's form solidified as it hung in front of her, like a puppet hanging from invisible strings. "And why not?" It asked. The creature's voice buzzed through her mind without ever passing through her ears. "It is *such* an appropriate form for you."

Emily fought to control her reactions as it loomed closer. The more she stared at it, the more she realized that she didn't quite understand what she was seeing. Part of her mind insisted the demon was no taller than herself, but the other part of her mind insisted that the demon must be thousands of miles tall... and yet, somehow, it fit into a chamber that couldn't be more than ten yards from floor to ceiling. Her head swam again as it smiled at her, a terrifying Joker-like smile, and hovered its way around the circle. Emily turned to follow, keeping it in sight at all times. The last thing she wanted was it hovering behind her.

"We know you, down in the Darkness," the creature said. It came to a halt, facing her. "You have been *noticed*."

"Oh," Emily said. This was *not* going as the book had suggested. "And what is said about me in the Darkness?"

"That you will be responsible for much change and misery," the demon said. It dropped to the ground and stood upright, towering over her. "It is always fun to watch someone become corrupted by good intentions. To think that she can change the world and yet stumble when it becomes clear that the only way to achieve real, lasting change is to slaughter everyone who gets in her way. You are far from the first person with lofty ambitions and hopes for change."

It leaned closer, giant glowing eyes meeting hers. "We see the future," it said. "You will bring much death. All of the probability lines are tangled around you."

Emily forced herself to think clearly. Divination—seeing the future through magic—was almost impossible, certainly on a large scale. She had suspected, from what she'd read, that the core problem was that the prophet was part of the prophecy; the mere existence of the prophecy changed the future to the point where the prophecy was rendered invalid. But a demon, disengaged from the human perception of time, might be able to see the future, at least in general terms. It was quite possible that the demon truly *could* look into her future.

But demons also lie, she reminded herself.

"You and he are very much alike," the demon said. Somehow, she doubted it meant Aurelius, who was watching from his circle. "Why do you *think* I chose this form?"

"To unnerve me," Emily said. She wondered if she should ask the question she wanted to ask, but she decided there was no point in trying to ask any further questions. It was quite possible that the demon would share anything it had seen in her mind with its true master, no matter what she'd been told. "I thank you..."

"You will fit in well here," the demon interrupted. It cackled, unpleasantly. "Why, you're almost one of us already."

It paused. "Tell me something," it added. "How do you know this is *real?*"

"What do you mean?"

"You're in a fantasy world, going to a boarding school to learn magic," the demon said. "How do you know this isn't a dream? That you didn't hit your head and you're currently in a coma in a hospital bed?"

Emily swallowed bile. She had wondered, in the first few days after her arrival at Whitehall, if she was in a dream, but she had never woken up. Besides, she *wanted* it to be real.

"I could prove otherwise," the demon said. "Just break the circle."

The demon's taunting voice snapped Emily out of her shock. "No," she said. "I think this is real. And even if it *isn't*, I *want* it to be real."

The demon laughed and darted forward, so quickly that Emily stumbled backwards, almost breaking the circle. It looked, for a moment, disappointed, like a dog that had been denied a bone. And then it smiled sweetly. Red liquid dripped from its misshaped teeth and vanished into nothingness before it hit the floor.

"My Ladyship," it said, in a tone no one could mistake for fawning. "Have you not forgotten something?"

Emily frowned, then lifted the vial and threw it out of the circle. The demon caught it in its mouth and swallowed, then suddenly seemed to grow larger and larger until the mere force of its presence threatened to push Emily out of the circle. Hastily, she knelt down and muttered the words of banishment again and again until the demon vanished in a flash of light. As the book had warned, she kept reciting the words for several moments afterwards, just in case it was trying to be clever. A single mistake could give it a chance to take her for itself.

Everything blurred for a long moment. When her vision steadied, she discovered Aurelius kneeling beside her, one hand resting on her shoulder. Emily had never hugged an older man before, but now she found herself burrowing into his robes and holding him tightly. Aurelius held her, gently, before releasing her. Emily hesitated, then stumbled to her feet, embarrassed at her own weakness. Her entire body felt tired and drained.

"I couldn't hear what you said to it," Aurelius said. "What did you say?"

Emily frowned, unsure of what she wanted to say. "You couldn't hear a word?"

"The demon can only be heard by the one who calls it, unless permitted to speak to others," Aurelius reminded her. "I heard nothing."

"It told me that I would change everything," Emily hedged. At least Aurelius wouldn't recognize the significance of the demon's chosen form. No one in the Nameless World had any exposure to Earth's popular culture, apart from Emily herself. "And that I would cause much death."

"You already have," Aurelius told her, bluntly. "Would Shadye have attacked Whitehall if you hadn't been there?"

"I... I don't know," Emily said.

Aurelius smiled at her, carefully erased the glyph from the floor, and helped her stumble out of the circle and back up the stairs. A large pot of soup awaited them in his office, resting on the table. Emily took the bowl he offered her and tested it, using the remainder of her magic, then sipped it gratefully, tasting chicken and vegetables and something very different. But she couldn't put her finger on it.

"When you are older," Aurelius added, "you could bind a number of demons to yourself. It will not be *safe*, but they will come in handy in tight spots."

Emily shuddered. The demon might be gone, but the horror of its appearance lingered on in her mind. It would have killed her, if it could, or ripped her life apart for the hell of it. The last thing she wanted to do was meet another demon. Maybe there were magicians who could handle them, maybe there were magicians who thought they could deal with devils and walk away unscathed, but she knew she wasn't one of them. It would be far better to leave demons thoroughly alone.

"Go back to Raven Hall and have a good night's sleep," Aurelius ordered, as she finished her soup. "And we will discuss something else next week."

"Thank you," Emily said. She hesitated. "But no more demons?"

"No more demons," Aurelius agreed.

Chapter Fifteen

EMILY HAD SPENT UNCOMFORTABLE NIGHTS BEFORE, BUT THIS WAS WORSE THAN ANY SHE'D endured at Whitehall. It seemed impossible to tell the difference between a nightmare and a waking world, to the point where she honestly wasn't sure if she was awake or asleep. The only constant was the demon's laughter and its mocking final words to her. She wasn't like it, she told herself, but part of her mind held a quiet nagging doubt.

She snapped awake, one hand coming up to cast a spell, as someone landed on her bed and grinned at her. Emily's vision swam—her throat was so dry, she probably was dehydrated—and then she realized that Claudia was smiling, her face alight with mischievous delight. Behind her, Frieda was looking nervous, twisting her hands together in her lap. She had to have been browbeaten into allowing Claudia to pass through the wards.

"You'll be coming today, won't you?" Claudia said. "It's going to be a special meeting."

It took Emily several moments to remember the quarrel. Claudia had asked her last week, after all, although she'd forgotten in the press of events. She gritted her teeth, forced herself to sit upright and reached desperately for the bottle of water she kept by her bed. One or two swigs of water left her feeling surprisingly human again. Claudia hopped backwards, but never took her eyes off Emily, leaving Emily feeling uncomfortable. She didn't like being watched while she climbed out of bed.

"I'll get a shower," she said, finally. It seemed easier than arguing. She swung her legs out from under the covers—she hadn't even bothered to undress when she returned to her bed, thankfully—and reached for her towel. "Where do we meet?"

"Somewhere secret," Claudia said. "I'll wait for you here and take you there myself."

Emily's stomach growled. "Maybe after breakfast," Claudia added. "But you'll have to beg the cooks for food."

"Oh," Emily said, embarrassed. She glanced at her watch. It was nearly twelve bells—noon, the part of her mind that recalled Earth insisted. She'd overslept quite badly. "Why did she"—she nodded towards Nanette's bed—"let me sleep?"

"It's the weekend," Claudia reminded her, dryly. "She would have kicked you out of bed earlier if you'd had classes."

Emily sighed, then walked into the washroom and took a hasty shower. The water helped wake her up properly, but she still felt rotten as she stumbled out and headed back to her bed. She wasn't best pleased to have either Claudia or Frieda there as she dressed, yet there didn't seem to be any polite way to tell them to get lost. As soon as she was dressed, Claudia took her arm and led her towards the kitchens, knocking loudly on the door. It was several minutes before anyone bothered to respond.

"No food outside eating hours," the cook said, as he opened the door. He was a middle-aged man with a bad-tempered face, wearing a long white uniform that hung down to his ankles. "Go away, unless you have been sent to work."

"My friend had permission to sleep in," Claudia said, bluntly. "She needs something to eat now, or I will be forced to discuss the matter with the Administrator."

There was a long pause while the cook eyed her suspiciously, then he stepped aside and allowed them into the kitchen. Emily couldn't help being reminded of the great kitchens she'd seen in Zangaria, although there was more magic involved in cooking in Mountaintop, she suspected. Large bowls of soup bubbled over fires, entire animals were roasted over spits... it smelled heavenly, at least to her hungry stomach. The cook produced a roast beef sandwich and a glass of milk from somewhere, then pointed to a table at the edge of the giant room. Emily took the plate and sat down gratefully. Claudia sat down facing her and chatted happily about nothing until Emily had finished, whereupon she took Emily's arm and practically dragged her out of the room.

"This is the outer edge of the school," she explained, after a long walk through increasingly empty corridors. "Beyond here, there lies nothing but the old caves. We have our lair here and..."

She paused, significantly. "You cannot talk about where we're based to anyone, understand?"

"I understand," Emily said. There *were* secret clubhouses in Whitehall, after all, although she suspected that most of them were well-known to the Grandmaster and his staff. Whitehall was thoroughly pervaded with magic, after all. "I won't say a word."

Claudia grinned at Emily, then pulled her into a stone wall. Emily had no time to object before she was dragged *through* the stone wall—an illusion, she realized with some annoyance—and into a large, but surprisingly warm chamber. There was a table at the center of the room, surrounded by comfortable chairs, while dozens of other armchairs were scattered around the chamber. A large fire blazed merrily in the fireplace, heating a cauldron someone had placed over the flames. As clubhouses went, Emily had to admit, it was quite spectacular.

"Welcome to the quarrel," Claudia said. Her grin grew brighter. "Your best friends for the rest of your life."

Emily would have preferred to sit at the back of the room and watch, rather than participate, but Claudia had other ideas. She moved Emily from person to person, introducing her to older students who seemed to have mixed feelings about Emily and younger students who eyed her with an alarming amount of hero-worship. A cacophony of names ran past her, all unfamiliar, all linked to various magical houses. Emily recognized a couple of the family names, but others were new to her. She was, she slowly realized, the only person in the chamber who didn't have a proper family name. Even the Shadows who seemed to be in charge of making the Kava and hot buttered toast were from magical families.

"This is Steven of Lansdale," Claudia said, introducing her to an older boy who eyed Emily with a calculating gaze. "He's the current master of the quarrel within Mountaintop, appointed by the masters outside the school. Do as he tells you while you're in this room."

Emily lifted an eyebrow, but said nothing.

"You will be held to your word, if you stay with us," Steven said. He wasn't unattractive, Emily conceded, but there was something about him that reminded her of Travis, who had never liked her before his death. She hoped it wasn't a hint that the *real* Steven had also been replaced by a Mimic. "You may not talk to anyone about our affairs outside this room, Lady Emily. You will also be expected to assist your brothers and sisters in the quarrel to the best of your ability."

Emily forced herself to meet his gaze. "And if I don't?"

"You will be expelled," Steven said, bluntly. "And if you misbehave within this chamber, you will be placed on probation. Repeated misbehavior will be counted against you; you may be unable to take up a place within the quarrel once you graduate."

He followed up with a dizzying series of rules and regulations that made Kingmaker or Ken sound simple and easy to understand. She was expected to show deference to senior members, but also call on their assistance if necessary. There were rules for raising matters at the table, rules for settling disputes among members and weighted voting systems that gave proportionally greater representation to the older members of the quarrel. Emily had a private suspicion that if the older members agreed, they could pool their votes and maintain command of the quarrel, even if the majority disagreed with them. But she didn't have time to do the math and work it out for certain.

Claudia dragged her over to the table as soon as Steven had finished, pointing out the seats that were reserved for the senior members and the seats that were left open for whoever got to them first. Despite that, Emily couldn't help noticing some jostling as older members uprooted some of the younger members to claim seats closer to the head of the table, where Steven was sitting. Finally, as Steven banged a piece of wood against the table, the Shadows started handing out mugs of Kava.

"Our first order of business is a new prospective member," Steven said. He indicated Emily with one hand, who suddenly found herself the center of attention. "I believe you will all know her, by now."

Emily sighed, inwardly. Fame was *not* a good thing if someone wanted to remain unnoticed.

"Please welcome her," Steven continued. He sounded surprisingly respectful, even though he was a senior student. "We also welcome two newcomers from the old families, who are here to learn as well as serve us."

Emily followed his pointing finger and looked at the two Shadows. They were both young, but they *looked* their ages, unlike Frieda. It took her a moment to realize that they'd both had proper food and medical care from birth, something that wouldn't have happened for a girl growing up in a poor household. Emily herself was something of a special case, but Alassa had definitely developed magic long before Imaiqah. Hell, she would probably have gone to Whitehall a year earlier if her father hadn't been so determined to try to have a male child instead.

The next few pieces of business were largely mind-numbingly boring. There was a brief overview of the World Games at the White City, given by a Fifth Year student who clearly fancied himself a devotee, followed by a report from the games subcommittee. Emily honestly wasn't sure, as the discussion ranged from topic to topic, if she was being offered a chance to join an absurdly powerful student council or merely a group of people who took themselves too seriously. But if they had ties to former members outside the school, she had a feeling it might be the former.

"One issue that has come to our attention is the reluctance of the Administrator to introduce classes covering the New Learning," Steven said. "Does anyone wish to argue the point?"

There was a long pause. "I believe the old ways are still the best," a girl—young woman—said, rising to her feet. She wore a dress that was so low-cut Emily was embarrassed to even look at her, although she understood the meaning behind it. This was not someone who considered herself vulnerable. "We would risk losing some of our customs and traditions if we embraced the new ways."

Emily frowned as several other students echoed her words. She knew what they were talking about—and, from the glances they cast at her, they knew she was to blame for the whole debate. The New Learning—English letters, Arabic numbers and much else besides—had started turning the Allied Lands upside down. Who knew what else would change as the craftsmen of Zangaria and the remaining Kingdoms started developing their own version of the scientific method?

"Emily," Steven said. His voice was mild, but she could hear an undercurrent of something else, something darker. "Perhaps you would care to comment on the matter?"

Emily took a breath as everyone looked at her. Some were interested, some were clearly dismissive... and some, the older ones, were openly angry. Emily didn't really blame them, not really. They'd spent *years* learning how to do everything from reading and writing to producing their own spells and now she'd undercut them, more or less by accident. But it was far from a complete disaster.

"The New Learning will spread, no matter what you do," she said. It would be years before there was any unified consensus on spelling, let alone grammar, but the basics were already well-established throughout the Allied Lands. "You would be well-advised to learn how to read and write in the new manner before too long, certainly if only to avoid having to keep translation spells permanently in place."

She took another breath and tried to gauge their reactions, but they were all skilled at hiding their feelings. Shaking her head, mentally, she went on.

"However, what you have learned already will not be wasted," she added. "The older books will still be written in the old style. You will have to be able to read them—and so will newer students."

"Well put," Steven said. "And do you feel Mountaintop should offer classes in the New Learning?"

"Yes," Emily said. The literacy level in Zangaria was staggeringly poor; even in the city-states, where there was a better educational system, it wasn't much better. "It will be a long time before *everyone* outside the wards knows how to read and write."

Steven smiled, then turned back to address the table. "Is there any other business?"

"It has been noted that Professor Zed has been unfairly unpleasant to one of his students," Claudia said. She carefully did *not* look at Emily as she spoke. "Something ought to be done about it."

Emily swallowed. Just how powerful *were* the quarrels?

"Unfairly unpleasant," Steven echoed. "That has to be pretty bad."

He was right, Emily knew. On Earth, Whitehall and Mountaintop would be shut down at once and half the staff probably thrown in jail for various forms of child abuse. In the small amount of time she'd been at Mountaintop, she'd seen students caned, paddled, turned into small hopping things and forced to do unpleasant chores as a form of detention. And Whitehall really wasn't much better.

But then, no school on Earth is so dangerous, she reminded herself. *A single mistake with magic could be disastrous—or lethal.*

"We will review the matter," Steven said. He looked oddly disappointed, although Emily wasn't sure why. "The inner council will continue to discuss issues; everyone else may go."

"Come on," Claudia said, as the students rose to their feet. "You're going to want to see this."

She pulled Emily through a curtain and into a makeshift spellchamber. Emily studied it as a handful of other students assembled, wondering at how they'd managed to construct it without the staff knowing about it. And then, as one of the older girls brought a younger—blindfolded—girl into the chamber, she realized the staff *did* know about it. Some of them were probably members of the quarrel themselves. They might even have a hand in picking new members.

"The purpose of this part of the meeting is to learn new spells," Claudia said. "Some of them simply aren't taught here, some of them are unique to the quarrel. You might find some of them very interesting."

Emily had her doubts. The blindfolded girl looked terrified as the older girl removed her blindfold. Emily's eyes narrowed as the older girl turned to face them, her face calm and very composed. But there was an underlying excitement in the way she held herself that bothered Emily in a manner she didn't quite understand.

"That's Nadine," Claudia said. "She's a Fifth Year—and one of the most capable students around. You could learn a great deal from her."

"This is Rose," Nadine said. Her voice was very precise. "She has volunteered to be our test subject for the day."

She cast a spell on the younger girl, who instantly fell into a trance. Emily shivered in horror, then watched with a growing sense of disbelief as Nadine demonstrated how to insert post-hypnotic commands into the girl's mind. Rose clucked like a chicken, crawled on the ground like a frog and recited limericks whenever Nadine said the right keywords.

Emily elbowed Claudia as Nadine started inviting others to practice with the spell. "Is this permitted?"

"You can do anything, as long as you don't make them late for class or inflict permanent harm," Claudia said. She didn't sound very concerned, just puzzled at Emily's attitude. "Nadine will have paid Rose a considerable sum to get her to volunteer..."

"I'd like to go back to Raven Hall," Emily said. She suspected she should stay with the quarrel, in hopes of gathering intelligence, but she couldn't bear to watch any longer. She'd had mind control spells cast on her and *hated* the experience. How was Nadine any different from Shadye? "How do I get back?"

"Just think of the hall and use a seeking spell," Claudia said. "But..."

Emily turned, walked through the curtain and left, leaving Claudia behind. For a moment, she thought Claudia would follow her, but as she passed through the illusionary wall it became clear that her dorm mate had no intention of leaving the quarrel. Emily suspected, bitterly, that Claudia really *wanted* to learn that spell. It would be quite useful, if one didn't have moral objections to using it. Or if the target had no ability to fight it off.

For long minutes, she just wandered through the empty corridors, lost in her own thoughts. It was nearly an hour before she recollected herself, then made her way back to Raven Hall, noting—absently—just how much work had gone into turning the caves and tunnels into a place where humans could live. There would be a way to reach the surface, she was sure, and then... she wasn't certain what she could do afterwards. If she broke through the wards, which would be difficult for a single magician, she would still have no idea where she was.

Don't get involved in quarrels, Master Grey had said.

Emily shook her head. She hadn't understood at the time, but she did now. She'd never been a joiner, but part of her would have loved to be asked to join a group. And yet, now she'd been offered it on a silver platter, she was horrified. Who knew what *else* the quarrel taught its members to do? And peer pressure alone would make sure that most of them just took part in the lessons, even if they were secretly horrified.

She walked back into Raven Hall and stopped, dead. She could hear giggling—and whimpering.

And the whimpering was coming from her bed.

Chapter Sixteen

EMILY HESITATED, UNSURE OF WHAT TO DO, THEN LIFTED A HAND IN A SPELL-CASTING POSE and took a step forward. The whimpering grew louder as she approached the bed and peered through the handful of privacy wards. Frieda was lying on her bed, tossing and turning and scratching herself madly. Her skin, always pale, was covered with unpleasant blotches where she'd scratched herself raw. Emily stared, then stepped forward, lowering her hand. It was easy to see that the girl had been hexed.

"Lie still," she said, as Frieda turned to stare at her. Blood was dripping from her arm, staining the bedclothes. "Please, just lie still."

The hex didn't fade. Emily gritted her teeth then cast the most powerful counter-spell she knew. She'd seen something like the itching hex before, in Martial Magic; the Sergeants had used it to ensure that anyone who was knocked down stayed down. It was a nasty little spell, almost impossible for the victim to remove. Emily would have had problems removing it herself, as a Third Year. There was no way Frieda could be expected to free herself from the hex.

"Lie still," Emily repeated, as the hex faded away. Now she had stopped twitching, it was clear that Frieda was hurt far worse than Emily had realized. Her scratches might become infected, if they weren't healed quickly. "Who did this to you?"

She heard a giggle and looked up to see one of the other Shadows, smirking at Frieda. Emily felt her temper snap. She *hated* bullies. They picked on people who were unable to defend themselves and attacked their self-esteem so comprehensively that they were never able to rise above the torment or found ways to strike back at their enemies. Emily reached out, casting a spell, and dragged the girl over to the bed. The Shadow's giggles faded away as she found herself looking at Emily's face. Emily wasn't even trying to disguise her anger.

"Why?" She demanded. "Why did you cast the spell?"

The Shadow—it dawned on Emily that she didn't even know the girl's name—giggled, despite being held by Emily's spell. "It's fun," she said, seriously. She smirked at Frieda, as if she expected Emily to share her amusement. "And it..."

Emily felt a wave of pure rage and slapped the Shadow, hard. She saw blood trickling down from the girl's jaw, but she felt no guilt, just an overpowering urge to *hurt* the girl. The spell holding the girl in place snapped as she fell backwards; Emily rose to her feet and towered over the girl, rather than use magic to catch her again. The girl tried to scramble backwards, her face torn between pain and surprise. She obviously hadn't expected Emily to be furious with her.

"Do you think *that* was funny?" Emily demanded. "Being picked on by someone bigger than you?"

She reached out and hauled the girl to her feet. It was something she could never have done on Earth, but two years of Martial Magic had given her more muscles than she'd ever thought possible. The girl felt heavier than she'd expected, but not heavy enough to keep Emily from pulling her upright.

"I could snap your neck or turn you into a frog and you couldn't stop me," Emily snapped, shaking the girl violently. She pushed the girl out into the center of the hall. "Would that be funny, too?"

"...N-no," the girl stammered. Magic crackled around her fingertips, but she was clearly unable to cast a spell. "I..."

Emily stared down at her, feeling her rage slowly being replaced with a cold burning anger—and horror. She'd seen how casually the older students used the younger ones, but this was different—or maybe she was just being naïve. Part of her was shocked at how easily she'd terrified the girl, but the other part of her felt it was no more than the girl deserved. Frieda certainly didn't deserve to be picked on; no one deserved to be picked on. And yet...

She sensed the surge of magic from behind her and jumped backwards as a flash of light passed through where she'd been, seconds ago. Helen was standing there, looking furious; behind her, Rook seemed equally angry. Part of Emily's mind noted that while they were close to Claudia, they hadn't been invited to the quarrel. The rest of her concentrated on defending herself as the two girls hurled spell after spell at her. Neither of them had any proper Martial Magic-style training, but they knew how to duel. It gave them an advantage in cramped confines, particularly as Emily didn't dare use any of the nastier spells she'd been taught.

"She's mine," Helen snapped. She threw a transformation spell at Emily that had more power than skill behind it. Emily jumped to one side and threw back one of her own, then hurled a hex at the floor. The resulting shockwave knocked Helen back on her ass, then sent her scurrying backwards to find cover. "You don't touch something that belongs to me!"

"You taught her that spell," Emily shouted back. In hindsight, it was clear that *someone* had to have taught the Shadow that spell. Why not Helen? The girl might have acted like Claudia's crony, but she wouldn't have stayed in school if she were stupid. "Why didn't you teach her not to pick on others, too?"

Helen looked uncomprehending; Rook scrambled over Olive's bed and threw herself at Emily. Emily dodged, too late. Rook crashed into her and knocked her to the ground, raising her fists rather than relying on magic. Emily hastily shaped a blasting spell in her mind and detonated it, wincing in pain as she took half of the blast herself. But it knocked Rook away from her before she could start pounding Emily's head into the stone floor. Helen threw something nasty at Emily, which missed, then stopped. Emily had no time to realize what that meant before magic flared around her and she found herself helpless, unable to move, too.

"I believe I told you," Nanette said sweetly, "that you are not allowed to fight in the dorms."

Emily wanted to protest the unfairness of it all, but she couldn't move a muscle. She honestly wasn't sure how she could even *breathe*. Nanette strode into view, eying first Helen, then Rook, then finally Emily, her face under very tight control. Emily recalled her first impressions of Nanette and felt cold, despite the spell. Part of her had wanted to impress the Head Girl.

"Several badly damaged beds, one cracked floor and a smashed mirror," Nanette added, darkly. "The costs will be billed to your families, I imagine, and I dare say the rest of Raven Hall will not be too pleased. And what, precisely, was worth breaking the rules?"

"She was attacking me," Helen's Shadow said. "All I did was..."

"We will discuss this in good time, Ten," Nanette said. She looked up at the frozen girls. "Helen and Rook will accompany me into my office, where the truth will be discovered; Emily will wait in the corner until I have spoken to the other girls."

Emily tried hard to break the spell as Nanette levitated her into the corner, but nothing worked. All she could do was wait, helplessly, all too aware of the other girls whispering behind her back as they cleaned up the mess. A stab of guilt tore at her as she realized they'd damaged several beds and property belonging to girls who hadn't been involved in the fight, although they'd done nothing to stop it. What would Void say, she asked herself silently, when he was presented with a bill for damages? It wasn't as if he had any *obligation* to pay for her mistakes.

She heard the sound of a sob, hastily choked off, behind her, before the spell suddenly collapsed. Emily stumbled, then fell to the ground as her body shuddered violently, grunting in pain as she banged her elbows against the floor. She heard, rather than saw, Nanette stride up behind her, tapping her feet impatiently. Feeling oddly vulnerable and isolated in a way she hadn't felt since her first experiments with pocket dimensions, she staggered to her feet and followed Nanette back to her office. The privacy wards around Helen and Rook's beds were so strongly in place that she could not see or hear anything inside their protections.

But it was clear that they'd done a *lot* of damage, she realized, grimly. One bed would probably have to be replaced, and another might need replacement. The looks some of the other girls were shooting her were far from friendly, although Lerida and Astra were eying her speculatively. Emily knew Lerida had never stopped her hero-worship, but Emily had no idea what motivated Astra. Perhaps she simply hadn't liked Helen and Rook and enjoyed seeing them taken down a peg or two.

"Inside," Nanette ordered.

Emily obeyed. She had never been in Nanette's office before and hadn't really wanted to go there, not after a couple of girls had told her horror stories about what happened to people invited to visit the Head Boy or Girl. It was surprisingly barren compared to Markus's office; there were no paintings, no books, merely a dark stone desk with a single chair. Emily realized, numbly, that she was expected to stand in front of the desk, rather than sit down.

Nanette closed the door behind them, activated a privacy ward and then strode around the desk and sat down, staring up at Emily. It was, Emily knew, a tactic to make her sweat before she started the lecture, but her awareness of what was actually going on didn't make her feel any better. No matter how much Ten had deserved to be scared out of her mind, the other girls hadn't deserved to have their property damaged by a savage fight. And Nanette didn't deserve the problems Emily had caused.

"Perhaps you could explain to me," Nanette said, after what felt like hours, "precisely what happened before I arrived?"

Emily took a breath and started to explain, leaving nothing out. She talked about discovering the hex on Frieda, she talked about Ten... and how Helen and Rook had attacked her. The Head Girl listened in silence, saying nothing, allowing Emily to save or damn herself with her own words. Her face was a blank, emotionless mask. Emily would have been impressed if her future at Mountaintop hadn't been on the line. Did they expel students for breaking the dorm rules?

"What you did was immensely stupid," Nanette said, when Emily had finished. "I am aware that there are no Shadows at Whitehall, but you should at least be aware that it is the duty of an older pupil to look after her Shadow. You should have taken your complaints to Helen."

Emily bit her lip to keep from scowling. "And would she have done anything about it?"

"Perhaps," Nanette said. "Ten's behavior would have reflected badly on *her*, after all, as you should know. She would have been forced to rebuke Ten, at the very least. It would also have been added to the girl's permanent record, if you chose to make a formal complaint instead of a private one. But you had no right to attempt to discipline Ten yourself."

"She inflicted harm on *my* Shadow," Emily said, feeling an odd burst of protectiveness. Her own thoughts mocked her. Had she not practically ignored Frieda since she'd first met the girl? She'd thought it was the best thing for her. Frieda was in her First Year, after all. She didn't need to go running around at Emily's slightest whim. "I had to cancel the hex myself..."

"And Helen should have disciplined Ten for it," Nanette said, coldly. "You should not have done anything yourself, Emily."

Emily gritted her teeth. It wasn't time to argue. "No," she said, shortly.

"Helen shouldn't have attacked you, either," Nanette conceded. There was an odd note in her voice, almost a hint of resentment. "I imagine she feels a certain protectiveness towards Ten, Emily. There were a considerable amount of strings pulled to ensure that Ten would become Helen's Shadow. Their families are related."

Emily blinked. "Why?"

"I imagine it had something to do with one young man marrying a young woman," Nanette said, tartly. "You do understand how children are produced, don't you?"

She smirked, suddenly, as Emily flushed. "Or did you mean the string-pulling?"

"Yes," Emily agreed.

"All students are expected to serve as Shadows," Nanette said. Her voice was back to being tightly controlled. "Certain well-connected students are pushed into taking Shadows from powerful families, providing them with some degree of protection and supervision other Shadows lack. It doesn't give them personal servants, but it does pay off in the future."

"I see," Emily said.

She shuddered. The discrepancies made sense now. No one would dare abuse a student from a powerful family, even if they had formal power over their Shadows; students like Claudia and Markus had probably never done more than clean clothes, make the beds, fetch the Kava and a handful of other minor tasks. But a student like Frieda would have no protection whatsoever. Emily could have used her as a test subject for all kinds of spells and she would have had to stand there and take it.

Nanette met her eyes. "But you should have taken more interest in *your* Shadow," she added, warningly. "I believe Frieda was considered isolated by the younger students because her Patron showed no interest in her."

"I understand," Emily said.

"I'd be surprised if you did, at least completely," Nanette said. "Whitehall has no Shadows, after all, merely roommates. You were not encouraged to develop friendships with older students."

"I did," Emily said. But she'd been unusual. "Should I spend more time with her?"

"Yes," Nanette said, flatly.

She took a breath. "Your behavior broke several of the rules," she said. "This creates something of a problem. I understand why you did what you did, but I cannot allow it to go unpunished."

Emily swallowed. Her mouth was suddenly very dry.

"I can handle it myself," Nanette added, "or you can insist on facing the Administrator instead. If the latter, I'll have to take you there now."

For a moment, she looked oddly nervous. "I would advise you to deal with me," she said. "I don't believe the Administrator would look kindly on the whole affair."

It took Emily a moment to realize what she was being told. Quite apart from whatever punishments were meted out to Emily, Helen and Rook, Nanette would look very bad for allowing a dorm spat to come to the Administrator's attention. She might lose her place as Head Girl or face punishment herself, just for not putting a stop to the disagreement before it turned violent. Emily felt a flicker of sympathy for the older girl. *She* might be able to get away unpunished, if Aurelius was keen to show her outright favoritism, but Nanette would have no such option. And besides, taking Emily to Aurelius would undermine her authority in the eyes of the other girls.

And she found herself, somewhat against her will, *liking* Aurelius. She didn't want to go to him and confess she'd broken a whole series of rules. He might stop trying to show her new magics or even deny her access to his library as a form of punishment, something she would consider worse than any beating. She didn't want to let him down.

She gritted her teeth, then but nodded.

"I'll deal with you," she said.

Nanette looked, just for a second, relieved. "You are being punished," she said, "for slapping a younger girl and fighting in the hall. Do you understand me?"

"Yes," Emily said, tonelessly.

"I have already punished Helen, Rook and Ten," Nanette continued, as she rose to her feet and stalked around the desk. "Once your punishment is complete, it is *over*. It is not to continue. You are not to recriminate with them and they are not to recriminate with you. If there is a second round of fighting, you will all regret it. Do you understand me?"

It was all Emily could do not to run. "Yes," she said, instead. "I understand."

She winced as she saw the small paddle in Nanette's hand. This was going to hurt.

"Bend over," Nanette ordered. "Place your hands on the desk and hold the position."

Emily did as she was told, gritting her teeth in anticipation. There was a long pause before the paddle struck her behind. And again. And again, until it was finally over.

"Stand up," Nanette ordered.

Emily forced herself to obey, tears streaming down her face as her hands moved to rub her behind. The fire was slowly fading, to be replaced by a dull ache that told her she wouldn't be sleeping comfortably over the next couple of days. She'd had worse, she told herself. The Sergeants had never intended to *hurt* their students in Martial Magic, but they'd often left her aching and bruised after a milling session or a long forced march through the countryside. But it was the humiliation of knowing she'd been walloped that felt the worst. Everyone in the hall would know what had happened to her.

"I would suggest you spend some time with your Shadow," Nanette said, once Emily had managed to calm herself. It sounded as though she were advising Emily to walk and water her pet. "You should talk to her, at the very least. And maybe even do something with her, once or twice a week. It would be better for her if you did."

Emily nodded, then and gratefully fled the room.

Chapter Seventeen

NONE OF THE OTHER GIRLS SPOKE TO EMILY AS SHE HOBBLED BACK TO HER BED, THEN CAST several privacy wards and lay down on the sheets. The dull ache wouldn't fade for quite some time, she knew from bitter experience, no matter what she did. None of the potions she had obtained over the last couple of weeks were intended to help with corporal punishment. Somehow, she had a feeling that the school's administration would frown on anyone who produced a pain-relief potion for sore bottoms.

She heard a cough as she lay down and turned her head to see Frieda, sitting on her bed and staring at Emily. "You... you did that for me?"

There was something so plaintive in her voice that Emily's heart broke. "Yes," she said, slowly. How could she confess that she'd never really understood she had an obligation towards Frieda until it was too late? She couldn't, could she? "I'm sorry."

Frieda looked surprised. "Why?"

"Because... because it was the right thing to do," Emily said. She cursed her own mistake under her breath. "And because doing that to you was awful."

Frieda lowered her eyes. "I'm used to it," she said. "It wasn't your fault."

Emily felt another stab of guilt at her words. She'd been bullied a little on Earth, but mainly she'd just been left alone–completely alone. It was funny, part of her mind noted, how it was easy to accept that it wasn't Frieda's fault she was bullied. But then, Frieda didn't seem to have any awareness that it *was* wrong. Gritting her teeth, Emily sat upright, despite the pain, and beckoned for Frieda to sit next to her.

Up close, the girl was thinner than Emily had realized. Throwing caution to the winds, Emily poked and prodded at her, then cast a handful of diagnostic spells. Frieda wasn't just thin, she was *emaciated*, practically on the verge of starvation. Her dress - and Emily's reluctance to peek - had hidden it far too well. Even using the simplest spells would drain her energy quite badly, Emily realized; it was one of the reasons students at Whitehall were almost always thin, despite being fed huge meals three times a day. And then there were the signs of physical abuse...

Emily wrapped her arm around Frieda, then started casting a number of Healing spells. One by one, the marks on Frieda's skin healed up. But the scars on Frieda's mind would remain.

"You don't have to do that," Frieda said softly, as if she couldn't believe anyone would do anything like it for her. "I..."

"Yes, I do," Emily said, studying Frieda's face. Her Shadow looked torn between hope and fear. "You need to eat more, really."

"I can't," Frieda said. "I don't have any money."

Emily stared at her. She was familiar, all too familiar, with being unable to afford lunch at school. The introduction of free lunches on Earth had been a lifesaver, literally, for her. And, as far as she knew, food was included in Whitehall's fees, even for scholarship children. She'd certainly never noticed Imaiqah limiting her intake...

"My scholarship doesn't cover it," Frieda admitted, lowering her eyes in shame. "All I can afford are the basics..."

Emily felt a hot spike of anger. Food didn't cost *that* much in the Allied Lands...
and even if it did, students like Frieda *needed* to eat, just to build up their magic.
How could anyone reasonably expect them to live and study magic on a starvation
diet? And no one had asked her to pay for the food *she* ate... she swore under her
breath, silently promising to raise the issue with whoever she had to, just to make
sure Frieda had enough to eat.

"It *will*," Emily said. If worst came to worst, she could pay for it herself. She had
plenty of money, after all. "What do you spend money on, anyway? I assume you do
your own accounting?"

"I have notes," Frieda said. She started to scramble to her feet, but stopped as if she
were afraid Emily would get upset if she moved. "Do you want to see them?"

"Just tell me," Emily said. She didn't have the time to parse out Frieda's handwriting. "What do you spend money on, weekly?"

"Books, clothes and my wand," Frieda said. "I had to have it replaced twice after...
after it got broken."

Was snapped, Emily translated, mentally. "But why do you need a wand?"

Frieda stared at her blankly, as if she'd suddenly started speaking French—or
English. "To channel my magic," she said, as if it was the most obvious thing in the
world. "I'm not... I'm not from one of the Great Houses."

Emily frowned. "What does *that* have to do with it?"

"I can't channel my magic properly," Frieda confessed. "I need the wand."

"You shouldn't," Emily said. "I..."

She stopped in horror as the full enormity of the trick Mountaintop had played
on its scholarship students dawned on her. There was no need for a wand, no matter where the student had come from; *Emily* had certainly never needed one and
she'd never known that magic was even possible until she'd been kidnapped into
the Nameless World. Imaiqah had never used a wand, while Alassa's magic had been
crippled until she'd learned to cast spells without using *her* wand. And it had been
Zed who had taught her how to use magic.

Emily stared down at her hands, thinking hard. She'd assumed—anyone would
have assumed—that Zed had tried to teach her properly, then given up. Alassa had
been one hell of a Royal Brat at the time, acting more like a dumb blonde cheerleader than bothering to develop her own mind. It hadn't been until Alassa had come
within millimeters of death that she'd grown up and started taking her studies seriously. But had Zed steered her towards dependence on the wand?

Emily knew the dangers. Using wands regularly, for everything, risked losing the
ability to cast spells without one. It was as problematic, in its own way, as being
unable to cast spells without hand gestures, which was why it was so hard to escape
the relatively simple freeze spell. And if Frieda had been kept from learning to use
magic without a wand...

It keeps her under control, she thought, numbly.

Emily shook her head in disbelief. A girl from a very poor mundane family wouldn't
know the dangers of using a wand. Her classmates from the Great Houses would be

taught the dangers before they ever entered Mountaintop, perhaps even taught that their ability to channel magic without a wand was something that couldn't be taught, only inherited from their parents. And by the time they figured out the truth, if they ever did, it would be too late.

"Tell me about your life," she said, instead. "Where were you born?"

"A village in the Cairngorms," Frieda said. She laughed, a little bitterly. "It never really had a name, not for us. It was just *The Village*. I was the youngest of nine children, and have five sisters. When the magician came looking for talent, my parents sent me with him quite willingly."

Emily shuddered. She'd *been* in the Cairngorms. The locals had more use for boy children than girl children, who couldn't do so much around the farm and eventually left to marry into a different family. Lady Barb had told her that unwanted children were sometimes sold to the highest bidder or simply exposed to the elements and left to die. It was a cruelly hard life, where one mouth could make the difference between making it through the winter or starving to death.

It was horrific. But the peasants had no choice.

Her eyes narrowed as a thought struck her. "Have you been home since then?"

Frieda shook her head. "It would be costly..."

Her voice trailed away as Emily glared. *She* had never wanted to go back to Earth, so she'd allowed herself to fall completely into the Nameless World. But then, there was nothing for her back home. Even if she knew how to get to Earth and come back safely, she would still refuse to go. Frieda, on the other hand, had been completely separated from her parents and brought to a whole new environment. Even if she'd *wanted* to go home, Emily suspected, she would have nothing in common with her family. They might even be scared of her.

Maybe they should be, Emily thought, darkly.

"I don't want to go back anyway," Frieda said. She sounded conflicted, as if she wasn't sure if she wanted to go back or not. "I was always the runt of the family."

Emily could well believe it. The more children a poor family had, the smaller the amount of food they had to go around. If Frieda was the youngest, she would have had the least amount of food... hell, she was lucky she hadn't died years ago through simple malnutrition. And it wouldn't even be the most horrific thing she'd seen in the mountains.

Maybe Mother Holly had had a point, after all. Reforming the social system that bound people to the mountains might be the only way to save lives.

"I understand," Emily murmured. She wrapped an arm around Frieda and gave her a tight hug. "How do you cast spells?"

"With my wand," Frieda said, softly.

Emily shook her head. "I mean, how do you input the spells into the wand?" Alassa had never been able to do it for herself, relying on her former cronies. "How were you taught to prime your wand?"

"Chanting," Frieda said. She picked up her wand and then started to chant a handful of words in a language Emily didn't recognize. "It works."

Emily felt the magic field twist around the wand as Frieda chanted. Was it some sort of mnemonic to shape and trigger the magic without letting the user know what was actually happening? Or what they were actually doing?

She frowned in puzzlement. There were no magic words, as such, when it came to basic charms. A magician could shout *Abracadabra* as loudly as he liked and nothing would happen, unless they had primed the spell to trigger upon hearing that word. But Frieda clearly seemed to believe it was possible... and what she'd just done suggested it *was* possible.

"So it would seem," Emily said, slowly. "Have you ever tried to cast magic without a wand?"

"It doesn't work," Frieda said.

"It should," Emily countered. "I never used a wand until I came to Mountaintop."

"You're the child of a Lone Power," Frieda objected. "You should be able to work magic without a wand."

Emily hesitated. "One of my best friends comes from a mundane family," she said. "And *she* can work magic without a wand."

She paused. "How do you cope in classes?"

"I..." Frieda swallowed and started to talk. "I don't do well."

Emily listened, feeling her sense of guilt grow stronger, as Frieda described the boarding school from hell. *Emily* had had some protection; Frieda had none. She'd been bullied incessantly since she'd arrived at Mountaintop for her preliminary year of preparatory studies, before going into First Year. *That* was something Whitehall would do well to copy, Emily noted, but Frieda had found it a foretaste of hell. The itching hex had been mild, compared to some of the other tricks that had been played on her.

"I'm stupid," Frieda concluded. "I don't deserve to be here."

"You are *not* stupid," Emily snapped. God knew she'd felt the same way from time to time, back when she'd been too hungry to study properly. It had taken her a long time to realize that she'd been beaten down by her own attitudes far more than anyone else, even her stepfather. "You just need to learn to study properly."

"They keep saying I should study harder," Frieda said. "But I can't..."

She broke off, bitterly.

"We'll study together," Emily promised. She hadn't realized she had an obligation, but she did now. And she was *damned* if she was allowing Frieda to remain in ignorance any longer, no matter the cost. If she could tutor Alassa as a First Year student, she could tutor Frieda as a Third Year. "And I will teach you magic."

And make sure you eat properly, she added, in the privacy of her own mind. There were potions Frieda would probably need, just to help her put on some weight. They were rarely used in Whitehall, but Emily knew how to make them. She'd just have to ask permission to make them herself if she couldn't get them from the infirmary.

Frieda stared up at her disbelievingly. "Really? You'd do that for me?"

"Yes," Emily said. She rose to her feet and started to pace, brushing against the edge of the wards. "I think I should have been doing it from the start."

"But..." Frieda lowered her eyes. "I'm not worthy of your time."

"Yes, you are," Emily said. It was going to be a problem, but she hadn't intended to do more than keep her ears open for a while longer. Besides, Frieda might make an excellent source of information. "And I should have been paying attention to you from the start."

She hesitated, before looking directly at Frieda and speaking with as much sincerity as she could. "I'm sorry, Frieda," she added. "The fault was mine."

Frieda still looked disbelieving. Emily wasn't too surprised. Somehow, she doubted that any of the older girls had ever bothered to apologize to her before. They would have been much more likely to use her as a servant, if not a slave. There was no way any of them would have bothered to teach her anything useful. And Emily was sure that most of the spells Frieda had been taught weren't intended to help her defend herself.

"When you came here," she asked suddenly, "what did they tell you about your future?"

"They said I'd marry a magician," Frieda said. "And that our children would be blessed."

She didn't seem to find the concept offensive. Emily wasn't surprised. Frieda would never have been able to choose her own husband, even if she'd never developed magic. Her father would have married her off for his best advantage, although there were few advantages to be had in a tiny village. Perhaps the best she could hope for was marrying the local headman's son. But that might have been thoroughly unpleasant... Emily remembered Hodge and shuddered.

But it was odd. Frieda might make a powerful magician if she was taught properly. She could be a Healer, or an Alchemist, or even a Combat Sorcerer. Maybe she would still have made a good healer if she remained restricted to a wand; basic healing spells could be cast with a wand, if necessary.

And yet, the whole idea of forcing common-born magicians to use a wand from the start was deeply offensive. It crippled them, all unknowingly, and weakened their potential power in the bargain. Why would anyone do that? The Allied Lands was permanently short of good magicians. There was nothing to gain in deliberately crippling Frieda or the others like her.

Just because you can't think of something doesn't mean that they can't, she reminded herself, sharply. Some of Imaiqah's moves on the Kingmaker board had made no sense until they'd exploded in Emily's face. *They may think they have a very good reason to keep the system in place.*

"We shall see," Emily said. "Do you have a copy of your timetable?"

Frieda nodded and reached for her bag, waiting at the end of her bed. "Here," she said, producing a sheet of torn parchment. "I had to repair it myself."

Emily sighed before she took it. Frieda had duties on Sunday, then classes all day on Monday.

"We'll use one of the spellchambers on Monday evening," Emily said, after a moment. It was her turn in the spellchamber, after all. She'd intended to practice other spells, but it was as good a time as any to start trying to teach Frieda how to use magic properly. "I want you to meet me there thirty minutes after classes end, all right?"

Frieda nodded. "I..."

She broke off as something–someone?–tapped against the privacy ward. Emily braced herself, before lowering the ward enough to see Helen standing there, looking annoyed and a little fearful.

"I wish to apologize for my Shadow's actions, Lady Emily," Helen said, bluntly. "She has been thoroughly punished for her misdeeds and I do not believe they will reoccur. I also wish to apologize for my own."

Emily wondered, suddenly, just what Nanette had said to Helen and Rook. A reminder that Emily had killed two Necromancers? Threats of dire punishment if she ever put Nanette in a position that could cost her the Head Girl's badge again? Or, perhaps, a droll warning against fighting in the hall?

"I accept," Emily said. She decided to swallow her pride. "I also wish to apologize for slapping your Shadow. I was out of line."

Helen nodded, then turned and walked away. Emily caught a glimpse of a frog hopping on Helen's bed before she replaced the privacy wards and turned to face Frieda.

The younger girl stared at her in astonishment. Frieda must *never* have heard anyone apologize for how she'd been treated in the past.

"We'd better go get something to eat," Emily said. She rubbed her bottom, decided she could sit on a hard chair without wincing too openly, then reached for a cloth to wipe her face. "Get changed into something that doesn't have blood on it, and make sure to get rid of the blood."

She paused as a nasty thought struck her. "You *do* know how to dispose of your blood safely?"

Frieda nodded, then scrambled to her feet and reached for the drawer under her bed. Emily watched numbly as she stripped off her top, revealing bones that were all too visible under her skin. How *could* it have passed unnoticed in a school of magic? No *wonder* her magic had been seen as weak. She would have had real trouble casting more than a handful of spells a day.

I'll speak to the Administrator, she promised herself. If nothing else, she was privately sure she could drop Void's name once or twice. He *had* paid her Whitehall fees, after all. And the Administrator, she suspected, wouldn't want to upset him openly. *And see if I can draw on my funds.*

Chapter Eighteen

As it happened, it was Monday morning before Emily was able to approach the Administrator. She *had* attempted to visit his office on Sunday, but the main door was locked and she had no idea where he slept. She'd taken the chance of leaving a note in the library, then spent most of the day reading a handful of books from his vast collection and making notes in her own private book. There were hints of ways to open communications over vast distances between two magicians that would have been very useful, when she'd been trapped in Zangaria. If she managed to master them...

Aurelius didn't look particularly surprised to see her when she knocked on his door, the following day. Emily couldn't help wondering what—if anything—he knew of the weekend's events, but she rather doubted he would say anything about it. What happened in Raven Hall *stayed* in Raven Hall, Nanette had said. Even if she *had* given Aurelius a private briefing, he wouldn't be inclined to admit it. Nanette's authority had been weakened enough already.

"Lady Emily," he said. "Shouldn't you be in class?"

"Not for another thirty minutes," Emily said. Warding, for whatever reason, started later than the other morning classes. One of her fellow classmates had joked that Professor Clifton always took longer than the other tutors to get out of bed in the morning. "I have a quick request for you, sir."

Aurelius lifted his eyebrows. "A request?"

"Yes, sir," Emily said. "My Shadow needs to be appropriately fed. I want to pay for her meals, as they do not seem to be included in her scholarship."

She'd wondered what Aurelius would make of her request, but the flicker that passed over his face told her nothing. Instead, he settled back in his chair and studied her thoughtfully, then smiled in approval.

"It speaks well of you that you care," he said. His tone wasn't mocking, but it stung. She knew she *hadn't* cared until it was almost too late. "But will your Shadow's pride survive it?"

"She needs to eat," Emily said, flatly. She understood—she'd always hated the thought of charity herself—but there was no room for pride now. "And I believe I have the funds to make it happen."

"I will inform the cooks that she is to eat as much as she wishes," Aurelius said. He gave her an odd little smile, as if he were expecting her to share a joke. "Your fees are in an awkward position right now, Emily, but we can certainly arrange for her to be fed properly."

Emily's eyes narrowed. "If it's that simple," she said, "why doesn't everyone get fed properly?"

"We do try to teach basic accounting here as well as magic," Aurelius said, slowly. "And it is the responsibility of Patrons to help their Shadows overcome certain problems."

Emily clenched her fists in genuine outrage. *She'd* been neglectful, but she was sure, now that she'd started looking for the signs, that other Patrons were outright abusive. Ten might have been pushed into Helen's care by her family, which might explain how angrily Helen had reacted when Emily had slapped her, but others had no such protection. And the Hall Supervisors didn't seem to care. Nanette certainly hadn't scolded Emily until the situation had already managed to get out of hand.

"The Patrons don't care," she said, fighting to keep her voice under control. "And you never even told me what being a Patron entailed."

"Authority is an odd thing," Aurelius said. "We do not grant it as a matter of right, but as a matter of determining who can be trusted to wield authority in the outside world. A taste of power could easily have turned you into a monster. You were given power over that young girl in the hopes you would learn how to use it."

"And who," Emily asked bitterly, "would protect her from *me?*"

"You," Aurelius said. "You have to learn self-restraint."

"I don't accept that," Emily said. She wanted to scream at him. "You gave me total authority over someone else, then... what would you have done if I'd abused her? Or worse?"

"You would not have become a prefect, let alone Head Girl," Aurelius said, flatly. "What is the point of giving you a test of character if you knew it was a test?"

"A secret test of character," Emily said, slowly. "*That's* what it is?"

"Yes," Aurelius said. "I would appreciate it if you didn't tell any of the other students about the true nature of the system. It would only upset them."

Emily could see the logic in it, from Aurelius's point of view. Give a student a chance to wield authority and see what they did with it. But it meant exposing Shadows, most of whom were completely defenseless, to older students who might take advantage of them, at the very least. And none of the Shadows were *that* young. It was all too easy to imagine other, more horrifying possibilities for abuse.

"I don't like the system," Emily said, flatly.

"Most people don't, when they realize what it entails," Aurelius told her. "It's what marks them out as students of quality."

"Many of those students will end up permanently victims," Emily snapped. "How many magicians have you lost because the system crushed their souls?"

"And those who overcome it will be great," Aurelius countered. "You don't learn through having everything given to you on a silver platter, Lady Emily. You learn from adversity, through meeting and overcoming challenges. Or was it different for you?"

Emily hesitated, then nodded reluctantly.

"There's something else I wanted to request," she said, slowly. "My father has left me very ignorant in a number of ways."

"That is true," Aurelius agreed.

Emily flushed, even though she knew it wasn't her fault. "I didn't know about the Shadows and I didn't know about... other matters," she said, softly. "Are there etiquette lessons for younger students? Something to tell them how to behave?"

"Those lessons are normally given by the Great Houses or Patrons," Aurelius said, thoughtfully. "But your father would not care for etiquette. I fancy anyone expecting him to bow as he enters their house would be very disappointed."

"Very disappointed," Emily agreed. Void had walked in and out of Whitehall without the Grandmaster's permission, a serious breach of etiquette. Even *she* knew that. "He never bothered to teach me how to act around other magicians."

"I will see what I can arrange," Aurelius said. "But you are in an odd position. You could not Shadow for anyone, not as a Third Year with a Shadow of your own. It might be better for you to learn from a quarrel mate. Have you chosen a quarrel yet?"

Emily shook her head.

"Then when you do, ask one of the older students for help," Aurelius said. "One of the girls, by preference. They tend to be more aware of etiquette than boys. It's no shame to admit ignorance to someone in the same quarrel. You're all in the group together."

Emily sighed. She'd had a feeling that the quarrels were far too much like social cliques on Earth—and nothing she'd seen at the first meeting had disproved it. Being a member was tempting, she had to admit; she'd hated the cliques on Earth, but perversely she'd also envied their camaraderie. But what would she be asked to do if she was a full member?

"I'll ask Claudia," she said. Perhaps she should ask Helen, if she didn't want to get any further involved with the quarrel, although she wasn't sure she would trust anything the other girl said. "I'm sure she could help."

"Smart choice," Aurelius said.

He paused. "I'll see you this weekend," he added, dryly. It was very clearly a dismissal. "And remember what I told you."

Emily rose to her feet, then walked out of the office and down towards the classroom, where students were already gathering outside the door. Professor Clifton was late, again. She sighed and joined the line, waiting as patiently as she could. It was several minutes past the deadline when the tutor arrived and swept into the classroom, followed by his students. At least *he* didn't seem to want Emily to sit in the front.

She sighed. Professor Clifton was definitely a drunkard. Emily had seen too many drunks in her time on Earth to miss the signs. At least he seemed to be an amiable drunk, unlike her mother or stepfather. But his nose was red, he slurred some of his words and he seemed to have great difficulty in focusing on any individual student. Perhaps it was for the best, she decided. Some of the girls in the class were quite attractive and she knew, from bitter experience, just how horrific it was to be stared at by a drunk.

"Be seated," Professor Clifton said. "In our previous classes, we have covered the techniques for producing an anchorstone. Have you all mastered the basic spell I taught you?"

Emily nodded, along with the other students. She'd been told never to visit the Professor's office outside class; fortunately, she'd managed to master the spell relatively quickly. It hadn't taken her long to recognize that some elements of producing anchorstones were related to the basic necromantic rite, although none of the other students seemed to have made the connection. Stone channeled magic, Emily knew. Done properly, it could channel a *vast* amount of magic.

"Good," Professor Clifton said. He paused, as though he wasn't quite sure what he intended to say, then waved a hand at the blackboard. A list of spell components appeared in front of them. "You have all mastered the basics, which allow you to tweak and control your own spells perfectly. This is something rather more complex."

Emily leaned forward, trying to parse out the spell components. Some of them were understandable, simple chains of spellwork rather like the ones she'd studied under Mistress Sun and Mistress Mauve, others were so complex she couldn't follow them properly. She disliked using spells she didn't understand, but there didn't seem to be a choice. The professor was already speaking.

"When you come to set up an establishment of your own," Professor Clifton said, "you will wish complete control over the use of magic within your territory. The wards we will be studying over the coming weeks are all related to magic detection, magic suppression and—if necessary—direct countering of magic spells. A basic anti-magic ward, if set up with due care and power, can prevent people from casting spells without your permission, at least long enough for you to deal with them. You would find it a very useful tool in defending your home."

Emily nodded. The whole system was rather akin to setting up an Internet message board, with different levels of permission for different users. It was considered rude to use magic in a magician's home without permission—and the wards would make sure that any attempt to use magic would be noted and logged. Now that she knew what the wards were designed to do, it was easier to parse out some of the more complicated pieces of spellwork. They effectively broke up and absorbed magic as soon as it was cast, preventing the spell from actually working.

She smiled. This was one thing she *definitely* intended to master as soon as possible. Unlike most of the students, she actually *did* have a home of her own, one that had too many servants and other visitors for her liking. She would need to master the wards simply to ensure that any unpleasant surprises the previous baron had left behind were removed before they exploded in her face. And besides, she liked the idea of preventing her guests from trying to harm or kill each other with magic. It made her wonder why there weren't such wards in Raven Hall.

Professor Clifton tapped his table, meaningfully. "You can start experimenting with your spellwork now," he said, addressing the class. "And remember to make sure you place the *entire* spell within the anchorstone. You don't want to have it leaking, or it will simply collapse into nothingness."

Emily sighed, then reached into her bag and produced her first true anchorstone. It didn't seem particularly impressive—it was no bigger than her fist—but she could sense the spell pulsing within the stone, just waiting to be activated. Extending it so it would spread through an entire room, let alone a small castle, would be complex, but she had several private thoughts about using her previous experiments with magical batteries to make the whole process considerably easier. Done properly, she wouldn't even need a team of Wardmasters to secure her home against intrusion.

She placed the stone on her desk, then glanced up at the blackboard, trying to memorize all the spell components. After a moment, she gave up and copied them down in her notebook, then started to try to put the spell together in her mind. It was fiendishly complex, far more than any of the wards she used for self-protection, but then those wards drew on her magic directly. These wards needed to draw magic from the local magic field.

But they leak too, she thought. It was the old problem of actually storing magic. The only way *she'd* found to store magic was through pocket dimensions. Given time, any ward would eventually collapse, no matter how strongly it was anchored, without proper maintenance. The only real exceptions to the rule were wards anchored to a nexus point, like Whitehall. In that case, there was an infinite supply of power for maintaining the wards without direct intervention.

But there were weaknesses too, she acknowledged. No sorcerer worthy of the name would be happy allowing someone else to control his wards, yet no sorcerer could control or manipulate Whitehall's wards for long. Emily had touched the user interface once, and the shock had almost killed her. And if Shadye hadn't been loose in the castle, she doubted she could have touched it at all.

She held the stone in one hand and concentrated as she tried to create the spell, uploading it into the stone. There was a brief moment when she thought she'd succeeded...

And then the spellware fragment simply came apart and evaporated. Emily swore under her breath, using several words she'd picked up from Lady Barb, and tried again. This time, the entire anchoring spell came apart.

"It isn't the easiest of spells to control," Professor Clifton said. Emily looked up to discover him standing in front of her desk. She hadn't even heard him approach. "You need to use a very gentle touch."

"Yes, sir," Emily said, cursing herself. Up close, the Professor's breath stank of alcohol. It was a mystery to her why he was still allowed to teach. A sadistic professor might be less dangerous than a drunkard in a magic school, where a single mistake could prove disastrous—or fatal. "Why doesn't it work?"

"You have to merge the two spells together," Professor Clifton explained. He picked up her anchorstone and examined it carefully, then inserted the spells himself. Drunkard or not, the spells fitted in perfectly. "It requires practice, practice and more practice."

He passed it back to her with a smile. "Try building the second set of spells in your mind," he added. "Get it down perfectly, then start tweaking the magic to fit it into the anchorstone. Right now, you're trying to do too much at once. This isn't a simple transfiguration spell, you know."

"Yes, sir," Emily said. He was right, she admitted to herself, even though it meant going back to first principles. It had taken months to learn to cast spells on automatic—and then, in some ways, she had limited herself, as if she'd started to use a wand. "I'll start again from scratch."

The professor nodded before turning to inspect several more students and their work, leaving Emily alone.

She concentrated, putting the spell together in her head. It didn't get any simpler, but not worrying about fitting the two spells together made it a little easier. The ward twisted and turned in her head–it wasn't one that could be safely anchored to her body–then faded out of existence. Emily did it again and again until she was sure she could run through all of the steps without any mistakes, then reached for the anchorstone and rebuilt the holding spell. As soon as it was ready, she reshaped the ward and shoved it into the stone. It held, long enough for her to feel convinced she was on the right track. And then, as before, it evaporated into nothingness.

But at least I'm getting somewhere, she thought.

She kept working on it until the class finally came to an end, then asked to borrow a pair of additional stones from Professor Clifton to continue practicing in private. Professor Clifton agreed, checked her anchorstone, then nodded approvingly. It helped that only a handful of other students had managed to create the ward perfectly. Emily thanked him gravely, then headed out of the door and down to the refectory. She'd arranged to meet Frieda for lunch.

"Hey," Claudia called, as she entered the refectory. "You left us very early."

"Yes," Emily said, irked. It had been two days since she'd left–and Claudia was only *now* speaking to her about it. "And so...?"

"We would like to have you as a member," Claudia said. "And so we brought you a gift."

She passed Emily a roll of parchment. Emily opened it to discover a list of instructions for several spells. Some of them she knew already, others were unfamiliar. One of them, she suspected, was the hypnotic spell.

"Come with us next weekend," Claudia asked. "You can learn with the rest of us."

"I suppose I could," Emily said, with a sigh. "But I don't know what I can offer in return."

Claudia snorted rudely. "When you're an older student, help mentor the younger ones," she said, dryly. "That's what the quarrel is for."

Chapter Nineteen

EMILY WAS MORE TIRED THAN SHE'D EXPECTED BY THE TIME ZED FINALLY LET HER OUT OF alchemy tutoring, but she managed to work up the energy to have a shower as soon as she returned to Raven Hall. His warnings about the dangers of some of the ingredients they'd worked with hung in her mind, to the point she'd almost forgotten about her agreement with Frieda. But thankfully she managed to remember before Frieda could either remind her or conclude that Emily had simply been making promises she had no intention of keeping.

The spellchamber attached to Raven Hall was little different from the ones she'd seen at Whitehall, although some of the confinement and protective spells were a little weaker, as if the older students were expected to maintain them themselves. Emily was surprised–it was an odd oversight–but chose to ignore it in favor of talking to Frieda. The younger girl looked starkly terrified after entering the chamber and closing the door. It puzzled Emily until she recalled just how the dueling classes had been used as excuses for bullying.

"Sit down on the mat," Emily said. She had no intention of trying any form of physical training, not until Frieda had put some more meat on her bones at the very least. "And put your wand away... no, give it to me."

Frieda looked reluctant, but surrendered her wand without a fight. Emily took the wand, placed it in her belt and leaned forward.

"Watch," she said, and cast a light globe into the air. "I've yet to find a spell that cannot be cast without a wand."

"But I need the wand," Frieda said, mournfully. "I..."

"No, you don't," Emily said. She was tempted to snap the wand in two, but she had a feeling that Frieda would react badly. "You just think you do. I want you to try to cast the spell without using a wand."

Frieda moved her hand in the air vaguely. Nothing happened.

"You're not concentrating on the spell," Emily said. Just how limited was Frieda's introduction to magic? Mistress Irene had slowly talked Emily through all of the stages, starting with the basics and moving on to more complex structures. "Try it again."

"I did," Frieda said, after a moment. There was a flare of unfocused magic, harmlessly absorbed by the wards, but nothing effective. "But it isn't working."

Emily thought, trying to recall lessons that had been both wondrous and extremely difficult at the same time. She'd had to learn to channel her magic before starting to actually put together a basic spell in her head. Logically, Frieda had to do the same, with some minor modifications... in fact, if her guess was correct, she'd been taught to keep the two parts of making a spell separate. It *was* an easier way to learn magic than the way Emily had been taught, but it was also very limited.

"I want you to close your eyes and think of a simple charm," Emily said, reaching out and taking Frieda's hands. "Pick a charm, any charm."

Frieda hesitated. "The glow charm," she said, as she closed her eyes. "They taught it to us first."

Emily nodded. "That will do," she said. It wasn't one that could become dangerous if overpowered, as far as she knew. "I want you to keep your eyes closed and think about how the charm *feels* when you create the spell. Don't try to chant, just think about how the charm feels in your wand. It will resonate against your magic. How does it feel?"

"Strange," Frieda said.

Emily smiled at her, reassuringly. "Hold that feeling in your head," she said, "and try to channel magic into the spell."

Frieda's hands shook. "It isn't working," she protested. "I can't *do* it."

"Try again," Emily said. She squeezed Frieda's hands lightly. "Focus on the feeling and..."

Magic flared around her. Emily smiled as the room was suddenly illuminated by a brilliant white glow of light.

"Open your eyes," she said. The spell wouldn't last long. "Hurry."

Frieda opened her eyes and stared. "I did that?"

"You did," Emily confirmed. "And without a wand."

She watched with some amusement as Frieda cast a whole series of spells into the air, starting with a brilliant light globe. The girl was almost giggling, even though some of her spells were strongly overpowered and others barely worked before fading back into nothingness and disappearing. Emily found herself smiling openly, remembering the wonder and joy she'd felt when she'd first cast a spell. Frieda, trapped by mental blocks that had been skilfully woven into her head, had never really felt the same way.

"You'll have to keep practicing," Emily said. She plucked the wand off her belt, held it in her hand for a long moment, then snapped it neatly in two. Frieda yelped, but didn't panic. "I have something for you."

She reached into her deep pocket and produced a wand she'd picked up earlier. "This is nothing more than a piece of wood," she said. As far as she could tell, there wasn't anything particularly special about any of the wands, although some were made of stone or iron instead of wood. "It just *looks* like a wand, but it won't work as one. I want you to carry it with you and cast all the spells you are ordered to do without using a proper wand."

Frieda stared at it. "Why...?"

"Because they always took your wand," Emily said, softly. "This way, you'll be able to surprise them when they do."

"I..." Frieda seemed stunned. "Do you mean I can fight?"

"There are probably spells to make it hard to lose a wand," Emily said, stroking the snake bracelet on her wrist. Hardly anyone had commented on it, although *that* was no surprise. She was far from the only student who wore jewellery. "You're surrounded by knowledge you can use to defend yourself, just waiting for you to pick it up. Why didn't you use it?"

"...Can't read," Frieda muttered, sullenly. "And no one would read to me."

Emily sighed. "I'll teach you some reading spells," she said. They never lasted very long, but they would suffice. "How did you learn from your books?"

Frieda shook her head, wordlessly.

"Maybe get someone to teach you the basics of reading too," Emily added, thoughtfully. She honestly had no idea who, in Mountaintop, would be interested in teaching a young girl to read, even if she was offered payment for her services. "But we will see."

She sat back, then started teaching Frieda a number of basic spells. Most of them were classed as harmless First Year pranks at Whitehall, an attitude that Emily had found horrific even before they were used on her. Turning someone into a toad seemed amusing, unless one happened to be the victim. Others were just as unpleasant... and perfectly normal, in a world of magic. Once she'd taught the spells, she added a number of basic countermeasures that would rapidly remove the original spell.

"You need to forget everything you were told about dueling," she warned. "The real world isn't fair. Nor do bloody-minded wizards give you a chance to raise your wand to defend yourself. Hit hard, hit fast and *keep moving!*"

Frieda swallowed. "But what if the spells don't work?"

"Test them," Emily said.

She took a breath, then decided she could take a risk. "Test one of the spells on me," she offered. "But *don't* try to alter the spellwork."

"I can't," Frieda said. "I was told..."

"Forget whatever you were told," Emily ordered, sharply. "Cast one of the spells on me."

Frieda raised a hand. Emily braced herself as light flared from Frieda's fingertips and swirled around Emily, then closed her eyes as the light merged into her very being. The sensation of having her entire body warped and twisted into something else was uncomfortable, but not particularly painful, somewhat to her surprise. There were other forms of transfiguration spells that were effectively methods of torture.

She opened her eyes to discover she was staring up at Frieda. A glance downwards revealed she had a green body and the entire room had suddenly become much larger. She hopped... and found herself halfway across the room. The spell, thankfully, protected her mind from being infected with the frog's mentality, but the experience was still uncomfortable. She gathered her thoughts, then shaped the counterspell in her mind. Her senses swam, once again, as she returned to human form. Keeping her eyes open had been a mistake.

"I... I did that?" Frieda asked. "Really?"

"Yes," Emily said, standing up and adjusting her dress. "You cast the spell; you turned me into a frog."

Frieda laughed for a moment before freezing in sudden horror, clearly expecting punishment of some kind. No doubt she'd been punished for doing what she'd been told before, Emily guessed, bitterly. It didn't matter to an abused child that it wasn't her fault that she'd been abused; abused children often blamed themselves for their suffering. And it just wasn't *right*.

"You did as you were told," Emily said, dryly.

"But... your clothes transformed too," Frieda said. "When I was turned into a pig, my clothes were left behind."

"Different spell," Emily said. Whitehall took a dim view of spells that left people running naked through the corridor. "And now you need to practice some of the other spells—just target them on the wards—after you do me one favor."

Frieda looked at her through shining eyes. "Anything," she said. "After this..."

"I taught you the freeze spell," Emily said. "I need you to cast it on me, then leave it in place until the bell rings for dinner."

"The freeze spell," Frieda said. "Why?"

"I need to master breaking it," Emily said. She'd been caught too often by the trick. "If I can't free myself by dinnertime, you can free me yourself."

She sat down and waited. Frieda cast the spell... and Emily froze. Magic crackled over her skin, then faded away. Emily tried to force herself to move, but not a single voluntary muscle would obey her orders. She privately suspected it was actually a form of stasis spell, rather than merely freezing someone in space, even though she could still think. Magic seemed to consider the mind partly disconnected from the body, after all. Logically, she shouldn't be able to think when she was a frog, because she had a frog's mind. But she *could* think...

It wasn't easy to think clearly when she was frozen. Partly, because it was unnatural; partly, because she was vulnerable and she *hated* being vulnerable. The spell was very easy to abuse, if someone was careful; it was far easier being a frog, rather than a frozen statue. But she knew it *was* possible to escape. Jade had done it, several times, when she'd frozen him.

She tried to close her eyes, remembered it was futile, then started to meditate, separating her mind from her body. It was what she'd told Frieda to do, more or less, with some modifications. If magic could be separated so a wand became necessary, was it possible to move all the way in the other direction? She concentrated desperately, recalling the sensations of the counterspell, then tried to trigger it. Everything went dark for a second...

And then she opened her eyes. She could move!

"You did it," Frieda cheered. "Can you teach me how to do it?"

"I can try," Emily said. Why had everything gone dark? She didn't feel as though she'd knocked herself out. And then she knew the answer and mentally kicked herself. She *had* wanted to close her eyes before breaking the spell. "But it's rather tricky."

Frieda giggled. "I've mastered more," she said. She paused. "Can I show these to others?"

"If you want," Emily said. Maybe it would make life a little better for the Shadows if they all learned to use magic without a wand. Or maybe someone would blame her for introducing the new/old technique. She shook her head. If there were consequences, she could take them. "But remember what I said about dueling."

"Thank you," Frieda said.

"Be careful who you teach," Emily warned. "Don't teach Ten anything."

Frieda giggled.

Emily rose to her feet on unsteady legs then walked around the chamber until she felt better.

"You can do more than simple deflecting charms," she told Frieda as she walked. "Your wand isn't a shield, nor should you be trying to use it as one. You need to learn to construct your own private wards, embedded in your magic. Once in place, they will remain there until they are knocked down or removed."

Frieda frowned. "I don't have to dodge everything?"

"You should," Emily warned. There *were* hexes that ate their way through personal wards, then attacked their target directly. She'd been taught quite a few in Martial Magic. "Don't ever let anyone hit you if you can avoid it."

She sighed, studying the younger girl. There was no way she would be a match for anyone physically, at least for quite some time. And she might never be a true Combat Sorceress, no matter how much magic she mastered. Lady Barb was the only woman Emily had met who had been able to keep up with the sergeants, either in magical or physical tussles.

"And try to get someone to watch your back too," she added. A person's back was always exposed, no matter how many protective wards they knew. "Maybe a friend... do you have someone you trust?"

"There's a few girls I do the laundry with," Frieda said. "And others I try to practice spells with, but we're kept very busy when we're not in class. And I don't know if I can trust them."

Under the circumstances, Emily decided, that was probably a wise attitude.

She hesitated, then allowed Frieda to test a few more spells on her. There was a variant on the freeze spell that merely trapped a person's feet to the floor–Emily couldn't resist pointing out how easy it was to escape by simply removing her shoes– and a darker spell that caused burning sensations, even though it inflicted no real harm. Frieda was laughing openly as she finished casting the third spell, then stumbled and almost collapsed. Emily stepped forward and held her, gently. Frieda felt alarmingly light in Emily's arms.

"You need to eat," she said. She'd spoken to Zed about specific potions and he'd agreed, reluctantly, to allow her to draw them from the school's supplies. Emily had managed to keep from demanding to know why they weren't made generally available, somehow. "And so do I."

She checked they hadn't left anything in the chamber–the remains of Frieda's wand were stuffed into her dress for later disposal–then allowed Frieda to lead her out of the room and down towards the refectory. Ten and Helen were outside, going to dinner too, but neither of them said anything and they passed in awkward silence.

Emily sighed, inwardly, then quietly resigned herself to an uncomfortable dinner. But it really didn't matter that much.

Frieda caught her arm as Helen and Ten walked into the refectory and held her back. "Why are you doing this?" She asked, quietly. "Why don't you just... use me?"

Emily shuddered. Frieda could have no idea just how many unfortunate implications were wrapped up in her words. Or perhaps she did. Someone who grew up on a farm would know the facts of life at a far earlier age than someone who had grown up in a city. And wouldn't have any illusions about her potential value to someone from a far higher social class. *And* she'd be too grand to fit in with her family if she ever went home.

"Because... because it's the right thing to do," Emily said.

She'd wondered if Frieda had been intended to spy on her, but that was clearly not the case. But instead... it was possible that she was intended as a subtle lure. The part of Emily that enjoyed helping people would love to spend more time teaching Frieda, even if it meant staying at Mountaintop for an additional year. She touched the rune between her breasts and shivered, knowing that she might be protected from subtle magic manipulation, but there was no protection from mundane manipulation. Aurelius had the measure of her all too well.

"No one else seems to feel that way," Frieda said, quietly. There was a bitterness in her voice that caused Emily a fresh pang of guilt. "You're the first to care about me."

"Maybe it gets better in later years," Emily said. She wasn't sure that was true, although Aurelius had hinted as much. The Shadows from poorer backgrounds would start at a lower level than the other Second Years. "Or maybe you would have gone elsewhere."

She shook her head as they walked into the dining hall. The cooks had definitely heard *something* from Aurelius; they placed a large dinner in front of Frieda, as well as a handful of potion vials. Emily watched as Frieda hesitated, then started to eat slowly and reluctantly.

"Take the green potion," Emily ordered. She knew from experience that it enhanced the appetite. The sergeants had made her drink them herself, once upon a time. "And then drink the others after the meal."

Frieda nodded and obeyed.

"I think we'll go over other subjects as well," Emily added, as Frieda ate. "I've never heard of Chanting. You might have something useful to teach me, too."

"It's not very common beyond Second Year," Helen said. She had been listening to their conversation in silence. Beside her, Ten looked a little betrayed. "I didn't take it at all."

Somehow, Emily wasn't surprised.

"Tell me what you did take," she said, trying to be friendly. Helen might be a useful source of information too. "And what it was like growing up in a Great House."

Helen smiled and started to talk.

Chapter Twenty

Y OU SHOULD KNOW SOME OF THE BASICS OF MAGICAL ETIQUETTE," ROBYN SAID, AS SHE CAST the privacy ward around the two chairs. She was a Fourth Year girl, freakishly tall even by Earthly standards. Claudia had recommended Robyn when Emily had asked for lessons in magical etiquette, then suggested they talked about it in the quarrel's clubhouse. Their oaths would keep the group from gossiping about it behind Emily's back afterwards. "I'm actually surprised your father taught you nothing."

"I was sixteen before I met another magician," Emily said, truthfully. She sat down and tried to look attentive despite her exhaustion. Classes had been growing harder over the last week. "I lived a very isolated life."

"Being in that Tower can't have been fun," Robyn said. She smiled. "I wonder if that should make you *my* Shadow."

Emily eyed her, darkly. If Robyn thought that Emily was going to be fetching and carrying for her, she was going to be rather disappointed.

"But never mind that," Robyn added, when Emily failed to rise to the bait. "My grandfather used to be a historian. Studying societies is second nature to me."

Emily leaned forward, interested. The Allied Lands had no real historians, apart from the History Monks, and *they* took vows of silence. There didn't seem to be any real historical method, certainly not outside some very specialised areas, and kings like Alassa's father seemed willing and able to rewrite history at will. She had a private suspicion that most of what the Allied Lands took for granted hadn't quite happened in the way they thought, if it had happened at all. For example, the current version of the coup in Zangaria boosted Alassa's involvement while minimizing Imaiqah's.

Robyn smiled in placation. "The principal difference between us and mundanes is that we wield power," she continued. "Each of us is far more formidable than any mundane army, even one armed with weapons designed to counter magic. The merest magician, even a simple student, can kill a mundane with a thought. We have power."

She paused, waiting for Emily to comment. Emily herself wasn't sure what to make of it. She'd been raised in a society where there was an accepted level of equality, but even *that* was a fairly new innovation by earthly standards—and there *was* no magic on Earth. Conversely, there was no real concept of true democracy in the Allied Lands. Even the most democratic city-state didn't offer the vote to *all* of its citizens.

And it would be hard for the mundanes to keep a magician in line, she knew. Emily had had no experience of magic at all when she'd come to the Nameless World, but she'd been able to turn people into animals or objects, freeze them in their tracks or even control them directly within six months. Someone like Void might as well be Superman as far as the locals were concerned, while Shadye would be more of a force of nature than anything merely *human*.

"But this gives us *pride*," Robyn said, after the pause had gone on too long. She made a show of glancing in both directions, then lowered her voice. "We act more like those strutting swordsmen we despise than we care to admit, with more dangerous weapons. Our society has evolved to control our pride and direct it in more useful directions."

She paused. "And so the core tenets of our society are *honor, obligation* and *respect*."

Emily drew in her breath sharply. Her stepfather had been fond of the word *respect*. He seemed to demand it from everyone, without good reason. King Randor also liked the word, although Emily knew he was far more deserving of respect. Someone who stayed on his throne in the midst of a snake pit of ambitious noblemen deserved admiration. But she also knew he'd tried to use her in the past and would continue to do so in the future.

"It isn't that bad," Robyn said. "But we do try to remember the concepts, no matter who we're dealing with."

She grinned. "When you are born, you assume an obligation to your parents and your family; when someone does you a favor, you assume an obligation to repay the favor at some later date. And thus we have *obligation*, the endless links between magicians that bind us together into a society. It would be a crime against *obligation* for you to act against your father, or me to act against my family. There isn't a magician alive who wouldn't understand your reluctance to swear oaths. Your father commanded it."

Emily nodded. She'd been surprised the quarrel had been satisfied with a gentleman's agreement, of sorts, rather than a sworn oath. But if they thought Emily had prior obligations, they wouldn't ask her to break them.

"It's considered very bad form to ask someone to deny an obligation," Robyn continued, warming to her subject. It was clear she rarely had a chance to discuss her personal field of study with anyone. "You wouldn't be asked to betray your family, no matter the situation, or turn against someone to whom you owe a debt."

"So no one would ever ask me to turn against... against my father," Emily said. "Because he *is* my father..."

"And the ties of blood are strong," Robyn said. She smiled, mischievously. "You may discover that, the more powerful the magician, the more reluctant he is to assume any form of obligation. I believe that most of the Lone Powers started out by deciding they no longer wanted to be woven into the warp and weft of our society. Your father cut himself off from his family and retreated to his Tower, only to start a new family of his own."

Emily could understand it. The more she considered the social networks, some visible, some hidden, running through Mountaintop, the more she realized the school was a microcosm of the entire magical side of the Nameless World. There were webs of obligations binding students and tutors together, with deals being made in the background to organize events long before they came into the open. Even the Shadow network made a strange kind of sense; it both prepared the newcomers for their role in society and ensured they couldn't really become a threat in their own right.

But it also seemed counterproductive. The Necromancers weren't *that* far from Mountaintop–and Shadye had almost punched through Whitehall and swept down into the Allied Lands. Shouldn't they be trying to muster as many fully-trained magicians as possible? It made very little sense.

She pushed the thought aside for later contemplation. Robyn was still talking.

"The next aspect of our society is *respect*," Robyn said. She smiled. "What do you imagine respect means?"

Emily had to think about it. *Respect* was one of the words she understood, but had difficulty putting into words. She respected the Grandmaster and many of her teachers at Whitehall–and Mountaintop, for that matter–yet she had never respected her parents or her stepfather.

"A feeling of understanding that someone is important," she hazarded, finally. She'd never make a writer. "Or... or respecting their ability to do something? Or..."

"Close enough," Robyn said. "We tend to consider it a form of acceptance that each and every magician, no matter how powerful, has feelings that should be taken into consideration. The basic rule against entering a magician's house without his permission is a form of *respect*. So, too, is honoring a master's right to teach his apprentice in any way he sees fit. *Respect*."

She paused. "Even the least of magicians can do very real harm, if provoked," she added. "It is generally considered unwise to fail to show the proper respect, even if he can barely light a fire with his magic. This doesn't stop magicians from fighting, unfortunately, but it does tend to limit our internal conflicts."

Emily nodded, slowly. "But respect isn't extended to mundanes?"

"Of course not," Robyn said. "They're not magicians."

She grinned, showing sharp teeth. "Is there a mundane alive who could beat a magician?"

Batman, Emily thought snidely. But Batman wasn't real.

"When you are awake, you will have wards that protect you from swords and spears, charms that protect you from poisons and spells that ensure your servants remain loyal to you," Robyn said, answering her own question. "When you are asleep, you have wards to keep out mundanes who might wish to do you harm. If you happened to die at mundane hands, you would die of your own carelessness, not because the mundane had the ability to kill you.

"And mundanes are weak, defenseless," she added. "Even the strongest of them could not fight off the least of control spells. You could make them do whatever you wanted."

Emily shuddered. It sounded like a nightmare... and yet it was also hellishly tempting. To go back to Earth, to show her stepfather exactly what it had been like growing up, how she'd felt helpless and utterly defenseless... part of her thought that was a very good idea. She could tear him to pieces, even without magic, after two years of the sergeants giving her personal combat training. Or she could...

No, she told herself, firmly. Doing anything like that would be giving in to madness and starting the fall towards becoming a dark wizard. Or worse, a Necromancer. *Besides, there's no way to Earth from here.*

"You will have seen how the quarrel discusses matters," Robyn said, unaware of Emily's thoughts. "That's a miniature version of how most of the Great Houses work. An adult magician, a trained magician, has a voice in the family council. The consensus will determine what the family does."

"So it's a form of democracy," Emily mused. But, in its own way, it was as restrictive as some of the others. "What would happen if someone was born to the family, but had no magic?"

"It doesn't happen," Robyn said. "If you have two magicians as parents, their children will certainly be magicians. Having one parent as a magician would be enough to ensure that the children were almost certainly magicians in their own right."

She eyed Emily speculatively. "Is that how you survived your early years? Your mother was a mundane?"

Emily shrugged. "My father never spoke of it to me," she said, which was true enough. She knew Void had servants in his Tower. No one seemed to have any problems accepting that he might have managed to get one of them pregnant. "I didn't develop magic until I was sixteen."

"Interesting," Robyn said. "I would have expected a Lone Power to try to encourage you to develop magic earlier and see if you could be nursed through puberty."

"I think he cared more about me than about his experiments," Emily said, a little tartly. It was well known that magicians who developed magic before puberty rarely survived growing into adulthood. Their magic was just too closely tied to their emotions, or so she'd heard, although she suspected the explanation was a little darker. "He wouldn't have wanted to risk my life."

"Good for him," Robyn said. "Do you understand *respect* now?"

"I think I do," Emily said.

"Your dorm mates have shown you quite a bit of respect," Robyn said. "But they're also bound to treat you as a normal student, as much as possible. They'd appreciate it if you treated them the same way."

She settled back in her chair and rolled her eyes as a shouting match broke out on the other side of the room. "Hang on," she said. "I may have to deal with that... discussion."

Emily sighed, then relaxed as two of the older students bore down on the combatants and separated them, allowing Robyn to stay in her chair. Magical society, Emily was starting to realize, was practically the *definition* of an armed society. Back on Earth, she'd been told that an armed society was a polite society; here, it would be literally true. Insult a magician and you might find yourself hopping on a lily pad—or dead. And even weaker magicians could be dangerous to stronger magicians.

But it isn't the same, she thought. *That only applies to magicians. There's no Sam Colt to make us all equal here.*

Robyn cleared her throat. "The final aspect of our society is *honor*," she said. "Unlike the other two, *honor* is, first and foremost, a deeply personal aspect. You are expected to uphold *respect* and *obligation* out of your love for society, but *honor* is something you are expected to do for yourself. It is only secondarily an aspect for relating to other magicians."

She paused. "You are expected to do the right thing, to build up a *reputation* for doing the right thing, because it is the best way to ensure you fit into society," she added. She nodded towards one of the younger students. "You understand that the Ashworth and Ashfall Families have been at war for the last two hundred years?"

Emily nodded. Markus had said as much, although he hadn't gone into details.

"They *hate* each other," Robyn said. "And yet few of the Ashworth Family would argue that Master Ashfall lacks personal honor. His reputation speaks well of him."

"I understand, I think," Emily said. "But doesn't that mean that he's merely managed to keep his sins buried?"

"You cynic," Robyn accused, lightly. "But you're right. He might well have managed to keep any lapses from getting out into the public eye."

She took a breath. "There are other aspects to honor," she added. "A tutor at this school would be quite within the bounds of honor to assign detention or a caning to any student who insulted him to his face. He would *not* be allowed to challenge that student to a duel, because there would be a colossal imbalance of power. No matter how much Professor Zed hates you, he cannot duel with you. Even if he survived—and you have killed two Necromancers—no one would ever respect him again."

Emily frowned. "But wouldn't I be considered an equal...?"

"You're a student," Robyn commented, darkly. "You would *not* be considered his equal. It might not be quite as bad as a twenty-year-old man beating up a six-year-old girl, but it would still be considered quite beyond the pale. I'm actually surprised the Dueling Mistresses have been facing you directly, even in training. Someone could use that against them in later life."

"I don't see how," Emily said. She didn't like dueling, but she was slowly improving. "It's just a training session."

"You'd be astonished at just how easily something innocent can become something else, if handled by the right person," Robyn said. "Their enemies would be hardly inclined to give them the benefit of the doubt."

She smiled. "But, on the other hand, *you* could challenge him," she added. "*That* would not be seen as a dishonorable act."

"But the outcome would be the same," Emily said. "Wouldn't it?"

"You would be regarded as having brought it on yourself," Robyn said. "As a student, you would be expected to understand that he knew much more magic than yourself—and yet you issued the challenge. If you won, well and good; if you lost, everyone will say that you were a stupid idiot who deserved to die."

And remove my genes from the gene pool, Emily thought. The magical society might not have the concept of genes—Zed's manipulation of Alassa's bloodline had been

plagued with simple ignorance—but they understood the need to remove idiots, particularly idiots blessed with the local version of deadly weapons. But then, truly
stupid magicians simply didn't last very long in any case.

"Honor is a tricky thing," Robyn explained. "If you are widely seen as dishonorable, your word will not be respected and you will not be welcome anywhere in
society. There are magicians who guard their honor as closely as certain ladies guard
their virtue. But all that's really necessary is to comport yourself in a decent manner
and remind yourself, from time to time, of your own honor."

"What else can you do," Emily mused, "that is actually dishonorable?"

"Break your word," Robyn said. "If you fail to keep your word, people will start
considering you a dishonorable person. There are quite a few other acts that are borderline permissible, but engaging in them costs you honor. For example, a marriage
can legally be consummated as soon as the girl is old enough to bear children, but
it is considered dishonorable to do so. It is also considered dishonorable to enter an
arranged marriage against the express will of one of the participants."

Emily's eyes narrowed. "How does that work?"

"Your father could betroth you to my brother," Robyn said. She shuddered. "Which
is a ghastly thought, really. My brother is twenty and still acts like he's eight. But your
father could make arrangements with my father for you to marry him. If you didn't
want to marry him, which would be quite understandable, you could say no and it
would be dishonorable for my brother to marry you."

"But there would be nothing stopping him from actually *doing* it," Emily said,
slowly. The whole concept was sickening. She had an awful feeling that her stepfather would have happily sold her for a few bottles of beer if it hadn't been thoroughly
illegal. "No law to forbid it..."

"You're a powerful magician," Robyn said. "I would not care to force you into
anything against your will."

She sighed. "Most betrothals are arranged before the children reach puberty," she
added, softly. "If the children, as young adults, feel they shouldn't be married, they
can say no."

"But there's no law forbidding it," Emily said, again. "Why not?"

"Because that would be a lack of *respect*," Robyn said. "One magician does not have
the right to tell another what he can do with his family."

Emily shuddered. The more she saw of magical society, the more she understood
why Void had wanted to leave it. And why she wanted to stay out of it too.

"Come on," Robyn said, as Steven banged the gavel. "There's dirty work afoot. But
there might be cakes, too."

Emily sighed and followed her back to the table.

Chapter Twenty-One

T HAT'S AN INTERESTING QUESTION," AURELIUS SAID. "MIGHT I ASK WHAT BROUGHT IT ON?"
Emily hesitated. She'd chatted to Claudia, then Helen, then even Rook and Ten. They'd all been surprisingly happy to talk to her about life in the Great Houses and, as far as she'd been able to tell, they'd been honest. Life in the Great Houses was better than life as a common-born magician, but it also carried so many obligations that Emily was surprised the entire society hadn't collapsed under its own weight. There were so many pitfalls waiting for an unwary magician that she was quite certain she didn't want to be part of it herself.

And then she'd asked why a patriarch had so much power over his family.

"I am being tutored in social etiquette," she said, finally. "And I discovered just how many arrangements a *paterfamilias* could make for his family."

"They do have a considerable amount of power," Aurelius agreed. "But then, they also inherit the family's obligations and debts."

"I know," Emily said, softly. "But does that give them the right to control their children's lives? Or to ensure that newcomers to their society are magically crippled?"

"Some would argue that they do," Aurelius said. "Others would point out that there's no way to make them follow outside laws."

Emily sighed. She was used to thinking in terms of a nuclear family; one mother, one father and a few children. But the Great Houses were almost clans in their own right; it was tricky, immensely so, to work out just who was related to whom. If they hadn't had a habit of integrating new blood from common-born magicians, Emily was sure, they would probably have had very real problems with incest and inbreeding by now. Markus had over a hundred relatives, all bearing the Ashfall name.

Maybe that's why they put so much weight on honor, she thought, sourly. *There's no other way to express their disapproval.*

"It's stupid," she said. It crossed her mind that saying it aloud could be a mistake, but she was too tired to care. "The Necromancers are pushing against the walls and they're fighting over... over who has the right to do what to whom."

"I quite agree," Aurelius said. "But convincing even a small number of magicians to work together, let alone accept another's leadership, is like herding fire drakes."

With the added disadvantage that those fire drakes have magic, Emily thought, remembering Lady Barb's frustration with the same problem. *You might be stronger than one of them, but all of them?*

He gave her a wintry smile. "It is good that you have come to recognize the flaws in the established order," he said. "But have you also come to understand why the established order exists?"

"I think so," Emily said, slowly. "It's to keep magicians from fighting each other too openly."

"Among other things," Aurelius agreed. He rose to his feet and turned to walk towards a door. "And, speaking of the Necromancers, there is something I want to show you."

Emily followed him through the door and down a long flight of stairs that seemed to reach down into the bowels of the Earth. Magic flickered and flared around her, some understandable privacy wards, others so soft and subtle she barely sensed their existence until it was too late. The rune on her chest burned suddenly—she gasped in pain, suddenly shocked into full awareness—as she moved further down the stairs. It was nearly a minute before the pain faded away. Aurelius, it seemed, had been so tightly focused on what was below him that he hadn't even looked back at her gasp.

She tested the magic, carefully. It wasn't focused on her, but more of a generalized *"don't look here"* sensation. Now that she knew it was there, she could just disregard it... and, as she kept moving, it faded away completely. All it did was help to keep the underground complex hidden.

"This is one of the most secure chambers in the world," Aurelius said, as they reached the bottom of the stairs. "And what I am about to show you is one of its greatest secrets."

He paused before turning to face her, his face illuminated by his light globe. "There are people who would look askance at you if they knew you'd been here," he told her. "You must never discuss it with anyone, ever. The consequences would be dire."

Emily watched him turn and walk through a doorway carved in stone, wondering what was worse than summoning demons. She followed him, curiosity winning over caution, and entered a large chamber, illuminated by a pearly white light that seemed to come from nowhere and everywhere. And, throughout the room, there were giant crystal structures, each one holding a figure—or a creature—trapped like flies in amber.

She found her voice. "What *is* this?"

"This is where we study the innermost workings of magic," Aurelius said. "And what the Faerie did to humans to make them monsters."

Emily peered into the first structure and froze. She was staring into the eyes of a male Gorgon, seemingly older than the Gorgon she knew. The mass of snakes surrounding its head were still, instead of the constant rustling motion Emily recalled, while his face was caught in a mask of terror. And someone, she saw, had been drilling into his skull. He was trapped on the verge of death.

The next structure held a white-faced man, completely bald and naked. There was nothing between his legs, while his pasty-white head was oddly inhuman. In all truth, she wasn't even sure it *was* male. She frowned, trying to think of what it could be, then looked a question at Aurelius. He smiled, then indicated the mouth. Two small fangs could be seen protruding from its upper jaw.

"A vampire," Aurelius said. "A deeply magical creature, bound by laws we do not fully understand. Strong, capable of shapeshifting into bats or mist, almost unstoppable save by magic or a wooden stake. And powerfully hypnotic. We've seen people become slaves and lure others to be eaten. Rumor has it that some of the mundane aristocrats are actually vampires, feeding on their populations."

They wouldn't need to bother to be vampires, Emily thought, remembering the Baron she'd displaced at Cockatrice. He'd been nothing more than a parasite with more power than concern for his people. But then, Robyn had made it clear that few magicians cared for the common folk. The only one she'd ever heard express genuine concern, without any regard for his own activities, was Master Tor. And wasn't *that* ironic? Master Tor had never liked Emily, and she tended to return the sentiment.

She looked up at Aurelius, dismissing the thought. "Why don't you do anything about it?"

"It isn't our problem," Aurelius said. "And besides, there are agreements. The Compact should not be threatened."

Emily frowned. "The Compact?"

"An agreement that we won't interfere openly in mundane society," Aurelius said. He led her to the next piece of crystal as he spoke. "We don't interfere in their affairs, they don't interfere in our affairs. And so the balance is maintained."

"And the real reason?" Emily asked. "I don't think King Randor could stop you if you wanted to march in and take over Zangaria."

Aurelius gave her a twisted smile. "Think about it," he said. "You'll figure it out."

Emily considered it for a long moment, then blinked in surprise as she looked into the third crystal. A girl stood inside, wearing a long white robe that reminded Emily of the first set of robes she'd been given, two years ago. Her face was tormented, as if she was struggling against something inside of her; her body looked to be on the cusp of womanhood. It was always tricky to estimate ages in the Allied Lands–people on Earth grew up faster–but Emily would have placed her age as somewhere around twelve.

"She developed magic when she was five," Aurelius said, softly. There was a bitter note in his voice. "At that age, Emily, one does not need to use complex spells to make things happen. But when she started growing into a woman she lost control of her magic. We had to seal her into a spell, trapping her forever."

He sighed. "Every magician both hopes for and dreads his children developing magic in childhood," he said. "It is always a sign of powerful magic, perhaps more powerful than any Lone Power, but so few of them survive the passage into adulthood. And we don't know why."

"They're scared," Emily said, without thinking.

Aurelius swung around to face her. "Why...?"

Emily swallowed. She wasn't sure she could answer without tipping off Aurelius that she hadn't been born on the Nameless World. But she knew he would never let her go without answering the question, not now.

"It's... it's something of a girl thing," she said, reluctantly. It wasn't a discussion she had ever envisaged having with anyone, let alone Aurelius. "As we grow into adulthood, we can be scared by the changes in our bodies. Some of us try not to eat in the hopes that our bodies won't change any further."

"I confess I have never heard of anything like it," Aurelius said, slowly. "But what does that have to do with developing magic?"

Emily wasn't surprised. The Allied Lands *feared* mental problems, particularly in magicians. And eating disorders, either brought on by fear or poor self-esteem, were a mental problem, if one that could be overcome. Besides, the Allied Lands weren't particularly fond of coddling children. Emily could imagine what sort of response a child would get if he or she insisted she wasn't eating something on a given day.

"Their magic is more responsive to their feelings," she said. "If they hate the changes in their bodies that much, their magic will try to bend and snap the bodies back to where they think they should be. And this kills them, because they don't know what they're doing..."

"Like a very poorly made de-aging potion," Aurelius said. "It's possible, I suppose." He took a breath. "Do you have a cure?"

"I don't think so," Emily said. She'd never had a chance to develop an eating disorder herself. "Nothing that will work here, in any case."

Aurelius gave her a sharp look, but quietly led the way past a whole series of crystal columns and into another room. Emily followed, seeing hundreds of creatures, some humanoid, some very strange to her eyes, trapped in Mountaintop. The next room held a skeleton so big it took her a long moment to comprehend what it actually was. But then, she'd never actually seen a dead dragon before.

"Dragons are powerfully magical," Aurelius said. There was a hint of heavy satisfaction in his voice. "And the older, the better."

He led her through another door into a much smaller chamber. One wall was crammed with potion bottles, filled with dozens of different liquids; the other three were bare, save for drawings of humans in various stages of dissection. There was no real photography in the Allied Lands, Emily reminded herself, as Aurelius waved her to a chair. The chair was positioned next to a medical table, like the one in Mistress Granite's classroom.

"Tell me something," Aurelius said, as he pulled a second chair over to the table and sat down facing her. "What would you say is the greatest threat to the Allied Lands?"

"The Necromancers," Emily said, at once. "They nearly won the war two years ago."

"True," Aurelius agreed. "And how far would you be prepared to go to stop the Necromancers?"

"As far as necessary," Emily said. She had no illusions about what the Necromancers would do to the Allied Lands. The population would become sources of food and magical sustenance, while the land itself would eventually be drained dry, leaving a barren wasteland behind. "What about you?"

"Some of us take the threat of the Necromancers very seriously," Aurelius said. He placed his elbows on the table. "Others... are more interested in private disputes than watching the barricades. They think the Necromancers are thousands of miles away and aren't likely to be a problem. Or that the Necromancers will eventually run out of energy and collapse into dust."

Emily couldn't dispute his words. She *knew* they were true.

Aurelius changed the subject, suddenly. "Do you have any long-term plans?"

"No," Emily said.

It wasn't something she had thought about, despite spending over two years in the Allied Lands. Everyone seemed to expect she would go back to Zangaria after graduation and take up her post as Baroness, then become Alassa's closest advisor when the Princess succeeded her father and took the throne. Quite a few people who remembered Alassa's time as a royal brat had been very pleased with even the slightest prospect of her having an advisor who couldn't be intimidated.

But there were other prospects. She was tempted to join Lady Barb in doing what she could for the common folk, or apply to become a tutor at Whitehall, or even try to become a librarian. And then there were all the innovations she planned to introduce through Imaiqah's father. She certainly had gleaned a few other ideas from Aurelius's books that she intended to use, once she returned to Whitehall. One of them would make banking a much more viable option.

"I ask because what I am about to show you will automatically bar you from becoming a healer," Aurelius said. "You will not be able to take advanced training, let alone apprentice with a qualified healer. They will ask you to swear certain things, and you will be unable to do so."

Emily considered it. Healing was *not* one of her strong subjects, even though Lady Barb had taken it in her first year. Mistress Granite hadn't been any better for her, she had to admit; it was clear that all tutors who tried to take Healing rapidly started snapping at their charges for even the slightest mistake. Lady Barb was respected by most of her students, but she certainly wasn't *liked*. Emily knew, without false modesty, that she had barely scraped through the Second Year exam. It was unlikely she would ever be a healer.

"I don't think I could be a healer," Emily confessed. She *liked* helping people, but she couldn't master the more complex spells. "Will it bar me from anything else?"

"No," Aurelius said. He took a breath. "Do you want to learn what I have to show you?"

Emily nodded, with some trepidation.

"Are you aware," Aurelius asked, "that the power to *heal* is also the power to *kill?*"

"Yes," Emily said, flatly. On Earth, doctors always made the worst criminals. The Allied Lands insisted on healers taking certain oaths before they practiced. Even so, Lady Barb had admitted once, there was plenty of scope for abuse. "You could kill someone without leaving a trace."

"There's more than that," Aurelius said. He met her eyes. "Healing can create... *obligations* between the healer and his client. To save a life can entail the highest of debts. The most potent of spells can have the strangest effects on both parties. Healers take oaths to forswear all such debts forevermore."

It dawned on Emily, suddenly, that he found the conversation as awkward as she did.

"I understand," she said.

"I doubt you do," Aurelius said. "These spells have been used for dreadful purposes in the past. And *you* won't be taking the oaths to prevent abuse."

He took a ragged breath. "But you need to know them," he said. "How were Necromancers killed before you arrived on the scene?"

"Poison," Emily said. No one had gone into details. Her eyes narrowed as she recalled just how inhuman Shadye had become, before his death. Had he still been human enough to be poisoned? "How...?"

"That is what I am about to show you," Aurelius said. "And others, too, if you wish it."

Emily stared down at her hands. The knowledge sounded dangerous—and she already knew far too many secrets. But she was also tempted. She'd been lucky with both Shadye and Mother Holly... and she wouldn't get lucky again, not like that. What if she had to trigger a colossal explosion in the middle of a city? Thousands of innocents would die at her hands.

And what, a nasty little voice asked at the back of her mind, *if it's a choice between killing them quickly, or allowing a Necromancer to use them as a power source?*

"Teach me," she said.

"Very well," Aurelius said. "This is a basic charm for healing the body—with a nasty little twist."

It was several hours before Emily stumbled back up the stairs and out into the corridors, cursing her own curiosity under her breath. Aurelius hadn't been joking when he'd said that some of the spells were very dangerous. If she'd realized just how *dark* some of them actually were, even though they were supposed to heal a mortally-wounded person, she would have had second thoughts. But she couldn't lose the knowledge now. One charm, one complex healing charm, would kill at her command. Another would slowly drain the victim's magic until they were left a powerless husk. A third would leave a dead body with no trace of any cause of death. Even a trained healer would be unsure of just what had happened to the victim.

And there was one she knew she didn't dare use. The obligations she would assume from using the spell were just too high.

Nanette nodded to her as she entered Raven Hall, but said nothing. Emily had no idea why the Head Girl stayed up, now she knew Emily was visiting the Administrator. It didn't look as though any of the other girls were out of bed, although Emily had heard that Helen and Rook had managed to get out of the Hall and roam the corridors for hours last week before being caught. The old tradition was still carried on.

Emily nodded back to Nanette, then slipped into her own bed and glanced at Frieda. The younger girl was sleeping, her face oddly relaxed in the semi-darkness. Emily felt a surge of affection that surprised her. She had never had a real sister, but she was starting to think of Frieda as a little sister who needed love and protection.

She smiled to herself, then activated the privacy wards. She was too tired to undress, so she lay down and closed her eyes. Sleep came quickly...

But her dreams, for the second time since she had arrived at Mountaintop, were dark and fearsome. And she knew, by mentioning knowledge that couldn't have come from the Allied Lands, that she might well have made a deadly mistake.

Chapter Twenty-Two

THE NEXT MONTH WENT BY FASTER THAN EMILY WOULD HAVE IMAGINED POSSIBLE, LARGELY because of her workload. There was no shortage of work from her tutors, then she had private lessons with Aurelius and Robyn and - finally - she had to practice spells and alchemy with Frieda.

Teaching was more difficult than Emily had ever imagined. She'd never really understood just how difficult it could be to truly understand a subject until she'd started teaching Frieda, but doing so had encouraged her to look back at her first lessons so she could remember how she'd been taught. It was a great deal easier to teach Frieda once she had a thorough understanding of the basics, and why they worked.

She'd asked Aurelius why the basics weren't covered thoroughly at either Whitehall or Mountaintop, and the older magician had pointed out that the Allied Lands needed practical magicians far more than it needed researchers. What she had been taught would suffice to make her a well-rounded magician when she graduated, but if she wanted to learn more she would have to apprentice herself to a master or hire a private tutor. It was an odd reflection of the somewhat skewed reaction the Allied Lands had to the looming threat of the Necromancers, but it made a certain kind of sense. She couldn't help finding it more than a little annoying, though. It was quite possible she wouldn't be able to progress in certain subjects without additional training.

Classes grew no easier, with the possible exception of Alchemy. Zed kept tutoring her in private and rarely said anything to her in class, apart from commenting on her latest disaster and helping her pass through the problematic stage. Some of the other students were actually starting to produce usable mixtures, although Zed cautioned that they weren't always stable and, as such, couldn't be trusted by builders and Wardmasters. The students didn't seem to mind. Two months of hard effort, punctuated with explosions, trips to the infirmary and harsh punishments for carelessness had finally started to pay off. Emily envied them and redoubled her own efforts. It still galled her that she wasn't doing as well as some of the others.

The real surprise had been Frieda. Their second lesson had been almost perfect; Frieda had mastered a series of charms without using her wand, while Emily had practiced breaking the freeze spell time and time again. She was uneasily aware that Frieda was hardly the strongest or most practiced of magicians–the spell, if cast by a tutor, might hold her anyway–but she was definitely making progress at casting spells without moving her hands. She'd also tried to cast other spells, only to discover it was far harder. Only the dispelling spell worked perfectly without a proper target.

And then Frieda had started teaching other students.

Emily hadn't realized it was happening until she'd seen several more wands snapped, and then left abandoned in waste bins. There was a standing order that all broken wands were to be handed in to the tutors–presumably to stop students realizing that they were little more than small sticks of wood–but no one seemed to be upset about losing the wands.

"I was teaching a few of my friends," Frieda confessed. "They can all cast spells without using wands now."

She swallowed, then went on before Emily could say a word. "*Please* don't tell anyone," she said. "I'll do anything..."

"Just... just be careful," Emily said. She wasn't sure what to make of it. "Whatever you do, be careful."

She was still mulling over the problem when she entered Mountaintop's library. It was strange compared to Whitehall's, but in some ways she found it more useful. Where Whitehall had one large chamber crammed with bookshelves, Mountaintop had hundreds of tiny compartments, each one filled with books divided by subject and year group. It was actually better-organized than Whitehall's library, Emily had to admit, but the librarians were stricter with the students and she'd had to appeal to Aurelius before she'd been allowed access to all of the compartments. But it was a dream come true in many ways. There were books on the shelves she hadn't been able to read at Whitehall.

She was sitting in one of the reading rooms, devouring a huge tome on ward-crafting, when she heard a cough and looked up. Nanette was standing there, seemingly torn between amusement and annoyance. Emily flushed in embarrassment. How long had Nanette been waiting for Emily to notice her presence?

"I'm sorry," she said, closing the tome. She didn't want Nanette looking over her shoulder as she read, although she was fairly sure the librarians were monitoring her choice of books. "I was miles away."

"I could tell," Nanette said, dryly. "Did you not hear the shouting?"

Emily frowned. "What shouting?"

"I'll take that as an answer," Nanette said. She folded her arms under her breasts. "Your Shadow is in some trouble, and your presence is requested."

"In trouble?" Emily repeated. She stood and returned the books to the trolley. The librarians had threatened baleful polymorphs to anyone to dared return a book to the bookshelves without permission. Given how many problems poorly-shelved books caused librarians, it was hard to blame them. "What happened?"

Nanette's lips twitched. "Apparently, she managed to turn Ten into a rather crabby crab," she said, darkly. "It was a trick."

"Oh," Emily said. It was hard for her to feel too sorry for Ten, who'd been thoroughly unpleasant to Frieda. But then, after Emily had slapped her, Ten hadn't even *looked* at Frieda. "And why?"

"I would hardly presume to guess," Nanette said, archly. "But I would advise you to handle the matter, as you *did* make your feelings clear on anyone else harming Frieda."

Emily nodded and followed Nanette through the twisting maze of corridors and book compartments, then down the stairs towards the dorms. Mountaintop didn't seem to alter its interior, unlike Whitehall, which was a blessed relief. The darkness alone made it hard to navigate, particularly when there were only one or two light globes in the corridor. Whatever spells they used to create the darkness, Emily had to admit, they were very effective. She frowned as she saw the proctor standing at the edge of Raven Hall. Had Frieda run afoul of one of them?

"Emily," Helen said, as soon as Nanette led Emily into the hall. "Your Shadow turned mine into a crab!"

"I know," Emily said. She hesitated, then asked the next question as delicately as she could. "Did you manage to turn her back?"

"Yes," Helen said. "But... you have to do something about this!"

Emily eyed her, blankly. "About what?"

"Some of the Shadows are revolting," Nanette said. There was a faint hint of amusement in her voice. "Or more revolting than usual. I've had several referred to me over the past week for fighting and hexing in the corridors."

"I thought that was an old school tradition," Emily said. She allowed her voice to harden. "Or does that only apply when the victims are unable to defend themselves?"

Nanette didn't bother to argue. "I would suggest that you... *deal* with Frieda," she said, sharply. "This isn't the time for the Shadows to find their wings."

"And Ten was badly shocked," Helen added. "She was just putting on her shoes, and *poof!*"

"I'll speak to Frieda," Emily said, tiredly. "But shouldn't you speak to Ten?"

"I will," Helen promised.

"And shouldn't the other Patrons," Emily asked Nanette, "have a word with their Shadows, too?"

"It will be done," Nanette said. "You speak to Frieda. I will speak to the rest of Raven Hall later tonight. This situation is growing beyond a mere joke."

Emily swallowed several responses that came to mind—starting with the suggestion that encouraging teenagers to play practical jokes on one another with magic wasn't always a bright idea, particularly when half of them had an overburdened sense of entitlement—and walked through the door into the sleeping chamber. Several beds were surrounded by privacy wards, but others were almost gleefully unshielded, as if the occupants were looking forward to listening to whatever Emily had to say. Emily glowered as she walked up to her bed and looked down at Frieda. The girl looked nervous, but defiant.

At least she didn't kill Ten, Emily thought, remembering just how close she'd come to killing Alassa. *There's that to be grateful for, at least.*

She stepped up and cast a series of privacy wards. The air thickened, just enough to keep peeking eyes from seeing anything. Emily sighed to herself—schoolchildren everywhere seemed to take unholy glee in hearing about their fellows being punished—then sat down beside Frieda. The younger girl didn't look at her.

"All right," Emily said, placing an arm around Frieda's shoulder. "What happened?"

Frieda looked at her and smiled, suddenly. "I did a few jobs for Angel," she said. "She taught me how to affix a spell to a person's shoe. Ten took hers off for the practical torture class"—PE, Emily translated mentally—"and I managed to sneak in and attach the spell before we were sent to change again. And then..."

She giggled. "It *worked!*"

"You turned her into a crab," Emily said, slowly. "Why?"

"She was being unpleasant again," Frieda said. "Just... whispering and muttering and insulting and... unpleasant."

"I'm sure she *was* unpleasant," Emily said. She rolled her eyes when she thought of Helen's outrage. Ten had cast such spells on Frieda herself. Clearly, bullying was only acceptable if done by Ten to Frieda, rather than the other way round. "But did you do the right thing?"

"She used to stick my pigtails to the chair," Frieda muttered. She looked down at the floor for a long moment. "Are you mad at me?"

Emily wasn't sure. On one hand, she didn't want to encourage Frieda to play nasty tricks on other students, no matter how much they deserved it. But on the other hand, they *did* deserve it. Ten had shown Frieda no respect whatsoever, which made it all the more likely that Frieda would want revenge, sooner rather than later. It wasn't enough to merely develop the ability to defeat open attacks. Frieda wanted to strike back at her tormentor.

A vision of Alassa's face, warped into eerie yellow stone, flashed through her mind. The prospect of something dangerous, perhaps even life-threatening, grew stronger the more students experimented with spells. Ten would want revenge, of course, and then Frieda would want revenge again and... Emily sighed, bitterly. The feud could easily get way out of hand.

"I think you should challenge her openly if you want to fight," Emily said. "How would you feel if you were putting your shoe on one moment and you were a crab the next?"

"I felt awful when I was walking down the corridor one moment and I was a frog the next," Frieda pointed out. Tears glittered in her eyes. "Where was anyone's compassion then? Or do you just want me to take it?"

Emily nodded in bitter understanding. Frieda was right. There was no point in talking about how wrong it was to hit back when the original hitter was still hitting.

"No," she said. "Just... just be careful."

Frieda nodded. "The Head Girl said you would deal with me," she said. "Why... because you defended me?"

"I think so," Emily said. "Stand up, please."

She took a breath as Frieda stood upright. The girl was still too thin, despite the potions and extra portions of food at mealtimes. There was no prospect of becoming fat anytime soon, Emily decided, as she was still painfully thin. Magic would burn up what calories didn't go towards repairing her body. She paused, unsure if she should do anything, then smacked Frieda's bottom lightly, several times. Frieda made no sound. Judging from the scans Emily had performed of her body, Frieda had almost certainly endured much worse long before she discovered she had magic.

"If anyone asks, tell them I beat you to within an inch of your life," Emily said, darkly. She knew a couple of spells that could produce bruises, without causing any actual pain. "Pretend it hurts to sit down."

Frieda giggled.

"And don't try to show off your wounds to anyone," Emily added.

"I'm not a *boy*," Frieda protested. "I wouldn't do *that*."

"Glad to hear it," Emily said. She motioned Frieda to her bed, then sighed. "And I would prefer not to have to do this again."

She looked up as the wards shook, suggesting that someone wanted to talk to her. Bracing herself, she stood and stepped through the wards, rather than taking them down. Nanette lifted an eyebrow when she saw Emily appear—she had probably not expected Emily to waste energy by leaving the wards in place—and waited.

Emily sighed. "Frieda deserves some privacy right now," she said. God knew she'd never wanted company after the first time she'd been punished. "And the matter has been dealt with, I think."

"Good," Nanette said. "There's a gathering in my office. Go now."

Emily sighed again, but did as she was told. Inside the office, all of the Third Year girls from Raven Hall and half of their Shadows had gathered, looking around nervously. None of them quite seemed to know what was happening, although one of the Shadows was rubbing her cheek where there was a nasty bruise. Emily looked past her to Rook and scowled, inwardly. Slapping someone's face could be dangerous even with healing magic.

Hypocrite, she told herself. Hadn't she slapped *Ten*?

Nanette slipped into her office and closed the door behind her. "I have heard from the Administrator," she said, bluntly. "The School Administration is quite upset about the recent outbreak of violence in the halls."

That was quick, Emily thought.

Or had there been more incidents she hadn't noticed? It was quite likely; she rarely paid any attention to anyone outside her year, apart from Frieda. The older students weren't encouraged to take any interest in younger students, apart from Shadows. They had reputations to maintain.

"They have... *requested* that we all keep a sharp eye on our Shadows," Nanette continued, carefully. She was treading on toes, Emily knew, even though she was the Head Girl. "Furthermore, in order to ensure that the students continue to learn the standard curriculum, First Years are now forbidden to use the spellchambers without supervision. There will also be dire penalties for any First Years who use magic in the corridors, with the single exception of light globes."

Emily bit her lip to keep herself from commenting. Claudia, surprisingly, was less restrained.

"Do these laws apply to *all* First Years," she asked, "or merely to the ones without family connections? Because, if it's the former, I can imagine a great many people being *thoroughly* upset at the decision. Their children have been taught to use magic properly from a very early age."

Nanette gave her a sharp look. "I would urge you to take that up with the Administrator," she said. Her voice dripped sarcasm. "I am absolutely *certain* that he will be interested in hearing *your* advice on how to run *his* school. It has been *years* since a student was publically flogged in the Great Hall."

Claudia scowled, but said nothing.

"To answer your question," Nanette continued, "the decree applies to all First Year students, without exception. Yes, I *know* the Great Houses will be upset. Their children"–her voice hardened–"gain an important part of their education by practicing spells in the corridors on unsuspecting or helpless victims. But this problem has gotten out of hand."

Emily remembered Shadye's attack on Whitehall, or the Mimic's steady consumption of staff and students, and wondered if Nanette knew what it was like to have a problem *really* get out of hand.

"You are to impress on your Shadows the importance of following these rules," Nanette cautioned. "There's a good chance that you may be blamed for any misbehavior on their part. I..."

"But that isn't *fair*," Olive said. She'd never said much to Emily, once she'd discovered that Emily didn't like *Ken* and hadn't played for any team at Whitehall. Outside classes, she was as obsessive about games as Alassa. "My Shadow doesn't *listen* to me. I can't be blamed for her misbehavior!"

"Then you have authority to *make* her listen," Nanette snapped. "Or do you think they merely assigned you a servant and nothing else?"

She fixed Olive with a look that made the younger girl take a step backwards. "I know Emily is new to our ways," she added. "But you were raised by a Great House. You should know your obligations as well as your rights. Take the girl in hand, teach her how to behave and take whatever steps necessary if she refuses to listen to you."

There was an uncomfortable pause. "This is a serious situation," she concluded, addressing everyone. "The tutors are out for blood. Don't give them the opportunity to take it from you. Go."

Emily turned and hurried out of the office, along with the other girls. It didn't bode well for the future, she knew, if what she suspected was true. The powers-that-be were responding to Frieda teaching spells and other forms of magical knowledge to the other Shadows. Emily wondered, suddenly, just how quickly the spells were spreading. If Frieda taught two people, then the three of them taught two more people each, and then the five of them... the spells might spread very rapidly. Hell, Frieda could concentrate on learning from Emily while her friends taught their other friends...

But they can't if they aren't allowed in the spellchambers, she thought, grimly. The ban on magic in the corridors was bad enough–at least they were allowed to make light globes–but the spellchambers were the only places they could practice. *They'd learn the theory; they wouldn't be able to practice.*

She pushed back the privacy wards and stepped through. Frieda was lying on her bed, reading a book with the aid of a spell. Emily smiled at her, then sat down on her bed and started to explain.

"I'll stay with you in a spellchamber," she concluded, "but you have to be careful. Your activities have been noticed."

"I don't care," Frieda said, defiantly. "This is something we *need* to do."

Chapter Twenty-Three

Y OU'RE DOING WELL IN YOUR STUDIES," AURELIUS SAID, AS THEY MET ONCE AGAIN IN HIS office. "But are you ready for the exams?"

Emily sighed. She hadn't seen Aurelius much over the last couple of weeks. He'd been occupied with the Sixth Year students, according to Nanette. She'd actually been starting to wonder if he'd decided to let her finish her exams before he taught her anything else, but he'd called her into his office a week before the exams were due to begin.

She gritted her teeth, feeling doom looming over her shoulder. She hated exams. Unlike Whitehall, Mountaintop had three sets of exams for each year, placed at the end of each trimester. If the exams hadn't been remorselessly practical, she would have wondered if the tutors used them to torture their students rather than check on just how many skills they'd learned over the past few months. As it was, the classes were getting even harder and the tutors were snapping at their students for the slightest hint of misbehavior.

"I think so," she said, slowly. "Do these exams count?"

"Of course they do," Aurelius said. He sipped his drink thoughtfully. "If you pass, you can move on to the next semester with a clean slate; if you fail, you have to spend the holidays making up for your failures."

"I see," Emily said. "And what happens if I fail completely?"

"We will be very disappointed in you," Aurelius said. "And you might have to repeat the year from scratch."

Emily sighed. Both Whitehall and Mountaintop placed more of a premium on exams than schools on Earth, but their exams seemed to be much better at gauging a student's actual progress rather than how much they could memorize for the exams and then forget afterwards. Failing an exam also carried serious consequences; she'd known students forced to repeat entire years at Whitehall. And failing the final sets of exams could be disastrous.

Aurelius placed his cup on his desk and leaned forward. "There's a more important reason I called you here today," he said. "Are you aware that many of our students will be going home for the holidays?"

"No," Emily said. Whitehall's students rarely left the building over the holidays between semesters. "Does that include the Shadows?"

"I believe that many of them will be going with their Patrons," Aurelius said. "The point, Lady Emily, is this. Do *you* want to go home?"

He meant Void's Tower, Emily realized after a moment's shock, rather than Earth. She had her castle in Cockatrice, but it didn't really feel like home, not compared to Whitehall itself. It was a tempting thought, she had to admit, yet it would also get her out of Mountaintop when the school would be almost empty, allowing her to explore at will. And besides, she didn't want to leave Frieda alone. Her Shadow had nowhere to go.

"I would prefer to stay and carry on with my studies," she said, casting a longing look towards the small library. "A break from classes would let me catch up with my reading."

Aurelius smiled. It had to be the right answer.

"I dare say that can be arranged," he said. "You'd do well to speak to Nanette about sleeping and eating arrangements over the holidays, but as you're a Third Year there won't be too many differences. And some of the tutors will remain in the school too."

Emily frowned. The tutors had definitely grown worse over the last few weeks, either because of the exams or the constant prank war in the corridors, no matter what edicts were issued by the administration. Professor Clifton had actually turned up to one class roaring drunk, while Mistress Granite had handed out detentions to her entire class after someone made a very off-color joke and everyone sniggered at the wrong time. Emily suspected the old lady had been rather more than just a little furious with all of them. The detention, which had involved cleaning the floors with toothbrushes, had been ghastly.

"I'm glad to hear that," she said, neutrally.

"I wouldn't have been glad at your age," Aurelius said, wryly. "The idea of being constantly watched would have been horrific."

He smiled, then sobered. "I shall make arrangements for you to stay over the holidays," he said. "You will be welcome, of course, to keep using my library. Or the main library."

"Thank you," Emily said.

"And that leads to a different point," Aurelius said, slowly. "Did you *have* to supervise the Shadows in the spellchambers?"

Emily had been expecting the hammer to fall for weeks. Indeed, she'd been rather surprised when *no one* had commented on it. Assuming Mountaintop's students were monitored as closely as Whitehall's, Aurelius and his staff should have a very good idea what the Shadows were doing and who was supervising them. Emily had honestly started to wonder if their forbearance was actually a tacit form of approval. Their *job* was to turn out strong magicians, after all.

"Yes, sir," she said. "Your edict did say they couldn't use the spellchambers without supervision."

"It did," Aurelius agreed. His voice was flat. "But did you consider the problems involved in teaching them different spells?"

"I thought that I was *meant* to help my Shadow learn," Emily said. Verbal fencing had never pleased her, if only because no one came right out and said what they meant. But she suspected she understood what Aurelius was doing. He was trying to pressure her into stopping it without actually *ordering* her to stop it. "That is precisely what I have been doing."

"True, true," Aurelius agreed. "But it is also upsetting the school's society."

Emily felt her temper start to fray. "Are you saying," she snapped, "that you actually approve of well-born students picking on common-born students? Because that's exactly what you had before I started teaching Frieda how to defend herself properly."

Aurelius looked awkward, his eyes downcast. He was caught between two different problems, she realized. "Our purpose is to teach the Shadows how to fit into our world," he told her. "It isn't so easy if they are already resistant to authority."

"I'm sure you could still teach them if you treated them decently," Emily said, wondering if she was about to get into real trouble and not quite caring. "They're living, breathing people, sir, not slaves or animals. Or is it just easier to come down on the Shadows than the students who bully them?"

She took an angry breath. "I don't *like* bullies, sir," she added. "And bullying is a very bad habit. Those students you allow to bully, those students who think that bullying is acceptable, will eventually pick on someone much bigger than themselves. And then they will die."

Aurelius scowled. "You do realize that *you* could be held accountable for their behavior?"

Emily's temper snapped. "And who will be held accountable for the bully's behavior?"

She recalled Sergeant Miles talking, once, about Sergeant Harkin, at the funeral they'd held for him after Shadye had attacked Whitehall. There was a fine line, he'd said, between forcing a student to grow stronger through adversity and outright bullying. It helped when the student had volunteered to be turned into a soldier, or a combat magician, but the line could still be crossed quite by accident. Emily had learned through adversity, through Alassa's attempts to bully her, yet she'd had more self-confidence than Frieda in *her* First Year. And, given how beaten down she'd been at the time, *that* was quite worrying.

"This isn't forcing them to learn to defend themselves," she said. "They don't even have the training to know where to *start* defending themselves. I had to teach them."

"You didn't answer my question," Aurelius said. "You do realize that *you* could be held accountable for their behavior?"

Emily glared at him. "If that's the price of doing the right thing," she said, eying the cane hanging from the wall, "I will gladly pay it."

"Your father would be proud," Aurelius said. There was a quiet amusement in his voice that puzzled her. Whose side was he actually on? "But I would advise you to be careful. You already have one pack of enemies on the other side of the mountains. I don't think you need any more."

Emily shrugged. Her innovations had earned her enemies throughout the Allied Lands, she knew, starting with guildsmen whose livelihoods had been upset by her work. The whole concept of enemies had been an abstract concept to her until she'd arrived in the Nameless World and made some deeply personal enemies. Zed probably spent days considering how best he could poison her, for one; many of the others were dead. She found it hard to care about new ones.

She toyed with the bracelet on her wrist, thoughtfully. In one sense, Aurelius was right; she didn't need more enemies. But on the other... she'd enjoyed teaching, more than she'd expected. She wasn't about to give it up for her own safety.

Aurelius gave her an odd smile. "I see you will not be dissuaded," he said. "Very well."

He settled back in his chair, sipping his drink.

Emily felt perplexed. Just whose side was he *on*? She'd been nerving herself up for punishment, either the cane or a thoroughly unpleasant detention, but he seemed to have dismissed the matter completely. Why?

She forced herself to sit back and sip her drink, waiting to see what he said next. It was quite possible he was merely trying to manipulate her into giving up without pressuring her... or that he secretly approved of what she was doing and wasn't actually planning to do anything effective to stop her. If he genuinely wanted more capable magicians...

She forced herself to relax, then watched him. She'd long since mastered the art of watching someone without making it obvious–her stepfather had forced her to learn–although she suspected he knew she was watching him. His face seemed to twitch between amusement, irritation and an odd desperation that made no sense at all. Why would he be *desperate*? He could remove Emily from Mountaintop any time he liked. Or he could try to find a way to force her to stop teaching the Shadows...

"Emily," Aurelius said slowly, "how do you *know* about how girls grow up?"

Emily blinked in surprise, thrown by the sudden change in subject. "I *am* a girl," she pointed out, puzzled. "I've lived through it."

"I suppose you would have done," Aurelius said, sardonically. His voice softened, but there was a hint of something else, something anxious, in his tone. "I meant... how did you know about girls having problems with coming to terms with the changes in their bodies?"

"I had problems," Emily said. "I think all girls have problems."

She had a nasty feeling she'd made a terrible mistake. The Allied Lands wasn't big on acknowledging any kind of mental disorder. And some of what she'd said was known on Earth, but not in the Allied Lands. Hell, it was quite possible that anorexia and body-image problems were First World issues. She'd certainly never heard of any girls from older times suffering from such issues... and *they'd* often had better excuses. The threat of being married off as soon as they developed their periods would have been enough to deter any of them from wanting to grow up.

Aurelius studied her for a long moment. "What makes you think that *all* girls have such problems?"

"Our bodies change more than male bodies," Emily said. She couldn't recall hearing of any boys suffering from anorexia. *They'd* always seemed more eager to grow into adulthood than girls. "We bleed, we suffer mood swings, we grow breasts and start preparing for childbirth... how many boys go through that, sir?"

She felt herself flushing and looked down at the ground. There was, as far as she could tell, no physical difference between a person born on Earth and a person born on the Nameless World. Alassa had some modifications worked into her genetic code–the Royal Bloodline–but she was still *human*. Logically, they should have the same problems–or at least the same potential for problems.

"None of us," Aurelius said, flatly. His voice went completely emotionless. "How do you overcome it?"

"You can't," Emily said. "I think you just have to endure. Knowledge helps."

She sighed. Her mother had never taught her about how her body would change as she grew older. If she hadn't been taught some information at school—and picked up even more from books and the Internet—she might have had some problems when she started puberty. And then her stepfather had started *looking* at her. Perhaps, if she'd had the option, she would have chosen to try to starve herself too. But she'd been dancing on the verge of starvation for far too long in any case.

"Your father didn't look for a cure?" Aurelius said. "Or something to help you survive?"

Emily's eyes narrowed in sudden understanding. He was talking about helping a child magician survive puberty. If Void had managed to discover a way to do just that, she realized in horror, and kept it to himself, the remainder of the magical community would be *furious*. How many children had been condemned to death because they'd grown into their teens, doomed by their own powers? But Void hadn't found anything, she knew all too well. Emily had survived reaching her teens because she'd had no powers at the time.

"I didn't develop magic until I was sixteen," Emily said, quietly. "I don't think my father did anything to prevent it."

"You had a standard education," Aurelius said. His voice was still flat. "I can tell you didn't develop powers as a child."

He paused. "But your father didn't develop anything?"

"Not as far as I know," Emily said, which was perfectly true. But somehow she couldn't really see Void raising a child. "I certainly don't think he did anything to me."

Something clicked in her mind. "The girl in the crystal," she said. "Whose child is she?"

Aurelius's face darkened in sudden anger. "Get out," he snapped. Magic flared around him as he lost control of his powers. "Now!"

Emily stared at him, suddenly feeling very slow and stupid. The girl was Aurelius's child, she had to be. And she'd taunted him with the prospect of something that would save her life. She would have happily slapped herself if she could take back the last few minutes of their conversation. The waves of magic spiralling around him were getting worse... Emily started to stand up, only to freeze when she sensed the full force of his presence for the first time. He *was* a terrifyingly powerful magician.

The Grandmaster might be a match for him, she thought, feeling like a rabbit looking up at a hawk, knowing that it might drop out of the sky at any moment, claws extended. *I...*

Aurelius glared at her. "Get out," he repeated. "*Now!*"

He made a gesture with his hand. Emily suddenly found herself flying through the air, then out the door and into the lobby, where she was unceremoniously dropped on the stone floor. She picked herself up off the floor, just in time to hear something smash against the wall inside his office before the door slammed shut.

Shaking, she leaned against the wall and waited for her heart to stop racing. It took her long moments to become aware of her sweat-soaked body again.

Idiot, she told herself, as she struggled to stand upright. *You utter idiot!*

Somehow, she managed to force herself to walk out into the darkened corridor. She was shaking so badly it took her several tries to generate a light globe; once she had, she followed it back to Raven Hall.

I've never seen Aurelius that furious, she thought as she stumbled through the corridors. *He'll probably refuse to talk to me again.*

And how could she blame him if he ordered her to go back to Whitehall after the exams?

You should have more concern for other people's feelings, a voice nagged at her. *Or didn't you realize that King Randor isn't exactly a normal father?*

Emily stumbled into the hall and staggered towards her bed. Nanette was sitting on *her* bed, reading a book; her eyes went wide when she saw Emily. She opened her mouth to say something, but Emily shook her head and erected privacy wards around her bed before the Head Girl could say a word. Frieda was, thankfully, sleeping—and snoring lightly. Emily pulled off her dress and fell into bed without bothering to don a nightgown. She felt too tired to do anything but sleep.

The following morning, Nanette cornered Emily and dragged her into her office.

"What happened?" She snapped. "And don't give me any nonsense about being punished."

"I said something stupid," Emily confessed. In hindsight, she couldn't believe how stupid she'd been. "And he threw me out of his office."

"You appear to have survived," Nanette said, dryly. "Clearly, it was something unconnected to the school, or you'd be in detention right now. But you survived."

Emily swallowed. "What should I do?"

Nanette shrugged. "I suggest you write him a note apologizing for whatever you said," she suggested. "Don't make any flamboyant gestures, I think; just write a simple apology and let him make the next move."

Emily nodded, slowly. "Is that what etiquette advises?"

"Usually," Nanette said. She frowned, meeting Emily's eyes. "What did you say to him?"

"I don't think I should tell you," Emily said. She had a feeling Aurelius would kill her for real if the news got out. "It's... personal."

"Then definitely write him a note, then stay out of his way until he calls you," Nanette said. "And *don't* tell anyone else, even your Shadow. Whatever you said had to be pretty bad."

Emily nodded. "It was," she said. Guilt nagged at her mind, mocking her. "And I feel like a bitch."

"Maybe you should," Nanette said, without sympathy. "Go eat breakfast, then write him that note. Or I won't be responsible for the consequences."

Chapter Twenty-Four

A URELIUS SAID NOTHING TO HER THAT DAY, EVEN AFTER SHE'D SENT HIM THE NOTE. NOR did he say anything as the week rolled on and exams began. Emily couldn't help feeling distracted by worry and guilt, even as she walked into the first examination room and saw Mistress Granite eying her with a gimlet eye and an utterly unforgiving expression. She would have sooner walked through Blackhall stark naked, without her magic, than endure the oppressive silence. If Nanette hadn't advised her to keep her distance, she would have gone to Aurelius and apologized in person.

By the time the exams finally came to an end, she was tired, depressed and not in the best of moods. The departure of almost all of the students from Raven Hall was definitely something of a relief. Nanette seemed to spend most of her time elsewhere, leaving Emily and Frieda alone. Emily would have liked the relative solitude if she hadn't been so worried about how badly she'd screwed up. Any hope of getting information out of Aurelius seemed to be completely gone.

At least Frieda doesn't seem to have noticed anything, Emily told herself. *But even if she did, what could she say?*

"I think it's time we went exploring," she said, to Frieda. The younger girl had been enjoying the break too, mainly practicing spells while Emily researched other countermeasures to the freeze charm. "Have you been in the lower tunnels?"

"I thought we weren't allowed to go there," Frieda said. "It's forbidden, isn't it?"

Emily shrugged. She'd asked at the quarrel and they'd said it wasn't forbidden, merely dangerous. Like so much else, Emily suspected, it was only forbidden if they were actually *caught*. Besides, she'd explored the woods and mountains around Whitehall. It was only fitting that she explored the tunnels of Mountaintop.

"I'm going to go," she said. She pulled off her dress, replacing it with trousers and a shirt designed for hard or dirty work. Once she had changed, she cast a series of spells to locate any tracking hexes that might have been attached to her person. There didn't seem to be any, as far as she could tell. "Come with me if you want."

She wasn't surprised when Frieda jumped up and started to change into her own work clothes. The change in the younger girl was astonishing; she'd moved from being frightened of Emily to being capable of actually sticking up for herself. Emily had a private feeling that Ten probably regretted it more than anyone else, even though she was probably getting private lessons from Helen, too. Frieda wouldn't forgive Ten in a hurry.

Outside, the darkened corridors seemed more oppressive than ever. Emily led the way towards the edge of the settled tunnels, keeping a careful eye out for tutors and proctors. The majority of teachers seemed to have left Mountaintop, but the remainder appeared to think that anyone who had stayed over the holidays was in desperate need of something to do. Nanette had warned her that they had a habit of prowling the corridors, looking for volunteers, and made it very hard for anyone to refuse to help. Emily had thought she was exaggerating, but Frieda had confirmed it was true. She'd been caught out, more than once, during the preparatory year.

They reached the edge of the school without incident and paused inside the gate. Emily had expected to have to pick the lock, but there was nothing more than a simple bolt, easily undone with magic. Given how many horror stories she'd been told about what lurked in the deeper tunnels, it seemed more than a little insecure. Emily puzzled over it, then understood once she stepped through the gate and the rune on her chest started to burn. There was an entire network of wards and runes covering the entrance, keeping out everyone who didn't have permission to enter. The spellwork was actually surprisingly elaborate compared to Whitehall's defenses. She didn't understand why they didn't use simpler spells.

"I can feel them," Frieda said. She looked scared for the first time in weeks. "Is that normal?"

"I think so," Emily said.

She frowned, studying the ebb and flow of the magic. The subtle magic seemed to be a variant on the magic she'd sensed earlier, just stronger. It hinted there was nothing to see through the gate, nothing worth visiting... anyone who looked at it without defenses, she realized slowly, might just walk past the entrance to the school without ever knowing it was there. She had a feeling it would work on supernatural vermin as well as human beings.

"This is something new," she said, carefully casting a marker spell. "You see, we don't have any maps of the tunnels and we could easily get lost down there. So..."

She demonstrated the spell for Frieda, then showed her how to mark her way. "The spell makes it much harder to get lost," she added. "But if we lose *those* markers, we can look for other ways through the tunnels by seeking out the gate."

"Clever," Frieda said. She looked at the ground. "I never thought about becoming lost."

Emily smiled. She'd looked at maps of the tunnels in the library, but one thing had become clear very fast. No two maps agreed on what was in the lower levels, below the school. She had a feeling that relying on one of the maps would have been disastrous, while trying to determine which one was actually accurate would take far too long. Instead, she'd remembered her lessons on how to lay a trail of magical breadcrumbs. The sergeants had deliberately allowed her Martial Magic class to get lost once, just to teach them the importance of marking their path. It had taught them all a harsh lesson.

"It's common sense," she said. "Didn't you have caves near your home?"

"I was never allowed out of the village," Frieda said. "Mother always said there were monsters in the forest."

"There are," Emily said, recalling the horrific night when Lady Barb had lingered on the edge of death. She'd seen all manner of creatures then, some very dangerous, before the sun had finally risen and banished them. "But they rarely come out during the day."

She shook her head, then looked around as they walked through the downwards-sloping tunnels. The stone walls were pitted and marked by hammers and chisels, rather than the smooth walls she'd seen inside the school, while some of the ceilings were so low she had to keep her head down to avoid banging it into the rock. No one had tried to make these tunnels fit for human-sized creatures, she realized, wishing she knew more about dwarves. Everything she'd read about them suggested they hated humans and preferred to remain deep below the ground, but there hadn't been much to read.

No one is really interested in studying their culture, she thought, sourly. *I wonder if they all have beards and spend their courting days trying to discover if they're chatting up a male or a female.*

The temperature fell rapidly as they continued slipping down the long passage-way, glancing into empty caves as they moved. A faint dampness in the air puzzled her until she looked into a cave and saw an underground river at the far end, racing through the caves to an unknown destination. Emily had a nightmarish image of a person falling in, only to be swept away under the rocky walls and lost forever. It was enough to convince her not to go anywhere near the water.

She paused, suddenly, as she heard something odd in the distance, and put her hand up to stop Frieda's movement, then tapped her lips to warn the younger girl to stay quiet. They'd been able to hear dripping water for a while, but this was different. It sounded almost like *breathing.* She exchanged a glance with Frieda before they fol-lowed the sound, leaving markers as they went along, until they reached a large cave. Inside, a giant creature lay on the rocky floor and slept, snoring loudly.

Frieda started. "What... what is *that?*"

"I have no idea," Emily said, very quietly. The creature seemed humanoid, a strange cross between a lizard and a gorilla. It was definitely several times her size. As far as she could tell, it didn't have any way to get out of the tunnels either. If she had problems walking through the labyrinth, a creature *that* size would find the passages utterly impassable. "But I don't think we should go any closer."

She took a final look, then tiptoed backwards as quietly as she could. The creature snorted loudly, but didn't show any signs of being aware of their presence. Emily let herself exhale in relief as soon as they were well up the tunnel.

Carefully, they continued to explore. It rapidly became clear that there were doz-ens, perhaps hundreds, of monsters stored in the caves, all sleeping peacefully. Emily couldn't help wondering if the dwarves—or Mountaintop - had shrunk the creatures using magic, then carried them down into the caves and released the spells. Trapped, the creatures would have no choice but to sleep...

But how did they eat?

"Maybe they eat unwary students," Frieda muttered, when Emily said that aloud. "We're not the first to explore the caves."

Emily had her doubts. Whitehall and Mountaintop might take a relaxed attitude to health and safety, but she couldn't see either school being casual about allowing students to become monster snacks. Perhaps the monsters were under a form of sleeping spell that prevented them from becoming too hungry, or perhaps they were just in some form of permanent hibernation. There was no way to be sure.

She hesitated as they reached another tunnel, this one leading further down into the bowels of the earth. Part of her wanted to go on, but the other part of her was uncomfortably aware that she had lost track of time and they might already have been missed. After a moment's deliberation, she led the way down the passageway, feeling odd sensations crawl over her skin. It took her a moment to realize she was sensing a very odd form of magic.

"Curious," she said. It felt oddly familiar, yet she was sure she'd never sensed anything like it in her life. "Can you feel the magic?"

"I think so," Frieda said. She sounded disturbed. "What *is* it?"

Emily shrugged. It wasn't a ward, she was sure, or she would have sensed it blocking their path. Or she would have walked right into it and been caught. And she was fairly sure it wasn't subtle magic, although she could make out a handful of glowing runes carved into the stone walls. Her protection would have warned her if the magic had been powerful enough to be dangerous. Instead, it was just... *there*.

And it ebbed and flowed downwards, deeper into the ground. Emily stopped, reminded herself that she was here to find out the secrets of Mountaintop, then forced herself to walk down the long passageway. The magic didn't seem to grow stronger, she noted, which puzzled her. It wasn't behaving in any logical fashion, even for magic. And there was something about it that bothered her on a very primal level.

They reached the bottom of the tunnel and looked out into a giant cave. There was nothing there, as far as Emily could tell, apart from inky darkness. No, she realized slowly, that wasn't quite right. The more they walked into the cave, the lighter it grew. There was a night-vision spell on the entire cave...

She dowsed the light-globes. Here, it seemed, night-vision spells *worked*. She puzzled over it for a long moment, then froze as she saw something—something—moving ahead of her in the semi-darkness. Frieda looked equally surprised as a hooded figure came into view. Emily grabbed her, pulling her well to the side, pressing them both against the wall. She held Frieda close, feeling the girl's heartbeat thumping in her chest, as the proctor walked past them, clearly on the prowl. He stopped, his head turning from side to side, as if he had sensed some hint of their presence.

Emily braced herself, uncertain of what to do. If they were caught, they'd be in trouble, but she had a feeling they were very close to one of Mountaintop's true secrets. There might be something worse in store for them than detention if they were caught down here. She considered trying to use magic on the proctor, but she knew it would be dangerous. If the spell failed, if the proctor was powerful enough to deflect it, they'd be caught red-handed assaulting a representative of the school. She doubted *that* would be taken lightly.

The proctor remained still, as if he were sniffing the air. Emily, raised on Tolkien and Rowling, couldn't help wondering if the proctor was even *human*. There was an odd sense around the hooded figure that felt strange, at least to her. He didn't seem to be looking around for anything out of place, merely sensing magic. Emily held Frieda tightly, silently praying the younger girl wouldn't panic. The only hope of getting out of the trap alive was to wait for the proctor to either catch sight of them or decide he had imagined whatever he had sensed and move onwards. The seconds became minutes, which felt like hours...

And then the proctor turned and walked away.

Emily let out a long sigh of relief, then helped Frieda to stand upright. The younger girl had clung to Emily's shirt so hard it had almost torn. Emily grunted in pain as she realized that Frieda had actually bruised her, then caught the girl's hand and led her back the way towards the school. *That* had been far too close.

I'll have to come back down here, she thought. *Alone.*

As soon as they reached the upper levels, she cast a night-vision spell of her own. It worked, barely. There just wasn't enough ambient light around for it to work properly, she decided, remembering Sergeant Miles's warnings. The spell drained more power in absolute darkness and wasn't entirely reliable. But it worked better in the caves than it did in Mountaintop itself.

"That was a *proctor*," Frieda said once they were well away from the caves. It was the first thing she'd said since the proctor had made its appearance. "What's he doing down there?"

Emily shrugged. "I have no idea," she said, untruthfully. Given the strange stream of magic and the proctor's location, she had the feeling he was guarding something. There was probably no shortage of students who wanted to explore the caves, the dangers of being eaten notwithstanding. Hell, it was probably safer to face the monsters than having an Alchemy class with students who had a habit of making their woks explode regularly. "I think I'll be coming back here."

Frieda looked hurt. "Without me?"

"I think you shouldn't be caught here," Emily said. She paused as they approached the gate. "And..."

She broke off as another form stepped out of the shadows. "Tell me," Mistress Granite said. "Is there a reason you were prowling through the caves?"

Frieda jumped. "I..."

"We were exploring," Emily cut in, smoothly. Being caught by Mistress Granite was bad, but nowhere near as bad as being caught by a proctor, if the rumors she'd heard were true. The quarrel's older members seemed determined to scare the younger ones with horror stories, few of which made sense. "I don't believe it is forbidden."

"It is *certainly* forbidden to newcomers," Mistress Granite snapped. "And it is *also* forbidden to go exploring without telling someone where you're going. Come with me."

Emily sighed, then allowed the tutor to march them both through the corridors. It was an odd coincidence that Mistress Granite had been waiting for them here, if it *was* a coincidence. And that didn't seem likely. King Randor had taught her, in one of his few lectures on statesmanship, that anything that looked like a coincidence probably wasn't. It was almost always the sign of someone plotting.

She sighed at the memory. Alassa's father was more than a little paranoid, Emily knew, but he had good reason to be. He'd almost lost his throne, daughter and brother two years ago—and if *she* hadn't been there, he would have lost everything.

"You should know better," Mistress Granite snapped, "than to take a First Year into the unknown. You could have been trapped down there."

"Trapped by what?" Frieda asked, innocently.

Mistress Granite glowered at her, then flung open the door to one of her classrooms. It looked a mess, Emily saw in alarm; there were empty potions bottles everywhere, tables and chairs stained with blood and even several half-dissected animals lying on desks. She honestly couldn't imagine Mistress Granite tolerating her students leaving her classroom in such a state. It was so unlike her that Emily was immediately sure of what had happened.

"Some... *pranksters* thought it was a good idea to turn my classroom into a mess," Mistress Granite said. She glared at Emily, as if she held her personally responsible. "You two will clean up this room, without magic. I expect to see it spotless before you get anything to eat."

She stamped out of the room, closing the door behind her. Frieda made a rude gesture at the door as it locked, then sighed in relief.

"I thought she was going to cane us," she said. "I..."

Emily snorted. "This way, she gets us to clean up her mess," she said. It wasn't much of a relief. "What happened here?"

"A few of us decided we really disliked old stony-face," Frieda said. "Does it matter?"

"It does if I have to clear up the mess," Emily pointed out, tartly. She sighed, then started to pick up potion bottles. The empty ones would have to be washed and cleansed of magic, the half-full ones would need to be discarded. Who knew how long exposure to the air would change the magic bottled inside? "I hope it was worth it to you."

Chapter Twenty-Five

Emily had hoped that Mistress Granite's detention would put an end to the matter, but somehow, that didn't seem to be the case. While there was no formal punishment beyond the detention, she was uncomfortably aware that Nanette and the remaining staff were watching her closely after their adventure in the caves. The Head Girl had spoken to her after they had finally finished cleaning the room, and given her a sharp lecture on exploring the caves with a First Year. Emily had nodded in all the right places, but continued to make plans to return underground. She *had* to know what was hidden in the darkness.

But it was several days before she could figure out a way to get back to the caves. They'd been missed, according to Nanette, when lunch had been served and they hadn't shown up to eat. Emily had attended lunch religiously, mainly to make sure Frieda ate, and their absence had been noted. Then the staff had discovered they weren't anywhere to be found in the school, and started to search. But they hadn't searched very hard.

They didn't have to, Emily thought, as she sat in the library and consulted more old maps and guides. Nothing was consistent, nothing agreed with anything else, but there were some useful flakes of detail. *All they had to do was set a guard on the gate and wait for us to come back. There was nowhere else we could go if we wanted to get back inside.*

In the end, she found herself enlisting Frieda and a handful of her young friends, probably the ones who had redecorated Mistress Granite's classroom. It awed and humbled her just how much magic the Shadows had learned, although their grasp of the basics was still shaky. If they caused a diversion, Emily would have at least an hour to slip back into the caves and see what the proctor had been guarding. If she used night-vision spells, rather than light globes, there was a good chance she could remain undetected.

Or so she hoped.

"Don't be caught," Emily warned. "I think they're reaching the limits of their patience."

Frieda nodded, seriously. "We'll be careful," she said. "But you shouldn't be going down there alone."

"I can't take you, either," Emily said. She rose, then checked her watch. "Make them spend time chasing you instead of me."

There was no guard on the gate when she arrived, which puzzled her. A single proctor standing there would have made it impossible for her to enter the caves. Instead, there was a complex network of wards, which—she had to admit—would have stopped any normal Third Year student. Emily, however, hadn't taken Martial Magic for two years without picking up several tricks that most students didn't learn until they entered Fifth Year. Recalling what Lady Barb had taught her, she carefully worked her way through the wards and allowed them to slam closed behind her. Breaking back in would be harder, but she knew she could handle it.

The caves felt colder, this time, as she cast the night-vision spell and waited for it to take effect. They looked odder, too; there were tiny sparkles of light running through the stone she hadn't seen before, when they'd been using light globes. But then, they would have been washed away by the glow. Emily checked the spell twice, then walked down the tunnel, leaving markers as she moved, making sure they were only visible to her.

She walked down the long corridor into the big cave and waited, heart thumping in her chest, for the proctor to appear. Nothing happened. It was possible, she decided, that the proctor had sensed the light globe... or that he had simply been on patrol when he'd caught a sniff of their presence. The books she'd looked at in the main library hadn't said anything about what the proctors actually were, merely that they were the guardians of the school. It could cover a multitude of sins, Emily knew. They might be homunculi, like Whitehall's Warden, or they could be something far darker. There were just too many possibilities.

Bracing herself, she slipped onwards. It rapidly became clear to her that there must be quite a lot of traffic through the caves; there was almost no dust, while the pathways had been swept clean of rubble. Indeed, as she walked further into the network, there were no places she had to lower her head. And yet, the only thing that was completely odd about the caves were the continual streams of magic, flowing through the stone like trickles of water. Emily had never felt anything like them in her life.

But they felt disturbing. And she wasn't sure why.

The next cave was smaller, yet illuminated by an eerie green glow shimmering down from high overhead. Emily looked up, automatically, then down towards the end of the cave. A solid door—a metal door—was set firmly in the stone, covered with so many runes that it practically *crackled* with subtle magic. Emily thought, for a hellish moment, that the rune on her chest was going to catch fire. The pain was so intense that it almost sent her to her knees before she managed to stumble back, away from the magic.

Shit, she thought, fighting down a whimper. There was so much subtle magic in the air that she had a feeling it was actually counterproductive. Indeed, it was reinforced by a dozen passive wards designed to keep out everything from teleportation to long-range magical spying. Most of them felt *old*, as if they had been created decades, perhaps centuries ago. Others felt much newer, even oddly familiar. Aurelius, she decided, must have had a hand in creating some of them.

She sat down and rubbed the rune as the pain slowly faded away, thinking hard. Maybe there was a reason for the seemingly lax security after all. She couldn't even *approach* the door with the rune carved on her chest—and if she hadn't had the rune, she wouldn't have even been able to *see* the door. There were ways to get closer, she was sure, but she had no idea what they were.

What the hell *was* it? Even the nexus chamber in Whitehall didn't have such an intensive level of security wards layered over it.

I could ask Frieda to try to open it, she thought, then shook her head, dismissing the idea. It would just land her Shadow in more trouble... for nothing. *She* wasn't part of Emily's mission, after all. *Or I could try to walk up to it again.*

Carefully, Emily rose to her feet and walked towards the door, trying hard to disregard the subtle magic altogether. It seemed to work, for a long moment, and then the pain resumed, worse than before. Emily screamed, then nearly fell to the ground, her shirt starting to catch fire. The rune couldn't dispel so much energy...

A strong hand caught her arm and pulled her back, away from the door. Emily shuddered; her entire body felt as though it had been tossed into a fire, then looked down at her treacherous shirt. It was intact. Her head pounded unpleasantly as she realized she'd *imagined* it catching on fire, although it might well have killed her. She knew enough about how sympathetic magic worked to realize she might just have set *herself* on fire if the pain lasted much longer.

And then she looked up. A hooded proctor stared back at her.

Shit, she thought, woozily.

At first, all she saw under the hood was darkness. Or so it seemed. The faintest hint of a chin revealed itself as the proctor hauled her to her feet, took a firm grip on her arm and pulled her towards the exit. Emily started to struggle, but rapidly discovered it was useless. The proctor wasn't just stronger than her, he was surrounded by a faint glow of the same strange magic running through the tunnels. She had a feeling that any spells she tried would rebound badly.

Or was that just an illusion created by magic, too?

The pain between her breasts slowly faded as they moved away from the hidden door and advanced back up the stairs. Emily tried to parse out another way of approaching the door as she weakened, feeling her legs threatening to cave in under her, then dismissed it as the proctor dragged her bodily into the school. There must have been a signal of some kind, Emily guessed, as Nanette was waiting for her by the gate. The Head Girl looked utterly furious.

"You idiot," she snapped, as the proctor let go of Emily's arm. "Didn't you remember me telling you *not* to go into the caves?"

Emily felt too tired to say anything. She stumbled and would have fallen if Nanette hadn't reached out and caught her arm. The Head Girl said something, but Emily's head was suddenly roaring with pain, and it was all she could do to remain awake. Nanette sighed, so loudly it had to be an act, then pushed something against Emily's lips. Throwing caution to the winds, Emily sipped gratefully, ignoring the danger. The potion made her feel a little better.

"You really shouldn't have gone down there," Nanette told her, angrily. "Being caught by a proctor so far out of bounds means having to face the Administrator. You're in deep trouble."

Emily swallowed. Aurelius hadn't written a response to the note she'd sent him—or called her into his office, even though they should both have more spare time during the holidays to study the more exotic branches of magic. Instead of having a pleasant conversation, she was likely to face him in a vile mood, one not made any better by whatever the Shadows had done to cause a diversion. She nodded ruefully, then forced herself to stand upright. The potion seemed to be working well enough to allow her to walk normally.

"I'd be surprised if you weren't expelled," Nanette snapped. "Do you realize just how poorly you acted?"

"Yes," Emily said, sharply. She wanted to lie down and sleep, not face Aurelius or Nanette or anyone else. "But the caves are fascinating..."

Nanette glared at her, then frog-marched Emily towards Aurelius's office. There was hardly anyone in the corridors until they reached the office lobby, where a pair of proctors stood, half-hidden in the darkness. Emily wondered spitefully if the bar on night-vision spells was intended to allow the proctors to sneak up on students and catch them out of bounds. Nanette told her to wait while she knocked on Aurelius's door and went inside; Emily wearily studied the two proctors. It was hard to be sure, but there was enough magic swirling around them to make her think of the Warden. Maybe they *were* homunculi. It *did* make a certain kind of sense.

"The Administrator is busy," Nanette said as she stepped out of the office. "Wait here until he calls for you."

Emily nodded and leaned against the wall, trying hard to compose herself. Being caught in the caves was potentially disastrous, not only because of the risk of expulsion. They might start to wonder if she'd deliberately *allowed* herself to be kidnapped, just so they would bring her into the school. But then they would start wondering how Emily had known there was a plot to kidnap her in the first place...

It felt like hours before she heard Aurelius calling for her. She forced herself to stand upright, reminded herself that she had faced two Necromancers and a Mimic, then walked into Aurelius's office, trying to keep her head held high. The cane rested on a chair, threateningly. She could hear the sound of sobs from the next room, but there was no one else in the office apart from Aurelius himself. He looked grim.

"Lady Emily," he said. He looked down at his paperwork, refusing to meet her eyes, as she stood in front of his desk and clasped her hands behind her back. "I owe you an apology."

Emily gaped. This was *not* what she'd been expecting.

"My... family situation is a secret," Aurelius continued. "I was careful not to let anything of my personal life slip out into society. When I thought you were taunting me, I overreacted and behaved poorly. My behavior was outrageous and I apologize without reservation."

He paused, waiting for her to speak.

"I behaved poorly, too," Emily said, carefully. She'd expected a lecture, or perhaps just a stern order to bend over the chair and prepare herself for a thrashing. Instead... she found herself torn between relief and fear, fear that something was going on she didn't understand. She'd had quite enough of that at Whitehall! "I should not have spoken so casually of something so important."

"I would not dispute that," Aurelius said. He gave her a thoughtful look. "My conduct was by far the worse, Lady Emily. I am charged with raising teenagers and turning them into functional members of society. I have dealt with everything from homesickness to temper tantrums and bullying far worse than anything you have seen. I know just how stupid and thoughtless teenagers can be. But I acted badly in assuming that you were being just as thoughtless, rather than ignorant."

"I didn't act well either," Emily said. "I..."

"You're the child," Aurelius said. "I'm the adult. I should have known better."

Emily felt a hint of irritation at being called a child. The Allied Lands had a flexible concept of adulthood, one that seemed to follow cultural rules rather than Earth's more legalistic approach. On one hand, men weren't really expected to be *mature* until they were in their earlier thirties; on the other hand, they were expected to adopt adult responsibilities from a very early age. The rules for girls didn't seem much different, at least in magical society, although they were different in the mundane side of the world. But then, magic could help people avoid consequences like unplanned pregnancies and sexually-transmitted diseases.

He looked up, meeting her eyes. "My daughter is trapped forever by magic," he said. "To release her is to kill her, to have her own powers kill her. Do you know *anything* that can be used to prevent others from dying in the same way?"

Emily swallowed. "You could teach them what to expect," she said, without much hope. She'd known what was happening to her, and she'd still had problems coping with growing into a young woman. "And you could try giving them potions to moderate their growth..."

"There's no potion that will leave someone a child forever," Aurelius said. "Their minds eventually rebel against such abuse."

There were worse things to be, Emily decided, than a teenage girl in a drunkard's house. She couldn't imagine growing to adulthood, mentally, while remaining trapped in the body of a child. The thought was unimaginably horrific, even if she did have magic; she'd be treated as a child for the remainder of her life. Everyone would look at her and *see* a child. And what if she wanted to form a relationship with someone her mental age? She could easily imagine her mind collapsing into madness as it struggled to cope with her body's refusal to age.

"Maybe their aging can be enhanced, instead," she mused. "Are there potions to make someone age faster?"

"Yes, though they tend to cause other problems," Aurelius said. "It might be worth trying, though. If we were desperate."

Emily nodded. "I'll think about it, sir," she said. "But you'd be experimenting on living people."

"There would be no other way to proceed," Aurelius said. "And if it saved their lives..."

He shook his head. "You're clearly exhausted," he said. "Come back here tomorrow morning, after breakfast. We have many topics to cover."

"Yes, sir," Emily said. She took a breath. "I thought I was in trouble..."

Aurelius lifted an eyebrow. It dawned on Emily's dulled mind that he'd been quietly letting her have a way out, either because he still intended to seduce her into joining him or as a form of apology for losing his temper. But it was too late to take back her words.

"My," Aurelius said, finally. "Do you *want* to be caned?"

Emily shook her head, firmly.

"It's funny," Aurelius said, with mock thoughtfulness. "I've only ever had one person say *yes* to that question, and he was a boy who was faced with the threat of spending several weeks serving as a test subject for First Year charms. Quite understandable, I suppose. It would be better to spend a few hours with a sore bottom then risk spending weeks in the infirmary as they try to figure out how to reverse a botched charm."

He pointed a finger at the door. "Go out, get something to eat and then go to bed early," he said. His face twisted into an odd little smile. "You'll need your energy tomorrow."

Emily nodded and fled the room. Outside, she found the nearest bathroom and stepped inside, casting a privacy ward as soon as the door was closed. Undoing the top of her shirt, she looked at the rune in the mirror. It looked as though someone had recently branded her flesh, just as a rancher would brand cattle. She touched it lightly, wincing at the pain. Lady Barb had told her it would heal quickly, if it was almost overpowered, but she hadn't quite realized just what she'd meant. There was no way to remove the rune from her flesh, even if she wanted it gone. And *that* meant she couldn't approach the hidden door without permission.

And that won't be granted, she thought, as she did up her shirt. It was a bitter thought. Without the rune, she could be manipulated; with it, she couldn't complete her mission for Whitehall. *They can afford to treat me lightly. There's no way I can get through that door.*

Gritting her teeth, she took down the ward and walked back to Raven Hall.

Chapter Twenty-Six

"THEY EXPELLED LUCILLE AND PALMA," FRIEDA SAID, WHEN EMILY RETURNED TO RAVEN Hall. There was no sign of Nanette, for which she was grateful. "The Administrator told them both that wreaking havoc was just not done—and then he *expelled* them."

"I'm sorry," Emily said. She remembered Lucille and Palma, two Second Year girls with a sense of mischief that outshone anyone she'd seen at Whitehall. "What will happen to them now?"

"I don't know," Frieda said. She shifted, uncomfortably. "And I got walloped by Professor Rugerson."

"I'm sorry about that too," Emily said. "What were you trying to do?"

"I had an idea for a prank in the Great Hall," Frieda said. "They caught me before I even started laying the oil."

"I don't want to know," Emily said. She sat down on the bed and reached for a bottle of energy potion. Lady Barb had warned her, more than once, that such potions could be dangerously addictive despite the taste, but she had no choice. She just felt too tired to do anything else. "And I probably shouldn't tell you to drink this."

She passed Frieda a bottle of pain-relief potion. The younger girl glanced at it, but shook her head.

"I've had worse," she said. She paused. "Can we go back to the spellchamber?"

Emily considered it briefly. She didn't want to risk getting into more trouble, not now, not when it would be a better idea to keep her head down and wait to see what happened. But, at the same time, she knew it would be a good idea to keep practicing her own spells, as well as keeping a sharp eye on Frieda. And she enjoyed spending time with the younger girl.

"Very well," she said. "Let me go into the washroom first, all right?"

The spellchamber had been modified slightly by one of the older students, they discovered when they stepped inside. A line of humanoid puppets—Emily couldn't help thinking of them as test dummies—stood against one wall, armed with everything from swords to crossbows and even pre-charged wands. She puzzled over them for a long moment, then started to practice putting her wards in place, then extending them away from her body. It gave her a form of in-depth defense, she'd discovered, and also made it harder for the nastier hexes to latch onto her magic and start chewing through her protections.

"The shielding spell isn't very good," Frieda said, as she carefully cast the spell. A shimmering wall of magic, no bigger than a mundane shield, appeared in front of her. "Why can't it be made bigger?"

"I think it would be spread too thin if you tried to make it bigger," Emily said. The general rule for protective wards was one ward, one hex. She'd also been taught to keep moving because no protective ward could stop *everything*. "And you'd also have the risk of being too attached to it, allowing it to drain your power."

"But someone could get a hex around it," Frieda complained. "It doesn't even cover *my* body, let alone yours."

"Try not to get hit, then," Emily said. She summoned a ward of her own and tested it, lightly. "Or should I charge *you* with breaking out of the freeze spell?"

Frieda shook her head. She'd never been able to break loose under her own power. Emily wasn't too surprised. Frieda was nowhere near capable of being able to cast spells without using her hands to help focus and guide the magic.

Magical combat isn't about exchanging spells one by one, in a civilised fashion, she recalled Sergeant Miles saying, once. *Magical combat is about exhausting or defeating your opponent as quickly as possible.*

She shook her head, feeling a sudden pang of loneliness. At Whitehall, there was always someone she could talk to, be it Lady Barb or Sergeant Miles. Some of the instructors liked her more than others, but she'd never really doubted they had her best interests at heart. Even Master Tor had shown redeeming features, although it had taken her time and reflection to realize they were there. But at Mountaintop... who could she talk to? Whatever she said might well end up being used against her.

And you weren't trying to sneak around at Whitehall, either, she reminded herself. *Here, you don't want to get caught doing anything you shouldn't. Again.*

She sighed. Sneaking around at Whitehall–breaking curfew and wandering around outside the dorms at night–had been part of the fun. Alassa had encouraged her to take part, pointing out that it was good training for later life. But at Mountaintop, it was dangerous, particularly after she'd been caught in the caves. Whatever was through that door had to be deadly secret, or they would never have put so much effort into warding it. And they'd barred her path quite effectively.

There was a loud bang. Emily jumped, then realized that Frieda had tossed a spell at her. "Why did you do that?"

"You're woolgathering," Frieda told her. "Come and play if you don't have spells of your own to practice."

"Who are you," Emily muttered, "and what have you done with Frieda?"

"Pardon?"

"Never mind," Emily said. The change in the younger girl was quite remarkable; perhaps, just perhaps, her life in the mountains hadn't been as bad as Emily had thought. She'd known other children on Earth who'd had decent families, but had remained permanently on the verge of starvation. "What do you want to play?"

She looked up as the door opened. Nanette stormed into the spellchamber. "Why... why are you *here*?"

Emily frowned. "Because there's nothing else to do?"

Nanette reddened with astonishing speed. "You were caught in the caves, breaking bounds, and he let you get *away* with it?"

"Yes," Emily said, pulling herself upright. She was tired of everyone's social pretensions, more tired than she cared to admit. "I think he thought I hadn't really committed a crime."

"Beyond being stupid enough to be caught by the proctors?" Nanette snapped. "How many allowances is he going to make for you?"

"I don't know," Emily said. She suddenly felt very tired, mentally if not physically. The potion she'd drunk seemed a distant memory. "I don't understand him."

"I do," Nanette said. "He wants to be MageMaster. He wants to be the master of the school."

Her eyes narrowed. "And he thinks you can help him reach his lofty goal."

Frieda leaned forward. "And he *told* you that?"

Nanette didn't look at the Shadow. "It's obvious," she said. "What other goal would be worth playing for?"

Emily smiled. "The ultimate defeat of the Necromancers?"

Nanette glared at her. "You shouldn't be teaching any of the First Years," she said. "And I think that quite a few other tutors are growing more than a little exasperated with you. The Administrator isn't all-powerful. He can't shield you forever."

Her face lapsed into a smile. "Perhaps I should teach you something instead. I think we should test each other, don't you?"

She motioned towards the wards. "Would you care to duel?"

"I thought I wasn't allowed to duel out of class," Emily said.

Nanette smirked. "You can duel with me, if you dare."

Emily hesitated. Jade had told her, once, that he'd had to test himself against another student who had challenged his authority, back during a group exercise. Emily had thought at the time that it was another piece of macho stupidity, but he'd insisted there was a serious point to it. *She* had not been convinced. Maybe she had the legal right to beat Frieda for talking back to her, yet that wouldn't make the younger girl *wrong*. How could it?

But Nanette seemed to want to duel...

She considered it, briefly. She'd tested herself against older students in Martial Magic and, all too often, found herself wanting. They were more practiced, more capable of establishing wards and casting spells with lightning speed—and often more capable at breaking spells than Emily herself. She'd done better as she'd grown older, but she'd often found herself outmatched. Her few victories had been very hard-won.

"Why?" She asked. "What do you gain from testing yourself against me?"

"That isn't the question you should be asking," Nanette taunted. "The question is what do *you* get from testing yourself against *me*?"

It struck Emily, suddenly, that Nanette was jealous. But jealous of what? Emily's reputation? The Administrator favoring her to the point he spared her a punishment Nanette certainly believed Emily deserved? Or something else? The whole point of the duel might not be so much about testing herself than about teaching Emily a lesson. But if Nanette believed Emily to be a favored student, injuring her could be a deadly mistake. She might just seek to humiliate Emily instead.

She was tempted to decline. But part of her was reluctant to surrender so easily. And besides, she might learn more about Nanette if she faced her in a dueling ring.

"Very well," she said. She inclined her head towards the ring. "Shall we?"

Frieda coughed. "Is this...?"

Nanette waved a hand at her. Frieda froze.

"I wouldn't expect a First Year of no parentage to understand," Nanette said, as Emily glared at her. "This is for the more powerful students."

Emily followed, feeling a cold simmering anger rise in her breast. Nanette was more than just jealous, she saw now; Nanette saw Emily as a challenge to her authority. What was the point of Nanette being Head Girl, Emily asked herself, if one or more of the students was exempt from her discipline? There might be no formal rule forbidding Nanette to reprimand or punish Emily, but if the Administrator favored her...

Or was there something else going on? Nanette might come from a powerful family—it was possible that the Head Girl was selected after careful negotiations between the families, rather than the basis of merit—but there were other students from powerful families, other students who might be able to get her in trouble if they felt they had been punished unjustly. It seemed unlike the girl Emily had come to know to risk her position in a personal feud, if that was what it was. The more she looked at the tangled web of magical politics, the less she felt she understood it.

Nanette reached the other side of the dueling ring and turned to face her. "We shall fight until one of us is immobilized," she said, grandly. It would have sounded more impressive if Emily hadn't known that first blood or death duels were strictly forbidden between students, no matter the provocation. The Dueling Mistresses had warned, in no uncertain terms, that issuing such a challenge could mean instant expulsion, even if the duel was never fought. "I will count to five, then we will begin."

Emily nodded, gathering herself. Nanette had more formal training in dueling, she was sure, but—perhaps—less experience in rough-and-tumble fighting. It might just give Emily an advantage... if, of course, she managed to get her spells off in time. Nanette paused, bowed in a manner that was more mocking than respectful, then started to count.

Emily threw a standard freeze charm as soon as Nanette reached five, then followed it up with several other spells, all relatively simple. Nanette blocked them all with contemptuous ease, then started tossing spells at Emily. Emily ducked and dodged as quickly as she could, trying to make it harder for Nanette to take aim at her. There were so many spells coming her way that she knew she didn't dare take more than one or two hits. They bounced off the wards, one almost reflecting right into Nanette's face before fading into nothingness. Emily noted it in passing as she cast a more complex spell of her own. A thought nagged at the back of her mind.

She finished her charm, then yanked on the magic as hard as she could. Nanette might have protected herself against all kinds of spells, but she hadn't thought to protect her boots! She fell over backwards as Emily's magic caught hold, hitting the ground hard enough to hurt. A moment later, her boots came off, revealing oddly pockmarked feet. Emily had no time to gloat before Nanette moved her hand and hit Emily with a wave of magic, knocking her back into the wards and pinning her against them. It wasn't quite enough to win the duel outright, but it trapped her...

Emily thought fast as Nanette pulled herself to her feet, her eyes glittering with fury. Being knocked down so easily had to be a blow to her pride. Emily cast a cancelation spell, then darted to one side and generated a whole series of illusions of herself, each one running in a different direction. Unlike Shadye, Nanette was experienced enough not to fall for the illusions. Emily ducked sharply as another wave of magic spilled through the air, wiping out her doppelgangers until only one Emily was left. Moments later, she was pinned back against the wards again.

Nanette advanced on her, slowly and steadily. "Is that the best you can do?" She asked. "I expected better from someone who has killed two Necromancers."

She lifted a hand and cast a series of spells, one after the other. Emily batted them away one by one, realizing that Nanette wasn't actually *trying* to immobilize her and win, merely to force her to expend energy. She wanted Emily to become completely drained. The thought spurred her on; she gritted her teeth, allowed a transfiguration spell to strike her wards and summoned a fireball. Nanette jumped back as the fireball launched from Emily's hand and flashed towards her, narrowly missing the outer edge of her wards. It struck the far side of the dueling ring and exploded, releasing a wave of heat.

Nanette stared at her. "Are you mad?"

Emily threw two more fireballs, carefully aiming to miss. The fireball was simple and unimaginative, Sergeant Miles had taught her, but it was also the most practical of the military spells. Nanette deflected the second fireball, just in time to have Emily hit her with a ward-breaking hex. Her body shimmered with green light as the hex burned through her wards one by one, ripping the spells apart. Emily thought for a moment that she'd won, then everything went dark.

Panic gibbered at the corner of her mind as she realized Nanette had struck her blind. It was one of the prank spells that was utterly forbidden at Whitehall.

She moved to one side blindly, desperately trying to cast the counterspell. It took two tries to make it work, far too long. Nanette had freed herself from Emily's hex, probably through dumping her wards completely and starting again, and threw back something nasty of her own. Emily felt her hair try to stand on end as magic crackled around her, but her wards managed to keep the spell away from her body. And then Nanette slammed her back into the circle's wards. Again.

Emily knew she was running out of magic, yet she didn't want to lose. Bracing herself, she recalled the spellwork she'd been taught in Wards and focused her mind. There was no anchorstone here to hold the spell in place; it wouldn't last more than a few seconds, at best. But it would be long enough. She looked up at Nanette, her face twisted with a rage and bitterness Emily didn't fully understand, and triggered the spell. A wave of... *nothingness* seemed to wash out from her as the anti-magic ward did its work.

Nanette's spell–and her wards–collapsed.

Emily launched herself forward as the older girl recoiled, stunned, and slammed her fist into Nanette's nose. The older girl hadn't thought to worry about physical attack, let alone protect herself. She fell backwards, with Emily landing on top of her.

For a long moment, Emily just stared down at Nanette. Nanette seemed equally surprised.

"Well," she said, finally. "Are you going to let me up, or are you going to ravish me instead?"

Emily felt her cheeks heat with embarrassment. She was suddenly very aware of just how Nanette's body was pressing against hers. But she knew better than to just roll off her, not now.

"Concede?" Emily asked, instead. She knew better than to let someone move before they had formally surrendered. "Give up?"

Nanette smiled, surprisingly. "I concede," she said. "Although someone could argue that was dirty fighting."

Emily shrugged. "There are no laws in war," she said, quoting Sergeant Harkin. "And if you're not cheating, you're not trying."

She rolled off Nanette and stumbled to her feet. Nanette sat up; sweat stained her dark hair and blood leaked from her nose. She'd been forced to fight harder than she'd expected, Emily decided, although something continued to nag her at the back of her mind. But she was too tired to think about it, let alone decide what it meant.

"I can help you clean up," she offered, feeling a hint of guilt. "Or..."

"Don't worry about it," Nanette said. "But can I ask you a favor?"

Emily lifted an eyebrow. "You can ask," she said. "But I may say no."

Nanette smiled. "Don't tell anyone about this duel. You may discover it reflects badly on you."

"Is that *really* why you want me to keep it to myself?" Emily asked. "Out of concern for me?"

Nanette shrugged. She would be mortally embarrassed if the school found out she'd been beaten by a Third Year. Her authority would be fatally undermined. But, Emily suspected, the fireballs alone would get her in real trouble if anyone found out she'd used them in a casual duel. And they'd certainly bent the rules against dueling without supervision. They both had good reasons to keep their mouths shut.

"You don't tell anyone and I won't tell anyone," Emily said. "Agreed?"

"Agreed," Nanette said. "And I will even throw in a lesson or two for Frieda in exchange for her silence."

"Good," Emily said.

Chapter Twenty-Seven

S OMEWHAT TO EMILY'S RELIEF, NANETTE STAYED OUT OF EMILY'S WAY AS THE HOLIDAYS came to an end. She had no idea what she should say to the older girl, or even where they stood now Emily had won a duel. Frieda pointed out that Emily might well have won more than just the duel, given that it had clearly been a grudge match, but Emily wasn't interested in supervising the dorm herself. Besides, questions would definitely be asked and she didn't want to have to answer them.

Eventually, the holidays came to an end. The students returned, just as they had at the start of the year, chatting happily about their vacations. Emily half-expected one of the tutors to assign essays on what the students did on their holidays, but–instead–the workload doubled, then tripled. The exams, it seemed, had separated the students who had genuinely advanced from those who had learned nothing. Emily found herself doing something she'd thought was impossible and working harder than ever before, fighting off exhaustion when she wasn't actually in class.

She wasn't the only one. Several students received detentions for falling asleep in class, two were told to stand up in the hopes of keeping themselves awake and a number of others resorted to various potions to keep up with their workload. Emily overhead Nanette lecturing Helen and Olive on the dangers of using such potions on a regular basis before she forced them both to pour their bottles down the sink. It was a waste, Emily thought, but she understood the potential risks. No magician could afford to become addicted to potions.

By the time Aurelius called her into his office, she felt like a nervous wreck.

"The second semester is always like that," Aurelius said, as soon as she sat down. She was too tired to try to hide it. "It's our way of weeding the weak from the strong."

"I think you're just working us too hard," Emily said. The only real break she'd had had come during dueling, where the disputes between First Year students had forced the dueling mistresses to put Emily to one side as they struggled to keep the peace. "I don't know how long we can keep up this pace."

"Long enough," Aurelius said. He smiled as he sipped his drink. "It does tend to become easier at the end of the first month, normally."

Emily sighed. She was tired, cranky and her wrists ached after spending hours writing out a particularly complex edit to a paper. If the magical typewriter had worked without needing the spells to be constantly replenished... she sighed. She'd drawn out plans for a typewriter that could work without magic, but the craftsmen had yet to turn her notes into a workable design, let alone something that could be mass-produced. But once she had a typewriter, she swore to herself, she was damned if she would look back.

"I hope you're right," she said, out loud. She was too tired for a proper conversation, let alone another lesson in dubious magics. "Is there any way I can get a detention that involves sleep?"

"Not unless you have an accident with a sleeping potion," Aurelius said, dryly. "When I was a lad, we had a practical joker who used to pretend to commit suicide by drinking the wrong potion, then having us carry him out as though he were dead. The tutors didn't see the funny side."

Emily shuddered. A single mistake would have had the joker carried out as though he were dead—and he *would* be dead. She didn't blame the tutors in the slightest.

"But enough of such pleasant thoughts," Aurelius said. "I called you here to learn something that is rarely taught to anyone outside Sixth Year Healers on the cusp of apprenticeships. I think you will find it interesting."

Emily nodded, fighting down a yawn.

"You will understand," Aurelius continued, dropping into a lecturing mode, "that there is a shifting scale of magic. There are simple spells, which are very understandable, then there are subtle magics, which are tricky and difficult to control or predict. You can sometimes muster a general idea of what to expect, but the more magic you use, the less predictable the results become."

He paused, then smiled mischievously. "Let me pose a question for you," he added. "Why can we swear oaths while mundanes *can't?*"

Emily considered it, tiredly. King Randor's noblemen had sworn loyalty to him and his lineage, which hadn't stopped them from plotting to overthrow their King and place his daughter in a gilded cage, warping and twisting her mind until she was their slave. The oaths hadn't killed them for daring to contemplate treason and no amount of legalistic hair-splitting could hide the fact that they *had* done rather more than just *contemplate* treason. If Emily hadn't been there, they would have won.

"We have magic," she said. "Our magic binds our words."

"Precisely," Aurelius said. "A mundane could swear oaths all he wanted, but nothing would *enforce* the oaths."

Emily frowned. "I thought there were spells to enforce such oaths..."

"Oh, there are," Aurelius said. "Spells of obedience, spells of enforced servitude... there are hundreds of them. But they all have one great weakness. Even when accepted willingly, they are not held firmly in place without an enchanted object. And the spells can sometimes be broken, even *by* mundanes."

Emily's fingers touched her shirt where it covered the rune. She'd had to carve it herself she'd been told, to make it a *part* of her. It couldn't be removed, whatever happened. The same, she reasoned, must be true of oaths. Something imposed on someone could be removed if the person could muster the will to defeat it, but something they chose freely would be part of them forever, just like their hair or eyes. And a mundane wouldn't have the magic to make an oath part of their very *being*.

"So it's a bad idea to be mean to someone under your control," she said. "They might break free and attack you."

"Precisely," Aurelius said. He shrugged. "But what makes us different from the mundanes?"

He went on before she could say a word. "Our power is woven into our very souls," he said, softly. "It is that which makes us different from them. We call the study of the interaction between magic and our souls *soul magic*. It is the least understood branch of magic and perhaps the most dangerous, at least on a personal level. You could do far worse than accidentally committing suicide if you meddled with your soul."

Emily nodded, slowly.

There was no shortage of cautionary tales at Whitehall about what happened to students who messed with magic without thinking through the consequences first. She'd been forced to read many of them after her misadventure with the pocket dimension and then write essays in which she had to locate the specific warning and explain why it was dangerous. One of them, she recalled, had featured a student who simply hadn't been able to muster the motivation to keep herself studying, even thought she knew it was important. She'd eventually cast a compulsion spell on herself to *make* herself study. And then she hadn't been able to stop, even to sleep or eat.

"There is no outside force that enforces oaths," Aurelius said, softly. "We do it to ourselves."

"That's why oaths are often sworn to leave loopholes," Emily said. "No one wants to bind themselves completely to someone else."

"Of course," Aurelius said. "But the person who swore the oath has to genuinely believe that the loophole is valid. If they don't, the oath remains in effect and it kills them. Or it destroys their magic. It is *that* which is most curious about the whole system."

"And the oaths also serve as drains on their magic," Emily said, slowly. The oath she'd offered the fairies from First Year was, she assumed, still valid. It hadn't impeded her studies, thankfully, but something more complex might make it harder for her to cast spells afterwards. "And any oath might conflict with any other."

She thought hard, then asked a different question. "What *does* happen if two oaths come into conflict?"

"You suffer the consequences of breaking one of them," Aurelius said. "Sometimes, the conflict isn't recognized at the start, no matter its nature. That's why so few magicians are comfortable swearing oaths."

Emily shuddered. If she'd sworn an oath to Void, and then a different one to Lady Barb, what would have happened if they'd pulled her in separate directions? It would have been disastrous for her personally, at the very least.

"There are other potential dangers," Aurelius added. "If you entangle your soul with someone else, that person will be bound to you for life. Done properly, you and your partner will be happily married; done poorly, one of you will be the master and the other will be the slave. And there will be no escape from such servitude."

"The last-ditch healing spell," Emily said, slowly. Aurelius had taught it to her, with strict warnings never to try to use it unless there was no other choice—and if she was willing to bear the consequences. If she saved a person's life using the spell, that person would be bound to her for the rest of her life. "That's a form of soul magic, isn't it?"

"Yes," Aurelius said, flatly. "And it extracts a huge price from its user."

Emily nodded. The concept of *obligation* had been devised, she suspected, partly in response to spells that demanded payment from both the caster and the target.

It was possible that the whole purpose of the concept was to make magicians aware that there was always a price, even if the price was nothing more than simply repaying one's debts. No wonder healers were expected to forswear all obligations for their work. The alternative was far worse.

Aurelius stood, then led her into another room. This one was completely bare save for a table, two stools and a crystal ball mounted on the table. Emily frowned, but sat where he indicated she should sit. The only crystal ball she'd seen was the one the Grandmaster used to monitor the interior of Whitehall.

He sat down and faced her.

"This is a meditation tool," he said. "It is a mirror, of sorts, allowing you to see the ebb and flow of your magic—and of your soul. What you see when you concentrate on your magic—as I assume you were taught—is a pale shadow of what you really are. But few students are encouraged to look beyond the very basics."

Emily peered into the ball, but saw nothing. "Why not?"

"It would give them ideas," Aurelius said. He inclined his eyebrows towards her, darkly. "And students already have far too many ideas merely from learning a handful of new spells."

Just like the First Years, Emily thought. *I taught them a handful of spells, and suddenly they're standing up for themselves.*

"Touch the ball," Aurelius said. "And close your eyes."

Emily obeyed, after checking the ball for unexpected spells. She felt a faint crackle of magic as her fingertips touched the crystal, but otherwise nothing. And then she realized it was all around her. It had always been there, merely beyond her perception. She could hear her heart pounding in her chest, pumping blood—and magic—through her body. Magic flowed through her veins, touching the rune she'd carved into her flesh and the places she knew served as power points, places she could use to draw out magic if necessary. And, most of all, it ebbed and flowed through her brain, ready to bend to her will.

"Don't try to twist the magic," Aurelius ordered, sharply. He sounded as though he were very far away. "Just... watch it."

"I know," Emily said, entranced. She didn't dare try to disturb it. "It's beautiful."

She meant every word. The magic *was* beautiful. She could practically see her own brain as she fell deeper into the power. And then she saw something shimmering through her mind, something translucent and solid at the same time. It had to be the oath she'd sworn to the fairies, she reasoned. If someone else happened to look at her in such a manner, would he know she'd sworn an oath? Or would he be unable to see her so clearly?

"It's also seductive," Aurelius said, softly. "You can fall so far into yourself that you cannot escape."

Emily barely heard him. Her magic was growing stronger, a roaring wave of power surrounding her, yet it felt oddly comfortable. She welcomed it as an old friend, something that had changed her life for the better. Part of her just wanted to surrender completely and allow it to absorb her...

She shook her head. It could not be allowed. Instead, she forced herself to concentrate until she managed to pull her mind and thoughts back out of herself. Her eyes snapped open.

For a moment, her mind was completely dazed, utterly unsure of what had just happened. And then she realized just how close she'd come to falling into her own power.

"That... that was strange," she said. She felt energetic and tired, happy and sad, enthusiastic and cautious... her thoughts and emotions made no sense. "I..."

"Most students have the same reaction at first," Aurelius told her. He seemed to be regarding her with approval, smiling warmly. "I would advise you not to try again for a few days."

Emily stared at him, rebelliously.

"You would run the risk of killing yourself," Aurelius said, flatly. "Or being lost forever."

He took a breath. "And if you don't take the dangers seriously," he added, "you will come far too close to death the next time you venture into your own mind."

"Very well," Emily said.

"This room is barred to all without me," Aurelius said. "I strongly advise you *not* to enter the room. We *will* try this again in a few days, Emily, but you are *not* to attempt this alone. Do you understand me?"

"Yes, sir," Emily said, carefully. "How much did you see?"

"Nothing," Aurelius said. "You would have seen everything, but I saw nothing. I would have had to touch your soul to see what you saw and that would be dangerous. Your father would not be pleased."

Emily nodded, then frowned. The crystal ball had seemed magic-less until she'd actually touched it, but now she could sense a faint haze of magic surrounding the table. It felt oddly familiar. And then she realized it felt a little like the magic surrounding the locked door and the proctors. Were they linked to Mountaintop though soul magic or was there something else, something more sinister, surrounding them?

The riddle of the ages, she thought, as she rose to her feet. *What hides beneath a proctor's hood?*

"There are books I wish you to read, if you have time," Aurelius said. "You'll find them on the desk in my library, clearly marked for your attention. Read them, consider them and expect a quiz when you next see me. You should be capable of answering some of the most important questions after reading the books."

"If I have time," Emily said.

She sighed. Zed and Mistress Mauve had both assigned piles of reading, leading to near-duels in the library between students fighting over the handful of copies of each book. The sooner they bought textbooks from the newly-formed printing houses, the better. But she did have an advantage, she thought mischievously. Most of the assigned texts were also included in Aurelius's library.

"I have also requested Mistress Mauve to teach you something new," Aurelius added. "But I advise you to be careful. She hates being told to break her lesson plans."

Emily swallowed, nervously. Mistress Mauve was almost certainly the most bad-tempered teacher in Mountaintop, particularly now. Yesterday, she'd torn into an unfortunate male student and questioned his competence, his parentage and his right to be at the school after he'd messed up a particularly complex charm. Charms might suffer one of the greatest accident rates in either Mountaintop or Whitehall, but Emily thought the tutor had overreacted. The thought of private lessons with Mistress Mauve was no more reassuring than private lessons with Zed!

But you survived those, she reminded herself. *You can survive Mistress Mauve, too.*

"One other thing," Aurelius said. Emily stopped at the door. "You are aware, of course, that I am not the supreme ruler of Mountaintop?"

Emily nodded. The MageMaster was the supreme ruler, she assumed, although hardly anyone had mentioned him apart from Nanette. It was almost as if they didn't want to say his name aloud and invoke him. But that was absurd. Saying a magician's name aloud, let alone his title, wouldn't bring him to her side.

"There are disputes among the staff about how to proceed," Aurelius said. "Some of them disagree with me."

"About what?" Emily asked. "About me being here?"

"Work it out," Aurelius said. He waved a hand at the door. "You may go."

Emily gave him a sharp look. "I should pay my respects to the MageMaster," she said, fighting to conceal her irritation. "Can I see him?"

"He's fighting for life," Aurelius said. "You shouldn't visit him, I think. If he gets better, I will introduce you to him."

He paused. "Now, go study," he said. "Or go get some sleep. You'll need it after touching your own soul."

"Yes, sir," Emily said.

She thought carefully as she walked her way back towards Raven Hall, almost tripping over a student who had been stuck to the floor. Clearly, the First Years were still waging their war despite the increased workload. Emily sighed, then released the student and kept walking, wondering which side the student was on. Or even if there *were* sides now.

But she knew, in the end, it didn't really matter.

Maybe that was what Aurelius was trying to warn me about, she thought, as she entered the hall and walked towards her bed. *Some of the other tutors want to take drastic action against the rebellious students.*

Chapter Twenty-Eight

E MILY," MISTRESS MAUVE SAID THE FOLLOWING DAY, "STAY BEHIND AFTER CLASS."
Emily nodded, trying to ignore the pitying looks several of the students sent her as the class was dismissed. Mistress Mauve had been in an even temper all day–thoroughly terrible–and had snapped and snarled at the class for hours. It hadn't helped any of them put their series of spells together, although Emily knew she'd done better than most and actually managed to get a full chain reaction before the spellware fell apart. But she didn't want to call attention to how she was being treated, so she remained seated until the classroom was completely empty.

"I have been ordered to teach you how to teleport," Mistress Mauve said. She sounded furious, although it didn't seem to be directed at Emily. "This is against my best advice as a teacher who has been tutoring young students in teleportation for the last two decades. You are quite formidably powerful, as befits your heritage, but your power reserves have yet to reach the stable levels required for regular teleportation."

"You don't have to teach me," Emily said. "I..."

"Don't be more stupid than you can help, girl," Mistress Mauve snapped. "I was ordered to teach you the theory and the spells, but I strongly advise you not to use them unless you are trapped and there's no other way out. The worst that can happen in that case, at least, is better than certain death without teleporting out."

Emily took a breath. "And what *is* the worst that can happen?"

"You scatter yourself into very tiny pieces," Mistress Mauve said. "Or you wind up in the heart of a mountain. Or you slam against wards designed to block teleportation and no one ever knows what happened to you."

She took a breath. "You will read these books and write an essay on the variables involved," she added. She passed Emily a sheet of parchment with a written authorization to enter one of the more restricted parts of the library. "I should expect it to be perfect, but as you are a Third Year student I will allow you three mistakes. Any further mistakes will result in punishment. Do you understand me?"

Emily didn't think that sounded particularly fair, but she knew better than to argue. She'd always intended to learn how to teleport, after all, and even knowing the *theory* might allow her to sidestep the normal rules. There were quite a few possible uses of her magical batteries that might make teleportation easier, if she had a battery set up and charged. Besides, it was clear that Mistress Mauve had been forced to teach her how to teleport. There was no point in complaining to her about it.

"Yes, Mistress," she said, instead.

"Good," Mistress Mauve said. She moved on at once. "Teleportation requires the use of several different pieces of spellwork, all of which must be triggered at the same time for the spell to work properly. Outside a nexus point, there is no such thing as an easy teleport. The spellcaster is required to envisage the destination, then the spells that move him from one part of the world to another, then finally the spells that will protect him from the ravages of the journey. It is quite difficult to practice the spells separately, let alone together. Very few magicians master teleporting until later in life."

Emily nodded. She'd wondered if teleportation was akin to transporter technology, where a person was broken down into a stream of energy and put back together at the far end, or something more like a personalized wormhole. Judging from Mistress Mauve's description, she would have bet on the latter. But there was no way to be sure.

"There is an additional spell that tests the waters at your destination," Mistress Mauve continued. "It makes sure that there is no strong magical field blocking access. If you should *fail* to cast it and jump into a ward, you will vanish and no one will ever see you again."

"So you said," Emily said.

"It bears repeating," Mistress Mauve snapped. "You must never forget that this is a raw piece of spellwork, put together on the go. You cannot treat it as a prank spell or something else that has been devised by teams of experts and then tested thoroughly until all of the glitches have been removed. One failure when you are casting the spell and *you will die*. If you play around with this spell, *you will die*. And if you act like an idiot while I'm trying to teach you, you will wish you were dead when I am finished with you."

She glared at Emily, then down at the table as if it had personally offended her. "This room should be heavily warded to prevent your classmates from causing havoc," she said. She held up a hand, then waved it in an odd gesture. The wards, which had been a background noise so low Emily had been barely aware of them, snapped out of existence. "Right now, there are no wards in the room. I want you to watch as I cast the first set of spells."

Emily marvelled at the tutor as she stood up, using magic to shove all the desks and chairs against the walls, then started to cast the spells, slowly and carefully. She'd known the woman was both powerful and disciplined, but she hadn't realized just *how* disciplined until she'd watched the chain of spellwork shimmer into existence. To cast the spells was hard enough, yet she was also showing Emily what she was doing...

There was a flash of light, then another. Mistress Mauve vanished from one side of the classroom and reappeared on the other side of the room. Emily frowned, grimly. She doubted she could hold the spells together long enough to actually trigger them, even if she did have a destination in mind. And how did she designate the arrival site within the spells?

"That was a very basic teleport," Mistress Mauve said, as she strode back to the desk. "Do you have any questions before we start to begin?"

"Yes," Emily said. "How do you designate your arrival site?"

"If you know where you are going, you can guide your magic naturally," Mistress Mauve said, flatly. "But if you don't, you have to weave your location into the spell, then the destination. You have to tell it where the destination is in relation to your starting point before you go anywhere. It isn't easy."

She seemed lost in thought for a long moment. "I imagine we will be going over the math in quite some detail," she added. "No student outside Sixth Year has mastered it. I highly doubt you will be the first."

Once she had finished talking, she started Emily on a series of exercises. None of them were easy, although Mistress Mauve showed a surprising amount of patience as Emily worked her way through them, only pointing out—once or twice—when Emily made a major mistake. By the time she was finished, Emily was having her doubts about ever getting the spells to work properly, at least before she'd left school. They were easily the most complex spells she'd yet seen... and to think that Void and Lady Barb had cast them with ease.

You have a lot to learn, she thought, bitterly. *And the sooner the better.*

She discovered, somewhat to her surprise, that the maths for calculating her destination *were* relatively easy. Earth had taught her quite a bit of math beyond that used by the Allied Lands, much of which was applicable to teleporting. It did require some imagination, along with the ability to think in three dimensions, but it was simple enough once she'd worked out what she was actually being told to do. But she still wasn't sure she understood how the spell actually *worked*.

"You need to focus your mind, then start testing the spells," Mistress Mauve said. "And be *careful*."

Emily obeyed, but mastering the chain of spells was almost impossible. No matter how she tried, she couldn't muster the spells, or even set them up inside a wand for later use. The tutor looked oddly confused—Emily's skill with the maths had baffled her—but talked Emily through each step, time and time again. But by the time her private lesson came to an end, Emily hadn't progressed very far.

"Do *not* practice these spells without my supervision," Mistress Mauve said. "I don't care who tells you to practice, or what they say about it. Do *not* practice them without me, or I won't be answerable for the consequences."

"I won't," Emily promised. She rose to her feet, then paused. "And thank you."

The teacher scowled at her. "I have never been ordered to teach a student spells that might well hurt her badly, if she managed to bungle the casting," she said. "Not until now, at least, and it does not sit well with me. If you master the spells, if you manage to use them safely, you can thank me then. Until then..."

She pointed at the door. "Out," she ordered. A wave of her hand replaced the wards around the classroom. "I'll see you in class tomorrow."

Emily stepped outside, right into the middle of a fight. Several students, First or Second Years, were battling it out, exchanging spells with more enthusiasm than skill. Emily hastily raised her wards, then did her best to sneak past the combatants before either side could take aim at her. But one girl, lying on the ground and crying heavily, caught her eye and forced her to stop. Shaking her head, Emily walked towards her, silently daring the combatants to try to stop her. Instead, they retreated in opposite directions.

She knelt down next to the girl and helped her to sit upright. "They hate me," the girl sobbed, tears staining her First Year robes. A large badge on her chest proclaimed her to be a member of one of the Great Houses. "They *really* hate me."

Emily gave her a quick once over. There was nothing wrong with the girl, apart from scraped knees, but the mildest injuries often seemed the most painful. She thought for a moment, then sighed inwardly and wrapped her arms around the girl. What had just happened to her? Or who, for that matter, had picked on her? But there had been a fight going on...

She sighed, then stood and helped the girl to her feet. "I'll walk you back to your dorm," she said, grimly. She *hated* bullies. The girl was clearly defenseless. She hadn't even had a wand in hand. "And then you can tell your Patron who did this to you."

The girl clung to Emily's robes as they walked through the darkened corridors. Two proctors passed, their hooded faces utterly invisible. Emily shivered as she felt the odd traces of magic surrounding them, but forced herself to look away. A handful of other students walked past them before they reached the hall, which was closed. Emily gently disengaged the girl from her robes, then pushed her towards the door and turned to walk back to her hall. Behind her, she heard the girl start to cry again.

There was no one else in sight until she finally reached Raven Hall, where Nanette stood at the door. Emily frowned—it was hardly dinnertime, let alone bedtime—then sighed as Nanette motioned for Emily to follow her into her office. They'd barely exchanged two words since the duel, choosing to ignore one another as much as possible. Emily had a nasty feeling that Nanette would have preferred to keep her distance and that her calling Emily now was not good news.

"Your Shadow has been causing more trouble," she said, bluntly. "It is suggested you deal with her."

Emily swore under her breath. The girl she'd rescued had been a First Year from one of the Great Houses. Had she been obnoxious when she'd been in charge, then utterly demoralized when the common-born First Years had learned how to fight back? Alassa had gone through much the same, Emily recalled, but *Emily* had never felt like making matters worse. And then she'd befriended Alassa instead of keeping her as an enemy.

You idiot, she told herself. *Didn't you realize that they would want to do more than just defend themselves?*

She sighed, then left the office and walked into the sleeping dorm. Frieda was standing in the Silent Corner, her hands on her head, next to two other Shadows. Emily guessed *their* Patrons were still in class. She called Frieda to her and watched the other girls shake. *They* would have to wait and, as Emily knew from bitter experience, the waiting could be worse than the punishment.

"You're getting out of control," she said, once she had erected a handful of wards. She understood the impulse to just hit back, to make the bullies become the bullied, but it would be disastrous. The Administrator had tried to warn her, she realized now. "You cannot keep hitting back at them."

Frieda eyed her, sullenly. "Traitor."

"And who," Emily demanded, fighting down her temper, "taught you to fight in the first place?"

"You," Frieda said. She lowered her eyes. "I'm sorry."

"So you should be," Emily said. "How long until this stops?"

"Until they stop treating us like... like dirt," Frieda said. She smiled, suddenly. "But we are winning, aren't we?"

"I don't think anyone wins such a war," Emily said. If she could move to Frieda's defense, what stopped the other Patrons from getting involved? Or the tutors simply running out of patience and expelling more students? "In the future, I want you to defend yourself, nothing more."

"You have to understand," Frieda pleaded. "They need to learn, too..."

"And when," Emily snapped, "does it stop?"

She understood. She understood all too well. But she also knew it couldn't go on.

"Frieda, listen to me," Emily said. "If this goes on, if none of the tutors will do anything to stop you, you'll become just as bad as they are. You'll become a worse bully than Ten!"

"How?" Frieda asked. She sighed, loudly and dramatically. "I don't have money or connections or..."

Wrong. Frieda had one, Emily knew; Emily herself. But Emily had her limitations. And she wouldn't be at Mountaintop next year. And if Aurelius was refusing to do anything about Frieda because of Emily, next year the younger girl would be horrifyingly vulnerable. Emily wondered, briefly, if she could convince Frieda to transfer to Whitehall. But what would happen to her there?

"And if the tutors do stop you, you'll wind up expelled," Emily snapped. To be expelled from Whitehall was her worst nightmare, even if she did have an entire barony to use as a home and base of future studies. She *loved* Whitehall. "Where would you go then?"

Frieda glowered at her. "Don't you understand?"

"Of course I understand," Emily said, wearily. "I understand the urge to just hit back and keep hitting. But I also understand that this isn't going to end well for anyone."

She took a breath. "Stay out of the fighting from now on," she ordered. "Please."

"I can try," Frieda said, reluctantly. She looked oddly hopeful for a second. "But what happens if I get attacked?"

"Defend yourself," Emily told her, meeting Frieda's eyes. Judging by the rules she'd been taught for dueling, goading someone younger into issuing a challenge was acceptable behavior. "And nothing more."

Frieda looked mutinous. "You say you're on my side, then you refuse to help me," she said, spitefully. Her words stung more than Emily cared to admit. "Which side are you on?"

"You need to worry about completing your schooling, learning how to master the magics that will let you have a place in this world and suchlike," Emily said. It sounded unconvincing and she knew it. "It isn't about sides."

She considered—quite seriously—draping Frieda over her knee. It was well within her rights as Frieda's Patron. But she didn't *want* to punish the girl, not really. She understood Frieda's feelings all too well. And besides, given how badly Frieda had been treated in life, Emily would have had to thrash the girl well beyond the line just to make an impression on her. She wouldn't - she couldn't - do that to anyone.

Shaking her head, she reached for a book and started to read. There would be time to visit the library later, after dinner, by which time everything would have calmed down a little and they could get their food in peace. If not... she cursed, not for the first time, the attitude the Nameless World showed to what Earth would unhesitatingly call bullying. Everyone in the whole affair needed more than a little attitude adjustment.

Starting with the tutors, she thought. Politics shouldn't play any role in how a school was run, although she wasn't naïve enough to think they didn't. Ten's parents had probably whined and moaned to her tutors after Frieda had started fighting back. And she would have been very surprised if Aurelius was the only tutor who had his eye on becoming MageMaster of Mountaintop. Whitehall's Grandmaster wielded staggering amounts of political power as well as his personal and positional power. It was hardly a stretch to think that the MageMaster might have similar amounts of power, a reward well worth any effort to take it.

And Aurelius brought me to Mountaintop, perhaps without the approval of all the tutors, she added, in the privacy of her own head. She couldn't imagine *Zed* happily agreeing to bring Emily to Mountaintop. *A gamble that could easily cost him all his hopes...*

She sighed in frustration, then lost herself in the book.

Chapter Twenty-Nine

E MILY CAREFULLY CAST THE FINAL SPELL - AND WAITED.
The mixture in her wok bubbled once, then came to a simmer. Magic flickered over the purple surface, easy to sense now that everything had fallen into place, then stabilized the liquid and held it steady. Emily let out a sigh of relief and raised her hand.

Zed turned and walked towards her table, his eyes shifting left and right as he checked on the other students. He never left anyone completely unwatched.

"Let me see," he said. He eyed Emily's wok, carefully. "It appears to be stable."

"Thank you, sir," Emily said, relieved.

Zed smiled. "Have you prepared the parchment and the contract?"

Emily scrabbled within her desk for the two pieces of parchment she'd prepared earlier, when it was clear she was approaching the final stage of producing *Manaskol*. One was blank, ready to be turned into a contract, while the other held a draft version of the contract she'd written in pencil. Zed took the latter, read it quickly, and then passed it back to her without comment. Several of the other students had made mistakes with *their* contracts that could have been disastrous, if he'd let them actually try to *make* the contracts magically binding. Emily reread it anyway, just to be sure. She wouldn't entirely put it past Zed to deliberately allow her to make a harmless, but humiliating mistake.

"Add the base liquid, then start writing the contract," Zed ordered. "And be *careful.*"

"Yes, sir," Emily said.

She dripped water into the wok until the mixture started to take on the consistency of ink, then lowered her wand into the liquid and triggered the spell. There was a surge of magic—for a moment, she thought she'd messed up again and it was about to explode—before the mixture stabilized again. Bracing herself, she retrieved an old-fashioned ink pen from her desk and lowered it into the mixture, sucking some of the ink into the container. And only then she placed the second piece of parchment on the desk and started to write.

"Any fool can sign a piece of paper," Master Tor had said, nearly a year ago. "In order to make a contract magically binding, the signer has to know what he's signing—and sign it in such a manner to make the magic bind itself to him."

Emily hadn't understood at the time just how complex the process of creating contracts actually was. It needed the magic ink—she kept the smile off her face at that thought—and very careful drafting, even now. Ironically, her introduction of English letters might lead to more contractual problems in the future if more people learned to read and write. There would certainly be many more contracts, she suspected, and the magic bound into the parchment made it possible for them to apply to mundanes. But the contracts were still not as reliable as sworn oaths.

She finished writing out the sheet of paper and dried it with a simple spell. The words looked loose and untidy compared to her normal handwriting—she wasn't used to using such a pen–but they were easy enough to read. Whoever signed the contract had to wear a black shirt for the next few hours or suffer an itchy nose, rather than any of the dire consequences Master Tor had warned were used to enforce more serious contracts.

Zed took the contract, examined it carefully, and smiled.

"Very good, Lady Emily."

Emily smiled back, then carefully bottled and labelled her *Manaskol*. Zed had already told the class they would be paid a small amount for each successful brew, based on how valuable it was to magical society. As soon as she was finished, she cleaned up her workspace and headed for the door, as Zed had dismissed the students who had completed their work before her. But she was called back. Emily flushed, while a handful of remaining students tittered.

"Come back here at the end of the period," Zed ordered. "We have much to discuss."

"Yes, sir," Emily said, checking her watch. There were twenty minutes until the class was officially supposed to end. "I'll be back."

She made her escape, then headed to the refectory for a mug of Kava and some fresh fruit. Inside, there were a handful of older students, some eying Emily with obvious curiosity. Emily kept her distance–some of the older students she'd met at the quarrel, both boys and girls, had seemed more interested in her than she liked–and found a couple of apples to eat, then sat down to cut them apart. Sergeant Harkin had insisted, firmly, that she try to eat at least two pieces of fruit a day. Emily had to admit she'd felt better since she'd started to follow the older man's advice.

The thought made her feel melancholy. She'd *killed* Sergeant Harkin–and even though she knew she'd had no choice, she still felt guilty. He'd been tough and fearsome and utterly merciless to his students, and yet she'd liked him. Unlike so many others, he hadn't been wrapped up in his own skill and strength or inclined to abuse it. Or, for that matter, to single Emily out for special treatment. It was pretty much the last thing she wanted.

She sighed, finished her drink and walked back to the alchemy classroom. Lerida, the only student left in the room looked rather distraught as she entered, the mixture in her wok having somehow turned into an ashy mess that was clearly useless for anything other than a teaching aid. Judging from Zed's dark expression, Lerida had messed up completely and had detention, as well as a long essay to write on precisely what she had done wrong. Emily felt a flicker of pity as Lerida made her escape, which she hastily pushed aside. Few of her schoolmates at Mountaintop wanted pity.

"You did well," Zed said, sounding as though each of the words cost him dearly. "It will take you months of practice to become a *reliable* brewer, at least of *Manaskol*, but you have successfully created your first batch. I believe you are now ready to move on to more advanced brews."

Emily winced. *Manaskol* had twenty-one steps, all of which had to be completed perfectly or the mixture would explode, evaporate or become a useless sludge. The thought of something worse, something that needed more steps to brew, was horrific.

But she wanted to master the art, no matter how many problems it caused her. The more she knew, the better the magician she would be.

"Thank you, sir," she said, out loud.

Zed nodded, then led the way into his private brewing chamber. A large tome sat on the desk, already opened at a specific recipe. Emily sat down when he indicated the chair, and started to read her way through a complex potion that seemed to have no understandable purpose. It looked as though the title had been carefully removed before the book had been placed on the desk. Puzzled, she glanced at the recipes to either side and found two recipes that were equally unmarked.

"Sir," she said slowly, "what is this potion meant to do?"

"You're meant to figure it out," Zed said. He jabbed a finger towards the single bookcase, then smiled at her, humorlessly. "You can consult the textbooks if you wish, but I expect you to work out precisely what the potion does and then justify your results to me."

Emily sighed as she returned her gaze to the tome. Professor Thande was fond of making them want to think—or so he put it—by telling them to figure out *why* they needed certain ingredients to make a certain potion, but he'd never given them a recipe and told them to work out what it *did*. That was supposed to be advanced work, if a student stayed at Whitehall for Fifth and Sixth Year. By then, they would either have a sense for what the potion was supposed to do, or be willing to put in a great deal of research for an answer that might well be meaningless.

She sighed, again, as she ran her gaze down the list of exotic ingredients. She'd never been a good cook—she'd never been able to afford the ingredients that would have allowed her to experiment—but alchemy was often completely counter-intuitive. Professor Thande's zany nature, she'd been told, was part of what made him such a successful alchemist. *He* would ask himself what would happen if he added Eye of Newt or Tongue of Bat to a brew, while Emily would dismiss the idea as worthless. But alchemy suggested it *wasn't* worthless...

"Yes, sir," she said. "Can I have a sheet of parchment?"

Zed produced several cheap sheets without comment. Emily took one and started to write down the ingredients she knew, then went to the bookcase. Every alchemical classroom had a set of standard reference works updated every five years by the Alchemist's Guild. Professor Thande had complained, quite often, that every five years wasn't often enough; Emily had a feeling that the printing press would ensure that new textbooks would be produced every year, if not every month. There was always a new alchemical discovery to study.

Scanning the shelves, she found one of the standard textbooks and started to look up the ingredients, one by one. The pattern that emerged in front of her, though, made little sense. It almost seemed to be a delayed action potion, yet there was a quite staggering amount of magic worked into the liquid, carefully bound together by alchemical processes she didn't even *begin* to understand. And the final component, the introduction of blood from the intended user, suggested that the potion was highly personalized.

She looked up at Zed and knew the answer. "This is the Royal Bloodline," she said. "Isn't it?"

The insight gave her new understanding. There were ingredients intended to promote muscle growth, shaping a child in the womb; ingredients intended to promote mental development, although there were limits to how far magic could enhance a person's mind. But all of them would only take effect in the next generation, not the current one. The person who drank the potion would draw no direct benefit from it. Only his or her children would reap the rewards.

If there aren't hidden drawbacks, Emily thought, as she returned the book to the shelf and walked back to the table. The Royal Bloodline had also rendered its users much less fertile. In the past, King Randor had no shortage of royal mistresses—the temptation to act like Henry VIII must have been overpowering—but he'd only had one child. Emily had no doubt that, if he'd had a bastard son, he would have acknowledged the boy and made him his heir. *They don't understand quite what they're doing.*

"It is," Zed said, flatly. "Or a much-improved version of it."

He had been sitting at his desk, marking essays, while she worked. Now, he rose to his feet and stalked towards her, then sat down facing her. Emily sensed magic crackling over him, like the sun peeking out behind the clouds, and braced herself. If he'd finally decided to take a little revenge...

"The Royal Bloodline was a dangerously-flawed creation at start," Zed said. He sounded more than a little frustrated, but his face was almost expressionless. "I would have preferred to produce a whole new version of it, but that was impossible."

Emily nodded. Lamarckian biology—the concept that any changes in a parent's body, such as having a hand cut off, would be passed down to the child—had been discredited long ago on Earth, but the Royal Bloodline made it work to some extent. King Randor might have been better served by adopting a child from a mundane bloodline, then ensuring that no one would ever know the child wasn't legitimate. It wouldn't have been hard to make it work, not with his mistresses and resources.

But it wouldn't have been a child of his blood.

"Instead, I looked at ways to improve the modifications without the weaknesses," Zed continued. "But many of the weaknesses were already forced into the bloodline. They could not be removed."

"I know," Emily said.

On Earth, there might have been options. She wasn't sure of the exact process for taking sperm, then ensuring that only the viable ones reached the egg, but she knew it was doable with modern technology. If King Randor had *any* viable sperm, Earth could probably have ensured he had a new child, perhaps more than one. But she knew it wasn't so practical in the Nameless World, even if King Randor had been prepared to consider the process. It was considered a source of pride to have as many children as possible. To be infertile was considered a great disgrace.

But his noblemen must guess the truth, she thought. They'd certainly known the King wouldn't have accepted Alassa as his Heir unless there was no choice. *They know how many lovers he's had.*

Zed studied her for a long moment, then nodded.

"This would also make the new children compatible with the old children," he told her. "The old modifications would be superseded by the newer modifications. And there would be no need for your partner to take the potion himself."

He paused. "You're a noblewoman of Zangaria," he added, almost casually. "You could drink the potion now, and join the Royal Family."

Emily stared at him. She didn't like being reminded of the obligations King Randor had foisted on her, particularly the worst of them. Sooner or later, she would have to produce a child, someone who could take the Barony of Cockatrice after her death. The thought of actually dating a boy... it felt less horrific than it had a year ago, she had to admit, but she still felt uncomfortable at the thought of exposing herself so openly. And to think that female magicians enjoyed a sexual freedom unknown to any other class in the Allied Lands.

And what, precisely, was *Zed* doing?

She had no idea if there were any laws concerning the Royal Bloodline in Zangaria, but she was fairly sure that adding herself to it without King Randor's permission would be awkward, at best. If she *was* adding herself to it. And why would *Zed* seek to offer her the bloodline unless there was a sting in the tail?

And even if he wasn't planning to use this against her—or King Randor—in some way, she doubted he had taken *everything* into account. The Nameless World had a better understanding of how to fiddle with genetics than Earth—they bred everything from horses to cattle—but they didn't always know what they were doing. It was easy to imagine her descendents paying the price for her folly.

"No, thank you," she said. "Besides, who would I marry?"

"There *are* potions that could change your gender permanently," Zed pointed out.

Emily blinked in surprise as she finally realized what he was telling her. She could change her gender, then become part of the Royal Bloodline and marry Alassa herself. It would utterly humiliate King Randor, Alassa and Emily. What better revenge could he possibly take?

"At the cost of screwing up my mind," she said, tartly. She'd looked into gender-bending potions when she'd realized just how badly King Randor had wanted a son. Why *not* force-feed Alassa something that would turn her into a man? But a madman on the throne was worse than a queen. "I think it would be a bad idea."

"As you wish," Zed said.

Emily took a breath, then asked the question that had been nagging at her mind since she'd discovered how Mountaintop used wands.

"Sir," she said, "did you deliberately teach Alassa to rely on a wand?"

"She was a very poor pupil," Zed said. It wasn't quite an answer. "I was unable to teach her the mental discipline she needed to cast spells without a wand. She was even unable to learn how to prime her wand without assistance. Sending her to Whitehall was a desperation move for King Randor."

"But it worked," Emily pointed out.

"After the brat was almost killed by an untrained magician," Zed pointed out. He gave Emily a dark look. "King Randor was furious at the thought of his daughter coming to harm. He might well have hired assassins if things had gone differently."

Emily swallowed. *She* had almost killed Alassa. If things had been slightly different, if she had killed Alassa, she would have started a civil war in Zangaria...

But Zed was right; Alassa *had* been a very poor pupil. If Emily hadn't been forced into tutoring her, the blind leading the blind, Alassa might never have progressed at all. Emily could easily believe that Alassa hadn't been able to learn magic properly—and Zed would have had no power to discipline her. But at the same time, it was remarkably convenient to have the only known magician in Zangaria's Royal Bloodline crippled by reliance on a wand. Zed might not have tried very hard to teach her.

"She isn't a poor pupil now," Emily said, instead. Alassa might not be as scholarly as Imaiqah or Emily, but she was far from stupid and she learned fast. And she had a competitive streak a mile wide. "She's growing into one of the most capable magicians in Whitehall."

"If she is allowed to complete her studies," Zed said, dismissively. He rose to his feet, towering over Emily. "You should be aware, purely for the sake of throwing a potion on troubled waters, that there are discontented rumblings among the tutors. Not all of them are happy right now and, without the MageMaster, there is no single will who can keep them all in line. You really should watch yourself."

Emily blinked. "Me?"

"You *are* a Child of Destiny, are you not?" Zed asked. "Children of Destiny cut both ways, young lady, and not everyone *wanted* you here in the first place. And the current situation is untenable. How many more students will be injured before the Great Houses start demanding action?"

Emily said nothing. Frieda hadn't listened to her half-hearted warnings. And, even if she would have, it wasn't just Frieda who was rebelling against the established order. Or fighting back against an insurgency...

She shook her head. What had she done?

Chapter Thirty

THE BLUNT TRUTH IS THAT MAGICIANS ARE MORE *MORAL* THAN MUNDANES," ROBYN SAID, several hours later. "We are simply more suited to rule."

Emily frowned. *That* was a change—or, perhaps, it hadn't really been a change at all.

Magicians were arrogant, as a general rule. She'd only ever met one magician who had expressed concern for mundanes he'd never met, Master Tor. He'd been doing it to make a point, Emily suspected, but he'd also been right. It wasn't good for mundanes to be ruled by a magician who was more interested in experiments than taking care of her people. But there weren't that many magicians who were also rulers.

"A mundane can break his oath without repercussion," Robyn continued. "A magician cannot break his oath without losing something very valuable to him. We are simply more trustworthy than mundanes."

Emily could see her point. King Randor's noblemen had turned on him, despite their sworn oaths to loyalty. And they'd come alarmingly close to overthrowing him and turning his daughter into a puppet. If Emily hadn't been there... but then, if Emily had never entered the Nameless World, they might not have needed to bother. Why set up puppet strings when the old Alassa wouldn't have troubled herself to interfere with their lives?

But she didn't *like* the concept. She had been raised to consider everyone as equals, regardless of wealth, skin color, gender or skill set. Practically speaking, she knew there was no such thing as true equality, but it was definitely the *ideal*. To have a group of people separated - placed on a pedestal - over the common herd offended her sense of right and wrong. Merit was far more important than birth.

And yet... magicians were practically a different order of life compared to commoners. Mundanes throughout the Allied Lands scrabbled in the dirt; magicians used magic to clean themselves, to make themselves healthy, to run hot and cold running water... all things mundanes couldn't do for themselves. And it was a rare mundane who could beat a magician in battle, sword against sorcery. And other magicians laughed at the magician who happened *lose* such a battle, pointing out that it ensured that the magician who lost was removed from the breeding pool. It bothered her more than she could say to acknowledge that there were any differences between magicians and mundane, but she had to admit they were there.

"Mundanes aren't idiots," she said. "And they have ways of making do without magic."

Robyn snorted. "And how would they cure themselves without the potions *we* produce?"

Medicine, Emily thought. She had a private suspicion that the Allied Lands *had* stumbled on medical science, to some degree, and every potion that could be brewed by a mundane might actually be a form of medicine. But while she had a vague idea how to produce penicillin, it wasn't something the Allied Lands *needed*. They'd be happier using potions.

But things would change soon, she was sure. She'd done her best to introduce the scientific method to Zangaria, along with gunpowder and steam engines. Even if she never offered them another idea, she would have changed the world beyond repair. There was no way King Randor and his fellow monarchs could put the genie back in the bottle, not now. And, as ideas were exchanged between her followers, trying to press the limits of what she'd taught them, she had no doubt that they would eventually crack all the secrets of Earth, all the science she'd never thought to study.

And if I had a copy of The Way Things Worked *it would be so much easier,* she thought, ruefully. If she'd had more practical experience, the world would have been turned completely upside down by now. *We'll just have to keep repeating the mistakes of the past.*

Robyn cleared her throat. "Oaths and obligations bind our society together," she said, calmly. "Mundane society does not have those advantages."

"I know," Emily said, suddenly feeling very tired. The hell of it was that Robyn was largely right. And yet she didn't *want* to agree with the older girl. There might have been mundanes who were shifty treacherous weasels, but she knew there were good and decent mundanes, too. Sergeant Harkin, for one, and Imaiqah's parents. "But that doesn't mean that all mundanes are evil."

"I didn't say evil," Robyn pointed out. "Just... less moral. And much less capable."

Emily felt her temper snap. "And how much opportunity do they have?"

Robyn raised her eyebrows. "I beg your pardon?"

"Imagine a girl born in a peasant village," Emily said. "She's brilliant, smart enough to take what has been invented before and improve on it, or develop a whole new theory of her own."

She took a breath. "But she will spend her early days, from dawn till dusk, working in the fields or cooking, cleaning and sewing for the men. She will be married off as soon as she can have children safely, then start churning them out as soon as she is in the marital bed. A word out of place will lead to a beating, so she learns to keep her opinions to herself. She will never have the education she needs to actually put her mind to work, so it will be completely wasted. And she will die, never having made a mark on the world."

Robyn frowned. "If she had magic," she said, "we would find her."

"She doesn't have to have magic to change the world," Emily argued. She recalled one of the lads from Alexis, who had taken Emily's half-formed ideas and produced a vastly superior printing press. "All she needs is a chance to develop herself to her full potential. And that is what she *won't* get."

She sighed. "A magician can balance children and a career," she said. "But a woman born to a peasant village will never be able to rest and actually use her *mind.*"

It was worse than that, she knew from bitter experience. Peasant culture was communal in ways the communists would have envied, but it was also very conservative and unwilling to accept new ideas. Someone who tried to stand apart from the herd would be isolated, cut down to size, or simply banished. And because their lives were so hardscrabble, there was little tolerance for anyone who might put on airs and graces. Even the merest hint of book-learning would be disliked, if not outright hated.

"And that makes us superior," Robyn said. She eyed Emily with frank puzzlement. "Do you really think that mundanes could be our equals?"

She waved her hand, casting a spell. A glimmering image of her face appeared, and then faded away. "How many of them could do *that*?"

Emily met her eyes. "We can have children," she said. "Steven and Marius"—she nodded towards the two Sixth Years, talking earnestly about something at the far side of the room—"cannot, at least not without perverted spells. Does that make them inferior to us, or superior? Or just different?"

She fought down her temper. This was *important*. "You can't judge a person on birth," she warned. "You have to give them the options they need to shine."

"You were born to a Lone Power," Robyn observed. "Why would *you* believe that people might be... equals?"

Emily cursed herself for getting too wrapped up in the argument to realize that she was treading in dangerous waters. "I was largely brought up by the servants," she lied, allowing a hint of bitterness to enter her voice. "My father had very little to do with me."

"Maybe he considered you a disappointment," Robyn said, nastily.

Maybe it was my fault my real father vanished, Emily thought, bitterly. *Would things have been better if he'd remained with my mother?*

She cursed under her breath. There was no way to know.

But Emily herself proved her point. Trapped in a poor household, forced to fend for herself just to eat and drink, she had never had a chance to shine. In the Nameless World, with friends and tutors who actually cared, she had grown and blossomed. And changed the world. How many others had the same intelligence as Imaiqah, but lacked the magic to take them out of their mundane lives and into Whitehall? Or had access to the tutors who could teach them how to read and write?

That will change, she swore to herself. One of her planned innovations for her Barony was to insist that everyone had at least *some* schooling—and it would be practical, too, with English letters and Arabic numerals. The guilds would hate it, at first, but it would eventually give them a far greater pool of potential recruits. But she'd have to fight to make sure there wasn't a teacher's guild. She had far too much experience, on Earth, with incompetent teachers being allowed to remain in place because they had tenure or it was too hard to sack them.

"My father is his own man," she said, as Robyn cleared her throat. "And I have never been allowed to forget it."

"Probably not," Robyn said. She sighed. "But you do realize my point?"

"I think it is a flawed point," Emily said, carefully. "You are claiming superiority based on an accident of birth, not on achievement. You might as well give one Ken team a colossal lead in points, then declare their inevitable victory a fair match. But it wouldn't be remotely fair."

She smiled, grimly. "Would it not be better to help people achieve their potential?" Robyn looked down at the table. "Do you feel we *could?*"

"I think we have to try," Emily said. Perhaps it was arrogant of her to start introducing concepts from Earth, but she hadn't felt she had a choice. The natural beauty of the Nameless World was more than offset by the lives lived by most of its population. Hot and cold running water alone would make one hell of a difference. "And we cannot start by declaring that magicians are insurmountably superior to mundanes."

"But we *are*," Robyn protested. "I could cast a spell and turn a mundane into a frog. But could he do that to me?"

"No," Emily said. "But that brings us back to the idea that a particular talent, an accident of birth, grants superiority. Does the ability to have children make a woman superior to a man?"

"My mother would argue it does," Robyn said. "I suspect my father would disagree."

She smiled, but there was a ragged edge to her smile. "But the gap between the two genders is not insurmountable," she said. "There are spells that can make a man capable of bearing a child, at least for some time, and potions that can cause a complete shift in gender. No power we know will make someone a magician if they do not already have the potential for magic.

"A weak man can build himself up and make himself strong," she added. "But a mundane cannot become a magician. At best, he can wield magical tools."

"But a mundane could produce a magical child," Emily countered, remembering Imaiqah. "I don't think that leaves them completely talentless."

"My children might be great magicians," Robyn said. "But should I bask forever in their reflected glory?"

She shrugged. "And even children who are expelled from Mountaintop or Whitehall rarely go back to their hometowns," she pointed out. They have tasted a better way to live."

Emily nodded, sourly. She had grown up in a world where hot and cold running water had been on tap, where there were health and safety regulations, excellent medical care and Internet access. In many ways, she was the only pupil whose living conditions had degraded since she had come to Whitehall, although she wouldn't have given it up for anything. But that wasn't true of anyone else. Even Alassa hadn't had hot and cold running water in her father's draughty castle. But that was likely to change.

She changed the subject. "Tell me about the MageMaster," she said. "What is he like?"

"Dying," Robyn said. "The last I heard, he was in his private quarters. But no one has been allowed in there since his illness was first reported."

She shrugged again. "I think there's going to be an almighty fight over who gets to succeed him after he passes on. Most of the tutors have already started jockeying for position and support among the Great Houses."

"But there can be only one," Emily said. She *knew* that the tutors were positioning themselves. "They can't *all* win."

"No, but they can make deals," Robyn said. "If they convince their supporters to support someone else, that person will have a better chance at winning. So the front-runners will try to make deals with the lesser candidates, then combine their votes in hopes of winning enough support to proceed and win the chair. And then spend the next decade paying off their debts."

Emily had to smile. "You seem to know a lot about it," she commented.

"Basic politics," Robyn said. She snorted. "I'm distressed your father kept you so ignorant, Emily. You should have been learning this as you drank your mother's milk."

"I have enough to keep track of," Emily said. The politics of Whitehall, the politics of Zangaria, the politics of the Allied Lands as a whole... they all started to blur together into one tiresomely complex mass. And then something changed and she had to start figuring them out all over again. "And my head starts to hurt when I think about it too much."

"Then bear this in mind," Robyn said. "No one, absolutely no one, reveals the true level of their involvement in *anything*, ever. You have to watch everyone to see who moves first, Emily, and yet you must always remember that whoever moves first may not be the most important person involved. And that everything comes with a price."

"Which might be enforced magically," Emily said.

She was about to say something else, but the bell rang, summoning them to the table. Robyn banished the privacy wards, rose, and led the way towards her seat, motioning for Emily to follow her. There was a logic to the seating pattern, Emily had been told, but it escaped her. The seniors sat at one end, yet the juniors were scattered around in accordance with some arcane procedure. She had a private suspicion that the procedure changed every day to allow the students to meet others in the quarrel.

"There is an issue we have to discuss," Steven said, when everyone had sat down and the table had been called to order. "The problem is the growth of... *disputes* among First Years."

"Hardly a problem," an older boy said. "First Years have been having disputes since time out of mind."

"How true," another boy said. "Weren't you the one who had a month's detention for accidentally booby-trapping the wrong classroom?"

"So I misread the timetable," the first boy said. "A minor accident..."

Steven banged the table. "This is not a conventional dispute," he said. "I think we are approaching the level of organized violence."

Emily winced. Steven was right.

"The fact remains," the first boy said, "that this isn't exactly uncommon. The new bugs have been learning all sorts of new spells just to keep up their fight. Some of them will make good recruits for us next year. Why, exactly, do we wish to discourage it?"

"Because matters are getting out of hand in a time when there is a political dispute," Steven said. Robyn had once said that he loved to hear himself talk and, Emily had to admit, she was probably right. "The Mage Master is dying and the tutors are starting to get more and more annoyed, while the proctors... well, the proctors are the proctors."

He looked around the room, his gaze alighting on Emily for several seconds before moving on. "I want each and every one of you to concentrate on stopping the fighting, if you see it happen," he said. "The last thing we want is a blanket reaction from the tutors, particularly the ones who want to impress the governors with just how firmly they can respond to any problems within the school. We're not talking about simple canings here!

"Yes, many of the students taking part will make good recruits," he added, "but only next year. Right now, they won't be much good to anyone if they're all expelled as a group, will they? Talk to them, warn them to stop being idiots and deal with them if they persist. Or there will be *real* trouble."

Robyn elbowed Emily. "He wants to be Head Boy," she muttered, using a charm to hide her words from everyone else. "It would look good on his resume."

Emily frowned. "I thought he was in Sixth Year," she replied. "How can he take Markus's place?"

"He can if he convinces enough of the tutors that he did something when Markus didn't," Robyn said. "The Head Boy is regarded as too easy-going right now."

Emily rolled her eyes. "What do they want?" she asked. "Markus to stand in the corridor and flog anyone who even looks at him funny?"

"Probably," Robyn told her. "This is politics. Each tutor has a good chance that they *won't* have to deal with the consequences. So they do their best to look tough. And whoever gets the job after the MageMaster dies will have to sort out the mess."

She sighed, and returned her attention to Steven.

Emily looked down at the table, trying to avoid a handful of accusing stares. It *was* her fault, even though she didn't think she'd really had a choice. She was damned if she was leaving Frieda as the victim. But... things had definitely got out of hand.

I'll have another word with her, she told herself. *And try to rein her in.*

Chapter Thirty-One

THERE'S ANOTHER NOTE FOR YOU," FRIEDA SAID, WHEN EMILY RETURNED TO RAVEN HALL. "I think it's from the Administrator. And I just finished washing your clothes."

"Thank you," Emily said. She'd never been comfortable around servants, even in Zangaria, and having Frieda *act* as a servant bothered her. "Pass me the note."

She took the envelope, opened it and read the handful of lines. Aurelius was inviting her, again, to his office after dinner. Emily sighed—she felt too tired to do anything more than fall into bed and sleep—but nodded to herself. If nothing else, she would definitely learn something new from the Administrator. It almost made up for having to deal with problems she wouldn't have to face at Whitehall.

"We need to talk," she said, firmly. She pulled Frieda onto the bed, then cast a privacy ward. "I want you to do nothing more than defend yourself in the future, understand?"

Frieda opened her mouth to argue, but Emily cut her off.

"You have been noticed," she said, sharply. She had no idea about how older students were allowed to handle her Shadow, but she rather doubted that any of the tutors would complain if Steven boxed Frieda's ears. "And this is going to cause you problems in the future. I want you to *stop!*"

She gritted her teeth. "I won't be here next year," she added. "You could be expelled, or simply held back a year, or even forced to take on binding oaths as a condition for you remaining in school. I want you to do nothing more than defend yourself."

Frieda looked oddly upset. "But why?"

"Because there's a fine line between defending yourself against bullying and becoming the bully," Emily said. Something clicked in her mind and she swore, inwardly. She'd coped with Alassa's early attempts at bullying because Whitehall's staff had stepped in when things had gone too far. But Mountaintop's staff hadn't done more than shrug until matters had gone way out of hand. "And you are on the verge of crossing that line!"

"I'm not," Frieda protested. "I just want to make it clear that I can defend myself."

"I think you've succeeded," Emily said. "But those people you are fighting have older brothers and sisters—and parents who have political and magical power. Do you think they will sit back and let you do anything you like, time and time again? These parents have real power and you are almost defenseless!"

Frieda stared at her, mulishly. "All the better that I make my mark now," she said, stubbornly. "If I can't win, I can at least fight until I am overwhelmed."

Fatalism, Emily thought, remembering her holiday in the Cairngorms. The locals had a fatalistic attitude to life—whatever happened, happened—that had bothered her more than she wanted to admit. But then, they had little hope of anything better in their lives, apart from passing their homes and farms to their children. They might regard defeat and death as the natural outcome of life and just content themselves with making it harder for either one to actually win.

"You have a bright future ahead of you," Emily said, although she wasn't sure that was true. But then, the quarrels would definitely want someone as powerful and capable as Frieda was becoming. "You shouldn't throw it away for a private feud."

"I don't know if I have a future," Frieda said, standing and pushing against the edge of the wards. There was a bitterness in her voice that tore at Emily's heart. There would have been no future for the younger girl without magic. "And why should I hold back now?"

"Because I said so," Emily snapped. "I can't stop you making the choice to keep fighting, if you want, but I have to remind you of the possible consequences."

She reached out and smacked Frieda's bottom, hard. "You will throw away everything I taught you if you keep acting like a child," she added. She hesitated, then decided to cast a spell to prove a point. "Listen to me, and listen well. If you keep doing what you're doing, other people are going to start doing *this*."

Frieda flipped over and flew upwards to the ceiling, her feet sticking firmly to the stone. Her dress, Emily noted, was charmed to keep it in place, even if she did end up upside down.

"And if I can overwhelm you so easily," Emily continued, "what could an older magician do?"

Frieda looked down at her. "I..."

"You could be turned into something else, permanently," Emily said. She put as much conviction into her voice as she could. "Or made to do whatever the magician wanted, or frozen in place, or trapped in a tiny room, or... "

She reversed the spell. "Please, Frieda. You must listen."

Frieda dropped down and landed next to Emily, her body shaking with outrage or shock.

"I care about you," Emily said, quietly. "Don't let this get any further out of hand."

She stood, dispelled the wards and walked out of the room, heading down to the refectory. Outside, the corridors felt tense, almost as dark and dangerous as Whitehall when the Mimic had roamed the school, hunting for victims. Several of the halls had stronger security precautions than Emily had expected, including wards intended to keep out uninvited guests. She shook her head in bitter disbelief, then cursed herself. It seemed to be her fate to be a disruptive influence wherever she went. As she made her way to the refectory she had the feeling that someone was shadowing her, a spell aimed at her back.

But nothing happened.

Dinner was simple enough, but the tables were separated and several groups of students were eating together, eying the other tables worriedly. Emily couldn't remember such an awkward dinner since the aftermath of the coup in Zangaria, where everyone had looked as though they expected everyone else to draw swords and start a massacre. Now, she suspected, a single hex would start a bloodbath, or someone would cough and someone else would take it as a sign to start a fight. She took a plate of food, ate it as silently as she could, then left the room, feeling–once again–as though someone had drawn targeting crosshairs on her back. The two proctors who passed her in eerie silence simply ignored her. But it was clear they were looking for trouble.

She reached Aurelius's office and knocked on the door. It was almost a relief when it opened and, after it closed behind her, the sensation of being watched faded away. Had someone been following her? Or was it just general paranoia, combined with a sense that no one would pick a fight inside the Administrator's territory? In Mountaintop, she reminded herself, they really *were* out to get her.

Or they will be when they work out that I caused the problem in the first place, Emily thought. Nanette knew, so she rather assumed the other seniors also knew. Perhaps Steven had been aiming his words at her specifically. *But what else could I have done?*

Aurelius stood by the bookcase, his back to her, reading a book. He put it down as she entered and turned to face her, his face lighting up into a smile of welcome. Emily smiled back, feeling oddly relieved to see him, then took her normal seat. Aurelius sat down facing her and crossed his legs. His robes glittered brightly under the light globe overhead.

"Emily," he said. "I understand that you have made progress with the teleportation spell?"

"Only a little," Emily said. She would have given her left arm for a spell-simulator, some way to practice casting a spell without actually casting it. A wand couldn't hold a spell as complex as teleportation. "But I have a long way to go."

"Knowing the basics will make it easier," Aurelius assured her. He smiled, then met her eyes. "I want to try something a little different today."

He paused. "Did your father ever tell you anything about foreseeing the future?"

"I was told it was impossible," Emily said. She had to smile. "Or at least it was impossible to do it *successfully*."

"I don't know about that," Aurelius said. He smiled back, inviting her to share a very weak joke. "I could predict that Founder's Day holds an excellent roast beef dinner to mark the birthday of our esteemed founder. And it does. I saw the cooks bringing in the beef myself after I approved the menu."

His smile grew wider. "But you're right. *Humans* cannot foretell the future with any accuracy. There is no way to get a *definite* picture of what will happen tomorrow, or even a few years in the future. Can you guess why?"

Emily had seen the dilemma before, in countless fantasy novels. "Because the existence of the prophecy itself changes the future," she said. "The prophecy would either have to be so vague as to be absolutely useless or it would simply never be allowed to come to pass."

She took a breath. "If a soothsayer predicted a lost war," she continued, "the government... ah, the *kingdom* would try to avoid the war, rather than fight it. They might make concessions instead of risking war. Or they might seek allies instead of fighting alone."

"That does assume," Aurelius pointed out, "that the future is *not* set in stone. That the war *can* be avoided. That there *is* something they can do to alter the future."

"Yes, sir," Emily said, reluctantly.

She didn't want to consider the possibility. The idea that, no matter what she did, her future was predetermined was horrific. Where was free will if even the outcome of her free choices was predictable and predicted? And she, of all people, had evidence that the many-worlds theory was correct. There was a different universe for every choice she made. Presumably, the same was true of *everyone* who could make a free choice. There would be trillions upon trillions of universes, some so nearly identical that they might merge back together, others so different that all hopes of rejoining their parent universe were gone.

But it would also make a joke of the thought of foretelling the future. The prophet might be right to say it would rain tomorrow, but in which universe?

"The only way to foretell the future is to use demons," Aurelius said. "They can give glimpses of a future, if you ask and pay the price. But their visions are often taken out of context, if your request is not precise enough or easily open to misinterpretation. As always, the golden rule of demons is...?"

He paused, clearly expecting an answer.

"That you never trust them completely," Emily said. The books had made that *very* clear, time and time again. "Whatever they say - whatever they do - can never be taken for granted."

"Correct," Aurelius said. "The only thing you can rely on, when demons are concerned, is that they will do their best to spite you. If you give them a tiny loophole, they will widen it to the point they can stick a knife in you. They may give you what you say you want, but they will do their level best to make sure you regret it."

Emily considered it. "So they will lie?"

"No," Aurelius said. "But they will tell the truth in a manner specifically designed to mislead. You have to think and rethink everything they tell you, and check everything carefully before you rely on it. At best, you will get a series of impressions of what *could* happen. There would be no guarantee that it actually *would* happen."

"I see, I think," Emily said. "Why do you want me to try to see the future?"

"You are a Child of Destiny," Aurelius said. "I think it would be time to see what your destiny actually *is*."

Emily hesitated. She knew she *wasn't* a Child of Destiny, not in the sense Aurelius meant, and the books had made her cautious where demons were concerned. But, at the same time, she was curious. Aurelius had shown her several levels of magic she hadn't even known existed, as well as having her taught spells years in advance of her powers. Why *not* take this final step? She thought, wrestling with her conscience, then surrendered to curiosity.

"Why not?" she asked. "How do we begin?"

Aurelius smiled, then led her back down into the summoning chamber. "You will use my blood again," he explained as he passed her a vial. "This time, though, the ritual is different and quite dangerous."

Emily listened without comment as he talked her through the second ritual. There would be no demon—no *visible* demon, at least. Instead, she would be appealing for insight into the future from one of the demons Aurelius had bound to him. Emily checked the books to make sure that the standard rule about not sharing anything it saw in her mind without specific permission was still in effect, then echoed everything back to him to make sure she had it straight. Here, at least, a mistake wouldn't prove fatal. She would merely have to start again.

"Sir," she said, "do people sell their souls to demons?"

"Yes," Aurelius said, bluntly. His tone discouraged further questions. "It never ends well."

He cleared his throat. "Sit there, and then begin."

Emily took a breath, then began the ritual. It was easy to see, now she was trying to use a spell that involved ritualistic chanting, why Mountaintop insisted on all students being taught to chant. She'd never sung, either on Earth or Whitehall, and her throat started to hurt within five minutes of starting. But she kept chanting until the magic thickened into a soupy haze that surrounded her. It was surprisingly unpleasant for a spell that wasn't actually aimed at hurting or transforming her... but then, if a demon were involved, it wouldn't be even remotely pleasant. She felt her vision start to fade moments later.

A demon is disconnected from time as humans see it, she thought, trying to hold back panic. *They may not see the specific future for me, but they will be able to garner an idea of what is important.*

"Show me my future," she ordered, as soon as she could no longer see. "I bring you blood, willingly donated from a man who is strong."

She broke the vial, allowing blood to dribble over her hands. Seconds later, she shuddered as she felt a leathery tongue licking her hands until they were completely clean. It was like having a dog licking her, only worse. Deep breathing, so deep she knew the entity in front of her was very far from human, echoed in her ears. If she hadn't been kneeling, she suspected she would have scrambled backwards, breaking the circle. And that would have ruined the ritual.

"Show me my future," she repeated. "I have brought you blood, willingly donated from a man who is strong..."

The world twisted around her... and she saw *things*. Some were visions, glimpses of potential futures, others were pieces of knowledge rather than images. They all seemed to blur together, as if she knew aspects of their context, but not everything. But then, the demon wouldn't want her to know *all* she was seeing, just enough to meet her demands. And it might well be misleading.

...Emily stands in the Great Hall of Whitehall, staring around in horror. Dead bodies lie everywhere, students and staff torn apart by monsters...

...There is a gaping emptiness at the heart of Whitehall...

...It is Alassa's wedding day. Blood stains the altar, her white dress is ripped and torn; in one hand, she holds a wand, in the other a staff. And she stares at Emily with accusation in her eyes...

...There is a gaping emptiness at the heart of Whitehall...

...A Necromancer stands in front of her, bright red eyes fearful. Emily faces him, lifting a hand, and then she dissolves into eerie, multicolored light. The Mimic drifts forward, ready to claim its prey...

...There is a gaping emptiness at the heart of Whitehall...

...Emily is kneeling on a stone floor, her hands and feet chained with cold iron. The spectators are booing loudly as her judges close in, joining hands in a fearsome ritual that will destroy her magic...

...There is a gaping emptiness at the heart of Whitehall...

...The grinning demon looms over her, strings dangling down from his fingertips and reaching past her to the world below. Emily wants to speak, but the words refuse to come from her lips. Instead, all she can do is wait...

...There is a gaping emptiness at the heart of Whitehall...

...She holds Imaiqah's dead body in her hands, feeling tears prickling at the corner of her eyes. And then she looks up and sees Melissa. She's crying, too...

...There is a gaping emptiness at the heart of Whitehall...

...Flames rush from house to house. The population flees...

...There is a gaping emptiness at the heart of Whitehall...

...A young man kisses her, nervously. Emily giggles; he looks offended, then disbelieving as she kisses him again. And then someone starts shouting at him...

...There is a gaping emptiness at the heart of Whitehall...

...The Gorgon stands, her back to a stone wall, her snakes poised and ready to petrify. But the hunters close in with mirrors and she falls below their swords...

...There is a gaping emptiness at the heart of Whitehall...

...There is a gaping emptiness at the heart of Whitehall...

...There is a gaping emptiness at the heart of Whitehall...

Emily snapped back as the visions came to an end. The final one haunted her. She knew what was at the heart of Whitehall, the nexus point. What if it was somehow snuffed out? Shadye might well have turned it into his own private source of power, given half a chance. She knew that was what he had in mind. Or did it mean something else?

...There is a gaping emptiness at the heart of Whitehall...

She opened her eyes. Her body felt too tired to move. Even breathing was a struggle. Aurelius knelt in front of her, holding out a hand, but Emily's vision blurred and she fell into darkness.

Chapter Thirty-Two

ITHINK," A FEMALE VOICE SAID TARTLY, "THAT YOU HAVE PUSHED THIS POOR GIRL QUITE FAR enough."

Emily heard the voice and, somehow, managed to force her eyes open. She felt tired and drained, yet awake and aware. Above her, a dark skinned woman waved a wand over her body with one hand and held a large gourd of potion with the other. As soon as she saw Emily was awake, she pressed the gourd against Emily's lips and motioned for her to suck. The potion, as always, tasted utterly foul. But it did help Emily to sit up.

She glanced around, curious. Aurelius was sitting next to her bed, looking downcast, although his eyes sparkled with a mischievous amusement. The woman—a healer, she guessed—glared daggers at him as she stepped back, then marched towards a large table covered with potion bottles. Emily watched in some alarm as she poured several potions into a glass, mixed them together with a spell and then turned to give Emily the glass. It smelled worse than she'd feared and the taste was appalling. She glowered at the woman, trying not to retch. No matter how bad potions tasted going down, they always tasted worse coming back up.

"You are suffering from excessive magical drain," the healer snapped crossly. "You slept for seven hours."

Emily looked for her watch. It was missing, along with her dress. Someone had taken her clothes and replaced them with a hospital gown. The only thing she'd been allowed to keep was the snake-bracelet.

The healer dropped a small bundle of clothing on the bed. "I would suggest you stay in bed over the next few days, but this... *person*"—she indicated Aurelius—"insists on walking you back to his office. Try not to cast any powerful spells over the next two weeks and, if anyone objects, refer them to me."

Emily sighed, inwardly, as the potions took effect. The jolt was rather like Kava, but there was a rough edge to it that promised pain when the effects finally wore off. It reminded her of some of the potions she'd used in Martial Magic, all of which left the user flat on their back afterwards. Probably the same brew, she decided, as she swung her legs over the side of the bed and stood. Her legs felt a little wobbly, but she could walk.

"I think we have a great deal to discuss," Aurelius said, as he held out a hand. Normally, Emily would have preferred to stand on her own, but right now she needed someone holding her arm. "And I have to make a proposal to you."

"A proposal?" Emily repeated. Her dulled mind honestly thought, for a handful of seconds, that he meant a real-life marriage proposal. Aurelius was old enough to be her grandfather; she knew that large age gaps between husband and wife were far from uncommon, but she had no intention of marrying someone more than a few years older - or younger. And then she realized he had something more professional in mind.

"Yes," Aurelius said. "I believe it will be to your advantage as much as to mine."

He turned his back long enough for her to swap her gown for a set of basic robes and strap her watch back over her wrist, then took her arm again. Emily wasn't sure she liked his touch—there was something unpleasantly possessive about it—but she couldn't say a word. He held her arm gently as they walked out the door and through a twisting maze of corridors, back to his office. Emily wasn't entirely surprised when he led her into yet another room, this one more of a comfortable sitting room than a library or administrative office. A small kettle hummed happily on a side table, the sound so electronic that she wondered if he'd managed to import something from Earth. But she knew that was unlikely, to say the least. He might have deduced Emily's true origins if he had any understanding of the basis of alternate worlds.

She wondered, as she sat down and fought the urge to close her eyes, if he *did* understand how demonic powers worked. It was quite logical; the demons might not be able to see precisely what would happen in any given timeline, but they would be able to see who might be important and what they might do. The whole Child of Destiny concept might have come from the demons and DemonMasters in the first place, a reflection of their unique ability to identify someone important and cut him loose from the herd. Emily had assumed that Shadye's plan was completely insane and that it would get him nowhere, apart from being devoured when the Harrowing discovered that its intended snack wasn't what she seemed. But the plan might have been workable after all.

Aurelius poured her a mug of Kava, which he passed to her without comment. Emily was somehow unsurprised to discover that there were two spoonfuls of sugar in it, just the way she liked her Kava in the morning. Aurelius had probably either kept an eye on her personally, or asked Nanette to make note of Emily's preferences. It was hard to tell, Lady Barb had told her more than once, which piece of information would be useful until it was found and slotted into place.

But I can't imagine a scenario where knowing what Kava I drink helps him win, she thought, as she took the mug gratefully and sipped. Her head still felt musty, but the potions and the Kava were driving her into an enhanced state of awareness. She would need to be somewhere near a bed when they finally worked their way out of her system. *Unless he's trying to manipulate me?*

Aurelius sat down facing her, his dark eyes suddenly very serious. "I do not know what you saw when the demon shared its insights with you," he said. "But it was clearly quite traumatic for you. Would you care to share them with me?"

"No, thank you," Emily said. She wanted to sit down and meditate, perhaps use a memory spell to go over the visions time and time again until she was absolutely sure what she'd been shown. But, taken out of context, just how useful could the visions be? "I'd prefer to consider them myself, first."

"As you wish," Aurelius said. He bowed his head in acknowledgement. "It is my duty to tell you, however, that while the DemonMasters may be gone, there are... experts who will be happy to help you try to interpret the visions. You would be well advised to seek their counsel."

And have them tell everyone what I saw, Emily thought. *Or would they have taken oaths of secrecy?*

She tried to think of a polite way to ask, but couldn't think of one that wouldn't reveal that she didn't trust him or his experts. Aurelius would be a fool if he thought anything else, she was sure, yet he might well think she was warming up to him. She didn't really want him to think any differently; he'd shown her knowledge and spells she hadn't known existed, but she was sure there was a hidden price tag. The bill might be about to come due.

Aurelius sipped his drink thoughtfully before speaking.

"There are some matters I must discuss with you, Lady Emily," he said, finally. "However, I must ask for your word that you will not discuss these matters with anyone else, at least until the day I die. They are quite sensitive."

Emily thought as fast as she could with a musty head. Giving her word wasn't exactly the same thing as giving a sworn oath, but being caught breaking her word could be disastrous, at least for her reputation. And that could come back to haunt her in later life. Aurelius would certainly make sure everyone knew *his* side of the story if she broke her word. Somehow, she doubted the magical community would listen to hers.

"I will not discuss them with anyone else, without your permission, unless lives are at stake," Emily said. She allowed her voice to sharpen. "I trust that will prove acceptable?"

Aurelius met her eyes, levelly. "It is not your right to determine if lives are at stake," he said, softly. "You should know better by now."

"I won't be in a position of having to choose between breaking my word and watching people die," Emily said, equally softly. "And I will be very careful how I make my decision."

"Very well," Aurelius said. "I accept your word."

He took a long breath. Emily realized, suddenly, that he was nervous.

"You are aware, of course, that the Allied Lands face a colossal threat," he said. "You of all people should be aware of just what threat the Necromancers pose."

Emily nodded, slowly.

"And yet the Allied Lands, as a whole, does not take the threat seriously," Aurelius continued, his voice growing louder as he pressed onwards. "It is barely two years since Whitehall was attacked and almost destroyed; two decades since we lost an entire country to the Necromancers. And yet the Allied Lands seems to choose to blind itself rather than actually prepare to fight!"

"And to cripple magicians who might be helpful," Emily added, sharply.

Aurelius didn't disagree. "Yes," he said. "A policy that is deeply flawed in many respects."

Emily had wondered why Whitehall and Mountaintop were such generalist academies when historical practice from Earth suggested that a master and apprentice system would be much more likely. But it did make sense. The Allied Lands needed

magicians so badly that it was prepared to throw education at every would-be magician it found, just to see what stuck. And the academies also provided what little
socialization some of the magicians received. They were—or they should have been—
outside the local power groups.

But something had gone wrong, she knew. The Fall of the Empire had wrecked a
great many carefully-calculated arrangements.

"It is badly flawed," Emily said, when it became clear he was waiting for a reply.
"But it seems to be the system you support."

"I am not the MageMaster," Aurelius said. He opened his hands, trying to project
trustworthiness and openness. "I do not have the power to change things, not yet."

He looked down at the table, then back up at her. "But if I become MageMaster,
Emily, a great many things can be changed."

Emily watched as he stood and started to pace.

"The Shadow system needs to be revised," he said, as he strode from one end of
the room to the other, magic crackling around his robes. "Many of the well-bred
Shadows learn nothing from it, while the common-born Shadows learn only how to
be slaves. For everyone who becomes a greater magician in their middle years, there
are ten who leave the school fit only to serve as servants to the Great Houses, to bear
their children in return for a lifestyle that does nothing to prepare them for war.
House Ashworth made no mistake in refusing to send their Heir to Mountaintop. It
would not have prepared her for her role as Matriarch of Ashworth."

"And that isn't the only problem," he added. "Mundanes may not be able to con-
tribute much against a Necromancer, but they can help in fighting off hordes of monsters raised to the Necromancer's cause. Or they can produce materials for war, even
if they can never deploy them. The Great Houses play their petty political games, the
Kingdoms and City-States struggle for power and position... while, slowly but surely,
the noose tightens around our necks. Whitehall isn't the only prospective bottleneck
between us and the Blighted Lands..."

He took a sharp, savage breath. "Whoever becomes MageMaster will be in a position to change the way of the world," he said. "I intend to reach that post and *use* it."

Emily looked down at the carpeted floor, trying to think. This was *it*, she realized
dully; this was his pitch, his proposal, his invitation to join him. Everything he'd done
for her, from showing her dangerous or forbidden magics, to letting her get away with
wandering out of the school's passageways into the underground tunnels, had been
leading up to this moment.

He was right. She *knew* he was right. The Allied Lands took the threat of the
Necromancers as seriously as King John of England had taken the threat of the
Ottoman Turks. Even King Randor, whose daughter had been caught up in Shadye's
attack on Whitehall, hadn't been as worried about the Necromancers as Emily
thought he should have been. And yet she couldn't help feeling that, if Aurelius had
wanted to make changes before hearing about Emily, he could have done so without
becoming the MageMaster.

She hesitated, then asked.

"Why now? Why not attempt to make the changes earlier?"

"You are aware, of course, that the quarrels pervade our society," Aurelius said. If he was offended by her question, he didn't show it. "Each of the tutors at Mountaintop, with a single exception, was appointed to the post because he or she had the backing of a powerful quarrel and strong connections within the Great Houses. They each represent a point of view—and not all of those points of view agree that we should make changes. But you... you *represent* change."

He stopped pacing and turned to face her. "I cannot make significant changes in our schooling because I do not have the power to override the other tutors," he told her. "Right now, with the MageMaster on the verge of death, there is no one with the power to impose his will on the staff. Or to make changes, if necessary. The school's policy is drifting."

"Which is why no one has done anything about... about Frieda," Emily said, slowly. She'd been surprised that no one had done anything violent, apart from a pair of expulsions that had had no real deterrent effect. "There's no consensus on what to do with her."

Aurelius nodded, once.

He sat down, still facing her, and rested his hands on his knees. "I have a proposal for you," he said. "You carry power and prestige, perhaps more than you know. Give me your support and, in exchange, I will arm you to face the Necromancers. I can show you how to use magics you can't even imagine, magics so dangerous that they were locked up centuries ago, and tricks that only an experienced combat sorcerer would know. I will be MageMaster, ready to implement the changes that would put an army at your back, ready to face the Necromancers once and for all.

"Or, if you want something else, I can meet your price. Special schooling and training in any subject you wish? Power? Wealth? A husband from a proven magical bloodline who will stabilize the wild power you inherited from your father? Or what would you like? I can give it to you."

Emily stared at him. "Why do you think I would tip the balance in your favor?"

Aurelius laughed, humorlessly. "You're the Necromancer's Bane," he said. "In two years, you have killed two Necromancers, upset a coup plot that was almost certain to succeed, introduced a whole new system of reading, writing, counting and riding horses... there are people all over the Allied Lands who pay vast sums of money for exclusive access to the words that come out of your mouth. If you made a public statement in my support, Emily, I guarantee you that people will *listen*."

"The girls in Raven Hall didn't treat me as anything special," Emily said, slowly. "They just treated me as one of them."

"I had cautioned them to treat you normally," Aurelius said. "And I wanted to see how you would act when pushed into a very different environment."

Emily's eyes narrowed. "Did you arrange for Ten to bully my Shadow?"

"That's something else I would like to change," Aurelius said, bluntly. "The current system squashes more great magicians than it produces."

"Yes," Emily agreed.

"Time is not on our side," Aurelius said. "The MageMaster could die at any moment—and, when he does, we have to have a viable successor in place. I shudder to think what would happen if the links to the wards passed to the wrong person—or no one. The school would be left defenseless."

And anyone watching from the outside could come in, Emily thought. Lady Barb and Master Grey had *said* they would be outside, hadn't they? *And what would happen then?*

"I would need to speak to my father," Emily hedged. She wanted—she needed—time to think, but she doubted she would be given the time. "I have not yet reached the age of majority."

Aurelius lifted his eyebrows. "You can't make a decision without consulting your father?"

"I am his daughter," Emily lied. She had only a hazy idea of just how much authority Void had over her—the Grandmaster knew perfectly well that Emily *wasn't* Void's daughter—but she doubted that Melissa or Claudia would be expected to make such a decision without consulting their fathers. "And I don't know what to say."

"I understand," Aurelius said. He looked, just for a second, disappointed. "Go back to your dorm, write your letter and enjoy the feast tonight. But I will need an answer soon. Time is not on our side."

"You said that already," Emily muttered.

"You're excused from classes for the next week in any case," Aurelius told her. He took a piece of parchment from a side table and scribbled on it, quickly. "I fear the healer was on the verge of cooking my intestines with a spell by the time you woke up. Give this note to the Head Girl. You're allowed to sleep as long as you like for the next week."

"Thank you, sir," Emily said.

"Go," Aurelius said. The urgency in his voice belied his words. "And write that letter!"

Emily nodded, then left the room.

Chapter Thirty-Three

IT WAS EARLY MORNING, ACCORDING TO EMILY'S WATCH, WHEN SHE FINALLY STUMBLED BACK into Raven Hall. Her head was starting to pound unpleasantly, suggesting that the potions and Kava were already starting to wear off. The effects hadn't lasted as long as she'd expected, part of Emily's mind noted; the healer might have deliberately given her a weaker dose. *She* clearly hadn't approved of Aurelius's plans for Emily.

She barely noticed Nanette until the older girl stepped right in front of her. "Are you all right?"

"I've been better," Emily managed. She pressed Aurelius's note into Nanette's hand, almost stumbling over and falling to the ground as she did so, then half-staggered towards her bed and sleep. "Tell Frieda not to wake me up..."

She fell onto the bed and into the darkness, her eyes slamming shut. Sleep must have claimed her, she recognized dully, because the next thing she remembered was opening her eyes to discover that she was practically bent over the bed. Her hazy mind struggled with the concept before she regained all of her memories and recalled just how badly she'd been drained the previous night. Aurelius had pushed her right to the limits of her endurance.

But she did feel better, she had to admit, as she rolled over and sat upright. Her robe was crumpled and stained with sweat, her hair felt a ghastly mess. Mindful of the healer's warnings, she pushed herself to her feet and glanced at her watch. It was mid-afternoon, when some of the girls would be in class and the others would be engaged in private study or trying to catch up on their sleep. She wondered if they'd seen her as they got out of bed—she hadn't had time to set up any privacy wards—and then decided it didn't matter. Instead, she stumbled towards the shower and undressed as soon as she was in the stall, then allowed the cool water to shock her awake.

She closed her eyes, enjoying the sensation of water washing her body clean, then started to think through everything the demon had shown her. Demons didn't lie, she had been told time and time again, but they could mislead. Anything could be used to imply anything, with a little bit of imagination, and if the books were to be believed demons had plenty of imagination and used it all to devise new ways to spite humans. The visions might have been taken completely out of context.

No, they were *taken out of context,* Emily thought, firmly. *And wondering about the original context will only drive me insane.*

The water started to turn icy cold, jerking her out of her thoughts. Hastily, she stepped out of the stall and towelled herself dry, then cursed herself under her breath. She'd forgotten to bring a gown and her clothes were all dirty. Angrily, she glanced out, discovered that the hall was still empty and ran out to her bed, stark naked. She tried to cast a privacy ward as soon as she arrived, but her head started to pound almost at once and she gave up. Instead, she pulled on her nightgown and dropped back into bed. But the door opened before she could close her eyes and get back to sleep.

"Emily," Frieda called, in delight. "You're back!"

"Of course I am," Emily said. "Where did you think I'd gone?"

"Well, Ferrell said you were expelled from school and Griselda said you were dead and Dune said you'd spent the night in Cockroach Hall with a *boy*, but Harris said you'd been in the infirmary and Hog backed him up," Frieda said. "His Patron is a Sixth Year brute who is supposed to be really good with healing charms, so he's working there to earn spare cash or something. The healer was in a right mood over you being there, he said."

"So she was," Emily said. She sighed, then leaned back into the sheets. "Let me sleep, would you?"

Her days fell into a quiet routine of rest, meals and chatting with Frieda about nothing in particular. Nanette visited from time to time, bringing books from the library, but rarely stayed to chat, while the remainder of the girls kept their distance. Emily wondered, as she slowly recovered her strength, if they thought she was contagious. The rumor mill had to be working overtime. By the time the weekend rolled around, and with it Founder's Day, she almost felt like herself again.

"You can't sleep now," Frieda said, sitting on the bed. Nanette stood nearby, looking amused. "There's a feast tonight, remember?"

"I may have heard something about it," Emily said, with great dignity. "I won't be attending."

"You *must*," Frieda said. "It's the event of the *year!*"

"I shouldn't go," Emily said. The dull ache at the back of her head was getting stronger. So was the urge to just shove Frieda away, physically. "I think I need to sleep."

"You can sleep, if you wish," Nanette said. "But it would be a shame to miss the feast."

Emily scowled, cursing her own weakness. She hadn't even been able to cast a simple privacy ward over the last week, let alone hold it in place. She'd have to teach Frieda how to produce them, she told herself, as she sat back upright and rubbed her forehead. When she touched her chest, she felt a dull ache between her breasts. The subtle magic used to help patients to heal had triggered her defenses.

Or, she asked herself, *did something else happen while I was asleep?*

"Fine," she snarled. She sighed, unwilling to admit her weakness, but knowing there was little choice. "Cast me a privacy ward, please."

Nanette nodded, then cast the spell and withdrew. Emily let out a breath she hadn't realized she'd been holding. If Nanette had wanted a little revenge for their grudge match of a duel, she would never have a better chance to humiliate Emily and shatter her reputation beyond repair. Except, no matter how cranky she was, Emily had a feeling that Nanette actually cared about her duties more than she cared to admit—or to show to anyone else.

And she'd have to be insane to piss off the Administrator, Emily thought, as she stood upright and pulled off her gown. *He would not take it kindly if she alienated me for good.*

"Your chest looks sore," Frieda said, softly. "Is that... is that *safe?*"

Emily looked down at the rune. It wasn't bleeding, but it was red and ugly against her pale skin. She cursed under her breath, wondering how anyone could hope to heal if they had runes to ward off subtle magic, then wondered just what else might have happened while she was unconscious. Had they done something else to her while she was asleep, or was she just being paranoid? It was quite possible that she'd had to be moved out of the chamber before anyone called the healers.

"I don't know," she said. Her head was starting to pound again. "And you might have to help me, later."

She bent down, ignoring Frieda's snicker, and retrieved a dress from the drawer. Claudia and Robyn had been giving her all kinds of advice on what to wear, pointing out that the feast was one of the most important social events in Mountaintop. They'd contradicted themselves so often that Emily had finally decided just to wear the blue dress she'd been given by Nanette, or whoever had picked up clothing for her. It suited her hair, she felt, while being surprisingly modest compared to some of the other magicians. She might have beaten off a would-be rapist, but she still didn't feel comfortable about showing so much flesh in public.

"You should tie up your hair," Frieda said. Unlike Emily, she had nothing more than a decent pair of dress robes to wear. "It would suit you."

"I prefer to leave it hanging down," Emily said. Long hair had been her only real vanity, back on Earth. Besides, going to have it cut was expensive. "What about yourself?"

"I'll stick with the pigtails," Frieda said. She jumped upright and twirled around, a motion that reminded Emily of Alassa. "Coming?"

Emily sighed. She knew she could probably refuse to go and make it stick—the healer had made that clear—but she was curious. And besides, she could simply walk out if the pain became unbearable. Gritting her teeth, trying to use a mental discipline without magic, she followed Frieda out of Raven Hall and down towards the Great Hall.

The interior of the hall took her breath away. In the center of the hall, a massive animal was being roasted on a spit, while smaller animals were being prepared for serving by the older students. High overhead, multicolored light globes hovered in the air, flicking and flaring in response to the magic running through the chamber. A dozen tables had been relocated to surround the cooking pit, while others had been pressed against the wall. It seemed to be a day where anyone could sit wherever they wanted, Emily decided, as Frieda caught her by the hand and pulled her towards one of the tables nearer the center. She sighed, then allowed the younger girl to have her head.

She sat down and was instantly served a glass of wine by one of the serving girls. Emily sniffed it, then shook her head and asked for water instead. Beside her, Frieda took several gulps of her wine, casually drinking it as though it were fruit juice. Emily pursed her lips in disapproval, torn between lecturing Frieda on the dangers of drinking and allowing the girl to have fun, just for once. She decided, finally, to tell the girl off for drinking tomorrow, after remembering that the Allied Lands had no age bar to drinking. Even children drank alcohol in mountain villages. It was the only way to live.

A wave of silence ran through the room, emanating from the High Table. Emily turned to see the tutors, wearing formal golden robes, lifting their glasses to their students. After a moment, she recalled her manners and lifted her own glass, then took a sip of water. There were places where drinking someone's health in water was considered offensive, she recalled from the more interesting etiquette lessons she'd had to endure, but Mountaintop wouldn't be one of them. The dangers of a drunken magician were all too clear.

Which raises the obvious question, Emily thought, as the serving girls returned with fresh glasses. *Why do they serve alcohol at all?*

She elbowed Frieda as the younger girl reached for a second glass. "No more wine," she said, firmly. She had to practically whisper in Frieda's ear to get her to hear her, with the spell still dampening the noise in the chamber. "Order fruit juice instead."

Frieda looked rebellious, but did as she was told.

A low tingle ran through the air, calling them to pay attention to Aurelius.

The Administrator rose to his feet slowly. Emily was mildly impressed as light glinted off his golden robes. *She'd* worn gold once or twice and she knew, without false modesty, that she'd looked more than a little absurd. But Aurelius managed to make it work. Wrapped in a haze of magic, he looked almost regal. The implications were not lost on her.

Recalling what he'd said, she lifted her eyes and scanned the tutors as they turned to look at Aurelius. It was clear, now, that he was right; there were at least three groupings among the tutors, some more aggressive and disinclined to support Aurelius than others. The only tutor who seemed above it all was Professor Zed, who sipped his drink absently as if he didn't have a care in the world. Emily had a private feeling that his presence at Mountaintop wasn't entirely an accident, but who had been behind it? Not Aurelius, she thought. *He* wouldn't have risked putting Emily next to a teacher who had an excellent motive to pick on her in the name of revenge.

"We are always charged with thinking of the future," Aurelius said. "We are the ones who must consider what will happen in the years to come. But in order to consider the future, we must consider the past. Where did we come from is just as important a question as where are we going?

"It has been over five hundred years since the caves were cleared of the dwarves," he continued, his words echoing around the chamber. "Since then, these hallowed halls have served as both our place of learning and our refuge. Even the Fall of the Empire did not deter us from turning out new students, ready to help bolster our society. Mountaintop stands ever ready to meet what the future will bring."

The students applauded, loudly. Emily clapped her hands too, although she had a feeling that Aurelius had deliberately spoken... maybe not nonsense, but boilerplate platitudes rather than anything useful. Or was he building up to something else, something more specific? She shivered uncomfortably as she remembered how King

Randor had told her she was going to be a baroness. Did Aurelius have something similar in mind? She prayed, silently, that he wasn't going to ask for her endorsement in front of the entire school.

"The future will bring many surprises," Aurelius said. "Our world changed two years ago—and we have hope and fear in equal measure. But we *will* meet the challenge of the future and emerge victorious, once again."

He sat down and smiled. "Serve the food," he ordered. "We will save the rest of the speeches for afterwards."

Emily had to smile as the students applauded again, then turned their attention to their plates as the servants handed round slices of meat, vast bowls of potatoes and great steaming jugs of gravy. Frieda piled her plate high as if eating were going out of style, then tucked in with a surprising amount of enthusiasm. Emily started to eat with more dignity, expecting the food to taste overcooked, like feasts in Zangaria. But it tasted better than she'd expected, good enough to encourage her to eat.

Frieda wasn't the only one to eat like a starving animal, she saw. The Shadows were *all* cramming themselves with food, as if they hadn't eaten anything over the last few days. It was quite possible, Emily realized dully, that they hadn't picked up on the benefits of eating full meals—or, more practically, that their Patrons hadn't provided them with funds to eat enough to keep themselves going. But the feast was a giant free-for-all. The Shadows could, for once, eat as much as they wanted.

Something else Aurelius will have to change, Emily thought. *The Shadows will need to be fed properly to make them effective magicians.*

She sighed. His offer was tempting, more than she cared to admit. If she'd been a free agent, she might well have accepted. Hell, *Void* might well have encouraged her to accept. But she had to make a report back to Whitehall and, so far, she knew she'd discovered very little. Unless she broke her word and told the Grandmaster about Aurelius's scheme...

The Grandmaster might approve, she thought, ruefully. The more she thought about it, the more she wondered if she could serve as a bridge between the two powerful magicians. *He knows the danger from the Blighted Lands as well as I do. And having the MageMaster on his side wouldn't hurt either of them.*

And then there was a surge of magic, far too close to her for comfort. Emily turned, just in time to see a plate of meat launch itself off the table and toss its contents towards another table. There were shouts and screams as the meat cascaded down. Emily glanced at Frieda, expecting to see a smirk and resolving not to let the younger girl defy her any longer, but her Shadow's mouth was wide with shock.

And then all hell broke loose as the targeted table retaliated.

Emily yelped in pain as a gravy jug exploded, sending steaming hot liquid everywhere, then stumbled backwards as a line of nasty-looking insects appeared from nowhere and started to advance towards her. Several of the other students at her table fired hexes indiscriminately, unwilling or unable to let the insult pass, even though none of them knew what had happened.

"Get under the table," Emily snapped, as more plates of food flew towards them. A half-eaten piece of roast pig slammed into the wall and disintegrated, showering chunks of meat over the unlucky diners. "Hurry..."

There was a roar, then screams of pain as the fire suddenly grew brighter–much brighter. Emily tried to raise a shield, but the pain in her head made it impossible. Instead, she caught Frieda's arm and dragged her towards the door. The tutors were trying to restore calm, yet they seemed to be having problems imposing their will. There were just too many hexes flying around for them to deal with *all* the casters.

She swore out loud as something thudded into her back–she didn't want to know what–and then pushed her way out of the door. Behind her, she felt waves of magic radiating outward, probably silencing the remaining combatants. The Grandmaster had done something similar, last year, when the students at Whitehall had threatened to panic.

"That wasn't me," Frieda said, frantically. "I didn't do it!"

Emily nodded. Whatever else Frieda was, she wasn't a liar. And besides, she would have to be insane to start something in the middle of the feast, let alone waste so much food either. But that raised a simple question. Who *had* done it?

"If it wasn't you," Emily said, "who did?"

The dull throbbing in her head grew louder. "We're going back to Raven Hall," Emily said. Judging from the other students running in all directions, she wasn't the only one who had come to the same conclusion. "I don't think the party is going to restart."

"Probably not," Frieda agreed. She looked shocked, as if she'd finally realized that the ongoing war was a disaster waiting to happen. "What... what happened?"

"Someone just decided to start a war," Emily guessed. She shook her head, feeling pieces of meat and gravy falling out of her hair, then led the way back to the hall. "And I really need to go to bed."

Chapter Thirty-Four

WAKE UP," A VOICE SNAPPED. "EMILY, *WAKE UP!*"
Emily opened her eyes. It felt as though she hadn't slept at all, although a quick glance at the clock in the far corner of the hall told her that it was early morning, nearly twelve hours after the disastrous feast. She rubbed her eyes before she looked up.

Frieda was securely held between the two Dueling Mistresses, her hands hidden behind her back. Emily stared, realizing dully that Frieda's hands were tied. She was in deep trouble.

"By order of the Administration," Mistress Hitam said, "Frieda, Daughter of Huckeba, is hereby expelled from the academy. You will now bid farewell to your Shadow."

Emily gathered herself, desperately. "She didn't do it," she said, cursing her headache. It was so hard to think clearly. "It wasn't her fault."

"The Administration has decided that her antics can no longer be tolerated," Mistress Hitam said. "She will be expelled without delay. *You* can consider yourself on suspension, young lady, until the academic investigation is completed. A proctor will bring you before the committee later in the day, whereupon you will be expected to answer questions. Your future at this institution hangs in the balance."

"But she didn't do it," Emily insisted. Her headache made it impossible to form a more coherent argument, but somehow she managed to stand up. "You can't expel her for a crime she didn't commit."

"She has served as the linchpin for offences against law and order," Mistress Hitam informed her. "And *your* involvement in this affair has yet to be determined."

She glowered at Emily. "Until the matter is resolved, you are forbidden to leave Raven Hall," she added. "Should you be caught out of bounds, you will be immediately expelled, without appeal. I urge you, if you wish to continue to study here, to do as I tell you."

"But..."

Mistress Hitam ignored her. Instead, she turned to face the other girls.

"You will leave Emily strictly alone until this matter is resolved," she stated. "Any offenders will be dragged into the inquiry, too."

She walked off, dragging Frieda with her. The Shadow's hands were firmly bound behind her back, making it difficult to use magic. As her head started to pound in earnest, Emily wondered why they hadn't turned her into something harmless. But she reasoned it was all about humiliation. Even if Frieda managed to remain at Mountaintop, no one would ever forget she'd been bound and marched around like a common criminal. She tried to find her voice, to find words to argue, but her head swum instead and she staggered and fell back on the bed.

"Sleep," a voice whispered. "And don't worry about a thing."

The voice must have been a spell, Emily realized, as she opened her eyes again. She felt better as her headache was gone, but once she looked at Frieda's bed, her heart plunged into despair. They'd even taken the damned bedding!

And where had they taken Frieda?

They said no one could leave during term-time, Emily thought, numbly. She sat up. Then removed the rest of her dress and swapped it for a robe. Her pretty blue dress had been stained, torn and utterly ruined. *So where have they taken her?*

She looked around and discovered a large bottle of water beside her bed, along with several smaller potion gourds. Wincing at the thought of tasting yet more potions, she performed a quick check and discovered that one of them—marked so she would drink it last—was a sleeping potion, potent enough to send her into darkness for nearly a day. How would that help her concentrate once the proctor came to fetch her? She couldn't take that now.

But she drank the others, then swallowed the water afterward as quickly as possible. It didn't improve the taste.

The hall was empty, she discovered, as she made her way to the washroom to answer the call of nature. She thought about going back to bed, but the thought of Frieda being expelled worried her enough to keep her awake. Perhaps she could bargain with Aurelius... she did have something he wanted, after all. Or she could send a note with Frieda asking the Grandmaster to consider offering her a place at Whitehall. She had a hell of a lot of potential for someone who had grown up in such a soul-crushing place to live.

The Dueling Mistress told you to stay here, her thoughts reminded her. *But I have somewhere to go if Mountaintop kicks me out.*

Her magic still felt odd when she reached for it, but the touch of the power against her mind was one hell of a confidence boost. She walked towards the door, half-expecting to walk into a ward keeping her trapped, yet nothing happened. Emily puzzled over it for a long moment, then decided that the tutors must have decided to tempt her into breaking her confinement, giving them an excuse to expel her. Shaking her head, she created a light globe—the effort wasn't painful, but it *was* draining—and walked down the corridor. Fortunately, she encountered no one until she reached Aurelius's office. A grim-faced woman she had never seen before was standing in front of it, her arms crossed under her breasts.

"The Administrator is busy," she said. She didn't seem to recognize Emily, which surprised her. But then, all of the portraits Emily had seen of herself were—at best—pitiful renditions of her true appearance. "You may make an appointment with me."

"I need to see him at once," Emily said. "This is *important.*"

"It's always important," the woman said. "If you've been sent here for punishment, report to Mistress Granite, who will handle you. If not..."

"Well," Emily interrupted crossly, "it's good to see that the school is maintaining its ability to punish students while everything else is in disarray."

"Discipline must be maintained," the woman said, firmly. "And I..."

She stopped as magic flickered around her. "You may enter," she said, in a very different tone of voice. "I apologize."

Emily blinked in surprise, then stepped through the door. She'd half-expected to step into a room crammed with students awaiting punishment, but the chamber was empty. The door to the inner office gaped open, invitingly, and she walked towards it. Inside, Aurelius was sitting at his desk, reading a long piece of paper. He didn't look happy.

"I believe you were told to stay in Raven Hall," he said. His words were disapproving, but his tone was more amused than annoyed. "Do you have a habit of only following the rules when it suits you?"

"I have yet to meet a magician who doesn't," Emily said, as she walked up to his desk and stood in front of it, clasping her hands behind her back to keep them from shaking. "Isn't magic all about breaking the normal rules?"

"Magic is *part* of the rules," Aurelius grunted. He looked up at her, darkly. "Why are you here, Lady Emily?"

"My Shadow has been expelled," Emily said. "I…"

"Yes," Aurelius agreed. "A number of staff worked together to organize the expulsion hearing, which was held only hours after the budding riot was finally quelled and the injured were carted off to the healers. They voted in favor of expulsion and took your Shadow Freda…"

"Frieda," Emily corrected.

"…into custody," Aurelius continued, ignoring her correction. "The expulsion cannot be countermanded by anyone short of the MageMaster."

Emily clenched her fists. "Where is she now?"

"In custody," Aurelius said. "And you will *not* be allowed to visit her."

"I thought you wanted my help," Emily snarled. "I could…"

"You cannot visit her because the terms of expulsion forbid it," Aurelius said. "I could not authorize you to visit her, Emily, because the other tutors have put her in the box. She will be sent home at the end of term unless she can find another placement. There's no shortage of Great Houses willing to hire servants with some magic of their own."

"Or she could go to Whitehall," Emily said. "I could write a letter and ask the Grandmaster to take her on."

"It won't do any harm if you write the letter," Aurelius said. "But she will have to live with the stigma of being expelled—and for good reason. I do not believe the Grandmaster would take her on willingly."

"It wasn't her who started the food fight," Emily said. "And…"

"That does not matter," Aurelius countered. "The tutors have voted to expel her as a dangerous and subversive influence. You should have taken her firmly in hand when you started to teach her."

Emily stared at him. "I…"

"You were given power over her to shape her footsteps and guide her ways," Aurelius said, flatly. "I thought you *understood*. She was there to learn from you as well as serve you. Instead, you placed a dangerous weapon in her hands without teaching her the morals of actually *using* it."

"And none of the well-born *children* had any such training?" Emily asked. "Or did they get told that it was all right to pick on the commoners?"

"This wasn't a single incident," Aurelius said, softly. "This was a whole series of incidents, some alarmingly close to dangerous. The decision cannot be reversed, save by the MageMaster."

Emily stared at him, wondering if he'd manipulated the whole situation to gain Emily's endorsement. If she offered to support him, would he undo the expulsion? Or would he try to smooth Frieda's path to Whitehall? Or... but cold logic suggested otherwise. If Aurelius couldn't undo the expulsion, couldn't even hold out *hope* of undoing the expulsion, what did it matter what she offered to do?

"But what," she asked bitterly, "should I have done?"

"Stopped her," Aurelius said, simply. "You were an only child, weren't you?"

Emily nodded. *That* wasn't really a secret.

"You were meant to be her big sister, but also her supervisor," Aurelius said. "But all you did was recklessly place a weapon in her hands. You had authority to deal with her in any way you saw fit, from assigning lines to smacking her in front of the entire hall. Instead, you chose not to supervise her at all."

He paused. "Perhaps you would have benefited from a similar system at Whitehall," he mused. "You would have learned how to be a Shadow before you learned to be a Patron."

"Half of the girls in Raven Hall seem to have been assigned to Patrons who gave them an easy time," Emily said. A moment of honestly made her clarify her statement. "The others never talked about their early years with me."

"One of them wasn't," Aurelius said. "And she became stronger than you realized, when you first met her."

Emily eyed him. "Who?"

Aurelius looked back at her. "Figure it out."

Emily put the puzzle aside for later contemplation, then forced herself to hold still. "I want to have Frieda either saved from expulsion or sent to Whitehall," she said. If there was any truth to what she'd been told about magical debts, the Grandmaster owed her one for saving his entire school. "What can I do to have her expulsion canceled?"

"You can't," Aurelius said, sharply. "Only the MageMaster can cancel the expulsion."

Emily met his eyes. "And can you become MageMaster quickly enough to arrange for her to return to classes, as if this never happened?"

"No," Aurelius said. "Not yet."

He looked down at his desk for a long moment. "There is nothing further that can be done for your Shadow. I suggest you go back to Raven Hall and wait." He gave her a long, level look. "You do not want the proctors hunting you down, Emily. The other tutors are quite eager to find an excuse to have you expelled, too."

"Then what was the point," Emily asked in frustration, "of having a Shadow in the first place?"

"I told you," Aurelius said. His voice was suddenly very cold. "To teach you how to use power—and when *not* to use power. We gave you power over that young girl—and, in doing so, we gave you a moral responsibility to *use* that power. The choices you made would define you. But you chose not to use your power at all."

He wrung his hands together as he spoke. "There are senior students who keep their Shadows hopping, sending them here and there until we have a quiet word with them about taking things too far," he added. "And there have been students who have crossed the line so blatantly that even the most well-connected student had to be expelled for gross misconduct. But you went to the opposite extreme. You were so reluctant to use your power that your Shadow drifted further and further out of control until she was expelled.

"You failed her, Emily. And you failed yourself, too."

"I didn't *ask* for her," Emily said.

"She didn't ask for *you*," Aurelius countered. "You had to learn to live with each other; she had to be your little sister and servant, you had to be her big sister and mistress. And you failed at both roles."

He sighed. "Go back to your hall," he ordered. "I dare say you will be called shortly to face the examination board. And believe me, they will ask so many questions that you will end up feeling as though you have been torn apart and then put back together again. Only the MageMaster could override their decision, and he isn't talking."

Emily nodded. "Thank you for your time," she said. "And..."

She shook her head. "I should go back to Whitehall," she said. Whatever her mission, she knew she couldn't stand Mountaintop any longer. "I can't stay here."

"The wards will keep you here," Aurelius said. "Only the MageMaster can lower the wards."

Only the MageMaster, Emily thought. He'd said it over and over again, reminding her that the MageMaster could do everything from reversing the expulsion to lowering the wards ahead of schedule. And she knew where to find the MageMaster. Perhaps she could ask him for help... if not for her, then for Frieda.

"Thank you, sir," she said. "I'll go back to my hall."

Outside, she nodded to the grim-faced woman and hurried along towards the MageMaster's quarters. She'd explored most of the open corridors with Frieda and had been surprised to discover that the MageMaster practically lived right *next* to the Administrator. But Mountaintop, despite being a labyrinth of passageways and corridors, didn't seem to change its interior to guide or confuse students. In some ways, Emily was almost disappointed. The spells she'd learned to help sneak around Whitehall were useless at Mountaintop. But at least this particular section of the school was brightly lit.

She paused as she turned the corridor, her instincts warning her to be careful. A single figure—Markus—stood in front of the door, looking at the ground. For a moment, she thought he was waiting for entry, then she realized he was on guard. But on guard for *what?*

Maybe they thought I would go to the MageMaster, she thought. Aurelius had been hinting–clumsily–that she should do just that. *Or maybe it's just a guard of honor.*

She braced herself, then walked into view, hastily devising and revising a plan in her head. It would have been simplest, she knew, to simply throw a spell at him before he realized she was there, but if he caught the spell and deflected it, he'd come after her for sure. And, if she was caught assaulting the Head Boy, the best she could hope for was expulsion. And *that* would mean having to wait in the cells until the wards were raised.

"Emily," Markus said, surprised. "Why are you here?"

Emily considered, briefly, trying to be seductive, but she knew she couldn't hope to pull it off. Instead, she decided to be honest.

"I need to talk to the MageMaster," she said, frankly. "Please, will you let me through?"

"I have strict orders not to let anyone through but staff," Markus said. He reached out and placed a hand on her shoulder as she wilted. "You can probably take your request to the Administrator..."

"I can't," Emily said, quietly. "I need the MageMaster to help me."

Markus nodded in sudden understanding, but his grip was firm. "I can't let you through," he said, softly. "My orders won't allow me to leave."

Emily reached up and took his hand in hers. It felt just like any other hand, hard and strong, but somehow it reminding her of how Jade had helped her to climb back when they had been exploring the mountains. And yet, part of her thrilled to the touch. There was something different about it now, and it scared as well as fascinated her. But there was no time to consider it...

"I'm sorry," she muttered, and cast the spell. "I really am sorry."

Markus froze. Emily stared at him, fighting down a strange sense of guilt as she released his hand. It wasn't the standard freeze spell, the one that could be broken, but a stasis spell. He would stand there, utterly unaware of time passing, until someone released the spell or it ran out of energy on its own. And he would be completely helpless...

She took one last look, then opened the door and stepped into the chamber. Inside, it was surprisingly warm, but dark. The only source of light was a dampened light globe hanging near the ceiling, flickering and dimming constantly, only to revive itself seconds later. And there was a strange smell in the air...

And magic. *Soul* magic.

"Make a light globe," a voice said, from out of the darkness. There was a hint of a chuckle, buried within a very old voice. "Ugly I may be, but you shouldn't have to be in the dark."

Emily tried to sense if the voice sounded well-meaning, then obeyed.

Chapter Thirty-Five

EMILY HAD EXPECTED THE MAGEMASTER TO LOOK LIKE THE GRANDMASTER. INSTEAD, HE was a little old man, with hair as white as snow. His eyes were bright blue, but so deeply recessed in his head that she couldn't help wondering if his body was slowly collapsing in on itself. The more she saw of him, the stranger he seemed. It was almost like looking at a humanoid alien rather than a living human being, or perhaps a desiccated Santa Claus.

"I don't get much company," the MageMaster said. He coughed loudly, a long hacking cough, then cleared his throat. His voice was soft, yet instantly trustworthy. "And who might you be?"

"Emily," Emily told him.

"The Necromancer's Bane," the MageMaster said. He looked up, twisting his head very slightly. "Step into the light, child. I want to see you."

Emily obeyed. It was hard to believe the MageMaster was anything but a kindly old man. She had to remind herself, sharply, that appearances could be very deceptive in the Nameless World. Magic alone made it easy for a young man to look old and vice versa. And then there were the problems caused by the lack of a proper diet... But, as she stepped closer, she realized the MageMaster was truly as old as he looked. His bed was surrounded by strands of translucent magic that flickered in and out of existence, forever linked to the magic running through the school.

"You're young," the MageMaster murmured. "How did they get you here?"

"Kidnap, of sorts," Emily said. "Sir...?"

"Aurelius was always trying to collect as many interesting and useful people as possible," the MageMaster said. He seemed to smile, although his face was so old it was difficult to be certain. "I remember one girl who he picked out and trained himself, pushing her into becoming a truly capable magician. And she would do anything for him. I believe he even used her as a spy, then rewarded her despite her lowly origins."

Lin, Emily thought. Something was nagging at the back of her mind. *Where is she?*

"He would have been able to do the same for you, if you had let him," the MageMaster added. "I know he was fascinated by you as soon as you made your appearance at Whitehall."

Emily shivered. She was old enough to understand that interest from a stranger was not always a good thing. "Why?"

"You are a powerful, yet inexperienced child of a magician," the MageMaster said. "Someone who could be shaped and molded as he saw fit. Someone who had ideas that could change the world. And someone with influence he could use to further his own agenda."

"He said he wanted to beat the Necromancers," Emily said, feeling oddly betrayed. But Aurelius had also directed her to the MageMaster. "Was it all a lie?"

"I dare say he understands the importance of defeating the Necromancers," the MageMaster said. "But he is keeping an eye on his own power base, too. I suppose it isn't too surprising. He is, after all, highly ambitious."

He smiled. "He wants to be MageMaster, you know," he added, to Emily's complete lack of surprise. "But *should* he be MageMaster?"

Emily shrugged.

"On one hand, he would certainly be a more proactive MageMaster," the MageMaster mused, softly. "But on the other hand, he would be far too disruptive to the established order."

"Is that a bad thing?" Emily asked. She looked down at his pale skin, so translucent she could almost see his skull. "From what I've seen of it, the established order could do with some disruption."

"Your father would say so," the MageMaster said. "But *he* is powerful enough to stand alone, free of all oaths and obligations and demands from his peers. How many others share that level of power?"

"Few," Emily said. "How do you know my father?"

"We had some great times, back in the day," the MageMaster said. "And some almighty arguments. How is the old goat?"

"He was fine, the last I heard," Emily said. She hadn't seen Void since he'd visited her before she'd left Whitehall for her work experience with Lady Barb. "But he doesn't show himself very often."

"He likes to keep himself to himself," the MageMaster said. He cackled, loudly. "I would never have expected him to have a *daughter*. Or were you a surprise?"

"Something like that," Emily admitted. She really didn't want to lie to the man.

"I wish he were here," the MageMaster said. He sighed, theatrically. "Being stuck in this wretched bed isn't much fun."

"I know," Emily said, quietly. She came closer, stepping forward until she was standing by the side of the bed. "I wondered if you were dead. Very few people even *mentioned* you at school."

"They won't let me die," the MageMaster said. There was a sudden tiredness in his voice that stunned her. He sounded like she did when she wanted to sleep, but her studies or potions kept her awake, only worse. Much worse. "This is my time to go, yet they won't let me die. They're too scared of what will happen when I lose my grip on the wards."

Emily leaned forward. "And what *will* happen?"

"They'll collapse, *obviously*," the MageMaster said. "They were never designed to have more than one person in command, one person serving as the linchpin of the school's defenses. And none of my predecessors wanted to take the risk of allowing the wards to be linked to a homunculus. They liked being in control."

He smiled, again. "If they have a proper candidate in mind to replace me, that person can take on the wards and let me go onwards into the next world. But as long as they don't have someone ready and waiting to take over, they will be forced to keep me alive."

He paused. "When he brought you here," he said, "did Aurelius force you to take any oaths?"

"No," Emily said.

The MageMaster surprised her by laughing. "Oh, that sly dog," he said. "I could almost approve if it wasn't for the sheer *risk* of the act. Talk about finding a loophole!"

"A loophole," Emily repeated. "A loophole in *what*?"

"Why, the rules of course," the MageMaster said. He sniggered, rather like a young schoolboy than a grown man. "Aren't they cute when they think they're getting away with something?"

He cleared his throat. "But why are you here, my dear?"

Emily made a face. "I've made a mess of things," she confessed. She wasn't sure what was forcing her to talk, apart from the certainty there was no one else who could help her. "My Shadow has been expelled and Aurelius said you were the only one who could undo the punishment. Or at least help me get her to a different school."

"That might be true," the MageMaster agreed. "But–and be honest–why do you *care*?"

"Because it's the right thing to do," Emily said. "Because I like the girl. And because the whole situation is partly my fault."

The MageMaster smiled. "Just *partly*?"

"Yes," Emily said, firmly.

The MageMaster looked up at her through tired blue eyes. "I will help you find her," he said. "But I need you to do something for me in exchange."

Emily knew she would consider almost anything. "What?"

"There's a web of magic surrounding me," the MageMaster said. "I want you to disentangle it, carefully. Once the web is disrupted, take the key from around my neck and put it around your own. I am *giving* it to you. It will be *yours*. Do you understand me?"

"No," Emily said. Caution warred with the urgent need to do something–anything. Her caution won. "What does it do?"

The MageMaster snorted. "What do keys normally do?"

"Unlock things," Emily said. "But where is the lock it opens?"

"Disrupt the web, take the key," the MageMaster ordered. "And then listen carefully to what I tell you to do."

Emily scowled. She hated being in a position where she had to act without knowing precisely what was going on. Who knew *what* disrupting the magic surrounding the MageMaster would do? But, at the same time, she had a feeling the MageMaster was trying to help her, in a very twisted way. And he would owe her if she did what he told her to do and unpicked the web of magic.

"It won't harm you," the MageMaster assured her. "And it is the only way you will ever manage to retrieve your Shadow."

Emily ground her teeth. "Very well," she said.

She held up a hand, then reached out with her mind and attacked the cobweb of magic. It was easily the strangest set of magics she'd encountered, so translucent that it was difficult to touch without careful spellwork... yet the second she figured out how to bring her power to bear against the magic, it started to crumble at her touch. The MageMaster let out a long gasp of pain, then twitched unpleasantly in his bed.

Emily started in astonishment. What had she done?

"Take the key," the MageMaster hissed. An alarm howled in the distance, sending chills down her spine. "Take the key and put it around your neck, then hide in the next room. When they take me away, follow the magic down into the caves. The key will get you through the locked door. You'll find your Shadow there. You'll have to hurry. And I'm sorry."

His body shook again as she removed the key. It didn't look special, nothing more than an iron key studded with runes dangling from a golden chain, but she felt a tingle of magic as soon as she placed it around her neck. Suddenly, the magics running through the room became a bit more obvious. The alarm wasn't just noise, she realized, as it grew louder. Every magician in the school would sense the distress.

"Hide," the MageMaster snapped. In the distance, Emily heard the sound of running feet coming towards her. "Hurry!"

Emily nodded, then slipped into the next room and cast a shielding ward around herself. It was just in time.

The door burst open and a long line of proctors flowed into the room, their black garb making them appear almost part of the shadows. Emily felt the key grow warm against her skin as the proctors surrounded the MageMaster, then lifted his bed and carried it out of the room. Magic ebbed and flowed around her as she heard the MageMaster complaining loudly, keeping their attention on him.

Emily felt an odd flicker of gratitude towards the older man. She wasn't quite sure what she'd done, but he'd done something to help her.

The key twisted against her hand like a living thing, but she refused to let it go. Magic had never seemed quite so understandable; now, she sensed thousands upon thousands of charms and spells extending through the network of caves that made up the school. She closed her eyes and concentrated, drawing on her new knowledge. There was something about the network that was uniquely fragile, compared to Whitehall. Didn't they have access to a nexus point?

They can't, she thought, numbly. No one had any doubt where Whitehall was located, not really. The school's nexus was an open secret. Even if the Grandmaster had tried to hide, it would be mind-numbingly obvious where the school had to be. *I would have sensed a nexus point if they had one.*

And that led to a different thought. *If they don't have a nexus point*, she asked herself, *what do they use instead?*

She canceled the ward before stepping back into the main room. The magic that had hovered over the MageMaster's bed was almost completely gone, the last traces fading away into nothingness as she watched. Emily quickly searched the room, but found nothing apart from a set of runes she recognized from her classes the previous year. One channeled magic into the room, while the other two were designed to help keep their target awake. And, beyond them, there were a set of runes she didn't recognize at all. She tried to work out what they did, but got nowhere. They were too advanced for her current level.

A nasty thought struck her and she froze. *If they were keeping him alive*, she thought, *did I just kill him?*

But he'd been alive when the proctors came for him...

She braced herself, then touched the key around her neck once again. This time, her awareness of the school came quicker, showing her the charms and spells that were slowly unlocking themselves. The MageMaster might not be dead, but the magic he'd anchored in place was coming apart at the seams. She concentrated and realized that the MageMaster had been entirely correct. The system was designed to have a living mind–a *single* living mind–as the linchpin. There was no way they could prevent the entire system from collapsing now, until they put someone else in the MageMaster's place...

And the key might just be the key to Mountaintop.

"I am giving it to you," the MageMaster had said. "It will be yours."

Ownership, Emily thought, as she opened the door. There was no sign of Markus. *He gave me ownership of the key as well as the key itself.*

She glanced up and down the corridor, but saw nothing. Had the proctors taken Markus, or had her spell collapsed, releasing him? But he hadn't charged into the room, intent on capturing Emily before it was too late. Perhaps he'd gone directly to Aurelius, to report his failure... but his failure would be self-evident. Even without the key, Emily could sense the wards were slowly starting to come apart. Mountaintop would soon be completely defenseless.

Pushing the thought aside, she cast a light globe and hurried down the corridor, trying to make her way to the caves. There were almost no students in the corridors and those she passed looked frightened, but unaware of Emily's involvement. A handful of staff passed her, escorting lines of young students back to their halls, yet they showed no interest in her either. Their eyes were as frightened as their students. Whatever happened, whatever they did, their world was about to change.

A proctor loomed up in front of her suddenly, grabbing for her arm. Emily tried to yank herself free, then brought up her knee to strike the proctor in the groin. The proctor showed no sign of any reaction to her blow. Instead, he turned and started to pull her back towards the offices.

Emily braced herself, then tugged at his hood. It came free. Hundreds of images from zombie movies flashed into her mind as she saw the gray flesh, preserved forever by a spell; she sensed the soul magic flickering and flaring around the proctor. The key felt warm against her chest. It was suddenly the easiest thing in the world to pull the magic from the proctor, sending him–it–crashing to the ground.

Emily recoiled in disgust as, free of the spell, the body started to decay into a puddle of rotting flesh. But, before the face had become utterly unrecognisable, the proctor hadn't seemed any older than Emily.

Death Magic, she thought. Had someone found a body, then cast preservation and reanimation charms on it and turned it into a proctor? Or was something more sinister underway? Shadye had used skeletons as servants, after all.

But there shouldn't have been any reason for Mountaintop to do the same. There was no shortage of living people who would be glad of the chance to work at a magic school.

She shuddered as she walked towards the gate leading into the caves. Magic crackled around the structure, clearly intended to keep the students from exploring the underground network, but it was pointless. The gate lay open in front of her. Emily's eyes narrowed, suspecting a trap, yet the more she looked, the more confident she was that there were no unpleasant surprises waiting for her. Whoever had opened the gate had been in so great a hurry that he hadn't bothered to seal it behind him.

New flickers of magic ran through the air, heading past her and down towards the secure door. Emily hesitated, one hand touching the key hanging around her neck, then started to walk towards the gate, alert for any traps. Someone could easily have hidden a security charm in the web of magic surrounding the entrance, relying on the sheer quantity of charms to hide its presence. But then she felt magic flickering *behind* her and spun around, just in time to deflect the freeze spell aimed at her back. She'd concentrated so hard on the threat in front of her that she hadn't sensed the person sneaking up behind her.

"Emily," Nanette said. Her voice sounded strong and confident, but there was an underlying worry that would have been alarming, under other circumstances. She could probably sense the school's wards collapsing, too. "I have orders to take you to a secure room and place you there until the proctors can judge you."

Emily stared at her, feeling the pieces slowly falling into place. The MageMaster had talked about a girl Aurelius had used as a spy, then rewarded. Nanette had no allegiances to any magical family, as far as she could tell; her office was certainly barren of portraits, compared to Markus's room. And her feet were pockmarked, something that magic could easily cure, if she'd had access to healers from a very early age.

"Please don't do anything stupid," Nanette added. "There isn't *time* for us to fight."

And they said Nanette was elsewhere last year, Emily thought, ignoring her. Nanette had *manipulated* her—and she'd done it so effectively, she must have had prior knowledge of Emily. *And the only person who could have done that was...*

She took a breath. "Hello, Lin."

Chapter Thirty-Six

M Y *NAME*," Nanette said, "is *Nanette.*"

"But you were Lin," Emily said. It was hard to connect the mousy little girl she barely recalled, a last remnant of the magic she had used to protect herself, with the strong and confident Nanette, but the more she considered the idea the more Emily was sure she was right. Nanette looked like an older version of Lin. "You spied on me at Whitehall."

"And you were brought here to take my place," Nanette said. She sounded jealous, of all things. "If I had had a free choice, I would have refused to accept you at Mountaintop."

"But Aurelius didn't give you a choice," Emily said, as more pieces of the puzzle fell into place. Aurelius had rewarded his spy, all right, by making her Head Girl. "You already knew me. Who else could be relied upon to make sure I did what I was told?"

She sighed. She'd assumed–*careless*, Sergeant Harkin's voice mocked her–that Nanette was from one of the Great Houses. It had seemed a reasonable assumption, as Markus had definitely received his post because of his family connections, but it was clearly in error. And some of Nanette's actions made more sense, now Emily realized just how far Nanette had to fall if something went badly wrong. *She* couldn't rely on her family to help her.

"You were his client," Emily said. Aurelius might have been telling the truth about the flaws in the system–he'd clearly understood its weaknesses–but he hadn't avoided exploiting them. Offering Nanette special lessons would have gone a long way towards making the girl devoted to him. "What else have you done for him?"

"It doesn't matter," Nanette said. "What have *you* done?"

Emily winced, suddenly understanding why Nanette was jealous. She'd seen Emily as a rival, not for a suitor, but for a father-figure. And Emily might have more to offer Aurelius than Nanette could ever hope to match. What was loyalty compared to the ideas that had reshaped the world and defeated two Necromancers? She had watched Emily grow closer to Aurelius, her wariness blossoming into an intellectual relationship, and grown more than a little concerned for her position. And why not?

"It doesn't matter either," she said. Part of her felt almost sorry for Nanette. The rest of her mind, recalling how Nanette had tried to kill her, told that part of her to shut up. "Where are my notes?"

"Somewhere safe," Nanette said. She smirked. "Copied, of course."

"Of course," Emily echoed. In truth, she wasn't surprised. "Why did you try to kill me?"

"I wanted to cover my tracks," Nanette admitted. "The Gorgon would have made a more than acceptable scapegoat."

"True," Emily sneered. She allowed her fury to show. She'd never realized just how much casual racism there was against Gorgons, not emotionally, until she'd heard the staff considering simply smashing the statue the Gorgon had become. "But your plan misfired."

"So it did," Nanette said. "No plan is ever perfect, Emily. All you have to do is adapt and improvise when all hell breaks loose."

She lifted a hand. "And now, I have to take you to your cell," she added. "I held back in our last encounter..."

"No, you didn't," Emily said, cursing under her breath. She wasn't sure how much magic she could summon, while Nanette was clearly at the top of her game. "I think you wanted to give me enough of a hammering to put me firmly in my place."

Nanette's eyes narrowed. "Did *he* tell you that?"

"I never told him about the duel," Emily said. Had Aurelius been using the wards in the school to monitor her? "Did you?"

"No," Nanette said.

She tossed her head. "You're nothing special," she added. "I watched you at Whitehall, and I watched you here at Mountaintop. You have the potential for power, but you lack the confidence–the arrogance–of a sorcerer. I honestly don't understand how your father didn't teach you to hold your head up high, or look people in the eye when you talk to them. I would have thought that a willing daughter would be a more than competent assistant for his work."

"I'm getting better," Emily said, defiantly. The key warmed for a long second, then cooled again as magic flared around them. "I had a great deal to learn."

"Or was your father abusive?" Nanette asked. "Mine used to beat me with a belt. My first use of magic was blasting him right out of the house. Why wouldn't a Lone Power be just as unpleasant to a daughter who clearly didn't develop magic as a child?"

That, Emily thought, was distressingly close to the truth. She had never realized until Hodge had tried to rape her and its aftermath, just how many scars had been left on her soul by her stepfather. Nanette was quite right, she had to admit; she'd merely blamed Emily's experiences on the wrong person.

But she was working to try to overcome her problems, now she knew what they were. The old Emily would never have dared allow herself to be kidnapped if she'd been offered a choice.

"I think my past is none of your concern," she offered, tartly. "Why was your father so unpleasant to *you*? Did he know what you were?"

"His people believe that a couple marries for life," Nanette said. She shrugged, although she never took her eyes off Emily. "When my mother died giving birth to a stillborn child who should have been my brother, my father went a little mad. I might have been more sympathetic if he hadn't taken it out on me."

"I'm sorry," Emily said. She'd gone looking for a father-figure too, in a way. "Nanette..."

She took a breath. "I have to find my Shadow," she said. "You shouldn't try to stop me."

"I have no choice," Nanette said. "*I* don't have a castle in Zangaria to call my own!"

"I could take you in," Emily offered. "It isn't as though I don't have the room."

Emily could have kicked herself a moment later. She wasn't sure where *that* had come from, but it was a workable option. With the proper oaths, Nanette might be a very useful source of assistance in her long-term plans. She was clearly intelligent enough to master magic at a very early age, if Aurelius had used her as a spy. And to pose as the harmless Lin when she'd been sharing a room with Emily and the Gorgon, or being pranked by other Second Years at Whitehall. It must have been humiliating to know she could easily best any of them, yet she had endured their taunts. And she'd completed her mission in the end.

She's a better spy than me, Emily thought, ruefully. *A week in place and she already had runes scattered through our room.*

"I don't think I can leave him," Nanette said. She lifted her hand and shot a spell at Emily, testing her defenses. Emily stepped to one side, rather than waste energy deflecting the spell, and allowed it to hit the gate. Magic flared behind her, then fell into nothingness. "And I don't trust you to keep your word."

"Tell me," Emily said. "Do you trust *him?*"

"He made me Head Girl," Nanette pointed out. "*That* must have cost him."

"It probably did," Emily conceded. She saw, all too clearly, just how strong a hold Aurelius had on Nanette. A little care and attention, a handful of advanced lessons... and he'd made himself an ally for life. "Nanette... Lin... you have to listen to me."

"No, *you* have to listen," Nanette said. She launched a second spell, a wide-band stunner that was weak, but almost impossible to dodge. Emily had to block it, gritting her teeth as her skin tingled before the spell faded away. "I have more training than you can imagine."

"I think I beat you before," Emily said, cheekily. She met Nanette's eyes and held them. Lady Barb had told her, more than once, that a show of confidence could defuse a fight before it even began. "And I have a few surprises too..."

Nanette didn't bother to respond. Instead, she tossed spell after spell at Emily, ranging from simple prank spells to nastier ones that could do real damage if they broke through Emily's defenses. Emily retaliated by creating a bubble shield around herself, using it as cover as she tried to get closer to Nanette, ducking or deflecting as many spells as she could before they could hit her.

Her enemy didn't seem amused by the handful of spells Emily threw back at her, all borderline lethal, but she didn't seem worried either. A fireball flashed past her and struck the stone wall, then exploded. She barely seemed to notice.

Emily gritted her teeth, feeling cold hatred swelling within her breast. *This* was the girl who had raided her notes, stolen her private thoughts, meddled with her mind and almost killed her and one of her friends. *This* was the girl who had almost pitched her headfirst into a feud with the Gorgon, a feud that could easily have killed them both; *this* was the girl who had tricked the Gorgon into petrifying both Emily and herself. Part of her was glad Nanette hadn't accepted her offer, even though it meant she had to waste time fighting her. The thought of beating her into a bloody pulp was almost hypnotic.

"You're running out of magic," Nanette said. "What *were* you and he doing that cost you so much?"

Well observed, Emily thought. She was only throwing a handful of spells at Nanette, while the older girl was firing them at her like bullets from a machine gun as if she had a limitless supply of energy. Last time, Emily had been caught by surprise; she'd never realized that harmless Lin had so much training. Now... she knew just how capable Nanette could be, and she still found herself wrong-footed. And she was so short of magic herself.

"He was showing me how to become the best," she said, hoping to lure Nanette into a foolish reaction. Duels had been lost before, she'd been told, because one duelist jeered the other into making a foolish move. "And how to be his favorite."

Nanette hissed, then threw a wave of magic at her. Emily was picked up and flung against the stone wall, held firmly in place by the spell.

I shouldn't have said that, she thought as Nanette stalked forward. The magic was so strong it was actually breaking the stone around her, now that the school's wards were falling apart. Emily recoiled as unpleasant crawling sensations moved over her skin, reaching under her dress to press against her bare flesh. The key flared, as the magic touched it, but did nothing.

"I will not let you replace me," Nanette said. "I think you got lucky."

Emily scrabbled for her magic, but nothing formed. Nanette had learned from her previous defeat, she thought, as she realized just what spells and wards Nanette had worked into her magic. It had to cost her dearly to hold the magic in place, but as long as she did, she could keep Emily helpless indefinitely. She could neither move enough to lash out at her or cast a spell.

"I think you beat Shadye through luck," Nanette remarked. "You don't have the power to beat me, so you certainly don't have the power to beat a Necromancer. And then the Grandmaster, not you, killed the Mimic. And I'd bet good money that you didn't kill the other Necromancer either. Or maybe you just killed her through poison and everyone thought you'd done something special."

Emily felt her bones starting to ache as Nanette pressed the magic against her chest. She tried desperately to think of an option, a way out of the trap, but nothing came to mind. The key didn't seem inclined to do anything to help, while she couldn't even break the wave of magic holding her in place. Nanette inched closer and closer, her eyes glinting with power and cold hatred. She wanted Emily dead, not for political purposes, but merely because she thought Emily had stolen Aurelius from her.

Desperately, she reached for the binding surrounding the Death Viper and released it. The snake bracelet became a snake, clinging to Emily's arm. She felt the surge of sensations as the familiar bond came back to life, then winced as the magic holding her tightened its grip.

"Tell me," Nanette said. "Do you honestly think I would fall for the same trick twice?"

The Death Viper lunged. Nanette lifted a hand to swat it away, but screamed in pain as she touched its poisoned scales. The magic holding Emily in place snapped out of existence as Nanette clutched her hand, and stumbled to the ground. She'd been lucky, part of Emily's mind noted dispassionately. If the Death Viper had bitten her, she would already be dead.

"It wasn't a fake," she said, quietly. Last year—it felt like decades ago—she'd used an illusion against an unknown opponent, someone she'd later assumed to be Lin. This time, the Death Viper had been real. "And..."

She broke off as Nanette convulsed in pain. The nasty part of her just wanted to wait and watch as the poison slowly killed the older girl, but the rest of her was horrified at the thought of watching a person die. Somehow, she managed to cast a stunning spell before using a cutting spell to slice Nanette's arm off at the elbow. She would hate Emily when she woke up, Emily knew, but it was better than death. Besides, the wound was already cauterized and a new arm could be grown through magic. She would be able to return to school if she wished.

"I'm sorry," Emily said, softly.

She recalled the serpent to her wrist, then tried to push it back into its bracelet form. But the magic refused to work, either because she was exhausted or because she could sense the snake's desire to remain in its normal form. Emily sighed, then picked up the snake and allowed it to rest on her shoulder, wrapping itself around her neck. For anyone else, it would be instantly fatal to allow a Death Viper so close to their brain. But as long as she was bonded to the snake, she knew it wouldn't be able to hurt her, even accidentally. The rotting touch was no threat to her.

Once, she knew, the mere thought of touching a snake would have been horrifying. Now, it felt natural.

She stroked the snake's head as she made her way down the carved passageways, past the monster lairs and into the large cavern before the sealed door. The key grew warm against her skin as she stepped towards the door; this time, her rune didn't even change at all as she reached the metal barrier. There was no sign of a keyhole; it took her several seconds to realize that she had to press the key against the metal and let the magic work. It was a long chilling moment before the door finally opened, allowing her into the hidden section of Mountaintop.

Inside, the air smelled musty, with a faint hint of decay, but it was brightly lit. Emily walked forward, down a stone corridor, and peered into the first chamber. It was empty, save for a stone table that reminded her of some of the stonework she'd seen in the Cairngorms. The next two chambers were the same, but the fourth held a girl lying on the table. Emily threw caution to the winds and ran towards the girl, recognizing the pigtails hanging down towards the floor.

"Frieda," she said.

The girl was in a trance, Emily realized, as she reached her side. She would have thought Frieda was dead, save for the steady rise and fall of her chest. Someone had changed her clothes, putting her into a white robe that clung to her body in odd places, as if it was designed to make her seem more of a child than a girl old enough to use magic. Emily paused, considering options, then tried to cast a dispersal spell. It didn't work.

"She will remain sleeping until the time is right," a familiar voice said. "And why are you here?"

Emily turned to see Aurelius, standing at the door with his arms crossed over his chest. His expression was grim, but calculating. Emily felt a flicker of fear as he studied her, no longer trying to be kind, and fought down the impulse to just slip away. If she hadn't known there was nowhere to go, she might well have run.

"I came to get my Shadow," she said, firmly. The key seemed to turn icy cold, as if it didn't want to be noticed. She had to fight the desire to remove it before her skin froze. "What are you doing to her?"

"Using her," Aurelius said. He beckoned to her to follow him, then turned and walked out of the door. When Emily didn't move, he turned back to her and sighed. "You *do* realize I can *make* you walk, don't you? There are no shortage of spells to compel obedience from unruly apprentices."

"I'm not your apprentice," Emily said.

"After today, you will be," Aurelius said. He turned again, his voice echoing back to her ears. "Or dead. Follow me."

Emily forced herself to follow him, despite her growing fear. The key was growing colder, while the magic surrounding them was changing, becoming something different. If Aurelius noticed, he showed no reaction. Instead, he simply led her down into a large chamber...

...And Emily stopped, frozen in utter horror at the sight that greeted her eyes.

"Welcome to the Heart of Mountaintop," Aurelius said. He didn't seem pleased or angry, merely amused. "A sight few have seen without swearing the right oaths."

Chapter Thirty-Seven

THE CHAMBER WAS HUGE, EASILY LARGE ENOUGH TO SERVE AS A SECOND GREAT HALL. People–former students, she suspected–drifted high overhead, their faces twisted in agony as they were drained of their magic. Two of them, she realized to her horror, were familiar, both part of Frieda's little rebellion. Below them, the MageMaster's dying body lay on a table, surrounded by a small army of proctors. They were kneeling, as if they were at prayer, or worshipping the dying man. None paid any attention to either Emily or Aurelius.

The process wasn't Necromancy, she realized as she forced herself to think straight. A Necromancer drew his victim's entire reserve of magic and life force out of his body in one wave of power, enough to drive the Necromancer insane if he hadn't already been mad as a hatter. Here, the process was clearly under some form of control, allowing their power to be siphoned off and inserted into the wards protecting the school.

"This is a giant ritual," she said, recalling the ritual chamber Lady Barb had shown her, hidden below her house. "But I thought rituals had to be voluntary..."

"They all swore their oaths," Aurelius said, softly. He rested a hand on her shoulder. "They promised to come back to Mountaintop and offer their power, if necessary. Their oaths keep them working for us, even if they are expelled. *This* is the cruel necessity at the heart of Mountaintop."

"You're sacrificing your students to power the school," Emily said. She took a sharp breath as she realized it was worse than that. "No, not *all* of your students. You're just sacrificing the common-born to maintain your power."

"The ones who cannot be fitted into our society," Aurelius said. "They swore oaths when they entered the school."

Emily's blood ran cold as she recalled the oath. *I will put my magic at the school's disposal, should I be called upon to serve...*

She'd assumed it meant fighting for the school. It had never crossed her mind that it might mean allowing herself to be used as a living power source.

"And," Emily asked, "did they know what they were swearing?"

"They knew the potential risks," Aurelius said. "Their oaths force them to open their power and allow it to be drained through the network."

"And when they're completely drained," Emily said slowly, "they become proctors."

"Yes," Aurelius said.

Emily rounded on him. "You said that you wanted to *fix* the system," she snapped. "This... this is horrifying!"

"There is no choice," Aurelius said. "We need a source of power to keep the school functional, Emily. There is no nexus point here, as you must have noticed, and the ones that remain active are heavily guarded. We see no option."

"You could make a deal with Red Rose," Emily said, desperately. "There's a nexus point there."

"They would not surrender it to us," Aurelius said. He gave her a long consider-ing look, then smiled coldly, without humor. "What would you suggest in its place?"

Emily shook her head. She couldn't think of anything... she understood their prob-lem, but *this* was no way to solve it. They had to go through hundreds of students a year, sacrificing them all just to keep the school operational. How the hell had they managed to operate during the days of the Empire? And why had they even set the school up in such a poor location in any case?

"You could take a little energy from *all* of the students," she said, after a moment. "You'd have less from each person, but collectively you might have enough..."

"Not enough," Aurelius said. "Or so we believe."

"I think you didn't mean a word you told me," Emily bit off. She jerked back-wards, forcing him to move his hand. "You don't give a shit about the common-born magicians."

"Only in the abstract," a weak voice said. The MageMaster lay on his back, but his head was turned towards the two younger magicians. "People are merely numbers if you have high ideals and low motives."

Aurelius glared at him. "And what did *you* do to change our society?"

The MageMaster took a rasping breath. His body was failing rapidly, even though the oddly *stretched* appearance was gone. The soul magic must have been working overtime just to keep him alive, she deduced, pushing his body well beyond breaking point. Now, just like the former proctor, his true age was catching up with him. And if he was old enough to consider Void a friend, he had to be in his second century.

"I did what I had to do," the MageMaster said. He twisted his head until he was looking directly at Aurelius. "Our society is fragile, but balanced. A push from you may send it tipping over in the wrong direction."

"It is already falling in the wrong direction," Aurelius hissed. "What will happen when the Necromancers come over the border?"

"They will be stopped," the MageMaster said.

"By whom?" Aurelius demanded. "You? You're a dead man! The only reason you're still alive..."

"...is so you could make sure there was a successor lined up before I died," the MageMaster interrupted, sneering. "And now you're playing your final card. You know I want to die. Here, you think I have no choice but to pass the wards to you."

Aurelius didn't look surprised at the accusation. "And do you have a choice?"

"You knew Emily could break the magic keeping me alive," the MageMaster said. "*She* never swore the oaths that prevented you from striking at me, directly. You never ordered her to kill me, but you knew I would ask her to undo the magic. Very clever. Quite cold-blooded, but very clever."

Emily stared at him. "I didn't mean to kill you..."

"Oh, don't be silly," the MageMaster rasped. "I knew what would happen even if you didn't. And besides, I would have died months ago if they hadn't kept me alive, the selfish bastards."

"We had no choice," Aurelius said, stiffly.

The MageMaster ignored him. "You must not become MageMaster," he said. His voice grew weaker as he spoke. "You are too calculating. There will be rebellion against you soon enough and... you..."

He paused, coughing. Bloody flecks appeared on his pillow.

"There is no other choice," Aurelius said. "Only one of the tutors has no agenda, Most Honored MageMaster. *He* would prefer to be working with his alchemical experiments, rather than make a bid for power."

Zed, Emily thought. Had he been working for King Randor because none of the Great Houses would consider sponsoring his experiments?

"You must not," the MageMaster said. "I..."

There was a sudden flare of magic, then nothing.

Emily stared, dully. The MageMaster had used up his remaining life to die on his own terms, having done the best he could to spite Aurelius. She honored him silently, then braced herself. She might have to run...

"The MageMaster is dead," Aurelius said, softly. Oddly, there was a hint of regret in his tone. "And I will take the wards."

He walked forward. The proctors made no attempt to bar his path as he strode to the bed and started searching the dead man's body. Emily stepped back, knowing it wouldn't be long before Aurelius realized she had the key, if he hadn't suspected it from how easily she'd managed to enter the hidden complex. Magic flickered and flared through her senses as the MageMaster's death accelerated the collapse of the wards. She heard a low roar in the distance, followed by a series of crashes. The sound made no sense to her.

Aurelius stepped backwards, then turned to face her. "Emily," he snarled, "give me the key!"

Emily turned and ran. She'd almost reached the door when his magic caught her and yanked her back, pulling her into the air and flipping her upside down. Her dress remained in place, thankfully, but the key fell down into the open air. The Death Viper hissed and tightened its grip on her neck. Aurelius's eyes went wide when he saw it—she couldn't imagine how he'd missed the snake earlier—but showed no other reaction. Instead, he merely held out a hand.

"Give me the key," he ordered.

"Fuck you," Emily shouted. She was too angry to care that she was upside down, even though she had the sensation that the people floating high overhead could look up—down—her dress. "He didn't want you to have it."

"Do you really think he meant for *you* to have it?" Aurelius said, sharply.

He gave it to me, Emily thought. But she suspected it wasn't a good idea to say that out loud, not when the MageMaster might have transferred ownership to her as well as physical custody. Aurelius met her eyes, then moved his hand in a complex pattern. Emily felt a dullness fall over her mind, but it snapped a moment later.

Emily allowed herself a moment of relief. Void's protection against certain spells still held true, it seemed.

"Interesting," Aurelius said. "What would you like in exchange for the key?"

"I don't think you can meet my price," Emily said. She tried to think of a way out, but nothing came to mind. Even the snake couldn't hope to bite a wary magician. "He believed you weren't suitable for the task."

Aurelius glared at her. "And what do *you* believe?"

"I think he was right," Emily said. "You claim to care about the common-born magicians—and yes, you gave one of them fantastic opportunities to prove herself. But you also sacrificed uncounted millions of them to power the school."

"Several hundred, at most," Aurelius said. He sounded irked, either by her defiance or her exaggeration. "Give me the key."

Emily—childishly—stuck out her tongue. A moment later, she screamed in pain as the torture curse hit her. Every atom of her body felt like it was on fire. Beside her, the snake was in agony too, either struck by the same curse or picking up on her pain through the familiar bond. She tried to focus her mind, telling herself that she was not going to stand for it, before the next wave of pain swept her thoughts away.

Aurelius stopped the pain after what felt like hours, watching dispassionately as Emily twitched and moaned, then cast the spell again. This time, if anything, the pain was far worse.

"There are nastier curses I can use," he said. The pain stopped, then started again. And again. "Give me the key!"

The spell holding Emily in place snapped, suddenly. Emily fell, his magic barely catching her before she hit the stone floor. The Death Viper hissed and uncurled from her neck, sliding down her shirt. He strode over to her and tore the key from her neck, then kicked her in the ribs. Emily gasped in pain, trying desperately to summon a painkilling spell or even just slip into a healing trance, but the pain made it impossible. Her stomach hurt so badly she had a nasty suspicion that he'd broken a rib or two. Or unleashed a curse that destroyed the stomach's lining, releasing the acid to burn its way through her body. Or...

"I don't think I like you anymore," she managed to say. She had to swallow hard to keep herself from throwing up. If she'd eaten since the ill-fated feast, she suspected she would have thrown up anyway, no matter how hard she tried to hold it in. "Is this how you will treat Nanette once she outlives her usefulness?"

"Be silent," Aurelius said. "If you will not help me, you will remain here until you swear your oaths."

He held the key in his hand, stroking it gently. Emily felt the magic twisting around him, drawn to the key, but it didn't seem *right*. She forced herself to lie still as the magic grew stronger, shimmering through in the air. Aurelius had taken the key by force; she hadn't given it to him willingly. And that, she suspected, would make all the difference. Aurelius held the key high in the air and started to chant loudly, using words from a language Emily didn't know. The magic grew stronger...

...And lashed out at him.

Aurelius screamed in pain and disbelief as the magic poured into his very soul. Emily stared, horrified, as his body flared with light, magic spilling everywhere. It wasn't *his* key, she thought numbly; he'd never anticipated the MageMaster transferring ownership as well as the key itself. And the only way to take ownership would have been to kill Emily and take the key from her corpse. If he'd thought of it before he took the key....

The noise grew louder. Emily looked up to see the expelled students screaming in pain, blood spilling from their eyes, ears and noses, falling to the chamber floor. She desperately tried to cast a spell to catch the nearest one, but her magic refused to respond. They were dying, she realized in horror; the network was killing them, rather than let them go.

She turned her attention back to Aurelius, just in time to see his body glow white and fall to the ground, releasing the last of his magic into the wards. The first MageMaster had built a remarkable safety precaution, she realized numbly, as she forced herself to her feet. Anyone who tried to use the key without permission would have their magic sucked out of them, leaving them powerless. Or dead.

She covered her ears as the screaming grew louder, then half-walked, half-crawled towards Aurelius. The former Administrator was lying on the floor, unconscious. She knelt down next to him and examined his body as best as she could, but most of the damage was clearly magical, rather than mundane wounds. Blood leaked from his nose, staining his robes. Emily, warily, picked up the key and felt it hum in approval. Magic crackled around it, inviting her to lift up the key herself and call the magic into her very soul. *She* could become MageMaster. *She* could take on the role, rather than risk passing the key to someone with a political agenda.

But she didn't want it. The MageMaster had never been able to leave Mountaintop permanently, just as the Grandmaster was tied to Whitehall. Part of her would be happy, reading books in the library and inviting the tutors to give her private lessons, but she was no longer the bookworm she'd once been. She knew there was a wider world outside, a world she wanted to explore. And change.

In the distance, someone cried out in shock. Emily cursed, remembering Frieda, and pulled herself to her feet. Her legs felt hideously unsteady as she stumbled towards the edge of the chamber and threw herself through the door, just in time to avoid more falling bodies. The school was no longer drawing power from its living batteries so carefully, she realized, as the key throbbed its protest below her fingers. Instead, it was trying to suck their power too quickly for the former students to recover, then dropping them when they died. It no longer had a living mind to tell it what to do.

It's flailing out of control, Emily thought, as she heard another dull roar in the distance. She ignored it as she pulled herself towards Frieda's chamber. *It won't be long before it runs out of power completely.*

The light globes high overhead flickered as she stumbled into Frieda's chamber. Her Shadow—her former Shadow, she suspected—was sitting upright, staring around wildly. Emily managed to stumble over to the table and hugged Frieda as tightly as she could. Her Shadow's eyes were wide with astonishment, relief, and something Emily couldn't bring herself to study too closely. Frieda had *known*, beyond a shadow of a doubt, that she was doomed.

"Emily," Frieda said. The lights dimmed again. This time, they remained dim. "What happened?"

"I'm not sure," Emily said. She replaced the key around her neck before helping Frieda to her feet. "How much do you remember?"

"They took me after the feast," Frieda said. "They just told me they were invoking my oaths, that I would spend the rest of my days feeding the school... then I just blanked out and the next thing I remember is waking up here. What did you do?"

"Won your freedom," Emily said, shortly. Several of the light globes snapped out of existence; the remaining ones grew brighter for long seconds, then started to fade again. "I think we'd better run."

She allowed Frieda to cast a light globe to illuminate their path as they made their way back towards the hidden door. Her magic wasn't responding to her will. The subtle magic protecting the door was still in evidence, Emily discovered; Frieda couldn't even *see* the door until Emily pulled her into it. Outside, she saw several proctors, lying on the ground. Their bodies were already decaying into dust.

And then there was another, louder, roar.

"I think the monsters are free," Frieda said, nervously. "And angry."

Emily shuddered. She still had no idea why Mountaintop had gathered the monsters, but it hardly mattered. The light globe Frieda had created would draw the creatures–the smaller ones, at least–to them like flies to rotting meat. She briefly considered going back into the hidden chamber, but there was no guarantee that they would be any safer there. Instead, she looked at Frieda, then unwrapped the Death Viper from her neck and placed it on the ground.

"That... that's a Death Viper," Frieda said, staring at the creature in horror. "I..."

"It won't bite you," Emily said, drawing on the bond to make sure the snake–she'd have to pick a name for it, someday–did as she said. "Just don't try to pick the snake up or you'll lose your hands. At least."

The snake sniffed the air. Emily closed her eyes, allowing herself to see through its senses. There were quite a few creatures nearby, some of them smart enough to be deterred by the Death Viper, others too stupid to realize that they should be afraid. At least the Death Viper could see in the dark... it crossed her mind, suddenly, that *that* little detail hadn't been in the books she'd read, after taking the viper as her familiar. But then, no one else had been stupid or desperate enough to try to form a familiar bond with a Death Viper.

"*Aurelius* would make a great name for the snake," she muttered. "Or is that too cruel?"

Beside her, Frieda snickered.

"Keep your magic at hand," Emily said. She knew her own was far from reliable. "As soon as you see a creature, use fire or light to scare it away. Only try to kill it if it comes too close. Understand?"

Frieda nodded.

"Then we need to start running," Emily said. She directed the snake to move ahead of them, sniffing for threats, then took Frieda's arm. "Let's go."

Chapter Thirty-Eight

EVEN STICKING TO THE SMALLER TUNNELS, THE WALK BACK UP TO THE GATE WAS NIGHT-marish. All sorts of creatures appeared out of nowhere, from giant centipedes to chimpanzee-sized creatures with sharp claws and sharper teeth, and lunged at them. They had to be deflected, deterred or destroyed. Fortunately, the Death Viper's mere presence scared away enough of the creatures for Frieda to finish the remainder or narrowly avoid their desperate attacks. By the time they finally reached the gate, they were both tired, drained, and far too aware that the wards protecting the school were gone.

Emily picked up the Death Viper and commanded it to hide under the remains of her shirt, then led Frieda through the gate and into the school. Absolute chaos greeted her eyes; Lady Barb and Master Grey stood in the midst of tutors and some of the older students, having a shouting match with their counterparts. The noise was so deafening that it was several moments before anyone noticed they'd made it back through the gate. Emily took advantage of the delay to close the gate and reseal the spells in place, leaving it firmly shut.

"Emily," Lady Barb said. "What happened?"

Emily was surprised to see her, then remembered that she and Master Grey had been waiting near Mountaintop. They'd probably located the school as soon as the defenses collapsed.

"She has the key," Master Grey said. He glowered at her, as if he couldn't quite believe what he saw. "And the school is falling down."

Frieda looked up at Emily, worriedly. "Is that true?"

"The magic is falling apart," Emily said. She knew the protective wards were already gone, but if they'd used magic to reinforce the caves, that magic might be about to come crashing down too. "I think it would be a good idea to abandon the caves."

"The students are already out," Markus said, as the tutors turned to look at Emily. The Head Boy gave her a look that suggested he hadn't forgotten or forgiven how she'd frozen him in place. "Where's the Administrator?"

"Down there," Emily said. It struck her, suddenly, that she hadn't sealed the hidden chamber below the school. For all she knew, Aurelius might be consumed by one of the creatures before he had a chance to wake up. "This was all his fault."

"The MageMaster is dead," Mistress Mauve said. "And she has the key."

Emily looked down at the key, resting on top of her shirt. "Yes, I do," she said. "And I have ownership too."

"Oh, *Emily*," Lady Barb said, sadly.

"We cannot allow you to keep the key," Mistress Mauve said.

"And I cannot allow you to keep using innocent people as power sources," Emily snapped back. "Didn't you *know* what was being done at your school?"

She scowled at the tutors. Only Zed seemed bemused, staring at Emily through calm blue eyes. The rest *had* to have known; they'd just never been able to speak of it. Even if they hadn't been told outright, they would have been able to deduce that *something* had happened to the expelled students, students who should have been held in the school until the end of term.

"We must have the key, and ownership," Professor Clifton said. For once, he didn't sound drunk. "Name your price."

Emily looked down at the key. She could *choose* the next MageMaster herself. Whoever took the key–and ownership–would almost certainly take the reins of power in the school, for what it was worth. Now she knew Mountaintop's secret, it was only a matter of time before common-born children were no longer allowed to go to the school. And then Mountaintop would be doomed.

Unless they find a new source of power, she thought. She could complete her experiments with magical batteries, then show the tutors how to produce them themselves. *Or they can try to talk to Red Rose. The nexus point there is wasted.*

"I will pass the key to a person of my choosing," she said, knowing that she didn't dare push them too far. They might just try to kill her and claim ownership through murder. She had no idea what the key would think of such an attempt. "In exchange, I want certain guarantees."

"Name them," Mistress Mauve said.

"I want you to release Frieda and anyone else who wants to leave from their oaths," Emily said. She had a feeling that not many would want to leave, even with the threat of being turned into a living power source. Mountaintop was still superior to the homes many of the students had left behind. "And then I want you to let us all"–she nodded to indicate Lady Barb and Master Grey–"leave without further ado."

She took a breath. "And I want you to find a new source of power," she added. "The one you have is unsustainable."

Mistress Mauve exchanged glances with Professor Clifton, who nodded. But the Charms Mistress didn't look convinced.

"You said you will choose the next keyholder," she said. "Who?"

"One of the staff," Emily said. "I will choose."

She briefly considered passing the key to Markus, but she had a feeling he wouldn't be able to keep it. He might have been Head Boy–and she had no complaints against him–yet he was also the Ashfall Heir. If Aurelius had been considered a danger with that much power in his hands, what would they think of the Ashfall Patriarch also being the MageMaster?

"Be careful," Lady Barb warned. "You may find yourself regretting the choice one day."

A dull rumble ran though Mountaintop. Emily touched the key and sensed that a section of spells holding the ceiling in place had finally collapsed, starting a cave-in. She hoped there were no students left in the hall. If there had been, they would have been crushed under the falling rock. Perhaps some students had been in detention when the alarms sounded and no one had thought to order them to the surface.

She clutched Frieda's hand and waited.

"We accept your terms," Mistress Mauve said. She glanced at her tutors until they had all nodded in agreement. "We will honor your requests."

Requests, Emily thought, sardonically. The key thrummed against her chest, demanding that she either use it herself or pass it on to someone else. It wouldn't be long before Mountaintop was completely beyond recovery. *As if they had a choice.*

"Do it now," Lady Barb advised. Another shudder ran through the school, followed by the sound of crashing masonry. "Hurry."

Emily hesitated, then made up her mind. She took the key from around her neck, silently bid farewell to the magics surrounding the wrought iron, then tossed it neatly to Zed. The Alchemist stared at her in disbelief, but managed to catch the key before it fell to the floor.

"I give the key to you," Emily said. An odd pressure—a weight she hadn't realized was there until it was gone—vanished from her mind. Moments later, she felt new thoughts washing out into the wards as ownership passed to Zed. "And please let me be the first to congratulate you."

Zed tossed her an unreadable look as he pulled the chain over his neck, one hand holding the key as if he didn't want to ever let it go. He didn't thank her. But, somehow, she hadn't expected it.

Emily sighed, feeling tiredness threatening to catch up with her again, then turned to walk towards the exit. The remaining tutors looked oddly relieved by the arrangement, although it didn't stop them from glaring daggers at Emily. But they didn't try to curse her and that was all that mattered. Lady Barb fell in beside her as she walked, eying Frieda curiously.

"You could have made a better choice," she said, as soon as they were out of earshot. "Why *Zed*?"

"It felt like the right thing to do," Emily said. It *did* feel like the right thing to do, but she honestly wasn't sure *why*. She'd have to sit down and think, hard, about why she'd dropped the key to the kingdom—literally—into the hands of a man who disliked her. "And it was my right to make the choice."

"Yes, it was," Lady Barb said. She generated a light globe. "I will have to stay here and settle matters, Emily. This light will lead you to the way out."

She paused, studying Emily closely. "Can you and your... friend make your way out of the caves? We'll meet you outside and take you home."

Emily nodded, then started to trudge up the passage that led to the main entrance. The school was badly damaged; a number of classrooms had been blown open by the protective wards snapping out of existence, and there were cave-ins *everywhere*. A faint smell in the air, wafting from the Alchemy section, suggested that several bottles of rare and expensive supplies had been smashed. She silently prayed there wouldn't be a spark before they were out of the caves.

She'd been stunned when she'd been brought in through the main entrance; this time, she was actually able to look around as they walked. There was nothing of the grandeur of Whitehall, merely a long tunnel lined with carved statues of strange, semi-human creatures. Emily couldn't help thinking of Easter Island, although the statues seemed to be even less human than the weird sculptures she remembered from TV documentaries. And they came to an end long before they finally reached the cave entrance and stepped outside, into the light.

"The entire school is here," Frieda said, as they walked out of the cave and saw the gathered students. "What will they do if the school falls apart completely?"

"Go to Whitehall, perhaps," Emily said, absently.

Below them, students were milling around, supervised by the Sixth Years. Emily looked for Nanette, but saw no sign of her. Had she been found and taken for healing—or had one of the creatures found and devoured her before anyone could save her life? There was no way to know. She looked up and saw barren mountains in the distance, long since swept clean of life. The sight reminded her of the mountains she'd seen during her journey to Whitehall, years ago. Had she flown over Mountaintop back then without knowing it?

She sat down on a stone and motioned for Frieda to sit next to her, rather than go and join the other students. God alone knew what they would say to her; they might be pleased, viewing the damage she'd inflicted, or they might be horrified. And they'd all sworn oaths to protect the school—and its secrets. Master Grey, in the end, hadn't been able to tell her anything useful, apart from a single warning.

The quarrel must have been another form of temptation, she thought, ruefully. It was odd, being courted by a group of older students, but it wouldn't have happened if she hadn't been famous. *I wonder if they truly wanted me, or if the Administrator pulled strings on my behalf.*

She touched the Death Viper below her shirt, then carefully worked the spell to return it to its bracelet form. As soon as it was harmless, she placed it over her wrist and sighed. It was a useful secret weapon—and she enjoyed playing with it, when she had the time—but it might not be a secret any longer. Anyone who took a look at Nanette's arm would know what had happened to her. Maybe they'd think it was just her very bad luck...

"Well," a deep voice said. The sound of students chatting cut off abruptly. "You do seem to have turned the world upside down—again."

"Void," Emily said.

She looked up. The sorcerer looked younger than she remembered, with long dark hair falling over an angular face. He wore a cloak, not unlike the proctors, although the hood was pulled down to show off his appearance. In his hand, he carried a device that looked like a small compass. Emily had a feeling it didn't show true north.

"The MageMaster remembered you," she said, softly. "I think he missed you."

"He should never have come here," Void said. He tossed the device into the air and caught it, neatly. "The power of the MageMaster isn't worth giving up one's freedom."

Emily frowned. She had never seen the Grandmaster leave Whitehall.

"He can't leave for very long," Void said, when she asked. "He carries the wards with him, Emily. They cannot be put aside on a whim."

"But there's the Warden," Emily protested.

"He's not human," Void said. There was a hint of disgust in his voice. "And besides, they rely on him too much for anyone's peace of mind. You can never trust a being formed of magic, Emily. They sometimes have their own agendas."

Emily sighed and changed the subject. "I think I messed up," she said. She looked at Frieda, her form utterly unmoving. "I nearly got her killed."

"We all make mistakes," Void said. He didn't sound as though he considered Frieda's life very important. But then, she'd never heard him express concern for anyone, not even Emily herself. "Did you learn anything interesting while you were here?"

"I saw hints of the future," Emily said, miserably. "Should I share them with others?"

"Depends," Void said. "Do you think they have a right to know what you saw, even knowing that the demon will have presented it to you out of context?"

"I don't know," Emily confessed.

She sighed, wanting nothing more than to go back to Whitehall and sleep. Context was important; she'd learned that on Earth. It was quite possible that the demon had shown her the visions to confuse her, or to make them come true by forcing her to act on them. Should she tell her friends she'd seen what could very well be their final days—or would the mere act of telling them ensure that the future she'd seen became reality?

"Then make up your mind and, if you want to tell them, tell them," Void advised. "But remember this, young lady. If you tell them, you will no longer be in control of the information. The Royal Brat will have an obligation to tell her father."

"She's grown up," Emily protested, defending her friend.

"She would still be a brat if she hadn't met you," Void said. "And she would still have to tell him, if he ever asked. I think her great-grandfather didn't like the thought of his family keeping secrets from him."

He smiled, then stepped backwards. "I'm proud of you, Emily."

"I failed so many people," Emily said. Now the excitement was over, she found herself second-guessing her decisions. Had she done the right thing by keeping the key, then passing it to Zed? Or should she have proclaimed herself MageMaster and dared them to try to unseat her? "I..."

"You found out the dread secret of Mountaintop," Void said. "And you made sure the plans of your enemies were thoroughly disrupted. Mountaintop will need years to recover from this little... mishap."

He smirked. "Lady Barb will be out soon," he told her. "Go back to Whitehall with her, have a hot bath and a long nap, and after that you can tell the Grandmaster everything that happened here. I have business to complete, but I dare say we will meet again soon enough."

"Wait," Emily said. She could sense the magic holding them out of time starting to fray, but she had no idea when she would see him again. Void chose his own times and places to appear. "I... I need to ask you something."

Void lifted an eyebrow, then waited.

"The... the Administrator implied that I might have inherited Shadye's possessions," Emily said. It still stung to contemplate the Grandmaster keeping *that* a secret from her. How much else might he have concealed that she had a right to know? "Is that true?"

"It's a possibility," Void said, thoughtfully. "I would certainly have expected some other Necromancer to take his lands by now and none of them have, as far as we know. It's possible there's a security measure surrounding it that can only be broken by the person who killed him."

He shrugged. "Or Shadye might just have tried to ensure his fortress could never be desecrated, even after his death. He wouldn't be the first sorcerer to try to keep his territory to himself."

"But he's dead," Emily said.

"It's rather unlikely that any Necromancer will be selfless," Void pointed out. He smiled at her, revealing sharp teeth. "I suggest you discuss the issue with the Grandmaster. He will have a much better idea of what, if anything, you might have inherited from Shadye. I would caution you not to expect much, though. Necromancers are not known for owning vast collections of magical artifacts."

Emily nodded. The average Necromancer wasn't a skilled magician, merely one who had decided to take a shortcut to power. Shadye had been little more than brute force wrapped in a limited amount of devilish cunning. Mother Holly had been smarter, Emily suspected; if she'd had more time and had less insanity, she might have managed to unite the mountains under her rule. But neither of them had had the power and control to become a Lone Power.

"I would just like to know what he kept there," she said, instead. "He might have tried to kidnap someone else before he came after me."

"He might," Void agreed. "But I saw no evidence of another ritual."

He reached out and squeezed her shoulder, gently. "I'm proud of you, Emily," he said again. "You've come a very long way."

Emily sighed, torn between a strange kind of pride—was this what it was like to have a father?—and guilt. "Did I do the right thing?"

"Always do the right thing," Void said. He turned and started to walk away, but his voice echoed in her head. "Even if it makes you bleed."

But that, she knew, was no answer.

Chapter Thirty-Nine

This is Whitehall," Emily told Frieda. "I think you will like it here."

Lady Barb cleared her throat and looked directly at Emily. "We've assigned you a spare room for the next few days," she said. "I believe that... Frieda would be better off sharing the room, at least until we decide what to do with her."

"She's my friend," Emily said. "And besides, where else can she go?"

Lady Barb nodded. "I suggest you sleep," she said, as she led them into the school and through a maze of corridors. Someone must have been altering the school's interior, Emily decided, because they didn't see a single student until they arrived in the dorms. "We'll have to have a long chat tomorrow."

"Understood," Emily said. It felt so *good* to step back into a Whitehall room, even though it was much smaller than Raven Hall. But then, there were only three beds in the room. "I have a great deal to tell you."

"I'm sure you do," Lady Barb said. She gave Frieda a long look, then nodded. "Make sure you both get plenty of sleep. We'll send you food when you awaken."

"You don't want us to leave the room," Emily said. She met her mentor's eyes. "Are we prisoners?"

"We would prefer not to let anyone know you're back until we decide what to tell them," Lady Barb said. "And I think you're smart enough to understand why."

She left the room. Emily tested the door and discovered, not entirely to her surprise, an alarm hex sliding into place. It wouldn't bar the way if she really wanted to get out, but it would make it impossible for her to leave without alerting Lady Barb. Muttering a curse under her breath, she turned to Frieda and motioned for her to take one of the beds. Frieda obeyed, gazing at Emily worshipfully. Emily sighed inwardly, then lay down on her bed and closed her eyes. Sleep fell over her like a shroud.

It felt like bare seconds before she opened her eyes, awakened by the smell of food. Frieda was devouring a large plate of bacon, eggs and toasted bread, wearing a robe someone had to have sent up from the school's supplies. Emily sat upright, then smiled at her former Shadow. Frieda looked embarrassed, but unrepentant. It was hard to blame her for eating when she had the chance.

Emily stumbled to her feet, walked into the washroom and showered, thoroughly. When she had finished, she found a spare robe hanging from the door and pulled it on, shaking her head in private amusement. They might be prisoners, of sorts, but it was a very comfortable cell, complete with a handful of books. And yet she knew it would pall soon enough.

"Don't worry about a thing," she said, as the door opened to reveal a servant carrying another plate of food. "No one will hurt you here."

Frieda's eyes were suddenly very serious. "I owe you my life," she said, as the servant retreated. "I would have died without you."

"You did get yourself into trouble," Emily reminded her. "Why *didn't* you listen to me?"

The younger girl reddened. "It... it wasn't what I wanted to hear," she confessed. "And I didn't really believe there was any choice."

"Don't do it here," Emily said. "This isn't Mountaintop."

"I won't," Frieda said. She met Emily's eyes. "My life is yours, you know."

"Your life is your own," Emily said. The devotion in Frieda's voice bothered her at a very primal level. "Just... just don't waste it, all right?"

They must have been under observation, for Lady Barb entered the room as soon as Emily had finished eating her breakfast. "I need you to come with me," she said, shortly. "Frieda will have to remain here, for the moment."

Emily sighed, then climbed to her feet and followed the older woman out of the room and through another twisting maze of corridors. This time, they saw several students as they walked, two of whom Emily knew from last year. They waved to her and, shyly, she waved back. It felt wonderful to react without fear of discovery.

"You'll be asked a great many questions," Lady Barb said, as they stopped outside the Grandmaster's office. "I suggest you answer as honestly and completely as possible."

"As if I would do anything else," Emily said. "And I have some questions of my own."

Lady Barb nodded, then opened the door. Inside, she saw the Grandmaster, Sergeant Miles, Master Grey—who scowled at her for a chilling moment—and two men she didn't recognize. She couldn't help wondering if one of them was Void, but neither of them radiated the sense of power she had grown to associate with the older sorcerer. Indeed, one of them was close to being a mundane. She took the seat in the center of the room and braced herself as best she could. There was no way this was going to be an easy discussion.

It took nearly three hours, according to her watch, before the first set of questions came to an end. Emily had a pounding headache by the time the Grandmaster called a halt, mainly from answering the same questions over and over again. She knew, from Martial Magic, that asking the same question repeatedly made it harder for someone to maintain a lie, but that was no consolation. It was enough to make her wish she'd never used a spell to ensure that truth spells simply didn't work on her.

Perhaps they should summon a demon, she thought, as Sergeant Miles chased the two strangers out of the room. *He could tell them the truth.*

"Here," Lady Barb said. She pushed a glass of fruit juice into Emily's hand. "Drink this, and relax."

Emily obeyed. The slightly bitter taste suggested that a painkilling potion had been slipped into the drink, but her head was too sore to care. Whatever it was, it worked; the pain slowly faded to a dull roar. Lady Barb sat next to her and waited, watching her patiently. The Grandmaster, his eyes hidden behind his cloth, seemed to be doing the same.

"Emily," Lady Barb said, "why Zed?"

"Because he had no attachment to any of the quarrels," Emily said. She'd taken the time to think of a justification, knowing that *someone* would ask that question.

But she hadn't taken that into account at the time. "He wasn't angling for the job, so he could reform Mountaintop without having to tend to the interests of one quarrel or another."

She paused. It was true... and yet she wasn't sure it was her *true* reason. Had she viewed it as a belated apology for getting him fired? Or as a way to keep him from continuing his experiments? But she had to admit he was a better man than she'd thought. It wasn't everyone who had seen a chance to poison the person responsible for destroying their reputation and chose to resist temptation.

And he will owe me, she thought, in the privacy of her own mind. *Who knows what that could be used for, in the future?*

"A reasonable argument," the Grandmaster said. "However, the consequences of damaging Mountaintop so badly may be disastrous for the Allied Lands."

Emily glowered at him. "They were using students to power their wards," she said. In hindsight, she had no idea why the founders had thought it was a good idea. The demand for power would have kept rising and, eventually, someone would have noticed that students—all commoners—were going missing. "They could not be allowed to continue."

Lady Barb coughed. "And you expect Zed to fix that problem?"

"I think he will look for alternatives," Emily said. "There are other nexus points they can access, if they're willing to work for them."

"Yes," the Grandmaster agreed. "But, until then, there will be a shortfall in trained combat magicians."

Emily felt a sudden flash of tired anger. "Are you blaming me for this?"

"No," the Grandmaster said. "But we may the only ones who *don't*. There will be consequences for this, Emily."

"I know," Emily said. "But would you have preferred me to do nothing?"

The Grandmaster shrugged, expressively.

"I will arrange for your... young friend to be enrolled in First Year," he said, instead of answering the question. "She will, I am sure, be a credit to the school."

"She has power, talent and determination," Emily agreed. "She will be great."

"And she seems quite taken with you," Lady Barb said. There was a hint of amusement in her voice. "You should be careful."

Emily sighed, then nodded.

"You pose a harder problem," the Grandmaster told her. "You might be well-advised to wait out the rest of the year rather than rejoin your friends."

Emily shook her head, mulishly. She'd never really had friends on Earth—she'd certainly had problems learning how to be a friend herself—but she'd missed her friends more than she cared to admit. Part of her wondered if they'd discovered they could remain friends without Emily; part of her was afraid to ask. It wanted her to slip away and never return to Whitehall out of fear of what she might find.

Angrily, she told that part of her to shut up.

"I would prefer to remain with them," she said, as evenly as she could. "I thought the schools followed the same basic curriculum."

"With some minor changes," the Grandmaster said. "I should warn you that you will have to be tested, then work very hard to catch up with your friends. You might be better advised to repeat the year, depending on your grades."

"Much of what you do in Third Year leads into the Fourth Year," Lady Barb put in. "You might not have an easy time of it."

"I'll take the chance," Emily said. "And besides, if I do badly, I can always repeat the year. Can't I?"

"You can," Lady Barb confirmed.

"Very well," the Grandmaster said. "We will give you a couple of days to recover, then have the class tutors run placement tests for you. If they say you have a reasonable chance of catching up and passing Third Year, you will be allowed to do so. But if they don't, Emily, you will be held back and start Third Year with the current Second Years."

Emily winced. Whitehall didn't really have a stigma attached to students who repeated a year—it was more important to master the basics than move on to later years without a solid grounding—but it would *hurt* to see her friends moving ahead without her. There was little contact between the years; they'd talk to her, she was sure, yet it wouldn't be the same.

"Very well," she said. She would just have to work hard. At least she'd spent plenty of time reading ahead, both at Whitehall and Mountaintop. "I'll do my best."

"I'm sure you will," the Grandmaster said. "I think a break to answer the call of nature would be appropriate here, don't you?"

"I have a question," Emily said, before he could motion her out of his office. "Why didn't you tell me that I might have inherited Shadye's lands?"

"We don't know if you have inherited anything," the Grandmaster said, slowly. "Magical ownership is a complicated issue at the best of times, Emily, and there was no reason to expect Shadye to own anything you could safely use. We expected a rival Necromancer to take Shadye's lands in short order, and were silently grateful when nothing happened. It didn't seem wise to risk upsetting the balance."

Emily felt her eyes narrow. "Would telling me have upset the balance?"

"Perhaps," the Grandmaster said. "We understand little of the magics surrounding ownership, Emily, as I hope would have been explained to you. You becoming aware you owned them might have triggered a free-for-all, if there was any reason to believe that Shadye owned anything worth taking. Or there might be nothing there, but the other Necromancers are merely concerned about the prospect of running into the Necromancer's Bane."

He sighed. "If you wish, we will take a trip to the Blighted Lands this summer," he added, "and see what might have been left there."

"I thought you couldn't leave the school," Emily said.

"I would have to pass the wards to Mistress Irene," the Grandmaster explained. "You could not go alone, young lady. I'd prefer to send a small army of magicians with you, but that would risk drawing too much attention."

Emily nodded. Shadye had deployed a vast army of orcs, goblins and other monsters to attack Whitehall, all of which had been bred in the Blighted Lands. Some of them would still be wandering around, looking for trouble. And then there were the other Necromancers. If she wasn't on the top of their list of people to kill, she would be very surprised.

"I could accompany you," Lady Barb said. "Sir..."

"We will see," the Grandmaster said. "I don't want to risk more people than strictly necessary."

He paused. "One final question, Emily. What happened to Aurelius?"

"I'm not sure," Emily confessed. "Or Nanette, who was also Lin. I last saw them both stunned and wounded, but they could have survived."

"I suppose," the Grandmaster said, clearly dissatisfied.

Emily toyed with the bracelet around her wrist, then looked up. "Will they be allowed to remain at Mountaintop?"

"It would depend on the new MageMaster," the Grandmaster reminded her. "Zed might believe that keeping them there is a sensible precaution. On the other hand, he knows how Aurelius schemed to evade his oaths and arrange the death of his predecessor. He might want Aurelius as far from Mountaintop as possible."

He sighed, heavily. "So passes glory. One day, we will be gone too."

"Of course," Lady Barb said, tartly.

She motioned for Emily to rise and follow her out the door. Outside, a pair of students were waiting to see the Grandmaster, looking more than a little guilty. Emily wondered what they'd done, then decided it wasn't important. All that mattered, now, was getting back to her friends and doing her level best to catch up with the rest of the Third Years.

"You did well," Lady Barb said, once they were alone. "I'm proud of you."

"Thank you," Emily said. She had come to think of Lady Barb as a mother, of sorts. Maybe not someone who would cosset and spoil her, but someone who would always be there to offer advice and help her solve her problems. Being away from her had hurt, too. "How many more questions will there be?"

"They'll sit down and have a solid think about what you told them," Lady Barb said. "And then they will devise new sets of questions and interview you again—and again. Once they think they know everything, they'll go off and write long, boring reports that no one will ever read."

She snorted as the corridor twisted around them. "I will be sending messages to the White Council and the Mediators," she added. "There will be no more common-born children sent to Mountaintop, at least until we obtain guarantees of their future safety. It won't stop the bastards trying to recruit more children, unfortunately, but it will make it harder for them."

Emily nodded. "Are you going to tell the world?"

"We will see," Lady Barb said. "I don't think full disclosure would suit everyone."

"Imaiqah could have gone there," Emily said. Two years ago, Imaiqah had been nothing more than a common-born magician, a person of wild blood, but no family connections in either world. If she'd gone to Mountaintop, what would have become of her? Would she have been floating in the hidden chamber when Emily broke in to free her Shadow? "How many others died since they started harvesting *children* for magic?"

"Too many," Lady Barb said. "But we also have to consider the long-term stability of the Allied Lands. You put Zed in power; wait and see, for a year, if he manages to come up with a new solution to the problem. Or try and devise a solution yourself. And if he doesn't come up with something new, Emily, *then* you pressure him into changing his ways."

"I see," Emily said, unhappily.

She didn't like it. The logic was clear, but she didn't like it.

"We all make compromises," Lady Barb said. She stopped outside a door, then smiled. "I took the liberty of making a few arrangements for you. Open the door."

Emily looked at her, but obeyed.

As Lady Barb turned to go, Emily heard Alassa calling out to her.

"Emily! Welcome home!"

"Thank you," Emily said, as her friends clustered around her. Alassa and Imaiqah gave her hugs; the Gorgon and Jade, more reserved, each shook her hand. "I..."

"Sit down," Alassa urged. Imaiqah pushed a mug of Kava into Emily's hand as Alassa continued. "We're sure you have a *lot* to tell us."

"I do," Emily said, feeling an unaccustomed lump in her throat. She had *friends*! Real friends! Friends who had taken time away from their studies to greet her! "And..."

She hesitated. The visions had never faded from her mind. If she told them what she'd seen, they would have the same problem she had, the problem of making sure that none of them came true. But the mere act of telling them could start them walking down the path that led to their deaths.

And yet... didn't they have a right to know?

"I have something to tell you," she said, finally. "But you have to give me your word that you will keep it a secret, at least for the moment. This *cannot* be shared with anyone else."

She waited, carefully erecting a pair of privacy wards around the small group. Imaiqah and Jade agreed at once; Alassa and the Gorgon, both responsible to their parents, hesitated before giving their words. Emily felt a flicker of guilt–she knew she was about to disturb them–and started to explain.

Chapter Forty

D EMONS ALWAYS LIE," THE GORGON SAID, ONCE EMILY HAD FINISHED. "CAN WE TAKE WHAT you saw for granted?"

"We can't," Jade said. He was the only one Emily *hadn't* seen die—or seemingly on the verge of death. "Even if it showed you true possibilities, it told you nothing useful."

"Like who I will marry," Alassa said, throwing a sharp glance at Jade. "Or when the wedding will actually take place."

"You had... what? *Twenty* suitors last year," Emily pointed out. "You could marry anyone."

"Not now," Alassa said. "My father has high hopes of a very important match."

"Or when any of us will die," Imaiqah said. Her face was pale, but her dark eyes were resolved. "The warnings are practically useless."

"Not entirely," the Gorgon said. "We know that one of them was centerd around Alassa's wedding. What about the others?"

"I don't think there was any focus," Emily said. The suggestion she would be a Mimic, one day, was terrifying. "The only one I had any location for was the one in the heart of Whitehall."

"There is a gaping emptiness at the heart of Whitehall," Jade mused. "Shadye went for the nexus point as soon as he broke into the castle. Maybe another Necromancer did - will do - the same thing."

That wasn't entirely accurate, Emily knew, but it was close enough. What would happen, she asked herself, if a Necromancer *did* manage to gain control of the nexus? Shadye had clearly believed the power would help him ascend to godhood, yet she doubted that all of the nexus points were in the Allied Lands. It was quite possible there were others within the territory controlled by the Necromancers. What had happened to those?

"We don't have enough details to speculate," the Gorgon said. Her snakes hissed in unison, showing her dismay. "All we can do is guess."

They fell into uneasy contemplation. Emily looked down at her hands, biting her lip. Perhaps it had been a mistake to tell them what she'd seen... but she hadn't really had a choice. They had a right to know... or, she wondered, was that what she told herself to make it feel better?

"Maybe you shouldn't get married," Imaiqah said, addressing Alassa. "You would be spared a wedding day..."

"I *have* to get married," Alassa said, "or the Line of Alexis will end with me. And then there will be civil war."

Jade cleared his throat. "Shouldn't we be taking this to the Grandmaster?"

"I wanted to discuss it with you first," Emily said. "But I think we may have no choice."

"If only we could study your memories directly," the Gorgon said.

Emily shook her head. Thanks to Void, anything short of demonic magic wouldn't work on her—and even then, she would have to give the demon permission to share what it saw in her head. She knew how to summon them now, how to bind them into a form she could tolerate, but it was too risky, even for this. And she knew it would take whatever permission she gave it, find a loophole and use her own words against her.

And what will they say, she thought, *if they knew I knew how to summon demons?*

"That isn't a possibility," she said.

Alassa clapped her hands together, once. "I think we need to start thinking about the future," she said. Like it or not"—she nodded to Emily—"we are in the heart of world-changing events. Our friend here has changed the world at least three times..."

"But who's counting?" Jade asked, mischievously. "Just once is more than most people manage."

Emily felt herself blush with embarrassment. Jade had always teased her lightly; in hindsight, she realized it had been a way of expressing his affection, even his attraction. Now... they were just friends, yet he still teased her. But he was right.

"We should form our own quarrel," Alassa said, firmly. "We wouldn't be limited to people from the Great Houses. We have royalty"—she tapped her chest between her ample breasts—"the merchant clans"—she nodded at Imaiqah—"and even a combat sorcerer and a Gorgon. And I'm sure we can find others, too."

Jade smiled. "You don't want to ask the tutors?"

"Too set in their ways," Alassa said. She rubbed her jaw, lightly. "It takes great force to make anyone like them change."

Emily frowned, inwardly. She liked the idea—there were advantages to it, as far as she could see—but it would mean giving up more of her time to be with others. She cursed herself for her own selfishness a moment later. They were her friends! She should spend time with them, not do her own thing. And she knew others who would be happy to join. Aloha, for one; Markus, perhaps, if he wasn't already pledged to a different quarrel. Perhaps she could even write to some of the Third Years she'd known at Mountaintop and invite them to join.

Nanette would have been perfect, she thought, *if she hadn't been evil. And where is she now?*

"This would be an interesting experiment," the Gorgon said, calling Emily's thoughts back to the room. "But do you think we could stand up to the Necromancers?"

Alassa looked at Emily. "Maybe," she said. "But we will fail if we *don't* try."

"True," Emily agreed. She thought, rapidly. Perhaps the vision had been a hint in the right direction, rather than a warning. "There might be a third way to kill Necromancers."

Jade looked at her. "Do tell?"

"I can't, not now," Emily said, flatly.

She ran her hand though her hair. "If we do this," she said, "we would need to create a secrecy agreement, an oath to keep our secrets to ourselves. And we would need some organization, too."

"Alassa can lead it," Imaiqah said. "She's good at taking command."

"You *were* the most competitive person in Second Year," Emily agreed. "But can you take command of this?"

"Not without risking it becoming tied to Zangaria," Alassa said, slowly. "*You* should take command."

Emily shook her head. She was no leader. The thought of taking command of anything was daunting, even though she was a noblewoman thanks to King Randor. But she had a feeling he'd planned to use Emily's inexperience to control her as soon as he'd offered her Cockatrice. He certainly hadn't trained her to serve as a baroness.

"I nominate Imaiqah," she said, instead. Her friend was clever, unassuming and very capable. "She can serve as our chairperson."

"Good thought," Jade said.

"We can hold the next meeting tomorrow," Alassa said. She looked at Emily. "When will you be returning to classes?"

"Next week, I hope," Emily said. She had no idea how well she would do on the tests. "And I have to move to a proper room. Madame Razz won't be pleased."

"Madame Razz isn't our housemother any longer," Alassa said. "Third Years have Madame Beauregard. She's tougher than Madame Razz."

"Joy," Emily said. Madame Razz had been tough, all right, and very short with any girls who forgot any of their possessions when they arrived at Whitehall. But she'd also been fair to the girls—and woe betide any boy who tried to enter their rooms without permission. "I'll have to speak to her soon, I think."

"No doubt," Alassa said. "It's good to see you again."

"You too," Emily said.

A bell rang through the school. Emily rose automatically, then remembered she didn't actually have classes to attend. Instead, she watched her friends leave, feeling an odd pang in her heart. Once they were gone, she released the Death Viper and stroked its head, trying to assuage her sense of abandonment. She knew better, and yet she still felt bad.

"I'm glad to see that little monster survived," Lady Barb said, as she stepped into the room. "Have you thought of a name?"

"Aurelius," Emily told her.

Lady Barb snorted. "Fitting," she said. She watched Emily change the snake back into a bracelet and pull it over her wrist. "The questioners have decided to call it a day, you'll be pleased to hear. You can spend the rest of the day in the library or providing assistance to some of your tutors."

"The library sounds fine," Emily said. She had some cross-referencing to do, but she thought she was on a solid path to finding a way to make a practical magical battery. The pocket dimensions she'd created could *store* power, yet discharging it in a controlled manner was a major headache. But she'd had an idea. "And then dinner?"

"I think you can return to the Great Hall," Lady Barb agreed. "We can move your young friend into a First Year room tomorrow."

"She'll like that," Emily said. There were no Shadows in Whitehall. Frieda would be able to concentrate on her studies rather than satisfying Emily's every whim. "And some better friends her own age won't be a bad thing."

"Just keep an eye on her," Lady Barb said. "I didn't like *everything* I heard at Mountaintop."

"I suppose not," Emily said.

The library was just as she remembered, although there were hundreds of students fighting over a handful of tomes that had yet to be duplicated by the budding printing presses. Emily found a table in the corner, then started to look for several books she knew were normally assigned to Fifth and Sixth Years. Thanks to Aurelius, she had to admit, she knew enough of the basic concepts to understand what she was reading, although the practice was still beyond her. She'd need help from an expert to actually complete her design.

Dinner was better than she recalled, although some of the stares from well-connected students suggested that *some* rumors had already leaked out. Emily did her best to ignore them; instead, she pointed out a few of her friends and acquaintances to Frieda, ending with Melissa and her cronies. She couldn't help wondering what Melissa thought of the rumors, assuming she'd heard any of them. If Markus hadn't been at Mountaintop, Melissa would have been in Raven Hall when Emily arrived. And who knew what would have happened then?

When dinner finally came to an end, she led Frieda back up the stairs to their room. Lady Barb had warned her that they would both have to be up early, Frieda to go to her first set of classes and Emily to answer yet more questions. She would have preferred to visit her friends, but sleep seemed more important. If she was lucky, she'd be sharing a room with one of them at the end of the week.

"I can't sleep," Frieda said, after they were in their beds. "This room feels so empty."

"I had problems sleeping when there were twenty girls in the hall," Emily confessed. She looked over at Frieda. "Would you like me to tell you a story?"

"My mother used to tell me stories," Frieda said, softly. "Do you think she's still alive?"

"I think so," Emily said, although she wasn't so sure. The Cairngorms were a harsh place to live, even for strong men. Frieda's mother could easily have died by now, her body buried beneath the trees and left to return to the land. "You could write her a letter, or even go see her..."

"I was never allowed to go," Frieda said, miserably. "They always said I was a burden."

"They wanted you to stay at Mountaintop," Emily said. Subtle magic, combined with the lingering awareness of the rejection, would have helped break the ties binding the students to their mundane families. "But Whitehall won't force you to stay here over the summer."

She hesitated before getting up and walking to Frieda's bed. "Move over," she said, as she sat down. "And I'll tell you a story."

"Please," Frieda said.

Emily thought, fast. Most of the stories she knew would require far too much explanation, or modification. But there were some that had universal appeal.

"Once upon a time," she said, "there was a magician who made chocolate. This man owned a vast factory on the edge of a very poor town. And in that town there lived a young boy..."

It wasn't quite the original, she knew. She'd often considered trying to recall stories from Earth and transcribing them, but it had seemed a pointless exercise. And yet, as she detailed the adventures of Charlie and four insufferable brats, Frieda relaxed and curled up against her. By the time Emily had detailed the unfortunate end of a very spoiled brat, Frieda was fast asleep.

"Sleep well," Emily murmured. "You're safe now."

And, with that, she closed her eyes and went to sleep.

Epilogue

THE CHAMBERS HE'D ONCE KNOWN LIKE THE BACK OF HIS HAND WERE IN RUINS.
Aurelius stumbled through the hidden sections of Mountaintop, feeling as though he was in an unending nightmare. The experiments of countless researchers had been left in ruins, while the wards were no longer even slightly responsive to his touch. There should have been light everywhere, he knew all too well, as he stumbled towards a hidden passageway leading up into another set of research chambers, but the light globes were gone. It cost him more than it should have done to produce one of his own.

He crawled up the stairs, fighting the growing temptation to just lie down and die. It was overpowering, a sense that he had not only been beaten, but beaten so comprehensively as to be beyond any hope of recovery. And yet he'd never given up before, no matter the problems he'd had to overcome to advance the Star Council's agenda. Whatever had happened—and his memory refused to remember what had taken place before his collapse—it could be overcome and he could recover.

There was no light in the research chamber either, he discovered as he forced his way through a door that was suddenly very resistant to his touch. He saw why as soon as he stood up; the magic that had once run through the room like water was gone, redirected to another part of the school. Panic yammered at the back of his mind as he thought of just *how* much magic had gone into Mountaintop, once upon a time. Had the corridors above his head caved in, now the magic was gone? Or had the other tutors decided to abandon him to his fate? Their oaths might just allow them to leave him to die...

Raw hatred surged through him as he staggered towards the crystal column. His daughter Renate had been there, trapped and held in stasis like a fly in amber. He'd loved her with all his heart, yet he'd been forced to watch helplessly as her own magic slowly tore her apart. In the end, the only way to save her life had been to deprive her of everything, even idle thought. It was no life for a young girl, but he couldn't bear to see her die. He couldn't kill her. He just couldn't do it.

But now her column was dark and, when he peered into the crystal, it was clear that the magic holding her in place had failed. Renate was dead. It should have held her in stasis forever...

...And then he heard someone behind him.

"You're stronger than I thought," a familiar voice said. "I would not have expected you to actually make it to this chamber."

"Cloak," Aurelius said. He tried to turn around, but his legs buckled under him and he fell to the hard stone floor. "What... what happened?"

"I believe a Child of Destiny can cut both ways," Cloak observed. "This one turned on you when you took her Shadow. Who would have thought her presence would be enough to convince the MageMaster to die?"

"Help me," Aurelius said. "I..."

"That would be a bad idea," Cloak said. "Your time is up."

Aurelius stared, wildly, as fire crackled around Cloak's fingertips. "But... but... *why?*"

"The existing order has to go," Cloak said. "I believe you know that, don't you? All your plans to reshape it into something more viable, something that could fight the Necromancers and change the world. But I fear that would interfere with *my* plans."

He lifted his hand and pointed a long finger at Aurelius's temple. "Goodbye," he said. "It hasn't been a pleasant time."

"Wait," Aurelius pleaded. He knew there was no way out. Cloak was far too powerful to beat in his weakened state. "Who *are* you?"

Cloak hesitated, then pulled back his hood.

Aurelius nearly fainted in shock. "You're..."

There was a brilliant flare of magic, then nothing. Nothing at all.

End of Book V

Emily will return in

Love's Labor's Won

Appendix - On Wands

There are two basic components to any magic spell. First, there is the spellwork, the structure of magic that shapes and directs the spell. Second, there is the *mana* produced by the magician, which needs to be channeled through the spellwork to actually make the spell take effect. Normally, as Emily was taught in *Schooled in Magic*, the spellwork should be handled in a magician's mind, to the point where she can cast spells instinctively. This requires considerable mental discipline, which is why a number of students were forced to keep working their way through First Year courses until they successfully completed the preparatory work.

However, Magicians in the Allied Lands discovered that someone could produce the spellwork ahead of time and store it in wood, thus allowing an untrained magician to channel magic into the wood and thus trigger the spell. In effect, the spell could be fired off as soon as the wand was raised, shaving seconds off the casting time. Both wands and staffs were developed to serve this purpose (there is nothing special about the wands, which are really nothing more than pieces of wood) and used by magicians. Indeed, the basic technique for priming a wand was so simple that a First Year student could use it.

This, however, had a serious effect on their ability to cast magic. Dependency on a wand made it incredibly difficult for them to cast magic without it, thus running the risk of accidentally binding one's magic. Therefore, students at Whitehall were largely forbidden to use wands for the first two years of their schooling and warned, in no uncertain terms, that they risked self-inflicted harm if they broke the rule. (Mountaintop, by contrast, wanted to limit the magic of common-born students, so encouraged them to use wands rather than learn to develop their own magic.)

By the time the students reached Third Year, they required more precise spellwork than before (in alchemy, in particular) so they were permitted to use wands. However, they were strongly encouraged not to slip into dependency.

There is no real difference between the use of wands and staffs, save one; the staff, being larger, is capable of holding more spellwork, allowing the magician to use magic to either do one complex spell or fire off a number of smaller spells in quick succession.

About the author

Christopher G. Nuttall is thirty-two years old and has been reading science fiction since he was five when someone introduced him to children's SF. Born in Scotland, Chris attended schools in Edinburgh, Fife and University in Manchester before moving to Malaysia to live with his wife Aisha.

Chris has been involved in the online Alternate History community since 1998; in particular, he was the original founder of Changing The Times, an online alternate history website that brought in submissions from all over the community. Later, Chris took up writing and eventually became a full-time writer.

Current and forthcoming titles published by Twilight Times Books:

Schooled in Magic YA fantasy series
Schooled in Magic—book 1
Lessons in Etiquette —book 2
A Study in Slaughter —book 3
Work Experience —book 4
The School of Hard Knocks —book 5
Love's Labor's Won—book 6

The Decline and Fall of the Galactic Empire military SF series
Barbarians at the Gates—book 1
The Shadow of Cincinnatus —book 2
The Barbarian Bride—book 3

Chris has also produced *The Empire's Corps* series, the *Outside Context Problem* series and many others. He is also responsible for two fan-made Posleen novels, both set in John Ringo's famous Posleen universe. They can both be downloaded from his site.

Website: http://www.chrishanger.net
Blog: http://chrishanger.wordpress.com
Facebook: https://www.facebook.com/ChristopherGNuttall